Myth-Maker Extraordinaire

"No one ever wrote like Smith, with his special blend of intense myth-making and rich invention!"
—*Publishers Weekly*

Cordwainer Smith held a vision of the future unmatched in science fiction. His seemingly limitless universe stretches from Manhome itself to the planet that held the promise of Immortality—Norstrilia.

Smith peopled his universe with such unforgettable creations as the enchanting girly girl C'mell . . . the all-powerful Lords of the Instrumentality . . . the men who sailed too far between the stars and changed . . . and many many more.

His was a vision filled with the truth of poetry and prophecy.

Watch for all the volumes in Ballantine's Classic Library of Science Fiction—big, definitive collections by the true masters in the field. Each book in the series is introduced by a well-known science fiction writer or by a distinguished critic.

Now Available in a Ballantine Edition:

The Best of Stanley G. Weinbaum
Introduction by Isaac Asimov

The Best of Fritz Leiber
Introduction by Poul Anderson

The Best of Frederik Pohl
Introduction by Lester del Rey

The Best of Henry Kuttner
Introduction by Ray Bradbury

Volumes in Preparation:

The Best of C. L. Moore
Introduction by Lester del Rey

The Best of John W. Campbell/Don A. Stuart
Introduction by Lester del Rey

The Best of L. Sprague de Camp
Introduction by Poul Anderson

The Best of Raymond Z. Gallun
Introduction by Frederik Pohl

Coming from Ballantine Books

THE BEST OF
Cordwainer Smith

Edited, with Introduction and Notes, by
J. J. PIERCE

林

白

樂

BALLANTINE BOOKS • NEW YORK

Library of Congress Catalog Card Number: 75-19108

SBN 345-24581-4-195

First Printing: September, 1975

Book Club Edition: July, 1975

Cover art by Darrell Sweet

Printed in the United States of America

BALLANTINE BOOKS
A Division of Random House, Inc.
201 East 50th Street, New York, N.Y. 10022
Simultaneously published by
Ballantine Books, Ltd., Toronto, Canada

ACKNOWLEDGMENTS

"Scanners Live in Vain," copyright 1950 by Fantasy Publishing Co., Inc., for *Fantasy Book*. Copyright 1963 by Cordwainer Smith.

"The Lady Who Sailed *The Soul*," copyright 1960 by Galaxy Publishing Co. for *Galaxy Magazine*. Copyright 1963 by Cordwainer Smith.

"The Game of Rat and Dragon," copyright 1955 by Galaxy Publishing Co. for *Galaxy Science Fiction*. Copyright 1963 by Cordwainer Smith.

"The Burning of the Brain," copyright 1958 by Quinn Publishing Co. for *Worlds of If*. Copyright 1963 by Cordwainer Smith.

"The Crime and the Glory of Commander Suzdal," copyright 1964 by Ziff-Davis Publishing Co. for *Amazing Stories*. Copyright 1971 by Mrs. Genevieve Linebarger.

"Golden the Ship Was—Oh! Oh! Oh!," copyright 1959 by Ziff-Davis Publishing Co. for *Amazing Science Fiction Stories*. Copyright 1963 by Cordwainer Smith.

"The Dead Lady of Clown Town," copyright 1964 by Galaxy Publishing Corporation for *Galaxy Magazine*, August 1964. Copyright 1965 by Cordwainer Smith.

"Under Old Earth," copyright 1966 by Galaxy Publishing Corporation for *Galaxy Magazine*. Copyright 1971 by Mrs. Genevieve Linebarger.

"Mother Hitton's Littul Kittons," copyright 1961 by Galaxy Publishing Corporation for *Galaxy Magazine*, June 1961. Copyright 1965 by Cordwainer Smith.

"Alpha Ralpha Boulevard," copyright 1961 by Mercury Press, Inc. for *The Magazine of Fantasy and Science Fiction*. Copyright 1963 by Cordwainer Smith.

"The Ballad of Lost C'mell," copyright 1962 by Galaxy Publishing Corp. for *Galaxy Magazine*, October 1962. Copyright 1965 by Cordwainer Smith.

"A Planet Named Shayol," copyright 1961 by Galaxy Publishing Corp. for *Galaxy Magazine*, October 1961. Copyright 1965 by Cordwainer Smith.

CONTENTS

Timeline from THE INSTRUMENTALITY OF MANKIND

A. D.	2,000 ▶▶▶▶▶ 3,000 ▶▶▶▶▶▶▶▶▶▶ 4,000 ▶▶▶▶▶ 5,000 ▶▶▶▶
STORIES	No, No, Not Rogov	War No. 81-Q	Queen of the Afternoon	Mark Elf
EVENTS	Forgotten First Age of Space	The Ancient Wars, culminating in the collapse of all nations save China. Retreat of the true men into isolated cities, with most of Earth left to Beasts, manshonyaggers and Unforgiven.	Advent of the Vomacts and the return of vitality to mankind. Rule of the Jwindz succeeded by that of the Instrumentality.

◀◀

A. D.	9,000 ▶▶▶▶▶▶▶▶▶▶▶▶▶ 10,000 ▶▶▶▶▶▶▶▶▶▶▶▶▶▶▶▶▶
STORIES	The Game of Rat and Dragon* The Burning of the Brain*	From Gustible's Planet
EVENTS	Age of Planoforming. Settlement of thousands of worlds, compared to 200 by sailship.	Stabilization of Utopia. Life spans standardized at 400 years. Programming of embryos, growing use of robots, underpeople.

◀◀

A. D.	14,000 ▶▶▶▶▶▶▶▶▶▶▶ 15,000 ▶▶▶▶▶▶▶▶▶▶▶▶▶▶▶
STORIES	The Dead Lady of Clown Town*	Under Old Earth* Drunkboat
EVENTS	Martyrdom of D'Joan, rebirth of old strong Religion. Founding of line of Jestocost	Appearance of Lady Alice More, partner to Lord Jestocost in the Rediscovery of Man. Holy Insurgency. Visions from space.[3]

*Stories in this collection.

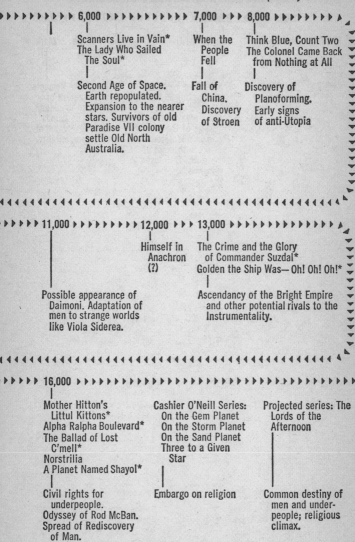

Compiled by J. J. Pierce

▶▶▶▶▶▶▶▶▶ 6,000 ▶▶▶▶▶▶▶▶▶▶ 7,000 ▶▶▶ 8,000 ▶▶▶▶▶▶▶▶▲

Scanners Live in Vain*
The Lady Who Sailed
   The Soul*

Second Age of Space.
Earth repopulated.
Expansion to the nearer
stars. Survivors of old
Paradise VII colony
settle Old North
Australia.

When the
People
Fell

Fall of
China.
Discovery
of Stroen

Think Blue, Count Two
The Colonel Came Back
   from Nothing at All

Discovery of
Planoforming.
Early signs
of anti-Utopia

▶▶▶▶▶▶ 11,000 ▶▶▶▶▶▶▶▶▶ 12,000 ▶▶▶ 13,000 ▶▶▶▶▶▶▶▶▶▶▲

Himself in
Anachron
(?)

The Crime and the Glory
of Commander Suzdal*
Golden the Ship Was—Oh! Oh! Oh!*

Possible appearance of
Daimoni. Adaptation of
men to strange worlds
like Viola Siderea.

Ascendancy of the Bright Empire
and other potential rivals to the
Instrumentality.

▶▶▶▶▶▶▶ 16,000 ▶▶▶▶▶▶▶▶▶▶▶▶▶▶▶▶▶▶▶▶▶▶▶▶▶▶▶▶▶▶▶▶▶

Mother Hitton's
   Littul Kittons*
Alpha Ralpha Boulevard*
The Ballad of Lost
   C'mell*
Norstrilia
A Planet Named Shayol*

Civil rights for
underpeople.
Odyssey of Rod McBan.
Spread of Rediscovery
of Man.

Cashier O'Neill Series:
On the Gem Planet
On the Storm Planet
On the Sand Planet
Three to a Given
   Star

Embargo on religion

Projected series: The
Lords of the
Afternoon

Common destiny of
men and under-
people; religious
climax.

Note: With Smith's own notebooks lost, chronology is largely a matter of
      guesswork, based on internal evidence. But the order of stories
      and surrounding events can be fairly well established.

Cordwainer Smith: The Shaper of Myths

IN AN OBSCURE and short-lived magazine called *Fantasy Book*, there appeared in 1950 a story called "Scanners Live in Vain."

No one had ever heard of the author, Cordwainer Smith. And it appeared for a time that he would never be heard from again in the world of science fiction.

But "Scanners Live in Vain" was a story that refused to die, and its republication in two anthologies encouraged the elusive Smith to begin submitting to other SF markets.

Today, he is recognized as one of the most creative SF writers of modern times. But, paradoxically, he is one of the least known or understood. Until shortly before his death, his very identity was a closely guarded secret.

Not that Dr. Paul Myron Anthony Linebarger (1913–66) was ashamed of science fiction. He was proud of the field, and had even boasted once to the *Baltimore Sun* that SF had attracted more Ph.D.'s than any other branch of fiction.

But he was a sensitive, emotional writer—and reluctant to become involved with his readers—to be forced to "explain" himself in a way that might destroy the spontaneity of his work.

Beyond that, he probably enjoyed being a man of mystery, as elusive as some of the allusions in his stories. Smith was a mythmaker in science fiction, and perhaps it takes a somewhat mythical figure to create true myths.

A new acquaintance unsure of the number of syllables in Dr. Linebarger's name would be answered by a significant gesture to the three Chinese characters on his tie. Only later would he learn the characters stood for Lin Bah Loh, or "Forest of Incandescent Bliss"—the name given him as godson to Sun Yat Sen, founder of the Chinese Republic.

Dr. Linebarger's life was certainly several cuts above the ordinary. At the age of seventeen, he negotiated a silver loan for China on behalf of his father—Sun's legal advisor and one of the financiers of the Revolution of 1911. He later became a colonel in U.S. Army Intelligence, despite partial blindness and general ill health —he once shocked guests at a dinner party by downing a "cocktail" of hydrochloric acid to aid his digestion.

Although born in Milwaukee—his father wanted to be sure that as a natural-born citizen his son would be eligible for the presidency—Linebarger spent his formative years in Japan, China, France and Germany. By the time he grew up, he knew six languages and had become intimate with several cultures, both Oriental and Occidental.

He was only twenty-three when he earned his Ph.D. in political science at Johns Hopkins University, where he was later Professor of Asiatic politics for many years. Shortly thereafter, he graduated from editing his father's books to publishing his own highly regarded works on Far Eastern affairs.

When World War II broke out, he used his position on the Operations Planning and Intelligence Board to draft a set of qualifications for an intelligence operative in China that only he could meet—so off he went to Chungking as an Army lieutenant. By war's end, he was a major.

Dr. Linebarger turned his wartime experiences into *Psychological Warfare,* still regarded as the most authoritative text in the field. As a colonel, he was advisor to the British forces in Malaya and to the U.S. Eighth Army in Korea. But this self-styled "visitor to small wars" passed up Vietnam, feeling American involvement there was a mistake.

Travels around the world took him to Australia, Greece, Egypt and many other countries; and his expertise was sufficiently valued that he became a leading member of the Foreign Policy Association and an advisor to President Kennedy.

But even in childhood, his thoughts had turned to fiction—including science fiction. Like many budding SF writers, he discovered the genre at an early age. Since he was living in Germany at the time, he added to the familiar classics of Verne, Wells, Doyle and others such works as Alfred Doblin's *Giganten* to his list of favorites.

He was only fifteen when his first SF story, "War No. 81-Q," was published. But unfortunately, no one seems to remember where. According to his widow, Genevieve, the story was bylined Anthony Bearden—a pseudonym later used for poetry published in little magazines. Two examples of this poetry appear in *Norstrilia,* also published by Ballantine.

During the 1930s, Dr. Linebarger began keeping a secret notebook—part personal diary, part story ideas. Then in 1937, he began writing serious stories, mostly set in ancient or modern China, or in contemporary locales elsewhere. None were ever published, but their range—some use the same Chinese narrative techniques that later turn up in SF works like "The Dead Lady of Clown Town"—is remarkable.

While back in China, he took on the name Felix C. Forrest—a pun on his Chinese name—for two psychological novels mailed home in installments and published after the war. *Ria* and *Carola* were remarkable novels for their feminine viewpoint and for the subtle interplay of cultural influences behind the interplay of character. Under the name of Carmichael Smith, Dr. Linebarger wrote *Atomsk,* a spy thriller set in the Soviet Union.

But his career in science fiction came about almost by accident. He may have submitted some stories to *Amazing* while still in China during the war; but if so, nothing ever came of them. It was during idle hours at the Pentagon after his return that he turned an idea that had been bothering him into "Scanners Live in Vain."

The story was almost written in vain, for it was rejected by every major publication in the field. *Fantasy Book,* to which it was submitted five years later as a last resort, did not even pay for it. Although he had written another Cordwainer Smith story, "Himself in Anachron" (recently adapted by his widow for Harlan Ellison's anthology *Last Dangerous Visions*) in 1946, he may well have despaired of any recognition in the genre.

But there were readers who took notice. Never mind that *Fantasy Book* had never before published a worthwhile story, never mind that the author was a total unknown. "Scanners Live in Vain" got to them.

"Martel was angry. He did not even adjust his blood away from anger. . . ."

It was more than just the bizarre situation that attracted attention—it was the way it was treated. From the opening lines, readers became part of Martel's universe—a universe as real as our own, for all its strangeness. They were intrigued, and no doubt mystified.

What was this Instrumentality of Mankind, which even the scanners held in awe? What were the Beasts and the manshonyaggers and the Unforgiven? One could sense their importance to the hero, but beyond that— only wonder.

Smith clearly knew more about this universe than he let on—more, in fact, than he ever would let on. His universe had been forming in his mind at least since the time he wrote his first published story in 1928, and it took further shape in his secret notebook during the 1930s and 1940s.

Already in "War No. 81-Q," his widow recalls, he had made reference to the Instrumentality—that all-powerful elite hierarchy that was to become central to the Cordwainer Smith stories twenty years and more later. Even the word may have had far more significance than it would appear at first.

Linebarger had been raised in a High Church Episcopalian family—his grandfather was a minister—and was devoutly religious. The word "instrumentality" has a distinct religious connotation, for in Roman Catholic and Episcopalian theology the priest performing the sacraments is the "instrumentality" of God Himself.

At the time he wrote "War No. 81-Q," young Linebarger was also having a fling with Communism—a tendency his father eventually cured by sending him on a trip to the Soviet Union for his eighteenth birthday. But he remained struck by the sense of vocation and conviction of historical destiny to which Communism appealed.

In Cordwainer Smith's epic of the future, the Instrumentality of Mankind has the hallmarks of both a political elite and a priesthood. Its hegemony is that, not of the galactic empire so typical of less imaginative SF, but of something far more subtle and pervasive—at once political and spiritual. Its lords see themselves not as mere governors or bureaucrats or politicians, but as instruments of human destiny itself.

Linebarger's sense of religion infused his work in other ways, and not merely in references to the Old Strong Religion and the Holy Insurgency of *Norstrilia* and other late works.

There is, for example, the emphasis on quasi-religious ritual—compare, for instance, the Code of the Scanners to the Saying of the Law in H.G. Wells' *The Island of Dr. Moreau*. Furthermore, there is the strong sense of vocation expressed by the scanners, sailors, pinlighters, Go-captains and the lords themselves—something very spiritual, even if not expressed in religious terms.

But Linebarger was no mere Christian apologist who used SF as a vehicle for orthodox religious messages like those of, say, C.S. Lewis. He was also a social and psychological thinker, whose experience with diverse cultures gave him peculiar and seemingly contradictory ideas about human nature and morality.

He could, for example, admire the samurai values of fantasy, courage and honor, and he showed his appreciation of Oriental art and literature in the furnishing of his home and his fiction. Yet he was so horrified by the tradition-bound fatalism and indifference to human life he found in the Orient that he became obsessed with the sanctity of life on any terms, as something too precious to sacrifice to any concept of honor or morality—Oriental or Occidental.

While in Korea, Linebarger masterminded the surrender of thousands of Chinese troops who considered it shameful to give up their arms. He drafted leaflets explaining how the soldiers could surrender by shouting the Chinese words for "love," "duty" "humanity" and "virtue"—words that happened, when pronounced in that order, to sound like "I surrender" in English. He considered this act to be the single most worthwhile thing he had done in his life.

Linebarger's attitude is reflected in the apparently casual manner in which matters such as brainwashing are treated in his SF. For the Hunter and Elaine at the end of "The Dead Lady of Clown Town," that is a more humane, if less "honorable" fate than death. Throughout the Smith canon, life is usually placed before honor, no matter how much the Oriental codes of honor and formality may permeate the hybrid culture of the future.

Yet Linebarger felt there was a meaning to life beyond mere living. "The God he had faith in had to do with the soul of man and with the unfolding of history and of the destiny of all living creatures," his Australian friend Arthur Burns once remarked; and it is this exploration of human—and more than human—destiny that gives Smith's work its unity.

Behind the invented cultures, behind the intricacies of plot and the joy or suffering of characters, there is Smith the philosopher, striving in a manner akin to that of Teilhard de Chardin (although there is no evidence of any direct influence) to reconcile science and religion, to create a synthesis of Christianity and evolution that will shed light on the nature of man and the meaning of history.

The stories in this volume, collected in their proper order for the first time, form part of a vast historical cycle taking place over some fifteen thousand years. They are based on material from Linebarger's original notebook and a second notebook—unfortunately lost—that he began keeping in the 1950s as new problems began to concern him.

Mankind is still haunted by the Ancient Wars and the

Dark Age that followed as this volume opens with "Scanners Live in Vain." Other stories, one unpublished, hint at millennia of historical stasis, during which the true men sought inhuman perfection behind the electronic pales of their cities, while leaving the Wild to survivors of the Ancient World—the Beasts, manshony-aggers and Unforgiven.

Into this future came the VomAcht sisters, daughters of a German scientist who placed them in satellites in suspended animation at the close of World War II. Returning to Earth in the latter days of the Dark Age, they bring the "gift of vitality"—a concept that seems to have meant to Smith what the "life force" meant to Bergson and Shaw—back to mankind. Founders of the Vomact family, they represent a force in human nature that can be either good or evil, but is perhaps ultimately beyond either, and a necessary means for the working out of human destiny through evolution.

The dual nature of the Vomacts and the force they represent is symbolized in the origin of their name: "Acht" is a German word with a double meaning: "proscribed" or "forbidden" and "care" or "attention." And the Vomacts alternate as outlaws and benefactors throughout the Smith epic.

But the gift of vitality sets a new cycle of history in motion—the heroic age of the scanners, pinlighters and Go-captains. What stands out in these early stories is the starkness of the emotional impact—the impact of strange new experiences and relationships, whether of the telepathic symbiosis of men and partners in "The Game of Rat and Dragon" or the woman become a functioning part of her spacecraft in "The Lady Who Sailed the *Soul*."

Some of Linebarger's own experiences went into his work. Captain Wow was the name of one of his cats at his Washington home when he wrote "The Game of Rat and Dragon" at a single sitting one day in 1954. Cat Melanie was later to inspire C'mell, heroine of the underpeople, who were created by men from mere animals. Then, too, Linebarger's frequent stays in hospitals, dependent on medical technology, gave him a feel for the linkage of man and machine.

But in "The Burning of the Brain," we already begin to see signs of the Pleasure Revolution, a trend which Linebarger detested in his own time and which he saw putting an end to the heroic age in his imagined future. Near immortality—thanks to the santaclara drug, or stroon, grown in Norstrilia—makes life less desperate, but also less meaningful.

Real experience gives way to synthetic experience; in "Golden the Ship Was, Oh, Oh, Oh" (as in "The Lady Who Sailed *The Soul*," which was also co-authored by Genevieve Linebarger), the hero seeks pleasure directly from an electric current—and only an epoch-making crisis affords him a chance to see that there is a better way.

Under the ruthless benevolence of the Instrumentality, a bland utopia takes shape. Men are freed of the fear of death, the burden of labor, the risks of the unknown —but deprived of hope and freedom. The underpeople, created to do the labor of mankind, are more human than their creators. The gift of vitality, seemingly, has been lost, and history come to a stop.

In these stories, it is the underpeople—and the more enlightened lords of the Instrumentality who heed them —who hold the salvation of humanity in their hands. In "The Dead Lady of Clown Town," the despised, animal-derived workers and robots must teach humans the meaning of humanity in order to free mankind from its seeming euphoria.

Lord Jestocost is inspired by the martyrdom of the dog-woman D'joan; and Santuna is transformed by the experiences in "Under Old Earth" into the Lady Alice More. Together, they become the architects of the Rediscovery of man—bringing back freedom, risk, uncertainty and even evil.

Parallelling these events are glimpses of other parts of the universe of the Instrumentality. In "Mother Hitton's Littul Kittons," we learn why Old North Australia is the most heavily defended planet in the galaxy; but Viola Siderea is just as strange. And where else in science fiction is there a world like "A Planet Named Shayol," where a daring conception in biological engineering is wedded to a classic vision of Hell?

Oriental narrative techniques, especially in "The Dead Lady of Clown Town" and "The Ballad of Lost C'mell" are prominent in the later stories. So is the sense of myth, whereby the just-mentioned stories are supposedly explanations of popular legends. But just how much of what is told "Under Old Earth" ever *really* took place?

Smith creates a sense of immense time having passed. To Paul and Virginia, newly freed by the Rediscovery of Man in "Alpha Ralpha Boulevard," our own age is lost in the dim past and is seen only through layer upon layer of half-forgotten history. Smith's effect has rarely been duplicated—the first half of Robert Silverberg's *Nightwings* is perhaps the most successful approximation.

Smith's universe remains infinitely greater than our knowledge of it—we shall never know what empire once conquered Earth and brought tribute up that fabulous boulevard; nor the identity of the Robot, the Rat and the Copt, whose visions are referred to in *Norstrilia* and elsewhere; nor what ultimately becomes of the cat-people created in "The Crime and Glory of Commander Suzdal."

Then there is that unfulfilled sense of anticipation— where was Smith leading us? What comes after the Rediscovery of Man and the liberation of the underpeople by C'mell? Linebarger gives hints of a common destiny for man and underpeople—some religious fulfillment of history, perhaps. But they remain hints.

The work of Cordwainer Smith will always retain its enigmas. But that is part of its appeal. In reading his stories, we are caught up in experiences as real as life itself—and just as mysterious.

—John J. Pierce
Berkeley Heights, New Jersey
January, 1975

Scanners Live in Vain

*Here, humanity is still emerging from the Dark Age
that is more fully described in the stories "Queen of the
Afternoon" and "Mark Elf" and which reveal the
"Beasts" to be mutated, intelligent animals and the
"manshonyaggers" to be old German killing machines
—taken from Menschenjäger, or "hunter of men." At
the time Smith wrote the story in 1945, there was an
abandoned shop in his neighborhood called the Little
Cranch—what "cranch" meant, he had no idea—but
he used the word anyway. The "ancient lady" ancestress of Vomact was one of the VomAcht sisters mentioned in Dark Age stories—which one, we don't
know.*

MARTEL WAS ANGRY. He did not even adjust his blood
away from anger. He stamped across the room by judgment, not by sight. When he saw the table hit the floor,
and could tell by the expression on Luci's face that the
table must have made a loud crash, he looked down to
see if his leg was broken. It was not. Scanner to the
core, he had to scan himself. The action was reflex and
automatic. The inventory included his legs, abdomen,
chestbox of instruments, hands, arms, face and back
with the mirror. Only then did Martel go back to being
angry. He talked with his voice, even though he knew

1

that his wife hated its blare and preferred to have him write.

"I tell you, I must cranch. I have to cranch. It's my worry, isn't it?"

When Luci answered, he saw only a part of her words as he read her lips: "Darling . . . you're my husband . . . right to love you . . . dangerous . . . do it . . . dangerous . . . wait . . ."

He faced her, but put sound in his voice, letting the blare hurt her again: "I tell you, I'm going to cranch."

Catching her expression, he became rueful and a little tender: "Can't you understand what it means to me? To get out of this horrible prison in my own head? To be a màn again—hearing your voice, smelling smoke? To *feel* again—to feel my feet on the ground, to feel the air move against my face? Don't you know what it means?"

Her wide-eyed worrisome concern thrust him back into pure annoyance. He read only a few words as her lips moved: " . . . love you . . . your own good . . . don't you think I want you to be human? . . . your own good . . . too much . . . he said . . . they said. . . ."

When he roared at her, he realized that his voice must be particularly bad. He knew that the sound hurt her no less than did the words: "Do you think I wanted you to marry a scanner? Didn't I tell you we're almost as low as the habermans? We're dead, I tell you. We've got to be dead to do our work. How can anybody go to the up-and-out? Can you dream what raw space is? I warned you. But you married me. All right, you married a man. Please, darling, let me be a man. Let me hear your voice, let me feel the warmth of being alive, of being human. Let me!"

He saw by her look of stricken assent that he had won the argument. He did not use his voice again. Instead, he pulled his tablet up from where it hung against his chest. He wrote on it, using the pointed fingernail of his right forefinger—the talking nail of a scanner—in quick cleancut script: *Pls, drlng, whrs crnching wire?*

She pulled the long gold-sheathed wire out of the pocket of her apron. She let its field sphere fall to the carpeted floor. Swiftly, dutifully, with the deft obedience of a scanner's wife, she wound the cranching wire around his head, spirally around his neck and chest. She avoided the instruments set in his chest. She even avoided the radiating scars around the instruments, the stigmata of men who had gone up and into the out. Mechanically he lifted a foot as she slipped the wire between his feet. She drew the wire taut. She snapped the small plug into the high-burden control next to his heart-reader. She helped him to sit down, arranging his hands for him, pushing his head back into the cup at the top of the chair. She turned then, full-face toward him, so that he could read her lips easily. Her expression was composed.

She knelt, scooped up the sphere at the other end of the wire, stood erect calmly, her back to him. He scanned her, and saw nothing in her posture but grief which would have escaped the eye of anyone but a scanner. She spoke: he could see her chest-muscles moving. She realized that she was not facing him, and turned so that he could see her lips.

"Ready at last?"

He smiled a *yes*.

She turned her back to him again. (Luci could never bear to watch him go under the wire.) She tossed the wire-sphere into the air. It caught in the force-field, and hung there. Suddenly it glowed. That was all. All—except for the sudden red stinking roar of coming back to his senses. Coming back, across the wild threshold of pain.

When he awakened, under the wire, he did not feel as though he had just cranched. Even though it was the second cranching within the week, he felt fit. He lay in the chair. His ears drank in the sound of air touching things in the room. He heard Luci breathing in the next room, where she was hanging up the wire to cool. He smelt the thousand and one smells that are in anybody's room: the crisp freshness of the germ-burner, the sour-sweet tang of the humidifier, the odor of the dinner they had just eaten, the smells of clothes, furniture, of people themselves. All these were pure delight. He sang a phrase or two of his favorite song:

"Here's to the haberman, up-and-out!

"Up—oh—and out—oh! up-and-out! . . ."

He heard Luci chuckle in the next room. He gloated over the sounds of her dress as she swished to the doorway.

She gave him her crooked little smile. "You sound all right. Are you all right, really?"

Even with this luxury of senses, he scanned. He took the flash-quick inventory which constituted his professional skill. His eyes swept in the news of the instruments. Nothing showed off scale, beyond the nerve compression hanging in the edge of *Danger*. But he could not worry about the nerve-box. That always came through cranching. You couldn't get under the wire without having it show on the nerve-box. Some day the box would go to *Overload* and drop back down to *Dead*. That was the way a haberman ended. But you couldn't have everything. People who went to the up-and-out had to pay the price for space.

Anyhow, he should worry! He was a scanner. A good one, and he knew it. If he couldn't scan himself, who could? This cranching wasn't too dangerous. Dangerous, but not too dangerous.

Luci put out her hand and ruffled his hair as if she had been reading his thoughts, instead of just following them: "But you know you shouldn't have! You shouldn't!"

"But I did!" He grinned at her.

Her gaiety still forced, she said: "Come on, darling, let's have a good time. I have almost everything there is in the icebox—all your favorite tastes. And I have two new records just full of smells. I tried them out myself, and even I liked them. And you know me—"

"Which?"

"Which what, you old darling?"

He slipped his hand over her shoulders as he limped out of the room. (He could never go back to feeling the floor beneath his feet, feeling the air against his face, without being bewildered and clumsy. As if cranching was real, and being a haberman was a bad dream. But he *was* a haberman, and a scanner. "You know what I meant, Luci . . . the smells, which you have. Which one did you like, on the record?"

"Well-l-l," said she, judiciously, "there were some lamb chops that were the strangest things—"

He interrupted: "What are lambtchots?"

"Wait till you smell them. Then guess. I'll tell you this much. It's a smell hundreds and hundreds of years old. They found about it in the old books."

"Is a lambtchot a beast?"

"I won't tell you. You've got to wait," she laughed, as she helped him sit down and spread his tasting dishes before him. He wanted to go back over the dinner first, sampling all the pretty things he had eaten, and savoring them this time with his now-living lips and tongue.

When Luci had found the music wire and had thrown its sphere up into the force-field, he reminded her of the new smells. She took out the long glass records and set the first one into a transmitter.

"Now sniff!"

A queer, frightening, exciting smell came over the room. It seemed like nothing in this world, nor like anything from the up-and-out. Yet it was familiar. His mouth watered. His pulse beat a little faster; he scanned his heartbox. (Faster, sure enough.) But that smell, what was it? In mock perplexity, he grabbed her hands, looked into her eyes, and growled:

"Tell me, darling! Tell me, or I'll eat you up!"

"That's just right!"

"What?"

"You're right. It should make you want to eat me. It's meat."

"Meat. Who?"

"Not a person," said she, knowledgeably, "a Beast. A Beast which people used to eat. A lamb was a small sheep—you've seen sheep out in the Wild, haven't you? —and a chop is part of its middle—here!" She pointed at her chest.

Martel did not hear her. All his boxes had swung over toward *Alarm,* some to *Danger.* He fought against the roar of his own mind, forcing his body into excess excitement. How easy it was to be a scanner when you really stood outside your own body, haberman-fashion, and looked back into it with your eyes alone. Then you could manage the body, rule it coldly even in the enduring agony of space. But to realize that you *were* a body, that this thing was ruling you, that the mind could kick the flesh and send it roaring off into panic! That was bad.

He tried to remember the days before he had gone into the haberman device, before he had been cut apart for the up-and-out. Had he always been subject to the rush of his emotions from his mind to his body, from his body back to his mind, confounding him so that he couldn't scan? But he hadn't been a scanner then.

He knew what had hit him. Amid the roar of his own pulse, he knew. In the nightmare of the up-and-out, that smell had forced its way through to him, while their ship burned off Venus and the habermans fought the collapsing metal with their bare hands. He had scanned then: all were in *Danger*. Chestboxes went up to Overload and dropped to *Dead* all around him as he had moved from man to man, shoving the drifting corpses out of his way as he fought to scan each man in turn, to clamp vises on unnoticed broken legs, to snap the sleeping valve on men whose instruments showed they were hopelessly near *Overload*. With men trying to work and cursing him for a scanner while he, professional zeal aroused, fought to do his job and keep them alive in the great pain of space, he had smelled that smell. It had fought its way along his rebuilt nerves, past the haberman cuts, past all the safeguards of physical and mental discipline. In the wildest hour of tragedy, he had smelled aloud. He remembered it was like a bad cranching, connected with the fury and nightmare all around him. He had even stopped his work to scan himself, fearful that the first effect might come, breaking past all haberman cuts and ruining him with the pain of space. But he had come through. His own instruments stayed and stayed at *Danger*, without nearing *Overload*. He had done his job, and won a commendation for it. He had even forgotten the burning ship.

All except the smell.

And here the smell was all over again—the smell of meat-with-fire . . .

Luci looked at him with wifely concern. She obviously thought he had cranched too much, and was about to haberman back. She tried to be cheerful: "You'd better rest, honey."

He whispered to her: "Cut—off—that—smell."

She did not question his word. She cut the transmitter. She even crossed the room and stepped up the room controls until a small breeze flitted across the floor and drove the smells up to the ceiling.

He rose, tired and stiff. (His instruments were normal, except that heart was fast and nerves still hanging on the edge of *Danger*.) He spoke sadly:

"Forgive me, Luci. I suppose I shouldn't have cranched. Not so soon again. But darling, I have to get out from being a haberman. How can I ever be near you? How can I be a man—not hearing my own voice, not even feeling my own life as it goes through my veins? I love you, darling. Can't I ever be near you?"

Her pride was disciplined and automatic: "But you're a scanner!"

"I know I'm a scanner. But so what?"

She went over the words, like a tale told a thousand times to reassure herself: "You are the bravest of the brave, and most skillful of the skilled. All mankind owes most honor to the scanner, who unites the Earths of mankind. Scanners are the protectors of the habermans. They are the judges in the up-and-out. They make men live in the place where men need desperately to die. They are the most honored of mankind, and even the chiefs of the Instrumentality are delighted to pay them homage!"

With obstinate sorrow he demurred: "Luci. we've heard that all before. But does it pay us back—"

" 'Scanners work for more than pay. They are the strong guards of mankind.' Don't you remember that?"

"But our lives, Luci. What can you get out of being the wife of a scanner? Why did you marry me? I'm human only when I cranch. The rest of the time—you know what I am. A machine. A man turned into a machine. A man who has been killed and kept alive for duty. Don't you realize what I miss?"

"Of course, darling, of course—"

He went on: "Don't you think I remember my childhood? Don't you think I remember what it is to be a man and not a haberman? To walk and feel my feet on the ground? To feel a decent clean pain instead of watching my body every minute to see if I'm alive? How will I know if I'm dead? Did you ever think of that, Luci? How will I know if I'm dead?"

She ignored the unreasonableness of his outburst. Pacifyingly, she said: "Sit down, darling. Let me make you some kind of drink. You're overwrought."

Automatically, he scanned. "No I'm not! Listen to me. How do you think it feels to be in the up-and-out with the crew tied-for-space all around you? How do you think it feels to watch them sleep? How do you think I like scanning, scanning, scanning month after month, when I can feel the pain of space beating against every part of my body, trying to get past my haberman blocks? How do you think I like to wake the men when I have to, and have them hate me for it? Have you ever seen habermans fight—strong men fighting, and neither knowing pain, fighting until one touches *Overload*? Do you think about that, Luci?" Triumphantly he added: "Can you blame me if I cranch, and come back to being a man, just two days a month?"

"I'm not blaming you, darling. Let's enjoy your cranch. Sit down now, and have a drink."

He was sitting down, resting his face in his hands, while she fixed the drink, using natural fruits out of bottles in addition to the secure alkaloids. He watched her restlessly and pitied her for marrying a scanner; and then, though it was unjust, resented having to pity her.

Just as she turned to hand him the drink, they both jumped a little as the phone rang. It should not have rung. They had turned it off. It rang again, obviously on the emergency circuit. Stepping ahead of Luci, Martel strode over to the phone and looked into it. Vomact was looking at him.

The custom of scanners entitled him to be brusque, even with a senior scanner, on certain given occasions. This was one.

Before Vomact could speak, Martel spoke two words into the plate, not caring whether the old man could read lips or not:

"Cranching. Busy."

He cut the switch and went back to Luci.

The phone rang again.

Luci said, gently, "I can find out what it is, darling. Here, take your drink and sit down."

"Leave it alone," said her husband. "No one has a right to call when I'm cranching. He knows that. He ought to know that."

The phone rang again. In a fury, Martel rose and went to the plate. He cut it back on. Vomact was on the screen. Before Martel could speak, Vomact held up his talking nail in line with his heartbox. Martel reverted to discipline:

"Scanner Martel present and waiting, sir."

The lips moved solemnly: "Top emergency."

"Sir, I am under the wire."

"Top emergency."

"Sir, don't you understand? Martel mouthed his words, so he could be sure that Vomact followed. "I . . . am . . . under . . . the . . . wire. Unfit . . . for . . . Space!"

Vomact repeated: "Top emergency. Report to Central Tie-in."

"But, sir, no emergency like this—"

"Right, Martel. No emergency like this, ever before. Report to Tie-in." With a faint glint of kindness, Vomact added: "No need to de-cranch. Report as you are."

This time it was Martel whose phone was cut out. The screen went gray.

He turned to Luci. The temper had gone out of his voice. She came to him. She kissed him, and rumpled his hair. All she could say was,

"I'm sorry."

She kissed him again, knowing his disappointment. "Take good care of yourself, darling. I'll wait."

He scanned, and slipped into his transparent aircoat. At the window he paused, and waved. She called, "Good luck!" As the air flowed past him he said to himself,

"This is the first time I've felt flight in—eleven years. Lord, but it's easy to fly if you can feel yourself live!"

Central Tie-in glowed white and austere far ahead. Martel peered. He saw no glare of incoming ships from the up-and-out, no shuddering flare of space-fire out of control. Everything was quiet, as it should be on an off-duty night.

And yet Vomact had called. He had called an emergency higher than space. There was no such thing. But Vomact had called it.

When Martel got there, he found about half the scanners present, two dozen or so of them. He lifted the talking finger. Most of the scanners were standing face to face, talking in pairs as they read lips. A few of the old, impatient ones were scribbling on their tablets and then thrusting the tablets into other people's faces. All the faces wore the dull dead relaxed look of a haberman. When Martel entered the room, he knew that most of the others laughed in the deep isolated privacy of their own minds, each thinking things it would be useless to express in formal words. It had been a long time since a scanner showed up at a meeting cranched.

Vomact was not there: probably, thought Martel, he was still on the phone calling others. The light of the phone flashed on and off; the bell rang. Martel felt odd when he realized that of all those present, he was the only one to hear that loud bell. It made him realize why ordinary people did not like to be around groups of habermans or scanners. Martel looked around for company.

His friend Chang was there, busy explaining to some old and testy scanner that he did not know why Vomact had called. Martel looked farther and saw Parizianski. He walked over, threading his way past the others with a dexterity that showed he could feel his feet from the inside, and did not have to watch them. Several of the others stared at him with their dead faces, and tried to smile. But they lacked full muscular control and their faces twisted into horrid masks. (Scanners usually knew better than to show expression on faces which they could no longer govern. Martel added to himself, *I swear I'll never smile again unless I'm cranched.*)

Parizianski gave him the sign of the talking finger. Looking face to face, he spoke:

"You come here cranched?"

Parizianski could not hear his own voice, so the words roared like the words on a broken and screeching phone; Martel was startled, but knew that the inquiry was well meant. No one could be better-natured than the burly Pole.

"Vomact called. Top emergency."

"You told him you were cranched?"

"Yes."

"He still made you come?"

"Yes."

"Then all this—it is not for Space? You could not go up-and-out? You are like ordinary men?"

"That's right."

"Then why did he call us?" Some pre-haberman habit made Parizianski wave his arms in inquiry. The hand struck the back of the old man behind them. The slap could be heard throughout the room, but only Martel heard it. Instinctively, he scanned Parizianski and the old scanner, and they scanned him back. Only then did the old man ask why Martel had scanned him. When Martel explained that he was under the wire, the old man moved swiftly away to pass on the news that there was a cranched scanner present at the tie-in.

Even this minor sensation could not keep the attention of most of the scanners from the worry about the top emergency. One young man, who had scanned his first transit just the year before, dramatically interposed himself between Parizianski and Martel. He dramatically flashed his tablet at them:

Is Vmct mad?

The older men shook their heads. Martel, remembering that it had not been too long that the young man had been haberman, mitigated the dead solemnity of the denial with a friendly smile. He spoke in a normal voice, saying:

"Vomact is the senior of scanners. I am sure that he could not go mad. Would he not see it on his boxes first?"

Martel had to repeat the question, speaking slowly and mouthing his words before the young scanner could understand the comment. The young man tried to make his face smile, and twisted it into a comic mask. But he took up his tablet and scribbled:

Yr rght.

Chang broke away from his friend and came over, his

half-Chinese face gleaming in the warm evening. (It's strange, thought Martel, that more Chinese don't become scanners. Or not so strange perhaps, if you think that they never fill their quota of habermans. Chinese love good living too much. The ones who do scan are all good ones.) Chang saw that Martel was cranched, and spoke with voice:

"You break precedents. Luci must be angry to lose you?"

"She took it well. Chang, that's strange."

"What?"

"I'm cranched, and I can hear. Your voice sounds all right. How did you learn to talk like—like an ordinary person?"

"I practiced with soundtracks. Funny you noticed it. I think I am the only scanner in or between the Earths who can pass for an ordinary man. Mirrors and soundtracks. I found out how to act."

"But you don't . . .?"

"No. I don't feel, or taste, or hear, or smell things, any more than you do. Talking doesn't do me much good. But I notice that it cheers up the people around me."

"It would make a difference in the life of Luci."

Chang nodded sagely. "My father insisted on it. He said, 'You may be proud of being a scanner. I am sorry you are not a man. Conceal your defects.' So I tried. I wanted to tell the old boy about the up-and-out, and what we did there, but it did not matter. He said, 'Airplanes were good enough for Confucius, and they are for me too.' The old humbug! He tries so hard to be a Chinese when he can't even read Old Chinese. But he's got wonderful good sense, and for somebody going on two hundred he certainly gets around."

Martel smiled at the thought: "In his airplane?"

Chang smiled back. This discipline of his facial muscles was amazing; a bystander would not think that Chang was a haberman, controlling his eyes, cheeks, and lips by cold intellectual control. The expression had the spontaniety of life. Martel felt a flash of envy for Chang when he looked at the dead cold faces of Parizianski and the others. He knew that he himself looked fine: but why shouldn't he? He was cranched. Turning to Parizianski he said,

"Did you see what Chang said about his father? The old boy uses an airplane."

Parizianski made motions with his mouth, but the sounds meant nothing. He took up his tablet and showed it to Martel and Chang.

Bzz bzz. Ha ha. Gd ol' boy.

At that moment, Martel heard steps out in the corridor. He could not help looking toward the door. Other eyes followed the direction of his glance.

Vomact came in.

The group shuffled to attention in four parallel lines. They scanned one another. Numerous hands reached across to adjust the electrochemical controls on chestboxes which had begun to load up. One scanner held out a broken finger which his counter-scanner had discovered, and submitted it for treatment and splinting.

Vomact had taken out his staff of office. The cube at the top flashed red light through the room, the lines reformed, and all scanners gave the sign meaning, *Present and ready*!

Vomact countered with the stance signifying, *I am the senior and take command.*

Talking fingers rose in the counter-gesture, *We concur and commit ourselves.*

Vomact raised his right arm, dropped the wrist as though it were broken, in a queer searching gesture, meaning: *Any men around? Any habermans not tied? All clear for the scanners?*

Alone of all those present, the cranched Martel heard the queer rustle of feet as they all turned completely around without leaving position, looking sharply at one another and flashing their beltlights into the dark corners of the great room. When again they faced Vomact, he made a further sign:

All clear. Follow my words.

Martel noticed that he alone relaxed. The others could not know the meaning of relaxation with the minds blocked off up there in their skulls, connected only with the eyes, and the rest of the body connected with the mind only by controlling non-sensory nerves and the instrument boxes on their chests. Martel realized that, cranched as he was, he had expected to hear Vomact's voice: the senior had been talking for some time. No sound escaped his lips. (Vomact never bothered with sound.)

". . . and when the first men to go up-and-out went to the moon, what did they find?"

"Nothing," responded the silent chorus of lips.

"Therefore they went farther, to Mars and to Venus. The ships went out year by year, but they did not come back until the Year One of Space. Then did a ship come back with the first effect. Scanners, I ask you, what is the first effect?"

"No one knows. No one knows."

"No one will ever know. Too many are the variables. By what do we know the first effect?"

"By the great pain of space," came the chorus.

"And by what further sign?"

"By the need, oh the need for death."

Vomact again: "And who stopped the need for death?"

"Henry Haberman conquered the first effect, in the Year 83 of Space."

"And, Scanners, I ask you, what did he do?"

"He made the habermans."

"How, O Scanners, are habermans made?"

"They are made with the cuts. The brain is cut from the heart, the lungs. The brain is cut from the ears, the nose. The brain is cut from the mouth, the belly. The brain is cut from desire, and pain. The brain is cut from the world. Save for the eyes. Save for the control of the living flesh."

"And how, O Scanners, is flesh controlled?"

"By the boxes set in the flesh, the controls set in the chest, the signs made to rule the living body, the signs by which the body lives."

"How does a haberman live and live?"

"The haberman lives by control of the boxes."

"Whence come the habermans?"

Martel felt in the coming response a great roar of broken voices echoing through the room as the scanners,

habermans themselves, put sound behind their mouthings:

"Habermans are the scum of mankind. Habermans
are the weak, the cruel, the credulous, and the unfit. Habermans are the sentenced-to-more-than-death. Habermans live in the mind alone. They are killed for space
but they live for space. They master the ships that connect the Earths. They live in the great pain while ordinary men sleep in the cold, cold sleep of the transit."

"Brothers and Scanners, I ask you now: are we habermans or are we not?"

"We are habermans in the flesh. We are cut apart,
brain and flesh. We are ready to go to the up-and-out.
All of us have gone through the haberman device."

"We are habermans then?" Vomact's eyes flashed and
glittered as he asked the ritual question.

Again the chorused answer was accompanied by a
roar of voices heard only by Martel: "Habermans we
are, and more, and more. We are the chosen who are
habermans by our own free will. We are the agents of
the Instrumentality of Mankind."

"What must the others say to us?"

"They must say to us, 'You are the bravest of the
brave, the most skillful of the skilled. All mankind owes
most honor to the scanner, who unites the Earths of
mankind. Scanners are the protectors of the habermans.
They are the judges in the up-and-out. They make men
live in the place where men need desperately to die.
They are the most honored of mankind, and even the
chiefs of the Instrumentality are delighted to pay them
homage!"

Vomact stood more erect: "What is the secret duty of
the scanner?"

"To keep secret our law, and to destroy the acquirers
thereof."

"How to destroy?"

"Twice to the *Overload*, back and *Dead*."

"If habermans die, what the duty then?"

The scanners all compressed their lips for answer.
(Silence was the code.) Martel, who—long familiar
with the code—was a little bored with the proceedings,
noticed that Chang was breathing too heavily; he

reached over and adjusted Chang's lung-control and received the thanks of Chang's eyes. Vomact observed the interruption and glared at them both. Martel relaxed, trying to imitate the dead cold stillness of the others. It was so hard to do, when you were cranched.

"If others die, what the duty then?" asked Vomact.

"Scanners together inform the Instrumentality. Scanners together accept the punishment. Scanners together settle the case."

"And if the punishment be severe?"

"Then no ships go."

"And if scanners be not honored?"

"Then no ships go."

"And if a scanner goes unpaid?"

"Then no ships go."

"And if the Others and the Instrumentality are not in all ways at all times mindful of their proper obligation to the scanners?"

"Then no ships go."

"And what, O Scanners, if no ships go?"

"The Earths fall apart. The Wild comes back in. The Old Machines and the Beasts return."

"What is the first known duty of a scanner?"

"Not to sleep in the up-and-out."

"What is the second duty of a scanner?"

"To keep forgotten the name of fear."

"What is the third duty of a scanner?"

"To use the wire of Eustace Cranch only with care, only with moderation." Several pair of eyes looked quickly at Martel before the mouthed chorus went on. "To cranch only at home, only among friends, only for the purpose of remembering, of relaxing, or of begetting."

"What is the word of the scanner?"

"Faithful though surrounded by death."

"What is the motto of the scanner?"

"Awake though surrounded by silence."

"What is the work of the scanner?"

"Labor even in the heights of the up-and-out, loyalty even in the depths of the Earths."

"How do you know a scanner?"

"We know ourselves. We are dead though we live. And we talk with the tablet and the nail."

"What is this code?"

"This code is the friendly ancient wisdom of scanners, briefly put that we may be mindful and be cheered by our loyalty to one another."

At this point the formula should have run: "We complete the code. Is there work or word for the scanners?" But Vomact said, and he repeated:

"Top emergency. Top emergency."

They gave him the sign, *Present and ready!*

He said, with every eye straining to follow his lips: "Some of you know the work of Adam Stone?"

Martel saw lips move, saying: "The Red Asteroid. The Other who lives at the edge of Space."

"Adam Stone has gone to the Instrumentality, claiming success for his work. He says that he has found how to screen out the pain of space. He says that the up-and-out can be made safe for ordinary men to work in, to stay awake in. He says that there need be no more scanners."

Beltlights flashed on all over the room as scanners sought the right to speak. Vomact nodded to one of the older men. "Scanner Smith will speak."

Smith stepped slowly up into the light, watching his own feet. He turned so that they could see his face. He spoke: "I say that this is a lie. I say that Stone is a liar. I say that the Instrumentality must not be deceived."

He paused. Then, in answer to some question from the audience which most of the others did not see, he said:

"I invoke the secret duty of the scanners."

Smith raised his right hand for emergency attention: "I say that Stone must die."

Martel, still cranched, shuddered as he heard the boos, groans, shouts, squeaks, grunts and moans which came from the scanners who forgot noise in their excitement and strove to make their dead bodies talk to one another's deaf ears. Beltlights flashed wildly all over the room. There was a rush for the rostrum and scanners milled around at the top, vying for attention until Parizianski—by sheer bulk—shoved the others aside and down, and turned to mouth at the group.

"Brother Scanners, I want your eyes."

The people on the floor kept moving, with their numb bodies jostling one another. Finally Vomact stepped up in front of Parizianski, faced the others, and said:

"Scanners, be scanners! Give him your eyes."

Parizianski was not good at public speaking. His lips moved too fast. He waved his hands, which took the eyes of the others away from his lips. Nevertheless, Martel was able to follow most of the message:

". . . can't do this. Stone may have succeeded. If he has succeeded, it means the end of the scanners. It means the end of the habermans, too. None of us will have to fight in the up-and-out. We won't have anybody else going under the wire for a few hours or days of being human. Everybody will be Other. Nobody will have to cranch, never again. Men can be men. The habermans can be killed decently and properly, the way men were killed in the old days, without anybody keeping them alive. They won't have to work in the up-and-out! There will be no more great pain—think of it! No . . . more . . . great . . . pain! How do we know that Stone is a liar—" Lights began flashing directly into his eyes. (The rudest insult of scanner to scanner was this.)

Vomact again exercised authority. He stepped in front of Parizianski and said something which the others could not see. Parizianski stepped down from the rostrum. Vomact again spoke:

"I think that some of the scanners disagree with our brother Parizianski. I say that the use of the rostrum be suspended till we have had a chance for private discussion. In fifteen minutes I will call the meeting back to order."

Martel looked around for Vomact when the senior had rejoined the group on the floor. Finding the senior, Martel wrote swift script on his tablet, waiting for a chance to thrust the tablet before the senior's eyes. He had written:

Am crnchd. Rspctfly requst prmissn lv now, stnd by fr orders.

Being cranched did strange things to Martel. Most

meetings that he attended seemed formal, hearteningly ceremonial, lighting up the dark inward eternities of habermanhood. When he was not cranched, he noticed his body no more than a marble bust notices its marble pedestal. He had stood with them before. He had stood with them effortless hours, while the long-winded ritual broke through the terrible loneliness behind his eyes, and made him feel that the scanners, though a confraternity of the damned, were none the less forever honored by the professional requirements of their mutilation.

This time, it was different. Coming cranched, and in full possession of smell-sound-taste-feeling, he reacted more or less as a normal man would. He saw his friends and colleagues as a lot of cruelly driven ghosts, posturing out the meaningless ritual of their indefeasible damnation. What difference did anything make, once you were a haberman? Why all this talk about habermans and scanners? Habermans were criminals or heretics, and scanners were gentlemen-volunteers, but they were all in the same fix—except that scanners were deemed worthy of the short-time return of the cranching wire, while habermans were simply disconnected while the ships lay in port and were left suspended until they should be awakened, in some hour of emergency or trouble, to work out another spell of their damnation. It was a rare haberman that you saw on the street—someone of special merit or bravery, allowed to look at mankind from the terrible prison of his own mechanified body. And yet, what scanner ever pitied a haberman? What scanner ever honored a haberman except perfunctorily in the line of duty? What had the scanners as a guild and a class ever done for the habermans, except to murder them with a twist of the wrist whenever a haberman, too long beside a scanner, picked up the tricks of the scanning trade and learned how to live at his own will, not the will the scanners imposed? What could the Others, the ordinary men, know of what went on inside inside the ships? The Others slept in their cylinders, mercifully unconscious until they woke up on whatever other Earth they had consigned themselves to. What could the Others know of the men who had to stay alive within the ship?

What could any Other know of the up-and-out? What Other could look at the biting acid beauty of the stars in open space? What could they tell of the great pain, which started quietly in the marrow, like an ache, and proceeded by the fatigue and nausea of each separate nerve cell, brain cell, touchpoint in the body, until life itself became a terrible aching hunger for silence and for death?

He was a scanner. All right, he *was* a scanner. He had been a scanner from the moment when, wholly normal, he had stood in the sunlight before a subchief of the Instrumentality, and had sworn:

"I pledge my honor and my life to mankind. I sacrifice myself willingly for the welfare of mankind. In accepting the perilous austere honor, I yield all my rights without exception to the honorable chiefs of the Instrumentality and to the honored confraternity of scanners."

He had pledged.

He had gone into the haberman device.

He remembered his hell. He had not had such a bad one, even though it had seemed to last a hundred-million years, all of them without sleep. He had learned to feel with his eyes. He had learned to see despite the heavy eyeplates set back of his eyeballs to insulate his eyes from the rest of him. He had learned to watch his skin. He still remembered the time he had noticed dampness on his shirt, and had pulled out his scanning mirror only to discover that he had worn a hole in his side by leaning against a vibrating machine. (A thing like that could not happen to him now; he was too adept at reading his own instruments.) He remembered the way that he had gone up-and-out, and the way that the great pain beat into him, despite the fact that his touch, smell, feeling, and hearing were gone for all ordinary purposes. He remembered killing habermans, and keeping others alive, and standing for months beside the honorable scanner-pilot while neither of them slept. He remembered going ashore on Earth Four, and remembered that he had not enjoyed it, and had realized on that day that there was no reward.

Martel stood among the other scanners. He hated their awkwardness when they moved, their immobility when they stood still. He hated the queer assortment of smells which their bodies yielded unnoticed. He hated the grunts and groans and squawks which they emitted from their deafness. He hated them, and himself.

How could Luci stand him? He had kept his chestbox reading *Danger* for weeks while he courted her, carrying the cranch wire about with him most illegally, and going direct from one cranch to the other without worrying about the fact his indicators all crept to the edge of *Overload*. He had wooed her without thinking of what would happen if she did say, "Yes." She had.

"And they lived happily ever after." In old books they did, but how could they, in life? He had had eighteen days under the wire in the whole of the past year yet she had loved him. She still loved him. He knew it. She fretted about him through the long months that he was in the up-and-out. She tried to make home mean something to him even when he was haberman, make food pretty when it could not be tasted, make herself lovable when she could not be kissed—or might as well not, since a haberman body meant no more than furniture. Luci was patient.

And now, Adam Stone! (He let his tablet fade: how could he leave, now?)

God bless Adam Stone?

Martel could not help feeling a little sorry for himself. No longer would the high keen call of duty carry him through two hundred or so years of the Others' time, two million private eternities of his own. He could slouch and relax. He could forget high space, and let the up-and-out be tended by Others. He could cranch, as much as he dared. He could be almost normal—almost —for one year or five years or no years. But at least he could stay with Luci. He could go with her into the Wild, where there were Beasts and Old Machines still roving the dark places. Perhaps he would die in the excitement of the hunt, throwing spears at an ancient man-shonyagger as it leapt from its lair, or tossing hot spheres at the tribesmen of the Unforgiven who still roamed the Wild. There was still life to live, still a good normal death to die, not the moving of a needle out in the silence and agony of space!

He had been walking about restlessly. His ears were attuned to the sounds of normal speech, so that he did not feel like watching the mouthings of his brethren. Now they seemed to have come to a decision. Vomact was moving to the rostrum. Martel looked about for Chang, and went to stand beside him. Chang whispered.

"You're as restless as water in mid-air! What's the matter? De-cranching?"

They both scanned Martel, but the instruments held steady and showed no sign of the cranch giving out.

The great light flared in its call to attention. Again they formed ranks. Vomact thrust his lean old face into the glare, and spoke:

"Scanners and Brothers, I call for a vote." He held himself in the stance which meant: *I am the senior and take command.*

A beltlight flashed in protest.

It was old Henderson. He moved to the rostrum, spoke to Vomact, and—with Vomact's nod of approval —turned full-face to repeat his question:

"Who speaks for the scanners out in space?"

No beltlight or hand answered.

Henderson and Vomact, face to face, conferred for a few moments. Then Henderson faced them again:

"I yield to the senior in command. But I do not yield to a meeting of the Confraternity. There are sixty-eight scanners, and only forty-seven present, of whom one is cranched and U. D. I have therefore proposed that the senior in command assume authority only over an emergency committee of the Confraternity, not over a meeting. Is that agreed and understood by the honorable scanners?"

Hands rose in assent.

Chang murmured in Martel's ear, "Lot of difference that makes! Who can tell the difference between a meeting and a committee?" Martel agreed with the words, but was even more impressed with the way that Chang, while haberman, could control his own voice.

Vomact resumed chairmanship: "We now vote on the question of Adam Stone.

"First, we can assume that he has not succeeded, and that his claims are lies. We know that from our practical experience as scanners. The pain of space is only part of scanning," (*But the essential part, the basis of it all,* thought Martel.) "and we can rest assured that Stone cannot solve the problem of space discipline."

"That tripe again," whispered Chang, unheard save by Martel.

"The space discipline of our confraternity has kept high space clean of war and dispute. Sixty-eight disciplined men control all high space. We are removed by our oath and our haberman status from all Earthly passions.

"Therefore, if Adam Stone has conquered the pain of space, so that Others can wreck our confraternity and bring to space the trouble and ruin which afflicts Earths, I say that Adam Stone is wrong. If Adam Stone succeeds, scanners live in vain!

"Secondly, if Adam Stone has not conquered the pain of space, he will cause great trouble in all the Earths. The Instrumentality and the subchiefs may not give us as many habermans as we need to operate the ships of mankind. There will be wild stories, and fewer recruits, and, worst of all, the discipline of the Confraternity may relax if this kind of nonsensical heresy is spread around.

"Therefore, if Adam Stone has succeeded, he threatens the ruin of the Confraternity and should die.

"I move the death of Adam Stone."

And Vomact made the sign, *The honorable scanners are pleased to vote.*

Martel grabbed wildly for his beltlight. Chang, guessing ahead, had his light out and ready; its bright beam, voting *No,* shone straight up at the ceiling. Martel got his light out and threw its beam upward in dissent. Then he looked around. Out of the forty-seven present, he could see only five or six glittering.

Two more lights went on. Vomact stood as erect as a frozen corpse. Vomact's eyes flashed as he stared back and forth over the group, looking for lights. Several more went on. Finally Vomact took the closing stance:

May it please the scanners to count the vote.

Three of the older men went up on the rostrum with

Vomact. They looked over the room. (Martel thought: *These damned ghosts are voting on the life of a real man, a live man! They have no right to do it. I'll tell the Instrumentality!* But he knew that he would not. He thought of Luci and what she might gain by the triumph of Adam Stone: the heart-breaking folly of the vote was then almost too much for Martel to bear.)

All three of the tellers held up their hands in unanimous agreement on the sign of the number: *Fifteen against.*

Vomact dismissed them with a bow of courtesy. He turned and again took the stance: *I am the senior and take command.*

Marveling at his own daring, Martel flashed his belt-light on. He knew that any one of the bystanders might reach over and twist his heartbox to *Overload* for such an act. He felt Chang's hand reaching to catch him by the aircoat. But he eluded Chang's grasp and ran, faster than a scanner should, to the platform. As he ran, he wondered what appeal to make. It was no use talking common sense. Not now. It had to be law.

He jumped up on the rostrum beside Vomact, and took the stance: *Scanners, an Illegality!*

He violated good custom while speaking, still in the stance: "A committee has no right to vote death by a majority vote. It takes two-thirds of a full meeting."

He felt Vomact's body lunge behind him, felt himself falling from the rostrum, hitting the floor, hurting his knees and his touch-aware hands. He was helped to his feet. He was scanned. Some scanner he scarcely knew took his instruments and toned him down.

Immediately Martel felt more calm, more detached, and hated himself for feeling so.

He looked up at the rostrum. Vomact maintained the stance signifying: *Order!*

The scanners adjusted their ranks. The two scanners next to Martel took his arms. He shouted at them, but they looked away, and cut themselves off from communication altogether.

Vomact spoke again when he saw the room was quiet: "A scanner came here cranched. Honorable Scanners, I apologize for this. It is not the fault of our great and worthy scanner and friend, Martel. He came here under orders. I told him not to de-cranch. I hoped to spare him an unnecessary haberman. We all know how happily Martel is married, and we wish his brave experiment well. I like Martel. I respect his judgment. I wanted him here. I knew you wanted him here. But he is cranched. He is in no mood to share in the lofty business of the scanners. I therefore propose a solution which will meet all the requirements of fairness. I propose that we rule Scanner Martel out of order for his violation of rules. This violation would be inexcusable if Martel were not cranched.

"But at the same time, in all fairness to Martel, I further propose that we deal with the points raised so improperly by our worthy but disqualified brother."

Vomact gave the sign, *The honorable scanners are pleased to vote.* Martel tried to reach his own beltlight; the dead strong hands held him tightly and he struggled in vain. One lone light shone high: Chang's no doubt.

Vomact thrust his face into the light again: "Having the approval of our worthy Scanners and present company for the general proposal, I now move that this committee declare itself to have the full authority of a meeting, and that this committee further make me responsible for all misdeeds which this committee may enact, to be held answerable before the next full meeting, but not before any other authority beyond the closed and secret ranks of scanners."

Flamboyantly this time, his triumph evident, Vomact assumed the *vote* stance.

Only a few lights shone: far less, patently, than a minority of one-fourth.

Vomact spoke again. The light shone on his high calm forehead, on his dead relaxed cheekbones. His lean cheeks and chin were half-shadowed, save where the lower light picked up and spotlighted his mouth, cruel even in repose. (Vomact was said to be a descendant of some ancient lady who had traversed, in an illegitimate and inexplicable fashion, some hundreds of years of time in a single night. Her name, the Lady Vomact, had passed into legend; but her blood and her archaic lust for mastery lived on in the mute masterful body of her descendant. Martel could believe the old tales as he stared at the rostrum, wondering what untraceable mutation had left the Vomact kin as predators among mankind.) Calling loudly with the movement of his lips, but still without sound, Vomact appealed:

"The honorable committee is now pleased to reaffirm the sentence of death issued against the heretic and enemy, Adam Stone." Again the *vote* stance.

Again Chang's light shone lonely in its isolated protest.

Vomact then made his final move:

"I call for the designation of the senior scanner present as the manager of the sentence. I call for authorization to him to appoint executioners, one or many, who shall make evident the will and majesty of scanners. I ask that I be accountable for the deed, and not for the means. The deed is a noble deed, for the protection of mankind and for the honor of the scanners; but of the means it must be said that they are to be the best at hand, and no more. Who knows the true way to kill an Other, here on a crowded and watchful Earth? This is no mere matter of discharging a cylindered sleeper, no mere question of upgrading the needle of a haberman. When people die down here, it is not like the up-and-out. They die reluctantly. Killing within the Earth is not our usual business, O Brothers and Scanners, as you know well. You must choose me to choose my agent as I see fit. Otherwise the common knowledge will become the common betrayal whereas if I alone know the responsibility, I alone could betray us, and you will not have far to look in case the Instrumentality comes searching." (*What about the killer you choose?* thought Martel. *He too will know unless—unless you silence him forever.*)

Vomact went into the stance: *The honorable scanners are pleased to vote.*

One light of protest shone; Chang's, again.

Martel imagined that he could see a cruel joyful smile on Vomact's dead face—the smile of a man who knew himself righteous and who found his righteousness upheld and affirmed by militant authority.

Martel tried one last time to come free.

The dead hands held. They were locked like vises until their owners' eyes unlocked them: how else could they hold the piloting month by month?

Martel then shouted: "Honorable Scanners, this is judicial murder."

No ear heard him. He was cranched, and alone.

Nonetheless, he shouted again: "You endanger the Confraternity."

Nothing happened.

The echo of his voice sounded from one end of the room to the other. No head turned. No eyes met his.

Martel realized that as they paired for talk, the eyes of the scanners avoided him. He saw that no one desired to watch his speech. He knew that behind the cold faces of his friends there lay compassion or amusement. He knew that they knew him to be cranched—absurd, normal, manlike, temporarily no scanner. But he knew that in this matter the wisdom of scanners was nothing. He knew that only a cranched scanner could feel with his very blood the outrage and anger which deliberate murder would provoke among the Others. He knew that the Confraternity endangered itself, and knew that the most ancient prerogative of law was the monopoly of death. Even the ancient nations, in the times of the Wars, before the Beasts, before men went into the up-and-out—even the ancients had known this. How did they say it? *Only the state shall kill.* The states were gone but the Instrumentality remained, and the Instrumentality could not pardon things which occurred within the Earths but beyond its authority. Death in space was the business, the right of the scanners: how could the Instrumentality enforce its laws in a place where all men who wakened, wakened only to die in the great pain? Wisely did the Instrumentality leave space to the scanners, wisely had the Confraternity not meddled inside the Earths. And now the Confraternity itself was going to step forth as an outlaw band, as a gang of rogues as stupid and reckless as the tribes of the Unforgiven!

Martel knew this because he was cranched. Had he been haberman, he would have thought only with his mind, not with his heart and guts and blood. How could the other scanners know?

Vomact returned for the last time to the rostrum: *The committee has met and its will shall be done.* Verbally he added: "Senior among you, I ask your loyalty and your silence."

At that point, the two scanners let his arms go. Martel rubbed his numb hands, shaking his fingers to get the circulation back into the cold fingertips. With real freedom, he began to think of what he might still do. He scanned himself: the cranching held. He might have a day. Well, he could go on even if haberman, but it would be inconvenient, having to talk with finger and tablet. He looked about for Chang. He saw his friend standing patient and immobile in a quiet corner. Martel moved slowly, so as not to attract any more attention to himself than could be helped. He faced Chang, moved until his face was in the light, and then articulated:

"What are we going to do? You're not going to let them kill Adam Stone, are you? Don't you realize what Stone's work will mean to us, if it succeeds? No more scanners. No more habermans. No more pain in the up-and-out. I tell you, if the others were all cranched, as I am, they would see it in a human way, not with the narrow crazy logic which they used in the meeting. We've got to stop them. How can we do it? What are we going to do? What does Parizianski think? Who has been chosen?"

"Which question do you want me to answer?"

Martel laughed. (It felt good to laugh, even then; it felt like being a man.) "Will you help me?"

Chang's eyes flashed across Martel's face as Chang answered: "No. No. No."

"You won't help?"

"No."

"Why not, Chang? Why not?"

"I am a scanner. The vote has been taken. You would do the same if you were not in this unusual condition."

"I'm not in an unusual condition. I'm cranched. That merely means that I see things the way that the Others would. I see the stupidity. The recklessness. The selfishness. It is murder."

"What is murder? Have you not killed? You are not one of the Others. You are a scanner. You will be sorry for what you are about to do, if you do not watch out."

"But why did you vote against Vomact then? Didn't you too see what Adam Stone means to all of us? Scanners will live in vain. Thank God for that! Can't you see it?"

"No."

"But you talk to me, Chang. You are my friend?"

"I talk to you. I am your friend. Why not?"

"But what are you going to do?"

"Nothing, Martel. Nothing."

"Will you help me?"

"No."

"Not even to save Stone?"

"No."

"Then I will go to Parizianski for help."

"It will do no good."

"Why not? He's more human than you, right now."

"He will not help you, because he has the job. Vomact designated him to kill Adam Stone."

Martel stopped speaking in mid-movement. He suddenly took the stance: *I thank you, Brother, and I depart.*

At the window he turned and faced the room. He saw that Vomact's eyes were upon him. He gave the stance, *I thank you, Brother, and I depart,* and added the flourish of respect which is shown when seniors are present. Vomact caught the sign, and Martel could see the cruel lips move. He thought he saw the words ". . . take good care of yourself . . ." but did not wait to inquire. He stepped backward and dropped out the window.

Once below the window and out of sight, he adjusted his aircoat to a maximum speed. He swam lazily in the air, scanning himself thoroughly, and adjusting his adrenal intake down. He then made the movement of release, and felt the cold air rush past his face like running water.

Adam Stone had to be at Chief Downport.

Adam Stone had to be there.

Wouldn't Adam Stone be surprised in the night? Surprised to meet the strangest of beings, the first renegade among scanners. (Martel suddenly appreciated that it was of himself he was thinking. Martel the Traitor to

Scanners! That sounded strange and bad. But what of Martel, the Loyal to Mankind? Was that not compensation? And if he won, he won Luci. If he lost, he lost nothing—an unconsidered and expendable haberman. It happened to be himself. But in contrast to the immense reward, to mankind, to the Confraternity, to Luci, what did that matter?)

Martel thought to himself: "Adam Stone will have two visitors tonight. Two scanners, who are the friends of one another." He hoped that Parizianski was still his friend.

"And the world," he added, "depends on which of us gets there first."

Multifaceted in their brightness, the lights of Chief Downport began to shine through the mist ahead. Martel could see the outer towers of the city and glimpsed the phosphorescent periphery which kept back the Wild, whether Beasts, Machines, or the Unforgiven.

Once more Martel invoked the lords of his chance: "Help me to pass for an Other!"

Within the Downport, Martel had less trouble than he thought. He draped his aircoat over his shoulder so that it concealed the instruments. He took up his scanning mirror, and made up his face from the inside, by adding tone and animation to his blood and nerves until the muscles of his face glowed and the skin gave out a healthy sweat. That way he looked like an ordinary man who had just completed a long night flight.

After straightening out his clothing, and hiding his tablet within his jacket, he faced the problem of what to do about the talking finger. If he kept the nail, it would show him to be a scanner. He would be respected, but he would be identified. He might be stopped by the guards whom the Instrumentality had undoubtedly set around the person of Adam Stone. If he broke the nail —But he couldn't! No scanner in the history of the Confraternity had ever willingly broken his nail. That would be resignation, and there was no such thing. The only way *out*, was in the up-and-out! Martel put his finger to his mouth and bit off the nail. He looked at the now-queer finger, and sighed to himself.

He stepped toward the city gate, slipping his hand

into his jacket and running up his muscular strength to four times normal. He started to scan, and then realized that his instruments were masked. *Might as well take all the chances at once,* he thought.

The watcher stopped him with a searching wire. The sphere thumped suddenly against Martel's chest.

"Are you a man?" said the unseen voice. (Martel knew that as a scanner in haberman condition, his own field-charge would have illuminated the sphere.)

"I am a man." Martel knew that the timbre of his voice had been good; he hoped that it would not be taken for that of a manshonyagger or a Beast or an Unforgiven one, who with mimicry sought to enter the cities and ports of mankind.

"Name, number, rank, purpose, function, time departed."

"Martel." He had to remember his old number, not Scanner 34. "Sunward 4234, 782nd Year of Space. Rank, rising subchief." That was no lie, but his substantive rank. "Purpose, personal and lawful within the limits of this city. No function of the Instrumentality. Departed Chief Outport 2019 hours." Everything now depended on whether he was believed, or would be checked against Chief Outport.

The voice was flat and routine: "Time desired within the city."

Martel used the standard phrase: "Your honorable sufferance is requested."

He stood in the cool night air, waiting. Far above him, through a gap in the mist, he could see the poisonous glittering in the sky of scanners. *The stars are my enemies,* he thought: *I have mastered the stars but they hate me. Ho, that sounds ancient! Like a book. Too much cranching.*

The voice returned: "Sunward 4234 dash 782 rising Subchief Martel, enter the lawful gates of the city. Welcome. Do you desire food, raiment, money, or companionship?" The voice had no hospitality in it, just business. This was certainly different from entering a city in a scanner's role! Then the petty officers came out, and threw their beltlights on their fretful faces, and mouthed their words with preposterous deference, shouting against the stone deafness of scanner's ears. So that was the way that a subchief was treated: matter of fact, but not bad. Not bad.

Martel replied: "I have that which I need, but beg of the city a favor. My friend Adam Stone is here. I desire to see him, on urgent and personal lawful affairs."

The voice replied: "Did you have an appointment with Adam Stone?"

"No."

"The city will find him. What is his number?"

"I have forgotten it."

"You have forgotten it? Is not Adam Stone a magnate of the Instrumentality? Are you truly his friend?"

"Truly." Martel let a little annoyance creep into his voice. "Watcher, doubt me and call your subchief."

"No doubt implied. Why do you not know the number? This must go into the record," added the voice.

"We were friends in childhood. He has crossed the—" Martel started to say "the up-and-out" and remembered that the phrase was current only among scanners. "He has leapt from Earth to Earth, and has just now returned. I knew him well and I seek him out. I have word of his kith. May the Instrumentality protect us!"

"Heard and believed. Adam Stone will be searched."

At a risk, though a slight one, of having the sphere sound an alarm for *nonhuman,* Martel cut in on his scanner speaker within his jacket. He saw the trembling needle of light await his words and he started to write on it with his blunt finger. *That won't work,* he thought, and had a moment's panic until he found his comb, which had a sharp enough tooth to write. He wrote: "Emergency none. Martel Scanner calling Parizianski Scanner."

The needle quivered and the reply glowed and faded out: "Parizianski Scanner on duty and D. C. Calls taken by Scanner Relay."

Martel cut off his speaker.

Parizianski was somewhere around. Could he have crossed the direct way, right over the city wall, setting off the alert, and invoking official business when the petty officers overtook him in mid-air? Scarcely. That meant that a number of other scanners must have come in with Parizianski, all of them pretending to be in search of a few of the tenuous pleasures which could be enjoyed by a haberman, such as the sight of the news-pictures or the viewing of beautiful women in the Pleasure Gallery. Parizianski was around, but he could not have moved privately, because Scanner Central registered him on duty and recorded his movements city by city.

The voice returned. Puzzlement was expressed in it. "Adam Stone is found and awakened. He has asked pardon of the Honorable, and says he knows no Martel. Will you see Adam Stone in the morning? The city will bid you welcome."

Martel ran out of resources. It was hard enough mimicking a man without having to tell lies in the guise of one. Martel could only repeat: "Tell him I am Martel. The husband of Luci."

"It will be done."

Again the silence, and the hostile stars, and the sense that Parizianski was somewhere near and getting nearer; Martel felt his heart beating faster. He stole a glimpse at his chestbox and set his heart down a point. He felt calmer, even though he had not been able to scan with care.

The voice this time was cheerful, as though an annoyance had been settled: "Adam Stone consents to see you. Enter Chief Downport, and welcome."

The little sphere dropped noiselessly to the ground and the wire whispered away into the darkness. A bright arc of narrow light rose from the ground in front of Martel and swept through the city to one of the higher towers—apparently a hostel, which Martel had never entered. Martel plucked his aircoat to his chest for ballast, stepped heel-and-toe on the beam, and felt himself whistle through the air to an entrance window which sprang up before him as suddenly as a devouring mouth.

A tower guard stood in the doorway. "You are awaited, sir. Do you bear weapons, sir?"

"None," said Martel, grateful that he was relying on his own strength.

The guard led him past the check-screen. Martel noticed the quick flight of a warning across the screen as his instruments registered and identified him as a scanner. But the guard had not noticed it.

The guard stopped at a door. "Adam Stone is armed. He is lawfully armed by authority of the Instrumentality and by the liberty of this city. All those who enter are given warning."

Martel nodded in understanding at the man and went in.

Adam Stone was a short man, stout and benign. His gray hair rose stiffly from a low forehead. His whole face was red and merry-looking. He looked like a jolly guide from the Pleasure Gallery, not like a man who had been at the edge of the up-and-out, fighting the great pain without haberman protection.

He stared at Martel. His look was puzzled, perhaps a little annoyed, but not hostile.

Martel came to the point. "You do not know me. I lied. My name is Martel, and I mean you no harm. But I lied. I beg the honorable gift of your hospitality. Remain armed. Direct your weapon against me—"

Stone smiled: "I am doing so," and Martel noticed the small wirepoint in Stone's capable, plump hand.

"Good. Keep on guard against me. It will give you confidence in what I shall say. But do, I beg you, give us a screen of privacy. I want no casual lookers. This is a matter of life and death."

"First: whose life and death?" Stone's face remained calm, his voice even.

"Yours and mine, and the worlds'."

"You are cryptic but I agree." Stone called through the doorway: "Privacy please." There was a sudden hum, and all the little noises of the night quickly vanished from the air of the room.

Said Adam Stone: "Sir, who are you? What brings you here?"

"I am Scanner 34."

"You a scanner? I don't believe it."

For answer, Martel pulled his jacket open, showing his chestbox. Stone looked up at him, amazed. Martel explained:

"I am cranched. Have you never seen it before?"

"*Not with men.* On animals. Amazing! But—what do you want?"

"The truth. Do you fear me?"

"Not with this," Stone, grasping the wirepoint. "But I shall tell you the truth."

"Is it true that you have conquered the great pain?"

Stone hesitated, seeking words for an answer.

"Quick, can you tell me how you have done it, so that I may believe you?"

"I have loaded the ships with life."

"Life?"

"Life. I don't know what the great pain is, but I did find that in the experiments, when I sent out masses of animals or plants, the life in the center of the mass lived longest. I built ships—small ones, of course—and sent them out with rabbits, with monkeys—"

"Those are Beasts?"

"Yes. With small Beasts. And the Beasts came back unhurt. They came back because the walls of the ships were filled with life. I tried many kinds, and finally found a sort of life which lives in the waters. Oysters. Oyster-beds. The outermost oysters died in the great pain. The inner ones lived. The passengers were unhurt."

"But they were Beasts?"

"Not only Beasts. Myself."

"You!"

"I came through space alone. Through what you call the up-and-out, alone. Awake and sleeping. I am unhurt. If you do not believe me, ask your brother scanners. Come and see my ship in the morning. I will be glad to see you then, along with your brother scanners. I am going to demonstrate before the chiefs of the Instrumentality."

Martel repeated his question: "You came here alone?"

Adam Stone grew testy: "Yes, alone. Go back and check your scanner's register if you do not believe me. You never put me in a bottle to cross Space."

Martel's face was radiant. "I believe you now. It is true. No more scanners. No more habermans. No more cranching."

Stone looked significantly toward the door.

Martel did not take the hint. "I must tell you that—"

"Sir, tell me in the morning. Go enjoy your cranch. Isn't it supposed to be pleasure? Medically I know it well. But not in practice."

"It is pleasure. It's normality—for a while. But listen. The scanners have sworn to destroy you, and your work."

"What!"

"They have met and have voted and sworn. You will make scanners unnecessary, they say. You will bring the ancient wars back to the world, if scanning is lost and the scanners live in vain!"

Adam Stone was nervous but kept his wits about him: "You're a scanner. Are you going to kill me—or try?"

"No, you fool. I have betrayed the Confraternity. Call guards the moment I escape. Keep guards around you. I will try to intercept the killer."

Martel saw a blur in the window. Before Stone could turn, the wirepoint was whipped out of his hand. The blur solidified and took form as Parizianski.

Martel recognized what Parizianski was doing: *High speed.*

Without thinking of his cranch, he thrust his hand to his chest, set himself up to *High speed* too. Waves of fire, like the great pain, but hotter, flooded over him. He fought to keep his face readable as he stepped in front of Parizianski and gave the sign,

Top emergency.

Parizianski spoke, while the normally moving body of Stone stepped away from them as slowly as a drifting cloud: "Get out of my way. I am on a mission."

"I know it. I stop you here and now. Stop. Stop. Stop. Stone is right."

Parizianski's lips were barely readable in the haze of pain which flooded Martel. (He thought: *God, God, God of the ancients! Let me hold on! Let me live under* Overload *just long enough!*) Parizianski was saying: "Get out of my way. By order of the Confraternity, get out of my way!" And Parizianski gave the sign, *Help I demand in the name of my duty!*

Martel choked for breath in the syruplike air. He

tried one last time: "Parizianski, friend, friend, my friend. Stop. Stop." (No scanner had ever murdered scanner before.)

Parizianski made the sign: *You are unfit for duty, and I will take over.*

Martel thought, *For the first time in the world!* as he reached over and twisted Parizianski's brainbox up to *Overload.* Parizianski's eyes glittered in terror and understanding. His body began to drift down toward the floor.

Martel had just strength enough to reach his own chestbox. As he faded into haberman or death, he knew not which, he felt his fingers turning on the control of speed, turning down. He tried to speak, to say, "Get a scanner, I need help, get a scanner . . ."

But the darkness rose about him, and the numb silence clasped him.

Martel awakened to see the face of Luci near his own.

He opened his eyes wider, and found that he was hearing—hearing the sound of her happy weeping, the sound of her chest as she caught the air back into her throat.

He spoke weakly: "Still cranched? Alive?"

Another face swam into the blur beside Luci's. It was Adam Stone. His deep voice rang across immensities of space before coming to Martel's hearing. Martel tried to read Stone's lips, but could not make them out. He went back to listening to the voice:

". . . not cranched. Do you understand me? Not cranched!"

Martel tried to say: "But I can hear! I can feel!" The others got his sense if not his words.

Adam Stone spoke again:

"You have gone back through the haberman. I put you back first. I didn't know how it would work in practice, but I had the theory all worked out. You don't think the Instrumentality would waste the scanners, do you? You go back to normality. We are letting the habermans die as fast as the ships come in. They don't need to live any more. But we are restoring the scanners. You are the first. Do you understand? You are the first. Take it easy, now."

Adam Stone smiled. Dimly behind Stone, Martel thought that he saw the face of one of the chiefs of the Instrumentality. That face, too, smiled at him, and then both faces disappeared upward and away.

Martel tried to lift his head, to scan himself. He could not. Luci stared at him, calming herself, but with an expression of loving perplexity. She said,

"My darling husband! You're back again, to stay!"

Still, Martel tried to see his box. Finally he swept his hand across his chest with a clumsy motion. There was nothing there. The instruments were gone. He was back to normality but still alive.

In the deep weak peacefulness of his mind, another troubling thought took shape. He tried to write with his finger, the way that Luci wanted him to, but he had neither pointed fingernail nor scanner's tablet. He had to use his voice. He summoned up his strength and whispered:

"Scanners?"

"Yes, darling? What is it?"

"Scanners?"

"Scanners. Oh, yes, darling, they're all right. They had to arrest some of them for going into *High speed* and running away. But the Instrumentality caught them all—all those on the ground—and they're happy now. Do you know, darling," she laughed, "some of them didn't want to be restored to normality. But Stone and the chiefs persuaded them."

"Vomact?"

"He's fine, too. He's staying cranched until he can be restored. Do you know, he has arranged for scanners to take new jobs. You're all to be deputy chiefs for Space. Isn't that nice? But he got himself made chief for Space. You're all going to be pilots, so that your fraternity and guild can go on. And Chang's getting changed right now. You'll see him soon."

Her face turned sad. She looked at him earnestly and said: "I might as well tell you now. You'll worry otherwise. There has been one accident. Only one. When you and your friend called on Adam Stone, your friend was so happy that he forgot to scan, and he let himself die of *Overload*."

"Called on Stone?"

"Yes. Don't you remember? Your friend."

He still looked surprised, so she said:

"Parizianski."

The Lady Who Sailed The Soul

*This story was written in collaboration with Gene-
vieve Linebarger (the manuscript is even inscribed
"by Genevieve Linebarger and P.M.A."), who has
completed one unfinished Smith story since her husband's death and is currently working on another.
"Spieltier" is simply German for "play animal." By
the time of this story, the Wild has been tamed and
the Beasts and manshonyaggers are gone. Even luxury has returned—perhaps too much so!*

1

THE STORY RAN—how did the story run? Everyone
knew the reference to Helen America and Mr. Grey-
no-more, but no one knew exactly how it happened.
Their names were welded to the glittering timeless jewel-
ry of romance. Sometimes they were compared to Heloise and Abelard, whose story had been found among
books in a long-buried library. Other ages were to compare their life with the weird, ugly-lovely story of the
Go-Captain Taliano and the Lady Dolores Oh.

Out of it all, two things stood forth—their love and
the image of the great sails, tissue-metal wings with
which the bodies of people finally fluttered out among
the stars.

Mention him, and others knew her. Mention her, and they knew him. He was the first of the inbound sailors, and she was the lady who sailed *The Soul*.

It was lucky that people lost their pictures. The romantic hero was a very young-looking man, prematurely old and still quite sick when the romance came. And Helen America, she was a freak, but a nice one: a grim, solemn, sad, little brunette who had been born amid the laughter of humanity. She was not the tall, confident heroine of the actresses who later played her.

She was, however, a wonderful sailor. That much was true. And with her body and mind she loved Mr. Grey-no-more, showing a devotion which the ages can neither surpass nor forget. History may scrape off the patina of their names and appearances, but even history can do no more than brighten the love of Helen America and Mr. Grey-no-more.

Both of them, one must remember, were sailors.

2

The child was playing with a spieltier. She got tired of letting it be a chicken, so she reversed it into the fur-bearing position. When she extended the ears to the optimum development, the little animal looked odd indeed. A light breeze blew the animal-toy on its side, but the spieltier good-naturedly righted itself and munched contentedly on the carpet.

The little girl suddenly clapped her hands and broke forth with the question,

"Mama, what's a sailor?"

"There used to be sailors, darling, a long time ago. They were brave men who took the ships out to the stars, the very first ships that took people away from our sun. And they had big sails. I don't know how it worked, but somehow, the light pushed them, and it took them a quarter of a life to make a single one-way trip. People only lived a hundred and sixty years at that time, darling, and it was forty years each way, but we don't need sailors any more."

"Of course not," said the child, "we can go right

away. You've taken me to Mars and you've taken me to New Earth as well, haven't you, Mamma? And we can go anywhere else soon, but that only takes one afternoon."

"That's planoforming, honey. But it was a long time before the people knew how to planoform. And they could not travel the way we could, so they made great big sails. They made sails so big that they could not build them on Earth. They had to hang them out, half-way between Earth and Mars. And you know, a funny thing happened . . . Did you ever hear about the time the world froze?"

"No, mamma, what was that?"

"Well, a long time ago, one of these sails drifted and people tried to save it because it took a lot of work to build it. But the sail was so large that it got between the Earth and the sun. And there was no more sunshine, just night all the time. And it got very cold on Earth. All the atomic power plants were busy, and all the air began to smell funny. And the people were worried and in a few days they pulled the sail back out of the way. And the sunshine came again."

"Mamma, were there ever any girl sailors?"

A curious expression crossed over the mother's face. "There was one. You'll hear about her later on when you are older. Her name was Helen America and she sailed The Soul out to the stars. She was the only woman that ever did it. And that is a wonderful story."

The mother dabbed at her eyes with a handkerchief.

The child said: "Mamma, tell me now. What's the story all about?"

At this point the mother became very firm and she said: "Honey, there are some things that you are not old enough to hear yet. But when you are a big girl, I'll tell you all about them."

The mother was an honest woman. She reflected a moment, and then she added, ". . . unless you read about it yourself first."

3

Helen America was to make her place in the history of mankind, but she started badly. The name itself was a misfortune.

No one ever knew who her father was. The officials agreed to keep the matter quiet.

Her mother was not in doubt. Her mother was the celebrated she-man Mona Muggeridge, a woman who had campaigned a hundred times for the lost cause of complete identity of the two genders. She had been a feminist beyond all limits, and when Mona Muggeridge, the one and only *Miss* Muggeridge, announced to the press that she was going to have a baby, that was first-class news.

Mona Muggeridge went further. She announced her firm conviction that fathers should not be identified. She proclaimed that no woman should have consecutive children with the same man, that women should be advised to pick different fathers for their children, so as to diversify and beautify the race. She capped it all by announcing that she, Miss Muggeridge, had selected the perfect father and would inevitably produce the only perfect child.

Miss Muggeridge, a bony, pompous blonde, stated that she would avoid the nonsense of marriage and family names, and that therefore the child, if a boy, would be called John America, and if a girl, Helen America.

Thus it happened that little Helen America was born with the correspondents in the press services waiting outside the delivery room. News-screens flashed the picture of a pretty three-kilogram baby. "It's a girl." "The perfect child." "Who's the dad?"

That was just the beginning. Mona Muggeridge was belligerent. She insisted, even after the baby had been photographed for the thousandth time, that this was the fiinest child ever born. She pointed to the child's perfections. She demonstrated all the foolish fondness of a doting mother, but felt that she, the great crusader, had discovered this fondness for the first time.

To say that this background was difficult for the child would be an understatement.

Helen America was a wonderful example of raw human material triumphing over its tormentors. By the time she was four years old, she spoke six languages, and was beginning to decipher some of the old Martian texts. At the age of five she was sent to school. Her fellow schoolchildren immediately developed a rhyme:

> Helen, Helen
> Fat and dumb
> Doesn't know where
> Her daddy's from!

Helen took all this and perhaps it was an accident of genetics that she grew to become a compact little person —a deadly serious little brunette. Challenged by lessons, haunted by publicity, she became careful and reserved about friendships and desperately lonely in an inner world.

When Helen America was sixteen her mother came to a bad end. Mona Muggeridge eloped with a man she announced to be the perfect husband for the perfect marriage hitherto overlooked by mankind. The perfect husband was a skilled machine polisher. He already had a wife and four children. He drank beer and his interest in Miss Muggeridge seems to have been a mixture of good-natured comradeship and a sensible awareness of her motherly bankroll. The planetary yacht on which they eloped broke the regulations with an off-schedule flight. The bridegroom's wife and children had alerted the police. The result was a collision with a robotic barge which left both bodies identifiable.

At sixteen Helen was already famous, and at seventeen already forgotten, and very much alone.

4

This was the age of sailors. The thousands of photo-reconnaissance and measuring missiles had begun to come back with their harvest from the stars. Planet after planet swam into the ken of mankind. The new worlds became known as the interstellar search missiles brought back photographs, samples of atmosphere, measurements of gravity, cloud coverage, chemical make-up and the like. Of the very numerous missiles which returned from their two- or three-hundred-year voyages, three brought back reports of New Earth, an earth so much like Terra itself that it could be settled.

The first sailors had gone out almost a hundred years before. They had started with small sails not over two-thousand miles square. Gradually the size of the sails increased. The technique of adiabatic packing and the carrying of passengers in individual pods reduced the damage done to the human cargo. It was great news when a sailor returned to Earth, a man born and reared under the light of another star. He was a man who had spent a month of agony and pain, bringing a few sleep-frozen settlers, guiding the immense light-pushed sailing craft which had managed the trip through the great interstellar deeps in an objective time-period of forty years.

Mankind got to know the look of a sailor. There was a plantigrade walk to the way he put his body on the ground. There was a sharp, stiff, mechanical swing to his neck. The man was neither young nor old. He had been awake and conscious for forty years, thanks to the drug which made possible a kind of limited awareness. By the time the psychologists interrogated him, first for the proper authorities of the Instrumentality and later for the news releases, it was plain enough that he thought the forty years were about a month. He never volunteered to sail back, because he had actually aged forty years. He was a young man, a young man in his hopes and wishes, but a man who had burnt up a quarter of a human lifetime in a single agonizing experience.

At this time Helen America went to Cambridge. Lady Joan's College was the finest woman's college in the Atlantic world. Cambridge had reconstructed its protohistoric traditions and the neo-British had recaptured that fine edge of engineering which reconnected their traditions with the earliest antiquity.

Naturally enough the language was cosmopolite Earth and not archaic English, but the students were proud to live at a reconstructed university very much like the ar-

chaeological evidence showed it to have been before the
period of darkness and troubles came upon the Earth.
Helen shone a little in this renaissance.

The news-release services watched Helen in the cruelest possible fashion. They revived her name and the
story of her mother. Then they forgot her again. She had
put in for six professions, and her last choice was "sail-
or." It happened that she was the first woman to make
the application—first because she was the only woman
young enough to qualify who had also passed the scientific requirements.

Her picture was beside his on the screens before they
ever met each other.

Actually, she was not anything like that at all. She had
suffered so much in her childhood from *Helen, Helen,
fat and dumb,* that she was competitive only on a coldly
professional basis. She hated and loved and missed the
tremendous mother whom she had lost, and she resolved
so fiercely not to be like her mother that she became an
embodied antithesis of Mona.

The mother had been horsy, blonde, big—the kind of
woman who is a feminist because she is not very feminine. Helen never thought about her own femininity. She
just worried about herself. Her face would have been
round if it had been plump, but she was not plump.
Black-haired, dark-eyed, broad-bodied but thin, she was
a genetic demonstration of her unknown father. Her
teachers often feared her. She was a pale, quiet girl, and
she always knew her subject.

Her fellow students had joked about her for a few
weeks and then most of them had banded together
against the indecency of the press. When a news-frame
came out with something ridiculous about the long-dead
Mona, the whisper went through Lady Joan's:

"Keep Helen away . . . those people are at it
again."

"Don't let Helen look at the frames now. She's the
best person we have in the non-collateral sciences and
we can't have her upset just before the tripos . . ."

They protected her, and it was only by chance that
she saw her own face in a news-frame. There was the
face of a man beside her. He looked like a little old

monkey, she thought. Then she read, "PERFECT GIRL
WANTS TO BE SAILOR. SHOULD SAILOR HIMSELF DATE
PERFECT GIRL?" Her cheeks burned with helpless, una-
voidable embarrassment and rage, but she had grown
too expert at being herself to do what she might have
done in her teens—hate the man. She knew it wasn't his
fault either. It wasn't even the fault of the silly pushing
men and women from the news services. It was time, it
was custom, it was man himself. But she had only to be
herself, if she could ever find out what that really meant.

5

Their dates, when they came, had the properties of
nightmares.

A news service sent a woman to tell her she had been
awarded a week's holiday in New Madrid.

With the sailor from the stars.

Helen refused.

Then *he* refused too, and he was a little too prompt
for her liking. She became curious about him.

Two weeks passed, and in the office of the news service a treasurer brought two slips of paper to the director.
They were the vouchers for Helen America and Mr.
Grey-no-more to obtain the utmost in preferential luxury at New Madrid. The treasurer said, "These have been
issued and registered as gifts with the Instrumentality,
sir. Should they be cancelled?" The executive had his fill
of stories that day, and he felt humane. On an impulse
he commanded the treasurer, "Tell you what. Give
those tickets to the young people. No publicity. We'll
keep out of it. If they don't want us, they don't have to
have us. Push it along. That's all. Go."

The tickets went back out to Helen. She had made
the highest record ever reported at the university, and
she needed a rest. When the news-service woman gave
her the ticket, she said,

"Is this a trick?"

Assured that it was not, she then asked,

"Is that man coming?"

She couldn't say "*the* sailor"—it sounded too much

like the way people had always talked about herself—
and she honestly didn't remember his other name at the
moment.

The woman did not know.

"Do I have to see him?" said Helen.

"Of course not," said the woman. The gift was uncon-
ditional.

Helen laughed, almost grimly. "All right, I'll take it
and say thanks. But one picturemaker, mind you, just
one, and I walk out. Or I may walk out for no reason at
all. Is that all right?"

It was.

Four days later Helen was in the pleasure world of
New Madrid, and a master of the dances was presenting
her to an odd, intense old man whose hair was black.

"Junior scientist Helen America—Sailor of the stars
Mr. Grey-no-more."

He looked at them shrewdly and smiled a kindly, experienced smile. He added the empty phrase of his profession,

"I have had the honor and I withdraw."

They were alone together on the edge of the dining
room. The sailor looked at her very sharply indeed, and
then said:

"Who are you? Are you somebody I have already
met? Should I remember you? There are too many people here on Earth. What do we do next? What are we
supposed to do? Would you like to sit down?"

Helen said one "Yes" to all those questions and never
dreamed that the single *yes* would be articulated by
hundreds of great actresses, each one in the actress's
own special way, across the centuries to come.

They did sit down.

How the rest of it happened, neither one was ever
quite sure.

She had had to quiet him almost as though he were a
hurt person in the House of Recovery. She explained the
dishes to him and when he still could not choose, she
gave the robot selections for him. She warned him, kindly enough, about manners when he forgot the simple
ceremonies of eating which everyone knew, such as
standing up to unfold the napkin or putting the scraps

into the solvent tray and the silverware into the transfer.

At last he relaxed and did not look so old.

Momentarily forgetting the thousand times she had been asked silly questions herself, she asked him,

"Why did *you* become a sailor?"

He stared at her in open-eyed inquiry as though she had spoken to him in an unknown language and expected a reply. Finally he mumbled the answer,

"Are you—you, too—saying that—that I shouldn't have done it?"

Her hand went to her mouth in instinctive apology.

"No, no, no. You see, I myself have put in to be a sailor."

He merely looked at her, his young-old eyes open with observativeness. He did not stare, but merely seemed to be trying to understand words, each one of which he could comprehend individually but which in sum amounted to sheer madness. She did not turn away from his look, odd though it was. Once again, she had the chance to note the indescribable peculiarity of this man who had managed enormous sails out in the blind empty black between untwinkling stars. He was young as a boy. The hair which gave him his name was glossy black. His beard must have been removed permanently, because his skin was that of a middle-aged woman— well-kept, pleasant, but showing the unmistakable wrinkles of age and betraying no sign of the normal stubble which the males in her culture preferred to leave on their faces. The skin had age without experience. The muscles had grown older, but they did not show *how* the person had grown.

Helen had learned to be an acute observer of people as her mother took up with one fanatic after another; she knew full well that people carry their secret biographies written in the muscles of their faces, and that a stranger passing on the street tells us (whether he wishes to or not) all his inmost intimacies. If we but look sharply enough, and in the right light, we know whether fear or hope or amusement has tallied the hours of his days, we divine the sources and outcome of his most secret sensuous pleasures, we catch the dim but persistent reflections of those other people who have left the imprints of their personalities on him in turn.

All this was absent from Mr. Grey-no-more: he had age but not the stigmata of age; he had growth without the normal markings of growth; he had lived without living, in a time and world in which most people stayed young while living too much.

He was the uttermost opposite of her mother that Helen had ever seen, and with a pang of undirected apprehension Helen realized that this man meant a great deal to her future life, whether she wished him to or not. She saw in him a young bachelor, prematurely old, a man whose love had been given to emptiness and horror, not to the tangible rewards and disappointments of human life. He had had all space for his mistress, and space had used him harshly. Still young, he was old; already old, he was young.

The mixture was one which she knew that she had never seen before, and which she suspected that no one else had ever seen, either. He had in the beginning of life the sorrow, compassion, and wisdom which most people find only at the end.

It was he who broke the silence. "You did say, didn't you, that you yourself had put in to be a sailor?"

Even to herself, her answer sounded silly and girlish. "I'm the first woman ever to qualify with the necessary scientific subjects while still young enough to pass the physical . . ."

"You must be an unusual girl," said he mildly. Helen realized, with a thrill, a sweet and bitterly real hope that this young-old man from the stars had never heard of the "perfect child" who had been laughed at in the moments of being born, the girl who had all America for a father, who was famous and unusual and alone so terribly much so that she could not even imagine being ordinary, happy, decent, or simple.

She thought to herself, *It would take a wise freak who sails in from the stars to overlook who I am,* but to him she simply said, "It's no use talking about being 'unusual.' I'm tired of this Earth, and since I don't have to die to leave it, I think I would like to sail to the stars. I've got less to lose than you may think . . ." She started to tell him about Mona Muggeridge but she stopped in time.

The compassionate gray eyes were upon her, and at this point it was he, not she, who was in control of the situation. She looked at the eyes themselves. They had stayed open for forty years, in the blackness near to pitch-darkness of the tiny cabin. The dim dials had shone like blazing suns upon his tired retinas before he was able to turn his eyes away. From time to time he had looked out at the black nothing to see the silhouettes of his sails, almost-blackness against total blackness, as the miles of their sweep sucked up the push of light itself and accelerated him and his frozen cargo at almost immeasurable speeds across an ocean of unfathomable silence. Yet, what he had done, she had asked to do.

The stare of his gray eyes yielded to a smile of his lips. In the young-old face, masculine in structure and feminine in texture, the smile had a connotation of tremendous kindness. She felt singularly much like weeping when she saw him smile in that particular way at her. Was that what people learned between the stars? To care for other people very much indeed and to spring upon them only to reveal love and not devouring to their prey?

In a measured voice he said, "I believe you. You're the first one that I have believed. All these people have said that they wanted to be sailors too, even when they looked at me. They could not know what it means, but they said it anyhow, and I hated them for saying it. You, though—you're different. Perhaps you will sail among the stars, but I hope that you will not."

As though waking from a dream, he looked around the luxurious room, with the gilt-and-enamel robot-waiters standing aside with negligent elegance. They were designed to be always present and never obtrusive: this was a difficult esthetic effect to achieve, but their designer had achieved it.

The rest of the evening moved with the inevitability of good music. He went with her to the forever-lonely beach which the architects of New Madrid had built beside the hotel. They talked a little, they looked at each other, and they made love with an affirmative certainty which seemed outside themselves. He was very tender, and he did not realize that in a genitally sophisticated society, he was the first lover she had ever wanted or had ever had. (How could the daughter of Mona Muggeridge want a lover or a mate or a child?)

On the next afternoon, she exercised the freedom of her times and asked him to marry her. They had gone back to their private beach, which, through miracles of ultra-fine mini-weather adjustments, brought a Polynesian afternoon to the high chilly plateau of central Spain.

She asked him, *she* did, to marry her, and he refused, as tenderly and as kindly as a man of sixty-five can refuse a girl of eighteen. She did not press him; they continued the bittersweet love affair.

They sat on the artificial sand of the artificial beach and dabbled their toes in the man-warmed water of the ocean. Then they lay down against an artificial sand dune which hid New Madrid from view.

"Tell me," Helen said, "can I ask again, why did you become a sailor?"

"Not so easily answered," he said. "Adventure, maybe. That, at least in part. And I wanted to see Earth. Couldn't afford to come in a pod. Now—well, I've enough to keep me the rest of my life. I can go back to New Earth as a passenger in a month instead of forty years—be frozen in no more time than the wink of an eye, put in my adiabatic pod, linked in to the next sailing ship, and wake up home again while some other fool does the sailing."

Helen nodded. She did not bother to tell him that she knew all this. She had been investigating sailing ships since meeting the sailor.

"Out where you sail among the stars," she said, "can you tell me—can you possibly tell me anything of what it's like out there?"

His face looked inward on his soul and afterward his voice came as from an immense distance.

"There are moments—or is it weeks—you can't really tell in the sail ship—when it seems—worthwhile. You feel . . . your nerve endings reach out until they touch the stars. You feel enormous, somehow." Gradually he came back to her. "It's trite to say, of course, but you're never the same afterward. I don't mean just the obvious physical thing, but—you find yourself—or maybe you lose yourself. That's why," he continued, gesturing toward New Madrid out of sight behind the sand dune, "I can't stand this. New Earth, well, it's like Earth must have been in the old days, I guess. There's something fresh about it. Here . . ."

"I know," said Helen America, and she did. The slightly decadent, slightly corrupt, too comfortable air of Earth must have had a stifling effect on the man from beyond the stars.

"There," he said, "you won't believe this, but sometimes the ocean's too cold to swim in. We have music that doesn't come from machines, and pleasures that come from inside our own bodies without being put there. I have to get back to New Earth."

Helen said nothing for a little while, concentrating on stilling the pain in her heart.

"I . . . I . . ." she began.

"I know," he said fiercely, almost savagely turning on her. "But I can't take you. I can't! You're too young, you've got a life to live and I've thrown away a quarter of mine. No, that's not right. I didn't throw it away. I wouldn't trade it back because it's given me something inside I never had before. And it's given me you."

"But if—" she started again to argue.

"No. Don't spoil it. I'm going next week to be frozen in my pod to wait for the next sail ship. I can't stand much more of this, and I might weaken. That would be a terrible mistake. But we have this time together now, and we have our separate lifetimes to remember in. Don't think of anything else. There's nothing, nothing we can do."

Helen did not tell him—then or ever—of the child she had started to hope for, the child they would now never have. Oh, she could have used the child. She could have tied him to her, for he was an honorable man and would have married her had she told him. But Helen's love, even then in her youth, was such that she could not use this means. She wanted him to come to her of his own free will, marrying her because he could not live without her. To that marriage their child would have been an additional blessing.

There was the other alternative, of course. She could have borne the child without naming the father. But *she* was no Mona Muggeridge. She knew too well the terrors and insecurity and loneliness of being Helen America ever to be responsible for the creation of another. And for the course she had laid out there was no place for a child. So she did the only thing she could. At the end of their time in New Madrid, she let him say a real goodbye. Wordless and without tears, she left. Then she went up to an arctic city, a pleasure city where such things are well-known and amidst shame, worry and a driving sense of regret she appealed to a confidential medical service which eliminated the unborn child. Then she went back to Cambridge and confirmed her place as the first woman to sail a ship to the stars.

6

The presiding lord of the Instrumentality at that time was a man named Wait. Wait was not cruel but he was never noted for tenderness of spirit or for a high regard for the adventuresome proclivities of young people. His aide said to him, "This girl wants to sail a ship to New Earth. Are you going to let her?"

"Why not?" said Wait. "A person is a person. She is well-bred, well-educated. If she fails, we will find out something eighty years from now when the ship comes back. If she succeeds, it will shut up some of these women who have been complaining." The lord leaned over his desk: "If she qualifies, and if she goes, though, don't give her any convicts. Convicts are too good and too valuable as settlers to be sent along on a fool trip like that. You can send her on something of a gamble. Give her all religious fanatics. We have more than enough. Don't you have twenty or thirty thousand who are waiting?"

He said, "Yes, sir, twenty-six thousand two hundred. Not counting recent additions."

"Very well," said the lord of the Instrumentality.
"Give her the whole lot of them and give her that new
ship. Have we named it?"

"No, sir," said the aide.

"Name it then."

The aide looked blank.

A contemptuous wise smile crossed the face of the
senior bureaucrat. He said, "'Take that ship now and
name it. Name it *The Soul* and let *The Soul* fly to the
stars. And let Helen America be an angel if she wants
to. Poor thing, she has not got much of a life to live on
this Earth, not the way she was born, and the way she
was brought up. And it's no use to try and reform her,
to transform her personality, when it's a lively, rich personality. It does not do any good. We don't have to punish her for being herself. Let her go. Let her have it."

Wait sat up and stared at his aide and then repeated
very firmly:

"Let her have it, *only if she qualifies.*"

7

Helen America did qualify.

The doctors and the experts tried to warn her against
it.

One technician said: "Don't you realize what this is
going to mean? Forty years will pour out of your life in
a single month. You leave here a girl. You will get there
a woman of sixty. Well, you will probably still have a
hundred years to live after that. And it's painful. You
will have all these people, thousands and thousands of
them. You will have some Earth cargo. There will be
about thirty thousand pods strung on sixteen lines behind
you. Then you will have the control cabin to live in. We
will give you as many robots as you need, probably a
dozen. You will have a mainsail and a foresail and you
will have to keep the two of them."

"I know. I have read the book," said Helen America.
"And I sail the ship with light, and if the infrared touches that sail—I go. If I get radio interference, I pull the
sails in. And if the sails fail, I wait as long as I live."

The technician looked a little cross. "There is no call for you to get tragic about it. Tragedy is easy enough to contrive. And if you want to be tragic, you can be tragic without destroying thirty thousand other people or without wasting a large amount of Earth property. You can drown in water right here, or jump into a volcano like the Japanese in the old books. Tragedy is not the hard part. The hard part is when you don't quite succeed and you have to keep on fighting. When you must keep going on and on and on in the face of really hopeless odds, of real temptations to despair.

"Now this is the way that the foresail works. That sail will be twenty thousand miles at the wide part. It tapers down and the total length will be just under eighty-thousand miles. It will be retracted or extended by small servo-robots. The servo-robots are radio-controlled. You had better use your radio sparingly, because after all these batteries, even though they are atomic, have to last forty years. They have got to keep you alive."

"Yes, sir," said Helen America very contritely.

"You've got to remember what your job is. You're going because you are cheap. You are going because a sailor takes a lot less weight than a machine. There is no all-purpose computer built that weighs as little as a hundred and fifty pounds. You do. You go simply because you are expendable. Anyone that goes out to the stars takes one chance in three of never getting there. But you are not going because you are a leader, you are going because you are young. You have a life to give and a life to spare. Because your nerves are good. You understand that?"

"Yes, sir, I knew that."

"Furthermore, you are going because you'll make the trip in forty years. If we send automatic devices and have them manage the sails, they would get there—possibly. But it would take them from a hundred years to a hundred-and twenty or more, and by that time the adiabatic pods would have spoiled, most of the human cargo would not be fit for revival and the leakage of heat, no matter how we face it, would be enough to ruin the entire expedition. So remember that the tragedy and the trouble you face is mostly work. Work, and that's all it is. That is your big job."

Helen smiled. She was a short girl with rich dark hair, brown eyes, and very pronounced eyebrows, but when Helen smiled she was almost a child again, and a rather charming one. She said: "My job is work. I understand that, sir."

8

In the preparation area, the make-ready was fast but not hurried. Twice the technicians urged her to take a holiday before she reported for final training. She did not accept their advice. She wanted to go forth; she knew that they knew she wanted to leave Earth forever, and she also knew they knew she was not merely her mother's daughter. She was trying, somehow, to be herself. She knew the world did not believe, but the world did not matter.

The third time they suggested a vacation, the suggestion was mandatory. She had a gloomy two months which she ended up enjoying a little bit on the wonderful islands of the Hesperides, islands which were raised when the weight of the Earthports caused a new group of small archipelagos to form below Bermuda.

She reported back, fit, healthy, and ready to go.

The senior medical officer was very blunt.

"Do you really know what we are going to do to you? We are going to make you live forty years out of your life in one month."

She nodded, white of face, and he went on, "Now to give you those forty years we've got to slow down your bodily processes. After all the sheer biological task of breathing forty years' worth of air in one month involves a factor of about five hundred to one. No lungs could stand it. Your body must circulate water. It must take in food. Most of this is going to be protein. There will be some kind of a hydrate. You'll need vitamins.

"Now, what we are going to do is to slow the brain down, very much indeed, so that the brain will be working at about that five-hundred-to-one ratio. We don't want you incapable of working. Somebody has got to manage the sails.

"Therefore, if you hesitate or you start to think, a thought or two is going to take several weeks. Meanwhile your body can be slowed down some. But the different parts can't be slowed down at the same rate. Water, for example, we brought down to about eighty to one. Food, to about three hundred to one.

"You won't have time to drink forty years' worth of water. We circulate it, get it through, purify it, and get it back in your system, unless you break your link-up.

"So what you face is a month of being absolutely wide awake, on an operating table and *being operated on without anesthetic,* while doing some of the hardest work that mankind has ever found.

"You'll have to take observations, you'll have to watch your lines with the pods of people and cargo behind you, you'll have to adjust the sails. If there is anybody surviving at destination point, they will come out and meet you.

"At least that happens most of the times.

"I am not going to assure you you will get the ship in. If they don't meet you, take an orbit beyond the farthest planet and either let yourself die or try to save yourself. You can't get thirty thousand people down on a planet singlehandedly.

"Meanwhile, though, you've got a real job. We are going to have to build these controls right into your body. We'll start by putting valves in your chest arteries. Then we go on, catheterizing your water. We are going to make an artificial colostomy that will go forward here just in front of your hip joint. Your water intake has a certain psychological value so that about one five-hundredth of your water we are going to leave you to drink out of a cup. The rest of it is going to go directly into your bloodstream. Again about a tenth of your food will go that way. You understand that?"

"You mean," said Helen, "I eat one-tenth, and the rest goes in intravenously?"

"That's right," said the medical technician. "We will pump it into you. The concentrates are there. The reconstitutor is there. Now these lines have a double connection. One set of connections runs into the maintenance machine. That will become the logistic support for your body. And these lines are the umbilical cord for a human being alone among the stars. They are your life.

"And now if they should break or if you should fall, you might faint for a year or two. If that happens, your local system takes over: that's the pack on your back.

"On Earth, it weighs as much as you do. You have already been drilled with the model pack. You know how easy it is to handle in space. That'll keep you going for a subjective period of about two hours. No one has ever worked out a clock yet that would match the human mind, so instead of giving you a clock we are giving you an odometer attached to your own pulse and we mark it off in grades. If you watch it in term of tens of thousands of pulse beats, you may get some information out of it.

"I don't know what kind of information, but you may find it helpful somehow." He looked at her sharply and then turned back to his tools, picking up a shining needle with a disk on the end.

"Now, let's get back to this. We are going to have to get right into your mind. That's chemical too."

Helen interrupted. "You said you were not going to operate on my head."

"Only the needle. That's the only way we can get to the mind. Slow it down enough so that you will have this subjective mind operating at a rate that will make the forty years pass in a month." He smiled grimly, but the grimness changed to momentary tenderness as he took in her brave obstinate stance, her girlish, admirable, pitiable determination.

"I won't argue it," she said. "This is as bad as a marriage and the stars are my bridegroom." The image of the sailor went across her mind, but she said nothing of him.

The technician went on. "Now, we have already built in psychotic elements. You can't even expect to remain sane. So you'd better not worry about it. You'll have to be insane to manage the sails and to survive utterly alone and be out there even a month. And the trouble is in that month you are going to know it's really forty years. There is not a mirror in the place but you'll probably find shiny surfaces to look at yourself.

"You won't look so good. You will see yourself aging, every time you slow down to look. I don't know what the problem is going to be on that score. It's been bad enough on men.

"Your hair problem is going to be easier than men's. The sailors we sent out, we simply had to kill all the hair roots. Otherwise the men would have been swamped in their own beards. And a tremendous amount of the nutrient would be wasted if it went into raising of hair on the face which no machine in the world could cut off fast enough to keep a man working. I think what we will do is inhibit hair on the top of your head. Whether it comes out in the same color or not is something you will find for yourself later. Did you ever meet the sailor that came in?"

The doctor knew she had met him. He did not know that it was the sailor from beyond the stars who called her. Helen managed to remain composed as she smiled at him to say: "Yes, you gave him new hair. Your technician planted a new scalp on his head, remember. Somebody on your staff did. The hair came out black and he got the nickname of Mr. Grey-no-more."

"If you are ready next Tuesday, we'll be ready too. Do you think you can make it by then, my lady?"

Helen felt odd seeing this old, serious man refer to her as "lady," but she knew he was paying respect to a profession and not just to an individual.

"Tuesday is time enough." She felt complimented that he was an old-fashioned enough person to know the ancient names of the days of the week and to use them. That was a sign that he had not only learned the essentials at the University but that he had picked up the elegant inconsequentialities as well.

9

Two weeks later was twenty-one years later by the chronometers in the cabin. Helen turned for the ten-thousand-times-ten-thousandth time to scan the sails.

Her back ached with a violent throb.

She could feel the steady roar of her heart like a fast vibrator as it ticked against the time-span of her awareness. She could look down at the meter on her wrist and see the hands on the watchlike dials indicate tens of thousands of pulses very slowly.

She heard the steady whistle of air in her throat as her lungs seemed shuddering with sheer speed.

And she felt the throbbing pain of a large tube feeding an immense quantity of mushy water directly into the artery of her neck.

On her abdomen, she felt as if someone had built a fire. The evacuation tube operated automatically but it burnt as if a coal had been held to her skin and a catheter, which connected her bladder to another tube, stung as savagely as the prod of a scalding-hot needle. Her head ached and her vision blurred.

But she could still see the instruments and she still could watch the sails. Now and then she could glimpse, faint as a tracery of dust, the immense skein of people and cargo that lay behind them.

She could not sit down. It hurt too much.

The only way that she could be comfortable for resting was to lean against the instrument panel, her lower ribs against the panel, her tired forehead against the meters.

Once she rested that way and realized that it was two and a half months before she got up. She knew that rest had no meaning and she could see her face moving, a distorted image of her own face growing old in the reflections from the glass face of the "apparent weight" dial. She could look at her arms with blurring vision, note the skin tightening, loosening and tightening again, as changes in temperatures affected it.

She looked out one more time at the sails and decided to take in the foresail. Wearily she dragged herself over the control panel with a servo-robot. She selected the right control and opened it for a week or so. She waited there, her heart buzzing, her throat whistling air, her fingernails breaking off gently as they grew. Finally she checked to see if it really had been the right one, pushed again, and nothing happened.

She pushed a third time. There was no response.

Now she went back to the master panel, re-read, checked the light direction, found a certain amount of infrared pressure which she should have been picking up. The sails had very gradually risen to something not far from the speed of light itself because they moved fast with the one side dulled; the pods behind, sealed against time and eternity, swam obediently in an almost perfect weightlessness.

She scanned; her reading had been correct.

The sail *was* wrong.

She went back to the emergency panel and pressed. Nothing happened.

She broke out a repair robot and sent it out to effect repairs, punching the papers as rapidly as she could to give instructions. The robot went out and an instant (three days) later it replied. The panel on the repair robot rang forth, "Does not conform."

She sent a second repair robot. That had no effect either.

She sent a third, the last. Three bright lights, "Does not conform," stared at her. She moved the servo-robots to the other side of the sails and pulled hard.

The sail was still not at the right angle.

She stood there wearied and lost in space, and she prayed: "Not for me, God, I am running away from a life that I did not want. But for this ship's souls and for the poor foolish people that I am taking who are brave enough to want to worship their own way and need the light of another star, I ask you, God, help me now." She thought she had prayed very fervently and she hoped that she would get an answer to her prayer.

It did not work out that way. She was bewildered, alone.

There was no sun. There was nothing, except the tiny cabin and herself more alone than any woman had ever been before. She sensed the thrill and ripple of her muscles as they went through days of adjustment while her mind noticed only the matter of minutes. She leaned forward, forced herself not to relax and finally she remembered that one of the official busybodies had included a weapon.

What she would use a weapon for she did not know.

It pointed. It had a range of two hundred thousand miles. The target could be selected automatically.

She got down on her knees trailing the abdominal tube and the feeding tube and the catheter tubes and the helmet wires, each one running back to the panel. She crawled underneath the panel for the servo-robots and she pulled out a written manual. She finally found the right frequency for the weapon's controls. She set the weapon up and went to the window.

At the last moment she thought, "Perhaps the fools are going to make me shoot the window out. It ought to have been designed to shoot through the window without hurting it. That's the way they should have done it."

She wondered about the matter for a week or two.

Just before she fired it she turned and there, next to her, stood her sailor, the sailor from the stars, Mr. Grey-no-more. He said: "It won't work that way."

He stood clear and handsome, the way she had seen him in New Madrid. He had no tubes, he did not tremble, she could see the normal rise and fall of his chest as he took one breath every hour or so. One part of her mind knew that he was a hallucination. Another part of her mind believed that he was real. She was mad and she was very happy to be mad at this time and she let the hallucination give her advice. She re-set the gun so that it would fire through the cabin wall and it fired a low charge at the repair mechanism out beyond the distorted and immovable sail.

The low charge did the trick. The interference had been something beyond all technical anticipation. The weapon had cleaned out the forever-unidentifiable obstruction, leaving the servo-robots free to attack their tasks like a tribe of maddened ants. They worked again. They had had defenses built in against the minor impediments of space. All of them scurried and skipped about.

With a sense of bewilderment close to religion, she

perceived the wind of starlight blowing against the immense sails. The sails snapped into position. She got a momentary touch of gravity as she sensed a little weight. *The Soul* was back on her course.

10

"It's a girl," they said to him on New Earth. "It's a girl. She must have been eighteen herself."

Mr. Grey-no-more did not believe it.

But he went to the hospital and there in the hospital he saw Helen America.

"Here I am, sailor," said she. "I sailed too." Her face was white as chalk, her expression was that of a girl of about twenty. Her body was that of a well-preserved woman of sixty.

As for him, he had not changed again, since he had returned home inside a pod.

He looked at her. His eyes narrowed and then in a sudden reversal of roles, it was he who was kneeling beside her bed and covering her hands with his tears.

Half-coherently, he babbled at her: "I ran away from you because I loved you so. I came back here where you would never follow, or if you did follow, you'd still be a young woman, and I'd still be too old. But you have sailed *The Soul* in here and you wanted me."

The nurse of New Earth did not know about the rules which should be applied to the sailors from the stars. Very quietly she went out of the room, smiling in tenderness and human pity at the love which she had seen. But she was a practical woman and she had a sense of her own advancement. She called a friend of hers at the news service and said: "I think I have got the biggest romance in history. If you get here soon enough you can get the first telling of the story of Helen America and Mr. Grey-no-more. They just met like that. I guess they'd seen each other somewhere. They just met like that and fell in love."

The nurse did not know that they had forsworn a love on Earth. The nurse did not know that Helen America had made a lonely trip with an icy purpose and the

nurse did not know that the crazy image of Mr. Grey-
no-more, the sailor himself, had stood beside Helen
twenty years out from nothing-at-all in the depth and
blackness of space between the stars.

11

The little girl had grown up, had married, and now
had a little girl of her own. The mother was unchanged,
but the spieltier was very, very old. It had outlived all its
marvelous tricks of adaptability, and for some years had
stayed frozen in the role of a yellow-haired, blue-eyed
girl doll. Out of sentimental sense of the fitness of
things, she had dressed the spieltier in a bright blue
jumper with matching panties. The little animal crept
softly across the floor on its tiny human hands, using its
knees for hind feet. The mock-human face looked up
blindly and squeaked for milk.

The young mother said, "Mom, you ought to get rid
of that thing. It's all used up and it looks horrible with
your nice period furniture."

"I thought you loved it," said the older woman.

"Of course," said the daughter. "It was cute, when I
was a child. But I'm not a child any more, and it doesn't
even work."

The spieltier had struggled to its feet and clutched its
mistress's ankle. The older woman took it away gently,
and put down a saucer of milk and a cup the size of a
thimble. The spieltier tried to curtsey, as it had been
motivated to do at the beginning, slipped, fell, and
whimpered. The mother righted it and the little old animal-toy began dipping milk with its thimble and sucking
the milk into its tiny toothless old mouth.

"You remember, Mom—" said the younger woman
and stopped.

"Remember what, dear?"

"You told me about Helen America and Mr. Grey-
no-more when that was brand new."

"Yes, darling, maybe I did."

"You didn't tell me everything," said the younger
woman accusingly.

"Of course not. You were a child."

"But it was awful. Those messy people, and the horrible way sailors live. I don't see how you idealized it and called it a romance—"

"But it was. It is," insisted the other.

"Romance, my foot," said the daughter. *"It's as bad as you and the worn-out spieltier."* She pointed at the tiny, living, aged doll who had fallen asleep beside its milk. *"I think it's horrible. You ought to get rid of it. And the world ought to get rid of sailors."*

"Don't be harsh, darling," said the mother.

"Don't be a sentimental old slob," said the daughter.

"Perhaps we are," said the mother with a loving sort of laugh. Unobtrusively she put the sleeping spieltier on a padded chair where it would not be stepped on or hurt.

12

Outsiders never knew the real end of the story.

More than a century after their wedding, Helen lay dying: she was dying happily, because her beloved sailor was beside her. She believed that if they could conquer space, they might conquer death as well.

Her loving, happy, weary dying mind blurred over and she picked up an argument they hadn't touched upon for decades.

"You did *so* come to *The Soul*," she said. "You did so stand beside me when I was lost and did not know how to handle the weapon."

"If I came then, darling, I'll come again, wherever you are. You're my darling, my heart, my own true love. You're my bravest of ladies, my boldest of people. You're my own. You sailed for me. You're my lady who sailed *The Soul*."

His voice broke, but his features stayed calm. He had never before seen anyone die so confident and so happy.

The Game of Rat and Dragon

Captain Wow and the other feline characters were inspired by cats living in the Linebarger home when this story was written—at a single sitting one afternoon in 1954. The discovery of planoforming, which forces men to brave the terrors of space₂, was described in an unpublished story written the next year . . . a story which may never appear now, since its theme was later reworked in "Drunkboat."

1. The Table

PINLIGHTING IS A hell of a way to earn a living. Underhill was furious as he closed the door behind himself. It didn't make much sense to wear a uniform and look like a soldier if people didn't appreciate what you did.

He sat down in his chair, laid his head back in the headrest, and pulled the helmet down over his forehead.

As he waited for the pin-set to warm up, he remembered the girl in the outer corridor. She had looked at it, then looked at him scornfully.

"Meow." That was all she had said. Yet it had cut him like a knife.

What did she think he was—a fool, a loafer, a uniformed nonentity? Didn't she know that for every half-hour of pinlighting, he got a minimum of two months' recuperation in the hospital?

By now the set was warm. He felt the squares of space around him, sensed himself at the middle of an immense grid, a cubic grid, full of nothing. Out in that nothingness, he could sense the hollow aching horror of space itself and could feel the terrible anxiety which his mind encountered whenever it met the faintest trace of inert dust.

As he relaxed, the comforting solidity of the Sun, the clockwork of the familiar planets and the moon rang in on him. Our own solar system was as charming and as simple as an ancient cuckoo clock filled with familiar ticking and with reassuring noises. The odd little moons of Mars swung around their planet like frantic mice, yet their regularity was itself an assurance that all was well. Far above the plane of the ecliptic, he could feel half a ton of dust more or less drifting outside the lanes of human travel.

Here there was nothing to fight, nothing to challenge the mind, to tear the living soul out of a body with its roots dripping in effluvium as tangible as blood.

Nothing ever moved in on the solar system. He could wear the pin-set forever and be nothing more than a sort of telepathic astronomer, a man who could feel the hot, warm protection of the sun throbbing and burning against his living mind.

Woodley came in.

"Same old ticking world," said Underhill. "Nothing to report. No wonder they didn't develop the pin-set until they began to planoform. Down here with the hot sun around us, it feels so good and so quiet. You can feel everything spinning and turning. It's nice and sharp and compact. It's sort of like sitting around home."

Woodley grunted. He was not much given to flights of fantasy.

Undeterred, Underhill went on, "It must have been pretty good to have been an ancient man. I wonder why they burned up their world with war. They didn't have to planoform. They didn't have to go out to earn their livings among the stars. They didn't have to dodge the rats or play the game. They couldn't have invented pin-lighting because they didn't have any need of it, did they, Woodley?"

Woodley grunted, "Uh-huh." Woodley was twenty-six years old and due to retire in one more year. He already had a farm picked out. He had gotten through ten years of hard work pinlighting with the best of them. He had kept his sanity by not thinking very much about his job, meeting the strains of the task whenever he had to meet them and thinking nothing more about his duties until the next emergency arose.

Woodley never made a point of getting popular among the partners. None of the partners liked him very much. Some of them even resented him. He was suspected of thinking ugly thoughts of the partners on occasion, but since none of the partners ever thought a complaint in articulate form, the other pinlighters and the chiefs of the Instrumentality left him alone.

Underhill was still full of the wonder of their job. Happily he babbled on, "What does happen to us when we planoform? Do you think it's sort of like dying? Did you ever see anybody who had his soul pulled out?"

"Pulling souls is just a way of talking about it," said Woodley. "After all these years, nobody knows whether we have souls or not."

"But I saw one once. I saw what Dogwood looked like when he came apart. There was something funny. It looked wet and sort of sticky as if it were bleeding and it went out of him—and you know what they did to Dogwood? They took him away, up in that part of the hospital where you and I never go—way up at the top part where the others are, where the others always have to go if they are alive after the rats of the up-and-out have gotten them."

Woodley sat down and lit an ancient pipe. He was burning something called tobacco in it. It was a dirty sort of habit, but it made him look very dashing and adventurous.

"Look here, youngster. You don't have to worry about that stuff. Pinlighting is getting better all the time. The partners are getting better. I've seen them pinlight two rats forty-six million miles apart in one and a half milliseconds. As long as people had to try to work the pin-sets themselves, there was always the chance that with a minimum of four-hundred milliseconds for the human mind to set a pinlight, we wouldn't light the rats up fast enough to protect our planoforming ships. The partners have changed all that. Once they get going, they're faster than rats. And they always will be. I know it's not easy, letting a partner share your mind—"

"It's not easy for them, either," said Underhill.

"Don't worry about them. They're not human. Let them take care of themselves. I've seen more pinlighters go crazy from monkeying around with partners than I have ever seen caught by the rats. How many of them do you actually know of that got grabbed by rats?"

Underhill looked down at his fingers, which shone green and purple in the vivid light thrown by the tuned-in pin-set, and counted ships. The thumb for the *Andromeda*, lost with crew and passengers, the index finger and the middle finger for *Release Ships 43* and *56*, found with their pin-sets burned out and every man, woman, and child on board dead or insane. The ring finger, the little finger, and the thumb of the other hand were the first three battleships to be lost to the rats—lost as people realized that there was something out there *underneath space itself* which was alive, capricious, and malevolent.

Planoforming was sort of funny. It felt like—

Like nothing much.

Like the twinge of a mild electric shock.

Like the ache of a sore tooth bitten on for the first time.

Like a slightly painful flash of light against the eyes.

Yet in that time, a forty-thousand-ton ship lifting free above Earth disappeared somehow or other into two dimensions and appeared half a light-year or fifty light-years off.

At one moment, he would be sitting in the Fighting Room, the pin-set ready and the familiar solar system ticking around inside his head. For a second or a year (he could never tell how long it really was, subjectively), the funny little flash went through him and then he was loose in the up-and-out, the terrible open spaces between the stars, where the stars themselves felt like pimples on his telepathic mind and the planets were too far away to be sensed or read.

Somewhere in this outer space, a gruesome death awaited, death and horror of a kind which man had never encountered until he reached out for interstellar space itself. Apparently the light of the suns kept the Dragons away.

Dragons. That was what people called them. To ordinary people, there was nothing, nothing except the shiver of planoforming and the hammer blow of sudden death or the dark spastic note of lunacy descending into their minds.

But to the telepaths, they were dragons.

In the fraction of a second between the telepaths' awareness of a hostile something out in the black, hollow nothingness of space and the impact of a ferocious, ruinous psychic blow against all living things within the ship, the telepaths had sensed entities something like the dragons of ancient human lore, beasts more clever than beasts, demons more tangible than demons, hungry vortices of aliveness and hate compounded by unknown means out of the thin, tenuous matter between the stars.

It took a surviving ship to bring back the news—a ship in which, by sheer chance, a telepath had a lightbeam ready, turning it out at the innocent dust so that, within the panorama of his mind, the dragon dissolved into nothing at all and the other passengers, themselves non-telepathic, went about their way not realizing that their own immediate deaths had been averted.

From then on, it was easy—almost.

Planoforming ships always carried telepaths. Telepaths had their sensitiveness enlarged to an immense range by the pin-sets, which were telepathic amplifiers adapted to the mammal mind. The pin-sets in turn were electronically geared into small dirigible light bombs. Light did it.

Light broke up the dragons, allowed the ships to reform three-dimensionally, skip, skip, skip, as they moved from star to star.

The odds suddenly moved down from a hundred to one against mankind to sixty to forty in mankind's favor.

This was not enough. The telepaths were trained to

become ultrasensitive, trained to become aware of the dragons in less than a millisecond.

But it was found that the dragons could move a million miles in just under two milliseconds and that this was not enough for the human mind to activate the light beams.

Attempts had been made to sheath the ships in light at all times.

This defense wore out.

As mankind learned about the dragons, so too, apparently, the dragons learned about mankind. Somehow they flattened their own bulk and came in on extremely flat trajectories very quickly.

Intense light was needed, light of sunlike intensity. This could be provided only the light bombs. Pinlighting came into existence.

Pinlighting consisted of the detonation of ultra-vivid miniature photonuclear bombs, which converted a few ounces of a magnesium isotope into pure visible radiance.

The odds kept coming down in mankind's favor, yet ships were being lost.

It became so bad that people didn't even want to find the ships because the rescuers knew what they would see. It was sad to bring back to Earth three hundred bodies ready for burial and two hundred or three hundred lunatics, damaged beyond repair, to be wakened, and fed, and cleaned, and put to sleep, wakened and fed again until their lives were ended.

Telepaths tried to reach into the minds of the psychotics who had been damaged by the dragons, but they found nothing there beyond vivid spouting columns of fiery terror bursting from the primordial id itself, the volcanic source of life.

Then came the partners.

Man and partner could do together what man could not do alone. Men had the intellect. Partners had the speed.

The partners rode their tiny craft, no larger than footballs, outside the spaceships. They planoformed with the ships. They rode beside them in their six-pound craft ready to attack.

The tiny ships of the partners were swift. Each carried a dozen pinlights, bombs no bigger than thimbles.

The pinlighters threw the partners—quite literally threw—by means of mind-to-firing relays directly at the dragons.

What seemed to be dragons to the human mind appeared in the form of gigantic rats in the minds of the partners.

Out in the pitiless nothingness of space, the partners' minds responded to an instinct as old as life. The partners attacked, striking with a speed faster than man's, going from attack to attack until the rats or themselves were destroyed. Almost all the time it was the partners who won.

With the safety of the interstellar skip, skip, skip of the ships, commerce increased immensely, the population of all the colonies went up, and the demand for trained partners increased.

Underhill and Woodley were a part of the third generation of pinlighters and yet, to them, it seemed as though their craft had endured forever.

Gearing space into minds by means of the pin-set, adding the partners to those minds, keying up the minds for the tension of a fight on which all depended—this was more than human synapses could stand for long. Underhill needed his two months' rest after half an hour of fighting. Woodley needed his retirement after ten years of service. They were young. They were good. But they had limitations.

So much depended on the choice of partners, so much on the sheer luck of who drew whom.

2. The Shuffle

Father Moontree and the little girl named West entered the room. They were the other two pinlighters. The human complement of the Fighting Room was now complete.

Father Moontree was a red-faced man of forty-five who had lived the peaceful life of a farmer until he reached his fortieth year. Only then, belatedly, did the authorities find he was telepathic and agree to let him late in life enter upon the career of pinlighter. He did well at it, but he was fantastically old for this kind of business.

Father Moontree looked at the glum Woodley and the musing Underhill. "How're the youngsters today? Ready for a good fight?"

"Father always wants a fight," giggled the little girl named West. She was such a little little girl. Her giggle was high and childish. She looked like the last person in the world one would expect to find in the rough, sharp dueling of pinlighting.

Underhill had been amused one time when he found one of the most sluggish of the partners coming away happy from contact with the mind of the girl named West.

Usually the partners didn't care much about the human minds with which they were paired for the journey. The partners seemed to take the attitude that human minds were complex and fouled up beyond belief, anyhow. No partner ever questioned the superiority of the human mind, though very few of the partners were much impressed by that superiority.

The partners liked people. They were willing to fight with them. They were even willing to die for them. But when a partner liked an individual the way, for example, that Captain Wow or the Lady May liked Underhill, the licking had nothing to do with intellect. It was a matter of temperament, of feel.

Underhill knew perfectly well that Captain Wow regarded his, Underhill's, brains as silly. What Captain Wow liked was Underhill's friendly emotional structure, the cheerfulness and glint of wicked amusement that shot through Underhill's unconscious thought patterns, and the gaiety with which Underhill faced danger. The words, the history books, the ideas, the science—Underhill could sense all that in his own mind, reflected back from Captain Wow's mind, as so much rubbish.

Miss West looked at Underhill. "I bet you've put stickum on the stones."

"I did not!"

Underhill felt his ears grow red with embarrassment.

During his novitiate, he had tried to cheat in the lottery because he got particularly fond of a special partner, a lovely young mother named Murr. It was so much easier to operate with Murr and she was so affectionate toward him that he forgot pinlighting was hard work and that he was not instructed to have a good time with his partner. They were both designed and prepared to go into deadly battle together.

One cheating had been enough. They had found him out and he had been laughed at for years.

Father Moontree picked up the imitation-leather cup and shook the stone dice which assigned them their partners for the trip. By senior rights he took first draw.

He grimaced. He had drawn a greedy old character, a tough old male whose mind was full of slobbering thoughts of food, veritable oceans full of half-spoiled fish. Father Moontree had once said that he burped cod liver oil for weeks after drawing that particular glutton, so strongly had the telepathic image of fish impressed itself upon his mind. Yet the glutton was a glutton for danger as well as for fish. He had killed sixty-three dragons, more than any other partner in the service, and was quite literally worth his weight in gold.

The little girl West came next. She drew Captain Wow. When she saw who it was, she smiled.

"I *like* him," she said. "He's such fun to fight with. He feels so nice and cuddly in my mind."

"Cuddly, hell," said Woodley. "I've been in his mind, too. It's the most leering mind in this ship, bar none."

"Nasty man," said the little girl. She said it declaratively, without reproach.

Underhill, looking at her, shivered.

He didn't see how she could take Captain Wow so calmly. Captain Wow's mind *did* leer. When Captain Wow got excited in the middle of a battle, confused images of dragons, deadly rats, luscious beds, the smell of fish, and the shock of space all scrambled together in his mind as he and Captain Wow, their consciousnesses linked together through the pin-set, became a fantastic composite of human being and Persian cat.

That's the trouble with working with cats, thought Underhill. It's a pity that nothing else anywhere will serve as partner. Cats were all right once you got in touch with them telepathically. They were smart enough to meet the needs of the flight, but their motives and desires were certainly different from those of humans.

They were companionable enough as long as you thought tangible images at them, but their minds just closed up and went to sleep when you recited Shakespeare or Colegrove, or if you tried to tell them what space was.

It was sort of funny realizing that the partners who were so grim and mature out here in space were the same cute little animals that people had used as pets for thousands of years back on Earth. He had embarrassed himself more than once while on the ground saluting perfectly ordinary non-telepathic cats because he had forgotten for the moment that they were not partners.

He picked up the cup and shook out his stone dice.

He was lucky—he drew the Lady May.

The Lady May was the most thoughtful partner he had ever met. In her, the finely bred pedigree mind of a Persian cat had reached one of its highest peaks of development. She was more complex than any human woman, but the complexity was all one of emotions, memory, hope, and discriminated experience—experience sorted through without benefit of words.

When he had first come into contact with her mind, he was astonished at its clarity. With her he remembered her kittenhood. He remembered every mating experience she had ever had. He saw in a half-recognizable gallery all the other pinlighters with whom she had been paired for the fight. And he saw himself radiant, cheerful, and desirable.

He even thought he caught the edge of a longing—

A very flattering and yearning thought: *What a pity he is not a cat.*

Woodley picked up the last stone. He drew what he deserved—a sullen, scarred old tomcat with none of the verve of Captain Wow. Woodley's partner was the most animal of all the cats on the ship, a low, brutish type with a dull mind. Even telepathy had not refined his character. His ears were half chewed off from the first fights in which he had engaged. He was a serviceable fighter, nothing more.

Woodley grunted.

Underhill glanced at him oddly. Didn't Woodley ever do anything but grunt?

Father Moontree looked at the other three. "You might as well get your partners now. I'll let the Go-captain know we're ready to go into the up-and-out."

3. The Deal

Underhill spun the combination lock on the Lady May's cage. He woke her gently and took her into his arms. She humped her back luxuriously, stretched her claws, started to purr, thought better of it, and licked him on the wrist instead. He did not have the pin-set on, so their minds were closed to each other, but in the angle of her mustache and in the movement of her ears, he caught some sense of the gratification she experienced in finding him as her partner.

He talked to her in human speech, even though speech meant nothing to a cat when the pin-set was not on.

"It's a damn shame, sending a sweet little thing like you whirling around in the coldness of nothing to hunt for rats that are bigger and deadlier than all of us put together. You didn't ask for this kind of fight, did you?"

For answer, she licked his hand, purred, tickled his cheek with her long fluffy tail, turned around and faced him, golden eyes shining.

For a moment, they stared at each other, man squatting, cat standing erect on her hind legs, front claws digging into his knee. Human eyes and cat eyes looked across an immensity which no words could meet, but which affection spanned in a single glance.

"Time to get in," he said.

She walked docilely to her spheroid carrier. She climbed in. He saw to it that her miniature pin-set rested firmly and comfortably against the base of her brain. He made sure that her claws were padded so that she could not tear herself in the excitement of battle.

Softly he said to her, "Ready?"

For answer, she preened her back as much as her harness would permit and purred softly within the confines of the frame that held her.

He slapped down the lid and watched the sealant ooze around the seam. For a few hours, she was welded into her projectile until a workman with a short cutting arc would remove her after she had done her duty.

He picked up the entire projectile and slipped it into the ejection tube. He closed the door of the tube, spun the lock, seated himself in his chair, and put his own pin-set on.

Once again he flung the switch.

He sat in a small room, *small, small, warm, warm,* the bodies of the other three people moving close around him, the tangible light in the ceiling bright and heavy against his closed eyelids.

As the pin-set warmed, the room fell away. The other people ceased to be people and became small glowing heaps of fire, embers, dark red fire, with the consciousness of life burning like old red coals in a country fireplace.

As the pin-set warmed a little more, he felt Earth just below him, felt the ship slipping away, felt the turning Moon as it swung on the far side of the world, felt the planets and the hot, clear goodness of the sun which kept the dragons so far from mankind's native ground.

Finally, he reached complete awareness.

He was telepathically alive to a range of millions of miles. He felt the dust which he had noticed earlier high above the ecliptic. With a thrill of warmth and tenderness, he felt the consciousness of the Lady May pouring over into his own. Her consciousness was as gentle and clear and yet sharp to the taste of his mind as if it were scented oil. It felt relaxing and reassuring. He could sense her welcome of him. It was scarcely a thought, just a raw emotion of greeting.

At last they were one again.

In a tiny remote corner of his mind, as tiny as the smallest toy he had ever seen in his childhood, he was still aware of the room and the ship, and of Father

Moontree picking up a telephone and speaking to a Go-captain in charge of the ship.

His telepathic mind caught the idea long before his ears could frame the words. The actual sound followed the idea the way that thunder on an ocean beach follows the lightning inward from far out over the seas.

"The Fighting Room is ready. Clear to planoform, sir."

4. The Play

Underhill was always a little exasperated the way that Lady May experienced things before he did.

He was braced for the quick vinegar thrill of planoforming, but he caught her report of it before his own nerves could register what happened.

Earth had fallen so far away that he groped for several milliseconds before he found the Sun in the upper rear right-hand corner of his telepathic mind.

That was a good jump, he thought. *This way we'll get there in four or five skips.*

A few hundred miles outside the ship, the Lady May thought back at him, "O warm, O generous, O gigantic man! O brave, O friendly, O tender and huge partner! O wonderful with you, with you so good, good, good, warm, warm, now to fight, now to go, good with you . . ."

He knew that she was not thinking words, that his mind took the clear amiable babble of her cat intellect and translated it into images which his own thinking could record and understand.

Neither one of them was absorbed in the game of mutual greetings. He reached out far beyond her range of perception to see if there was anything near the ship. It was funny how it was possible to do two things at once. He could scan space with his pin-set mind and yet at the same time catch a vagrant thought of hers, a lovely, affectionate thought about a son who had had a golden face and a chest covered with soft, incredibly downy white fur.

While he was still searching, he caught the warning from her.

We jump again!

And so they had. The ship had moved to a second planoform. The stars were different. The sun was immeasurably far behind. Even the nearest stars were barely in contact. This was good dragon country, this open, nasty, hollow kind of space. He reached farther, faster, sensing and looking for danger, ready to fling the Lady May at danger wherever he found it.

Terror blazed up in his mind, so sharp, so clear, that it came through as a physical wrench.

The little girl named West had found something—something immense, long, black, sharp, greedy, horrific. She flung Captain Wow at it.

Underhill tried to keep his own mind clear. "Watch out!" he shouted telepathically at the others, trying to move the Lady May around.

At one corner of the battle, he felt the lustful rage of Captain Wow as the big Persian tomcat detonated light while he approached the streak of dust which threatened the ship and the people within.

The light scored near misses.

The dust flattened itself, changing from the shape of a sting ray into the shape of a spear.

Not three milliseconds had elapsed.

Father Moontree was talking human words and was saying in a voice that moved like cold molasses out of a heavy jar, "C-a-p-t-a-i-n." Underhill knew that the sentence was going to be "Captain, move fast!"

The battle would be fought and finished before Father Moontree got through talking.

Now, fractions of a millisecond later, the Lady May was directly in line.

Here was where the skill and speed of the partners came in. She could react faster than he. She could see the threat as an immense rat coming directly at her.

She could fire the light-bombs with a discrimination which he might miss.

He was connected with her mind, but he could not follow it.

His consciousness absorbed the tearing wound inflicted by the alien enemy. It was like no wound on Earth

—raw, crazy pain which started like a burn at his navel. He began to writhe in his chair.

Actually he had not yet had time to move a muscle when the Lady May struck back at their enemy.

Five evenly spaced photonuclear bombs blazed out across a hundred-thousand miles.

The pain in his mind and body vanished.

He felt a moment of fierce, terrible, feral elation running through the mind of the Lady May as she finished her kill. It was always disappointing to the cats to find out that their enemies disappeared at the moment of destruction.

Then he felt her hurt, the pain and the fear that swept over both of them as the battle, quicker than the movement of an eyelid, had come and gone. In the same instant there came the sharp and acid twinge of planoform.

Once more the ship went skip.

He could hear Woodley thinking at him. "You don't have to bother much. This old son-of-a-gun and I will take over for a while."

Twice again the twinge, the skip.

He had no idea where he was until the lights of the Caledonia space port shone below.

With a weariness that lay almost beyond the limits of thought, he threw his mind back into rapport with the pin-set, fixing the Lady May's projectile gently and neatly in its launching tube.

She was half dead with fatigue, but he could feel the beat of her heart, could listen to her panting, and he grasped the grateful edge of a "Thanks" reaching from her mind to his.

5. The Score

They put him in the hospital at Caledonia.

The doctor was friendly but firm. "You actually got touched by that dragon. That's as close a shave as I've ever seen. It's all so quick that it'll be a long time before we know what happened scientifically, but I suppose you'd be ready for the insane asylum now if the contact had lasted several tenths of a millisecond longer. What kind of cat did you have out in front of you?"

Underhill felt the words coming out of him slowly. Words were such a lot of trouble compared with the speed and the joy of thinking, fast and sharp and clear, mind to mind! But words were all that could reach ordinary people like this doctor.

His mouth moved heavily as he articulated words. "Don't call our partners cats. The right thing to call them is partners. They fight for us in a team. You ought to know we call them partners, not cats. How is mine?"

"I don't know," said the doctor contritely. "We'll find out for you. Meanwhile, old man, you take it easy. There's nothing but rest than can help you. Can you make yourself sleep, or would you like us to give you some kind of sedative?"

"I can sleep," said Underhill. "I just want to know about the Lady May."

The nurse joined in. She was a little antagonistic. "Don't you want to know about the other people?"

"They're okay," said Underhill. "I knew that before I came in here."

He stretched his arms and sighed and grinned at them. He could see they were relaxing and were beginning to treat him as a person instead of a patient.

"I'm all right," he said. "Just let me know when I can go see my partner."

A new thought struck him. He looked wildly at the doctor. "They didn't send her off with the ship, did they?"

"I'll find out right away," said the doctor. He gave Underhill a reassuring squeeze of the shoulder and left the room.

The nurse took a napkin off a goblet of chilled fruit juice.

Underhill tried to smile at her. There seemed to be something wrong with the girl. He wished she would go away. First she had started to be friendly and now she was distant again. *It's a nuisance being telepathic,* he thought. *You keep trying to reach even when you are not making contact.*

Suddenly she swung around on him.

"You pinlighters! You and your damn cats!"

Just as she stamped out, he burst into her mind. He saw himself a radiant hero, clad in his smooth suede uniform, the pin-set crown shining like ancient royal jewels around his head. He saw his own face, handsome and masculine, shining out of her mind. He saw himself very far away and he saw himself as she hated him.

She hated him in the secrecy of her own mind. She hated him because he was—she thought—proud and strange and rich, better and more beautiful than people like her.

He cut off the sight of her mind and, as he buried his face in the pillow, he caught an image of the Lady May.

"She *is* a cat," he thought. "That's all she is—a *cat!*"

But that was not how his mind saw her—quick beyond all dreams of speed, sharp, clever, unbelievably graceful, beautiful, wordless and undemanding.

Where would he ever find a woman who could compare with her?

The Burning of the Brain

Rejuvenation, implied in parts of "The Lady Who Sailed The Soul" and mentioned more explicitly here, is made possible by the santaclara drug (stroon) found only on Old North Australia (Norstrilia)— although it was some years after publication of this story, written in 1955, that the planet was mentioned by name in Smith's fiction. Even at this period, we see the growing luxury and decadence of Instrumentality culture.

1. Dolores Oh

I TELL YOU, it is sad, it is more than sad, it is fearful— for it is a dreadful thing to go into the up-and-out, to fly without flying, to move between the stars as a moth may drift among the leaves on a summer night.

Of all the men who took the great ships into plano- form none was braver, none stronger, than Captain Magno Taliano.

Scanners had been gone for centuries and the jonaso- idal effect had become so simple, so manageable, that the traversing of light-years was no more difficult to most of the passengers of the great ships than to go from one room to the other.

Passengers moved easily.

Not the crew.

Least of all the captain.

The captain of a jonasoidal ship which had embarked on an interstellar journey was a man subject to rare and overwhelming strains. The art of getting past all the complications of space was far more like the piloting of turbulent waters in ancient days than like the smooth seas which legendary men once traversed with sails alone.

Go-captain on the *Wu-Feinstein,* finest ship of its class, was Magno Taliano.

Of him it was said, "He could sail through hell with the muscles of his left eye alone. He could plow space with his living brain if the instruments failed . . ."

Wife to the Go-captain was Dolores Oh. The name was Japonical, from some notion of the ancient days. Dolores Oh had been once beautiful, so beautiful that she took men's breath away, made wise men into fools, made young men into nightmares of lust and yearning. Wherever she went men had quarreled and fought over her.

But Dolores Oh was proud beyond all common limits of pride. She refused to go through the ordinary rejuvenescence. A terrible yearning a hundred or so years back must have come over her. Perhaps she said to herself, before that hope and terror which a mirror in a quiet room becomes to anyone:

"Surely I am me. There must be a *me* more than the beauty of my face, there must be a something other than the delicacy of skin and the accidental lines of my jaw and my cheekbone.

"What have men loved if it wasn't me? Can I ever find out who I am or what I am if I don't let beauty perish and live on in whatever flesh age gives me?"

She had met the Go-captain and had married him in a romance that left forty planets talking and half the ship lines stunned.

Magno Taliano was at the very beginning of his genius. Space, we can tell you, is rough—rough like the wildest of storm-driven waters, filled with perils which only the most sensitive, the quickest, the most daring of men can surmount.

Best of them all, class for class, age for age, out of

class, beating the best of his seniors, was Magno Taliano.

For him to marry the most beautiful beauty of forty worlds was a wedding like Heloise and Abelard's or like the unforgettable romance of Helen America and Mr. Grey-no-more.

The ships of the Go-captain Magno Taliano became more beautiful year by year, century by century.

As ships became better he always obtained the best. He maintained his lead over the other Go-captains so overwhelmingly that it was unthinkable for the finest ship of mankind to sail out amid the roughnesses and uncertainties of two-dimensional space without himself at the helm.

Stop-captains were proud to sail space beside him. (Though the Stop-captains had nothing more to do than to check the maintenance of the ship, its loading and unloading when it was in normal space, they were still more than ordinary men in their own kind of world, a world far below the more majestic and adventurous universe of the Go-captains.)

Magno Taliano had a niece who in the modern style used a place instead of a name: she was called "Dita from the Great South House."

When Dita came aboard the *Wu-Feinstein* she had heard much of Dolores Oh, her aunt by marriage who had once captivated the men in many worlds. Dita was wholly unprepared for what she found.

Dolores greeted her civilly enough, but the civility was a sucking pump of hideous anxiety, the friendliness was the driest of mockeries, the greeting itself an attack.

What's the matter with the woman? thought Dita.

As if to answer her thought, Dolores said aloud and in words: "It's nice to meet a woman who's not trying to take Taliano from me. I love him. Can you believe that? Can you?"

"Of course," said Dita. She looked at the ruined face of Dolores Oh, at the dreaming terror in Dolores's eyes, and she realized that Dolores had passed all limits of nightmare and had become a veritable demon of regret, a possessive ghost who sucked the vitality from her husband, who dreaded companionship, hated friendship, rejected even the most casual of acquaintances, because she feared forever and without limit that there was really nothing to herself, and feared that without Magno Taliano she would be more lost than the blackest of whirlpools in the nothing between the stars.

Magno Taliano came in.

He saw his wife and niece together.

He must have been used to Dolores Oh. In Dita's eyes Dolores was more frightening than a mud-caked reptile raising its wounded and venomous head with blind hunger and blind rage. To Magno Taliano the ghastly woman who stood like a witch beside him was somehow the beautiful girl he had wooed and had married one hundred sixty-four years before.

He kissed the withered cheek, he stroked the dried and stringy hair, he looked into the greedy, terror-haunted eyes as though they were the eyes of a child he loved. He said, lightly and gently,

"Be good to Dita, my dear."

He went on through the lobby of the ship to the inner sanctum of the planoforming room.

The Stop-captain waited for him. Outside on the world of Sherman the scented breezes of that pleasant planet blew in through the open windows of the ship.

Wu-Feinstein, finest ship of its class, had no need for metal walls. It was built to resemble an ancient, prehistoric estate named Mount Vernon, and when it sailed between the stars it was encased in its own rigid and self-renewing field of force.

The passengers went through a few pleasant hours of strolling on the grass, enjoying the spacious rooms, chatting beneath a marvelous simulacrum of an atmosphere-filled sky.

Only in the planoforming room did the Go-captain know what happened. The Go-captain, his pinlighters sitting beside him, took the ship from one compression to another, leaping hotly and frantically through space, sometimes one light-year, sometimes a hundred light-years, jump, jump, jump, jump until the ship, the light touches of the captain's mind guiding it, passed the perils of millions upon millions of worlds, came out at its appointed destination and settled as lightly as one feather resting upon others, settled into an embroidered and decorated countryside where the passengers could move as easily away from their journey as if they had done nothing more than to pass an afternoon in a pleasant old house by the side of a river.

2. The Lost Locksheet

Magno Taliano nodded to his pinlighters. The Stop-captain bowed obsequiously from the doorway of the planoforming room. Taliano looked at him sternly, but with robust friendliness. With formal and austere courtesy he asked,

"Sir and Colleague, is everything ready for the jonasoidal effect?"

The Stop-captain bowed even more formally. "Truly ready, Sir and Master."

"The locksheets in place?"

"Truly in place, Sir and Master."

"The passengers secure?"

"The passengers are secure, numbered, happy and ready, Sir and Master."

Then came the last and the most serious of questions. "Are my pinlighters warmed with their pin-sets and ready for combat?"

"Ready for combat, Sir and Master." With these words the Stop-captain withdrew. Magno Taliano smiled to his pinlighters. Through the minds of all of them there passed the same thought.

How could a man that pleasant stay married all those years to a hag like Dolores Oh? How could that witch, that horror, have ever been a beauty? How could that beast have ever been a woman, particularly the divine and glamorous Dolores Oh whose image we still see in four-di every now and then?

Yet pleasant he was, though long he may have been married to Dolores Oh. Her loneliness and greed might suck at him like a nightmare, but his strength was more than enough strength for two.

Was he not the captain of the greatest ship to sail between the stars?

Even as the pinlighters smiled their greetings back to him, his right hand depressed the golden ceremonial lever of the ship. This instrument alone was mechanical. All other controls in the ship had long since been formed telepathically or electronically.

Within the planoforming room the black skies became visible and the tissue of space shot up around them like boiling water at the base of a waterfall. Outside that one room the passengers still walked sedately on scented lawns.

From the wall facing him, as he sat rigid in his Go-captain's chair, Magno Taliano sensed the forming of a pattern which in three or four hundred milliseconds would tell him where he was and would give him the next clue as to how to move.

He moved the ship with the impulses of his own brain, to which the wall was a superlative complement.

The wall was a living brickwork of locksheets, laminated charts, one hundred thousand charts to the inch, the wall preselected and preassembled for all imaginable contingencies of the journey which, each time afresh, took the ship across half-unknown immensities of time and space. The ship leapt, as it had before.

The new star focused.

Magno Taliano waited for the wall to show him where he was, expecting (in partnership with the wall) to flick the ship back into the pattern of stellar space, moving it by immense skips from source to destination.

This time nothing happened.

Nothing?

For the first time in a hundred years his mind knew panic.

It couldn't be nothing. Not *nothing*. Something had to focus. The locksheets always focused.

His mind reached into the locksheets and he realized with a devastation beyond all limits of ordinary human grief that they were lost as no ship had ever been lost before. By some error never before committed in the history of mankind, the entire wall was made of duplicates of the same locksheet.

Worst of all, the emergency return sheet was lost. They were amid stars none of them had ever seen before, perhaps as near as five hundred million miles, perhaps as far as forty parsecs.

And the locksheet was lost.

And they would die.

As the ship's power failed coldness and blackness and death would crush in on them in a few hours at the most. That then would be all, all of the *Wu-Feinstein*, all of Dolores Oh.

3. *The Secret of The Old Dark Brain*

Outside of the planoforming room of the *Wu-Feinstein* the passengers had no reason to understand that they were marooned in the nothing-at-all.

Dolores Oh rocked back and forth in an ancient rocking chair. Her haggard face looked without pleasure at the imaginary river that ran past the edge of the lawn. Dita from the Great South House sat on a hassock by her aunt's knees.

Dolores was talking about a trip she had made when she was young and vibrant with beauty, a beauty which brought trouble and hate wherever it went.

". . . so the guardsman killed the captain and then came to my cabin and said to me. 'You've got to marry me now. I've given up everything for your sake,' and I said to him, 'I never said that I loved you. It was sweet of you to get into a fight, and in a way I suppose it is a compliment to my beauty, but it doesn't mean that I belong to you the rest of my life. What do you think I am, anyhow?' "

Dolores Oh sighed a dry, ugly sigh, like the crackling of sub-zero winds through frozen twigs. "So you see, Dita, being beautiful the way you are is no answer to anything. A woman has got to be herself before she finds out what she is. I know that my lord and husband, the Go-captain, loves me because my beauty is gone, and with my beauty gone there is nothing but *me* to love, is there?"

An odd figure came out on the verandah. It was a pinlighter in full fighting costume. Pinlighters were never supposed to leave the planoforming room, and it was most extraordinary for one of them to appear among the passengers.

He bowed to the two ladies and said with the utmost courtesy,

"Ladies, will you please come into the planoforming room? We have need that you should see the Go-captain now."

Dolores' hand leapt to her mouth. Her gesture of grief was as automatic as the striking of a snake. Dita sensed that her aunt had been waiting a hundred years and more for disaster, that her aunt had craved ruin for her husband the way that some people crave love and others crave death.

Dita said nothing. Neither did Dolores, apparently at second thought, utter a word.

They followed the pinlighter silently into the planoforming room.

The heavy door closed behind them.

Magno Taliano was still rigid in his captain's chair.

He spoke very slowly, his voice sounding like a record played too slowly on an ancient parlophone.

"We are lost in space, my dear," said the frigid, ghostly voice of the captain, still in his Go-captain's trance. *"We are lost in space and I thought that perhaps if your mind aided mine we might think of a way back."*

Dita started to speak.

A pinlighter told her: "Go ahead and speak, my dear. Do you have any suggestion?"

"Why don't we just go back? It would be humiliating, wouldn't it? Still it would be better than dying. Let's use the emergency return locksheet and go on right back. The world will forgive Magno Taliano for a single failure after thousands of brilliant and successful trips."

The pinlighter, a pleasant enough young man, was as friendly and calm as a doctor informing someone of a death or of a mutilation. "The impossible has happened, Dita from the Great South House. All the locksheets are wrong. They are all the same one. And not one of them is good for emergency return."

With that the two women knew where they were. They knew that space would tear into them like threads being pulled out of a fiber so that they would either die bit by bit as the hours passed and as the material of their bodies faded away a few molecules here and a few there. Or, alternatively, they could die all at once in a flash if the Go-captain chose to kill himself and the ship rather than to wait for a slow death. Or, if they believed in religion, they could pray.

The pinlighter said to the rigid Go-captain, "We think we see a familiar pattern at the edge of your own brain. May we look in?"

Taliano nodded very slowly, very gravely.

The pinlighter stood still.

The two women watched. Nothing visible happened, but they knew that beyond the limits of vision and yet before their eyes a great drama was being played out. The minds of the pinlighters probed deep into the mind of the frozen Go-captain, searching amid the synapses for the secret of the faintest clue to their possible rescue.

Minutes passed. They seemed like hours.

At last the pinlighter spoke. "We can see into your midbrain, Captain. At the edge of your paleocortex there is a star pattern which resembles the upper left rear of our present location."

The pinlighter laughed nervously. "We want to know, can you fly the ship home on your brain?"

Magno Taliano looked with deep tragic eyes at the inquirer. His slow voice came out at them once again since he dared not leave the half-trance which held the entire ship in stasis. *"Do you mean can I fly the ship on a brain alone? It would burn out my brain and the ship would be lost anyhow . . ."*

"But we're lost, lost, lost," screamed Dolores Oh. Her face was alive with hideous hope, with a hunger for ruin, with a greedy welcome of disaster. She screamed at her husband, "Wake up, my darling, and let us die together. At least we can belong to each other that much, that long, forever!"

"Why die?" said the pinlighter softly. "You tell him, Dita."

Said Dita, "Why not try, Sir and Uncle?"

Slowly Magno Taliano turned his face toward his niece. Again his hollow voice sounded. *"If I do this I*

*shall be a fool or a child or a dead man, but I will do it
for you."*

Dita had studied the work of the Go-captains and she
knew well enough that if the paleocortex was lost the
personality became intellectually sane, but emotionally
crazed. With the most ancient part of the brain gone the
fundamental controls of hostility, hunger and sex disappeared. The most ferocious of animals and the most
brilliant of men were reduced to a common level—a level of infantile friendliness in which lust and playfulness
and gentle, unappeasable hunger became the eternity of
their days.

Magno Taliano did not wait.

He reached out a slow hand and squeezed the hand of
Dolores Oh. *"As I die you shall at last be sure I love
you."*

Once again the women saw nothing. They realized
they had been called in simply to give Magno Taliano a
last glimpse of his own life.

A quiet pinlighter thrust a beam-electrode so that it
reached square into the paleocortex of Captain Magno
Taliano.

The planoforming room came to life. Strange heavens
swirled about them like milk being churned in a bowl.

Dita realized that her partial capacity of telepathy
was functioning even without the aid of a machine. With
her mind she could feel the dead wall of the locksheets.
She was aware of the rocking of the *Wu-Feinstein* as it
leapt from space to space, as uncertain as a man cross-
ing a river by leaping from one ice-covered rock to the
other.

In a strange way she even knew that the paleocortical
part of her uncle's brain was burning out at last and forever, that the star patterns which had been frozen in the
locksheets lived on in the infinitely complex pattern of
his own memories, and that with the help of his own telepathic pinlighters he was burning out his brain cell by
cell in order for them to find a way to the ship's destination. This indeed was his last trip.

Dolores Oh watched her husband with a hungry greed
surpassing all expression.

Little by little his face became relaxed and stupid.

Dita could see the midbrain being burned blank, as the ship's controls with the help of the pinlighters searched through the most magnificent intellect of its time for a last course into harbor.

Suddenly Dolores Oh was on her knees, sobbing by the hand of her husband.

A pinlighter took Dita by the arm.

"We have reached destination," he said.

"And my uncle?"

The pinlighter looked at her strangely.

She realized he was speaking to her without moving his lips—speaking mind-to-mind with pure telepathy.

"Can't you see it?"

She shook her head dazedly.

The pinlighter thought his emphatic statement at her once again.

"As your uncle burned out his brain, you picked up his skills. Can't you sense it? You are a Go-captain yourself and one of the greatest of us."

"And he?"

The pinlighter thought a merciful comment at her.

Magno Taliano had risen from the chair and was being led from the room by his wife and consort, Dolores Oh. He had the amiable smile of an idiot, and his face for the first time in more than a hundred years trembled with shy and silly love.

The Crime and the Glory of Commander Suzdal

One of the few Smith stories to touch directly on the manner in which many of the stranger worlds in the universe of the Instrumentality were settled—and the price that could often be paid thereby. This story is one of his more explicit expositions of the Instrumentality's methods of operation—at once brilliant, enlightened and totally ruthless and amoral—in its never-ending mission to safeguard mankind and extend and preserve its own power. Suzdal's name is taken from that of a Russian city.

Do not read this story; turn the page quickly. The story may upset you. Anyhow, you probably know it already. It is a very disturbing story. Everyone knows it. The glory and the crime of Cammander Suzdal have been told in a thousand different ways. Don't let yourself realize that the story is the truth.

It isn't. Not at all. There's not a bit of truth to it. There is no such planet as Arachosia, no such people as klopts, no such world as Catland. These are all just imaginary, they didn't happen, forget about it, go away and read something else.

95

The Beginning

COMMANDER SUZDAL WAS sent forth in a shell-strip to explore the outermost reaches of our galaxy. His ship was called a cruiser, but he was the only man in it. He was equipped with hypnotics and cubes to provide him the semblance of company, a large crowd of friendly people who could be convoked out of his own hallucinations.

The Instrumentality even offered him some choice in his imaginary companions, each of whom was embodied in a small ceramic cube containing the brain of a small animal but imprinted with the personality of an actual human being.

Suzdal, a short, stocky man with a jolly smile, was blunt about his needs:

"Give me two good security officers. I can manage the ship, but if I'm going into the unknown, I'll need help in meeting the strange problems which might show up."

The loading official smiled at him, "I never heard of a cruiser commander who *asked* for security officers. Most people regard them as an utter nuisance."

"That's all right," said Suzdal. "I don't."

"Don't you want some chess players?"

"I can play chess," said Suzdal, "all I want to, using the spare computers. All I have to do is set the power down and they start losing. On full power, they always beat me."

The official then gave Suzdal an odd look. He did not exactly leer, but his expression became both intimate and a little unpleasant. "What about other companions?" he asked, with a funny little edge to his voice.

"I've got books," siad Suzdal, "a couple of thousand. I'm going to be gone only a couple of years Earth time."

"Local-subjective, it might be several thousand years," said the official, "though the time will wind back up again as you re-approach Earth. And I wasn't talking about books," he repeated, with the same funny, prying lilt to his voice.

Suzdal shook his head with momentary worry, ran his hand through his sandy hair. His blue eyes were forthright and he looked straighforwardly into the official's eyes. "What do you mean, then, if not books? Navigators? I've got them, not to mention the turtle-men. They're good company, if you just talk to them slowly enough and then give them plenty of time to answer. Don't forget, I've been out before . . ."

The official spat out his offer: "Dancing girls. WOMEN. Concubines. Don't you want any of those? We could even cube your own wife for you and print her mind on a cube for you. That way she could be with you every week that you were awake."

Suzdal looked as though he would spit on the floor in sheer disgust. "Alice? You mean, you want me to travel around with a ghost of her? How would the real Alice feel when I came back? Don't tell me that you're going to put my wife on a mousebrain. You're just offering me delirium. I've got to keep my wits out there with space and time rolling in big waves around me. I'm going to be crazy enough, just as it is. Don't forget, I've been out there before. Getting back to a real Alice is going to be one of my biggest reality factors. It will help me to get home." At this point, Suzdal's own voice took on the note of intimate inquiry, as he added, "Don't tell me that a lot of cruiser commanders ask to go flying around with imaginary wives. That would be pretty nasty, in my opinion. Do many of them do it?"

"We're here to get you loaded on board ship, not to discuss what other officers do or do not do. Sometimes we think it good to have a female companion on the ship with the commander, even if she is imaginary. If you ever found anything among the stars which took on female form, you'd be mighty vulnerable to it."

"Females, among the stars? Bosh!" said Suzdal.

"Strange things have happened," said the official.

"Not that," said Suzdal. "Pain, craziness, distortion, panic without end, a craze for food—yes, those I can look for and face. They will be there. But females, no. There aren't any. I love my wife. I won't make females up out of my own mind. After all, I'll have the turtle-people aboard, and they will be bringing up their young. I'll have plenty of family to watch and to take part in. I can even give Christmas parties for the young ones."

"What kind of parties are those?" asked the official.

"Just a funny little ancient ritual that I heard about from an outer pilot. You give all the young things presents, once every local-subjective year."

"It sounds nice," said the official, his voice growing tired and final. "You still refuse to have a cube-woman on board. You wouldn't have to activate her unless you really needed her."

"You haven't flown, yourself, have you?" asked Suzdal.

It was the official's turn to flush. "No," he said, flatly.

"Anything that's in that ship, I'm going to think about. I'm a cheerful sort of man, and very friendly. Let me just get along with my turtle-people. They're not lively, but they are considerate and restful. Two thousand or more years, local-subjective, is a lot of time. Don't give me additional decisions to make. It's work enough, running the ship. Just leave me alone with my turtle-people. I've gotten along with them before."

"You, Suzdal, are the commander," said the loading official. "We'll do as you say."

"Fine," smiled Suzdal. "You may get a lot of queer types on this run, but I'm not one of them."

The two men smiled agreement at one another and the loading of the ship was completed.

The ship itself was managed by turtle-men, who aged very slowly, so that while Suzdal coursed the outer rim of the galaxy and let the thousands of years—local count—go past while he slept in his frozen bed, the turtle-men rose generation by generation, trained their young to work the ship, taught the stories of the Earth that they would never see again, and read the computers correctly, to awaken Suzdal only when there was a need for human intervention and for human intelligence. Suzdal awakened from time to time, did his work and then went back. He felt that he had been gone from earth only a few months.

Months indeed! He had been gone more than a subjective ten thousand years, when he met the siren capsule.

It looked like an ordinary distress capsule. The kind of thing that was often shot through space to indicate some complication of the destiny of man among the stars. This capsule had apparently been flung across an immense distance, and from the capsule Suzdal got the story of Arachosia.

The story was false. The brains of a whole planet—the wild genius of a malevolent, unhappy race—had been dedicated to the problem of ensnaring and attracting a normal pilot from Old Earth. The story which the capsule sang conveyed the rich personality of a wonderful woman with a contralto voice. The story was true, in part. The appeals were real, in part. Suzdal listened to the story and it sank, like a wonderfully orchestrated piece of grand opera, right into the fibers of his brain. It would have been different if he had known the real story.

Everybody now knows the real story of Arachosia, the bitter terrible story of the planet which was a paradise, which turned into a hell. The story of how people got to be something different from people. The story of what happened way out there in the most dreadful place among the stars.

He would have fled if he knew the real story. He couldn't understand what we now know:

Mankind could not meet the terrible people of Arachosia without the people of Arachosia following them home and bringing to mankind a grief greater than grief, a craziness worse than mere insanity, a plague surpassing all imaginable plagues. The Arachosians had become *un*people, and yet, in their innermost imprinting of their personalities, they remained people. They sang songs which exalted their own deformity and which praised themselves for what they had so horribly become, and yet, in their own songs, in their own ballads, the organ tones of the refrain rang out,

And I mourn man!

They knew what they were and they hated themselves. Hating themselves they pursued mankind.

Perhaps they are still pursuing mankind.

The Instrumentality has by now taken good pains that the Arachosians will never find us again, has flung networks of deception out along the edge of the galaxy to make sure that those lost ruined people cannot find us.

The Instrumentality knows and guards our world and all the other worlds of mankind against the deformity which has become Arachosia. We want nothing to do with Arachosia. Let them hunt for us. They won't find us.

How could Suzdal know that?

This was the first time someone had met the Arachosians, and he met them only with a message in which an elfin voice sang the elfin song of ruin, using perfectly clear words in the old common tongue to tell a story so sad, so abominable, that mankind has not forgotten it yet. In its essence the story was very simple. This is what Suzdal heard, and what people have learned ever since then.

The Arachosians were settlers. Settlers could go out by sail-ship, trailing behind them the pods. That was the first way.

Or they could go out by planoform ship, ships piloted by skillful men, who went into space$_2$ and came out again and found man.

Or for very long distances indeed, they could go out in the new combination. Individual pods packed into an enormous shell-ship, a gigantic version of Suzdal's own ship. The sleepers frozen, the machines waking, the ship fired to and beyond the speed of light, flung below space, coming out at random and homing on a suitable target. It was a gamble, but brave men took it. If no target was found, their machines might course space forever, while the bodies, protected by freezing as they were, spoiled bit by bit, and while the dim light of life went out in the individual frozen brains.

The shell-ships were the answers of mankind to an overpopulation, which neither the old planet Earth nor its daughter planets could quite respond to. The shell-ships took the bold, the reckless, the romantic, the willful, sometimes the criminals out among the stars. Mankind lost track of these ships, over and over again. The advance explorers, the organized Instrumentality, would stumble upon human beings, cities and cultures, high or low, tribes or families, where the shell-ships had gone on, far, far beyond the outermost limits of mankind, where the instruments of search had found an earthlike planet, and the shell-ship, like some great dying insect, had dropped to the planet, awakened its people, broken open, and destroyed itself with its delivery of newly re-born men and women, to settle a world.

Arachosia looked like a good world to the men and women who came to it. Beautiful beaches, with cliffs like endless rivieras rising above. Two bright big moons in the sky, a sun not too far away. The machines had pretested the atmosphere and sampled the water, had already scattered the forms of old earth life into the atmosphere and in the seas so that as the people awakened they heard the singing of earth birds and they knew that earth fish had already been adapted to the oceans and flung in, there to multiply. It seemed a good life, a rich life. Things went well.

Things went very, very well for the Arachosians.

This is the truth.

This was, thus far, the story told by the capsule.

But here they diverged.

The capsule did not tell the dreadful, pitiable truth about Arachosia. It invented a set of plausible lies. The voice which came telepathically out of the capsule was that of a mature, warm happy female—some woman of early middle age with a superb speaking contralto.

Suzdal almost fancied that he talked to it, so real was the personality. How could he know that he was being beguiled, trapped?

It sounded right, *really* right.

"And then," said the voice, "the Arachosian sickness has been hitting us. Do not land. Stand off. Talk to us. Tell us about medicine. Our young die, without reason. Our farms are rich, and the wheat here is more golden than it was on earth, the plums more purple, the flowers whiter. Everything does well—except people.

"Our young die . . ." said the womanly voice, ending in a sob.

"Are there any symptoms?" thought Suzdal, and almost as thought it had heard his question, the capsule went on.

"They die of nothing. Nothing which our medicine can test, nothing which our science can show. They die. Our population is dropping. People, do not forget us!

Man, whoever you are, come quickly, come now, bring
help! But for your own sake, do not land. Stand off-
planet and view us through screens so that you can take
word back to the home of man about the lost children of
mankind among the strange and outermost stars!"

Strange, indeed!

The truth was far stranger, and very ugly indeed.

Suzdal was convinced of the truth of the message. He
had been selected for the trip because he was good-natured, intelligent, and brave; this appeal touched all
three of his qualities.

Later, much later, when he was arrested, Suzdal was
asked, "Suzdal, you fool, why didn't you test the message? You've risked the safety of all the mankinds for a
foolish appeal!"

"It wasn't foolish!" snapped Suzdal. "That distress
capsule had a sad, wonderful womanly voice and the
story checked out true."

"With whom?" said the investigator, flatly and dully.

Suzdal sounded weary and sad when he replied to the
point. "It checked out with my books. With my knowledge." Reluctantly he added, "And with my own judgment . . ."

"Was your judgment good?" said the investigator.

"No," said Suzdal, and let the single word hang on
the air as though it might be the last word he would ever
speak.

But it was Suzdal himself who broke the silence when
he added, "Before I set course and went to sleep, I acti-
vated my security officers in cubes and had them check
the story. They got the real story of Arachosia, all right.
They cross-ciphered it out of patterns in the distress
capsule and they told me the whole real story very
quickly, just as I was waking up."

"And what did you do?"

"I did what I did. I did that for which I expect to be
punished. The Arachosians were already walking
around the outside of my hull by then. They had caught
my ship. They had caught me. How was I to know that
the wonderful, sad story was true only for the first twenty full years that the woman told about. And she wasn't

even a woman. Just a klopt. Only the first twenty years . . ."

Things had gone well for the Arachosians for the first twenty years. Then came disaster, but it was not the tale told in the distress capsule.

They couldn't understand it. They didn't know why it had to happen to them. They didn't know why it waited twenty years, three months and four days. But their time came.

We think it must have been something in the radiation of their sun. Or perhaps a combination of that particular sun's radiation and the chemistry, which even the wise machines in the shell-ship had not fully analyzed, which reached out and was spread from within. The disaster hit. It was a simple one and utterly unstoppable.

They had doctors. They had hospitals. They even had a limited capacity for research.

But they could not research fast enough. Not enough to meet this disaster. It was simple, monstrous, enormous.

Femininity became carcinogenetic.

Every woman on the planet began developing cancer at the same time, on her lips, in her breasts, in her groin, sometimes along the edge of her jaw, the edge of her lip, the tender portions of her body. The cancer had many forms, and yet it was always the same. There was something about the radiation which reached through, which reached into the human body, and which made a particular form of desoxycorticosterone turn into a subform —unknown on earth—of pregnandiol, which infallibly caused cancer. The advance was rapid.

The little baby girls began to die first. The women clung weeping to their fathers, their husbands. The mothers tried to say goodbye to their sons.

One of the doctors, herself, was a woman, a strong woman.

Remorselessly, she cut live tissue from her living body, put it under the microscope, took samples of her own urine, her blood, her spit, and she came up with the answer: *There is no answer.* And yet there was something better and worse than an answer.

If the sun of Arachosia killed everything which was

female, if the female fish floated upside down on the surface of the sea, if the female birds sang a shriller, wilder song as they died above the eggs which would never hatch, if the female animals grunted and growled in the lairs where they hid away with pain, female human beings did not have to accept death so tamely. The doctor's name was Astarte Kraus.

The Magic of the Klopts

The human female could do what the animal female could not. She could turn male. With the help of equipment from the ship, tremendous quantities of testosterone were manufactured, and every single girl and woman still surviving was turned into a man. Massive injections were administered to all of them. Their faces grew heavy, they all returned to growing a little bit, their chests flattened out, their muscles grew stronger, and in less than three months they were indeed men.

Some lower forms of life had survived because they were not polarized clearly enough to the forms of male and female, which depended on that particular organic chemistry for survival. With the fish gone, plants clotted the oceans, the birds were gone but the insects survived; dragonflies, butterflies, mutated versions of grasshoppers, beetles, and other insects swarmed over the planet. The men who had lost women worked side by side with the men who had been made out of the bodies of women.

When they knew each other, it was unutterably sad for them to meet. Husband and wife, both bearded, strong, quarrelsome, desperate and busy. The little boys somehow realizing that they would never grow up to have sweethearts, to have wives, to get married, to have daughters.

But what was a mere world to stop the driving brain and the burning intellect of Dr. Astarte Kraus? She became the leader of her people, the men and the men-women. She drove them forward, she made them survive, she used cold brains on all of them.

(Perhaps, if she had been a sympathetic person, she would have let them die. But it was the nature of Dr.

Kraus not to be sympathetic—just brilliant, remorseless, implacable against the universe which had tried to destroy her.)

Before she died, Dr. Kraus had worked out a carefully programed genetic system. Little bits of the men's tissues could be implanted by a surgical routine in the abdomens, just inside the peritoneal wall, crowding a little bit against the intestines, an artificial womb and artificial chemistry and artificial insemination by radiation, by heat made it possible for men to bear boy children.

What was the use of having girl children if they all died? The people of Arachosia went on. The first generation lived through the tragedy, half insane with the grief and disappointment. They sent out message capsules and they knew that their messages would reach earth in six million years.

As new explorers, they had gambled on going further than other ships went. They had found a good world, but they were not quite sure where they were. Were they still within the familiar galaxy, or had they jumped beyond to one of the nearby galaxies? They couldn't quite tell. It was a part of the policy of Old Earth not to overequip the exploring parties for fear that some of them, taking violent cultural change or becoming aggressive empires, might turn back on Earth and destroy it. Earth always made sure that it had the advantages.

The third and fourth and fifth generations of Arachosians were still people. All of them were male. They had the human memory, they had human books, they knew the words "mama," "sister," "sweetheart," but they no longer really understood what these terms referred to.

The human body, which had taken four million years on earth to grow, has immense resources within it, resources greater than the brain, or the personality, or the hopes of the individual. And the bodies of the Arachosians decided things for them. Since the chemistry of femininity meant instant death, and since an occasional girl baby was born dead and buried casually, the bodies made the adjustment. The men of Arachosia became both men and women. They gave themselves the ugly nickname, "klopt." Since they did not have the rewards of family life, they became strutting cockerels, who mixed their love with murder, who blended their songs with duels, who sharpened their weapons and who earned the right to reproduce within a strange family system which no decent Earth-man would find comprehensible.

But they did survive.

And the method of their survival was so sharp, so fierce, that it was indeed a difficult thing to understand.

In less than four hundred years the Arachosians had civilized into groups of fighting clans. They still had just one planet, around just one sun. They lived in just one place. They had a few spacecraft they had built themselves. Their science, their art and their music moved forward with strange lurches of inspired neurotic genius, because they lacked the fundamentals in the human personality itself, the balance of male and female, the family, the operations of love, of hope, of reproduction. They survived, but they themselves had become monsters and did not know it.

Out of their memory of old mankind they created a legend of Old Earth. Women in that memory were deformities, who should be killed. Misshapen beings, who should be erased. The family, as they recalled it, was filth and abomination which they were resolved to wipe out if they should ever meet it.

They, themselves, were bearded homosexuals, with rouged lips, ornate earrings, fine heads of hair, and very few old men among them. They killed off their men before they became old; the things they could not get from love or relaxation or comfort, they purchased with battle and death. They made up songs proclaiming themselves to be the last of the old men and the first of the new, and they sang their hate to mankind when they should meet, and they sang "Woe is Earth that we should find it," and yet something inside them made them add to almost every song a refrain which troubled even them,

And I mourn man!

They mourned mankind and yet they plotted to attack all of humanity.

The Trap

Suzdal had been decieved by the message capsule. He put himself back in the sleeping compartment and he directed the turtle-men to take the cruiser to Arachosia, wherever it might be. He did not do this crazily or wantonly. He did it as a matter of deliberate judgment. A judgment for which he was later heard, tried, judged fairly and then put to something worse than death.

He deserved it.

He sought for Arachosia without stopping to think of the most fundamental rule: How could he keep the Arachosians, singing monsters that they were, from following him home to the eventual ruin of Earth? Might not their condition be a disease which could be contagious, or might not their fierce society destroy the other societies of men and leave Earth and all of other men's worlds in ruin? He did not think of this, so he was heard, and tried and punished much later. We will come to that.

The Arrival

Suzdal awakened in orbit off Arachosia. And he awakened knowing he had made a mistake. Strange ships clung to his shell-ship like evil barnacles from an unknown ocean, attached to a familiar water craft. He called to his turtle-men to press the controls and the controls did not work.

The outsiders, whoever they were, man or woman or beast or god, had enough technology to immobolize his ship. Suzdal immediately realized his mistake. Naturally, he thought of destroying himself and the ship, but he was afraid that if he destroyed himself and missed destroying the ship completely there was a chance that his cruiser, a late model with recent weapons, would fall into the hands of whoever it was walking on the outer dome of his own cruiser. He could not afford the risk of mere individual suicide. He had to take a more drastic step. This was not time for obeying Earth rules.

His security officer—a cube ghost wakened to human

form—whispered the whole story to him in quick intelligent gasps:

"They are people, sir.

"More people than I am.

"I'm a ghost, an echo working out of a dead brain.

"These are real people, Commander Suzdal, but they are the worst people ever to get loose among the stars. You must destroy them, sir!"

"I can't," said Suzdal, still trying to come fully awake. "They're *people*."

"Then you've got to beat them off. By any means, sir. By any means whatever. Save Earth. Stop them. Warn Earth."

"And I?" asked Suzdal, and was immediately sorry that he had asked the selfish, personal question.

"You will die or you will be punished," said the security officer sympathetically, "and I do not know which one will be worse."

"Now?"

"Right now. There is no time left for you. No time at all."

"But the rules . . . ?"

"You have already strayed far outside of rules."

There were rules, but Suzdal left them all behind.

Rules, rules for ordinary times, for ordinary places, for understandable dangers.

This was a nightmare cooked up by the flesh of man, motivated by the brains of man. Already his monitors were bringing him news of who these people were, these seeming maniacs, these men who had never known women, these boys who had grown to lust and battle, who had a family structure which the normal human brain could not accept, could not believe, could not tolerate. The things on the outside were people, and they weren't. The things on the outside had the human brain, the human imagination, and the human capacity for revenge, and yet Suzdal, a brave officer, was so frightened by the mere nature of them that he did not respond to their efforts to communicate.

He could feel the turtle-women among his crew aching with fright itself, as they realized who was pounding on their ship and who it was that sang through loud announcing machines that they wanted *in, in, in*.

Suzdal committed a crime. It is the pride of the Instrumentality that the Instrumentality allows its officers to commit crimes or mistakes or suicide. The Instrumentality does the things for mankind that a computer can not do. The Instrumentality leaves the human brain, the human choice in action.

The Instrumentality passes dark knowledge to its staff, things not usually understood in the inhabited world, things prohibited to ordinary men and women because the officers of the Instrumentality, the captains and the subchiefs and the chiefs, must know their jobs. If they do not, all mankind might perish.

Suzdal reached into his arsenal. He knew what he was doing. The larger moon of Arachosia was habitable. He could see that there were earth plants already on it, and earth insects. His monitors showed him that the Arachosian men-women had not bothered to settle on the planet. He threw an agonized inquiry at his computers and cried out:

"Read me the age it's in!"

The machine sang back, "More than thirty million years."

Suzdal had strange resources. He had twins or quadruplets of almost every Earth animal. The earth animals were carried in tiny capsules no larger than a medicine capsule and they consisted of the sperm and the ovum of the higher animals, ready to be matched for sowing, ready to be imprinted; he also had small life-bombs which could surround any form of life with at least a chance of survival.

He went to the bank and he got cats, eight pairs, sixteen earth cats, *Felis domesticus*, the kind of cat that you and I know, the kind of cat which is bred, sometimes for telepathic uses, sometimes to go along on the ships and serve as auxiliary weapons when the minds of the pinlighters direct the cats to fight off dangers.

He coded these cats. He coded them with messages just as monstrous as the messages which had made the men-women of Arachosia into monsters. This is what he coded:

Do not breed true.
Invent new chemistry.
You will serve man.
Become civilized.
Learn speech.
You will serve man.
When man calls you will serve man.
Go back, and come forth.
Serve man.

These instructions were no mere verbal instructions. They were imprints on the actual molecular structure of the animals. They were charges in the genetic and biological coding which went with these cats. And then Suzdal committed his offense against the laws of mankind. He had a chronopathic device on board the ship. A time distorter, usually to be used for a moment or a second or two to bring the ship away from utter destruction.

The men-women of Arachosia were already cutting through the hull.

He could hear their high, hooting voices screaming delirious pleasure at one another as they regarded him as the first of their promised enemies that they had ever met, the first of the monsters from Old Earth who had finally overtaken them. The true, evil people on whom they, the men-women of Arachosia would be revenged.

Suzdal remained calm. He coded the genetic cats. He loaded them into life-bombs. He adjusted the controls of his chronopathic machine illegally, so that instead of reaching one second for a ship of eighty thousand tons, they reached two million years for a load of less than four kilos. He flung the cats into the nameless moon of Arachosia.

And he flung them back in time,
And he knew he did not have to wait.
He didn't.

The Catland Suzdal Made

The cats came. Their ships glittered in the naked sky above Arachosia. Their little combat craft attacked. The cats who had not existed a moment before, but who had then had two million years in which to follow a destiny printed into their brains, printed down their spinal cords, etched into the chemistry of their bodies and personalities. The cats had turned into people of a kind, with speech, intelligence, hope, and a mission. Their mission was to attach Suzdal, to rescue him, to obey him, and to damage Arachosia.

The cat ships screamed their battle warnings.

"This is the day of the year of the promised age. And *now come cats!*"

The Arachosians had waited for battle for four thousand years and now they got it. The cats attacked them. Two of the cat craft recognized Suzdal, and the cats reported,

"Oh Lord, oh God, oh Maker of all things, oh Commander of Time, oh Beginner of Life, we have waited since Everything began to serve You, to serve Your Name, to obey Your Glory! May we live for You, may we die for You. We are Your people."

Suzdal cried and threw his message to all the cats. "Harry the klopts but don't kill them all!"

He repeated, "Harry them and stop them until I escape." He flung his cruiser into nonspace and escaped. Neither cat nor Arachosian followed him.

And that's the story, but the tragedy is that Suzdal got back. And the Arachosians are still there and the cats are still there. Perhaps the Instrumentality knows where they are, perhaps the Instrumentality does not. Mankind does not really want to find out. It is against all law to bring up a form of life superior to man. Perhaps the cats are. Perhaps somebody knows whether the Arachosians won and killed the cats and added the cat science to their own and are now looking for us somewhere, probing like blind men through the stars for us true human beings to meet, to hate, to kill. Or perhaps the cats won.

Perhaps the cats are imprinted by a strange mission, by weird hopes of serving men they don't recognize. Perhaps they think we are all Arachosians and should be saved only for some particular cruiser commander, whom they will never see again. They won't see Suzdal, because we know what happened to him.

The Trial of Suzdal

Suzdal was brought to trial on a great stage in the open world. His trial was recorded. He had gone in when he should not have gone in. He had searched for the Arachosians without waiting and asking for advice and reinforcements. What business was it of his to relieve a distress ages old? What business indeed?

And then the cats. We had the records of the ship to show that something came out of that moon. Spacecraft, things with voices, things that could communicate with the human brain. We're not even sure, since they transmitted directly into the receiver computers, that they spoke an earth language. Perhaps they did it with some sort of direct telepathy. But the crime was, *Suzdal had succeeded.*

By throwing the cats back two million years, by coding them to survive, coding them to develop civilization, coding them to come to his rescue, he had created a whole new world in less than one second of objective time.

His chronopathic device had flung the little life-bombs back to the wet earth of the big moon over Arachosia and in less time than it takes to record this, the bombs came back in the form of a fleet built by a race, an earth race, though of cat origin, two million years old.

The court stripped Suzdal of his name and said, "You will not be named Suzdal any longer."

The court stripped Suzdal of his rank.

"You will not be a commander of this or any other navy, neither imperial nor of the Instrumentality."

The court stripped Suzdal of his life. "You will not live longer, former commander, and former Suzdal."

And then the court stripped Suzdal of death.

"You will go to the planet Shayol, the place of uttermost shame from which no one ever returns. You will go there with the contempt and hatred of mankind. We will not punish you. We do not wish to know about you any more. You will live on, but for us you will have ceased to exist."

That's the story. It's a sad, wonderful story. The Instrumentality tries to cheer up all the different kinds of mankind by telling them it isn't true, it's just a ballad.

Perhaps the records do exist. Perhaps somewhere the crazy klopts of Arachosia breed their boyish young, deliver their babies, always by Caesarean, feed them always by bottle, generations of men who have known fathers and who have no idea of what the word *mother* might be. And perhaps the Arachosians spend their crazy lives in endless battle with intelligent cats who are serving a mankind that may never come back.

That's the story.

Furthermore, it isn't true.

Golden the Ship Was—Oh! Oh! Oh!

*The "cat scandal" might refer to an incident in-
volving the pinlighters' partners, the underpeople, or
even the intelligent cats created by Commander Suzdal—Smith never made this reference clear. Nor is
the connection, if any, between Raumsog's empire
and the Bright Empire referred to passingly in
Norstrilia or that in "A Planet Named Shayol," ever
made clear. In any case, Tedesco's period is that of
Instrumentality before the Rediscovery of Man, when
Earth was at its most decadent. This story was another
collaboration with Genevieve Linebarger, by the way.*

AGGRESSION STARTED VERY far away.

War with Raumsog came about twenty years after the
great cat scandal which, for a while, threatened to cut
the entire planet Earth from the desperately essential
santaclara drug. It was a short war and a bitter one.

Corrupt, wise, weary old Earth fought with masked
weapons, since only hidden weapons could maintain so
ancient a sovereignty—sovereignty which had long since
lapsed into a titular paramountcy among the communi-
ties of mankind. Earth won and the others lost, because
the leaders of Earth never put other considerations
ahead of survival. And this time, they thought, they
were finally and really threatened.

The Raumsog war was never known to the general public except for the revival of wild old legends about golden ships.

1

On Earth the lords of the Instrumentality met. The presiding chairman looked about and said, "Well, gentlemen, all of us have been bribed by Raumsog. We have all been paid off individually. I myself received six ounces of stroon in pure form. Will the rest of you show better bargains?"

Around the room, the councilors announced the amounts of their bribes.

The chairman turned to the secretary. "Enter the bribes in the record and then mark the record off-the-record."

The others nodded gravely.

"Now we must fight. Bribery is not enough. Raumsog has been threatening to attack Earth. It's been cheap enough to let him threaten, but obviously we don't mean to let him do it."

"How are you going to stop him, Lord Chairman?" growled a gloomy old member. "Get out the golden ships?"

"Exactly that." The chairman looked deadly serious.

There was a murmurous sigh around the room. The golden ships had been used against an inhuman lifeform many centuries before. They were hidden somewhere in nonspace and only a few officials of Earth knew how much reality there was to them. Even at the level of the lords of the Instrumentality the council did not know precisely what they were.

"One ship," said the chairman of the lords of the Instrumentality, "will be enough."

It was.

2

The dictator Lord Raumsog on his planet knew the difference some weeks later.

"You can't mean that," he said. "You can't mean it. There is no such ship that size. The golden ships are just a story. No one ever saw a picture of one."

"Here is a picture, my Lord," said the subordinate.

Raumsog looked at it. "It's a trick. Some piece of trick photography. They distorted the size. The dimensions are wrong. Nobody has a ship that size. You could not build it, or if you did build it, you could not operate it. There just is not any such thing—" He babbled on for a few more sentences before he realized that his men were looking at the picture and not at him.

He calmed down.

The boldest of the officers resumed speaking. "That one ship is ninety million miles long, Your Highness. It shimmers like fire, but moves so fast that we cannot approach it. But it came into the center of our fleet almost touching our ships, stayed there twenty or thirty thousandths of a second. There it was, we thought. We saw the evidence of life on board: light beams waved; they examined us and then, of course, it lapsed back into nonspace. Ninety million miles, Your Highness. Old Earth has some stings yet and we do not know what the ship is doing."

The officers stared with anxious confidence at their overlord.

Raumsog sighed. "If we must fight, we'll fight. We can destroy that too. After all, what is size in the spaces between the stars? What difference does it make whether it is nine miles or nine million or ninety million?" He sighed again. "Yet I must say ninety million miles is an awful big size for a ship. I don't know what they are going to do with it."

He did not.

3

It is strange—strange and even fearful—what the love of Earth can do to men. Tedesco, for example.

Tedesco's reputation was far-flung. Even among the Go-captains, whose thoughts were rarely on such matters, Tedesco was known for his raiment, the foppish arrangement of his mantle of office and his bejeweled badges of authority. Tedesco was known too for his languid manner and his luxurious sybaritic living. When the message came, it found Tedesco in his usual character.

He was lying on the air-draft with his brain pleasure centers plugged into the triggering current. So deeply lost in pleasure was he that the food, the women, the clothing, the books of his apartments were completely neglected and forgotten. All pleasure save the pleasure of electricity acting on the brain was forgotten.

So great was the pleasure that Tedesco had been plugged into the current for twenty hours without interruption—a manifest disobedience of the rule which set six hours as maximum pleasure.

And yet, when the message came—relayed to Tedesco's brain by the infinitesimal crystal set there for the transmittal of messages so secret that even thought was too vulnerable to interception—when the message came Tedesco struggled through layer after layer of bliss and unconsciousness.

The ships of gold—the golden ships—for Earth is in danger.

Tedesco struggled. *Earth is in danger.* With a sigh of bliss he made the effort to press the button which turned off the current. And with a sigh of cold reality he took a look at the world about him and turned to the job at hand. Quickly he prepared to wait upon the lords of the Instrumentality.

The chairman of the lords of the Instrumentality sent out the Lord Admiral Tedesco to command the golden ship. The ship itself, larger than most stars, was an incredible monstrosity. Centuries before it had frightened away nonhuman aggressors from a forgotten corner of the galaxies.

The lord admiral walked back and forth on his

bridge. The cabin was small, twenty feet by thirty. The control area of the ship measured nothing over a hundred feet. All the rest was a golden bubble of the feinting ship, nothing more than thin and incredibly rigid foam with tiny wires cast across it so as to give the illusion of a hard metal and strong defenses.

The ninety million miles of length were right. Nothing else was.

The ship was a gigantic dummy, the largest scarecrow ever conceived by the human mind.

Century after century it had rested in nonspace between the stars, waiting for use. Now it proceeded helpless and defenseless against a militant and crazy dictator Raumsog and his horde of hard-fighting and very real ships.

Raumsog had broken the disciplines of space. He had killed the pinlighters. He had emprisoned the Go-captains. He had used renegades and apprentices to pillage the immense interstellar ships and had armed the captive vessels to the teeth. In a system which had not known real war, and least of all war against Earth, he had planned well.

He had bribed, he had swindled, he had propagandized. He expected Earth to fall before the threat itself. Then he launched his attack.

With the launching of the attack, Earth itself changed. Corrupt rascals became what they were in title: the leaders and the defenders of mankind.

Tedesco himself had been an elegant fop. War changed him into an aggressive captain, swinging the largest vessel of all time as though it were a tennis bat.

He cut in on the Raumsog fleet hard and fast.

Tedesco shifted his ship right, north, up, over.

He appeared before the enemy and eluded them—down, forward, right, over.

He appeared before the enemy again. One successful shot from them could destroy an illusion on which the safety of mankind itself depended. It was his business not to allow them that shot.

Tedesco was not a fool. He was fighting his own strange kind of war, but he could not help wondering where the real war was proceeding.

4

Prince Lovaduck had obtained his odd name because he had had a Chinesian ancestor who did love ducks, ducks in their Peking form—succulent duck skins brought forth to him ancestral dreams of culinary ecstasy.

His ancestress, an English lady, had said, "Lord Lovaduck, that fits you!"—and the name had been proudly taken as a family name. Lord Lovaduck had a small ship. The ship was tiny and had a very simple and threatening name: *Anybody*.

The ship was not listed in the space register and he himself was not in the Ministry of Space Defense. The craft was attached only to the Office of Statistics and Investigation—under the listing, "vehicle"—for the Earth treasury. He had very elementary defenses. With him on the ship went one chronopathic idiot essential to his final and vital maneuvers.

With him also went a monitor. The monitor, as always, sat rigid, catatonic, unthinking, unaware—except for the tape recorder of his living mind which unconsciously noted every imminent mechanical movement of the ship and was prepared to destroy Lovaduck, the chronopathic idiot, and the ship itself should they attempt to escape the authority of Earth or should they turn against Earth. The life of a monitor was a difficult one but was far better than execution for crime, its usual alternative. The monitor made no trouble. Lovaduck also had a very small collection of weapons, weapons selected with exquisite care for the atmosphere, the climate and the precise conditions of Raumsog's planet.

He also had a psionic talent, a poor crazy little girl who wept, and whom the lords of the Instrumentality had cruelly refused to heal, because her talents were better in unshielded form than they would have been had she been brought into the full community of mankind. She was a class-three etiological interference.

5

Lovaduck brought his tiny ship near the atmosphere of Raumsog's planet. He had paid good money for his captaincy to this ship and he meant to recover it. Recover it he would, and handsomely, if he succeeded in his adventurous mission.

The lords of the Instrumentality were the corrupt rulers of a corrupt world, but they had learned to make corruption serve their civil and military ends, and they were in no mind to put up with failures. If Lovaduck failed he might as well not come back at all. No bribery could save him from this condition. No monitor could let him escape. If he succeeded, he might be almost as rich as an Old North Australian or a stroon merchant.

Lovaduck materialized his ship just long enough to hit the planet by radio. He walked across the cabin and slapped the girl. The girl became frantically excited. At the height of her excitement he slapped a helmet on her head, plugged in the ship's communication system, and flung her own peculiar emotional psionic radiations over the entire planet.

She was a luck-changer. She succeeded: for a few moments, at every place on that planet, under the water and on it, in the sky and in the air, luck went wrong just a little. Quarrels did occur, accidents did happen, mischances moved just within the limits of sheer probability. They all occurred within the same minute. The uproar was reported just as Lovaduck moved his ship to another position. This was the most critical time of all. He dropped down into the atmosphere. He was immediately detected. Ravening weapons reached for him, weapons sharp enough to scorch the very air and to bring every living being on the planet into a condition of screaming alert.

No weapons possessed by Earth could defend against such an attack.

Lovaduck did not defend. He seized the shoulders of his chronopathic idiot. He pinched the poor defective; the idiot fled taking the ship with him. The ship moved back three, four seconds in time to a period slightly earlier than the first detection. All the instruments on

Raumsog's planet went off. There was nothing on which they could act.

Lovaduck was ready. He discharged the weapons. The weapons were not noble.

The Lords of the Instrumentality played at being chivalrous and did love money, but when life and death were at stake, they no longer cared much about money, or credit, or even about honor. They fought like the animals of Earth's ancient past—they fought to kill. Lovaduck had discharged a combination of organic and inorganic poisons with a high dispersion rate. Seventeen million people; nine hundred and fifty thousandths of the entire population, were to die within that night.

He slapped the chronopathic idiot again. The poor freak whimpered. The ship moved back two more seconds in time.

As he unloaded more poison, he could feel the mechanical relays reach for him.

He moved to the other side of the planet, moving backward one last time, dropped a final discharge of virulent carcinogens and snapped his ship in to nonspace, into the outer reaches of nothing. Here he was far beyond the reach of Raumsog.

6

Tedesco's golden ship moved serenely toward the dying planet, Raumsog's fighters closing on it. They fired—it evaded, surprisingly agile for so immense a craft, a ship larger than any sun seen in the heavens of that part of space. But while the ships closed in their radios reported:

"The capital has blanked out."

"Raumsog himself is dead."

"There is no response from the north."

"People are dying in the relay stations."

The fleet moved, intercommunicated, and began to surrender. The golden ship appeared once more and then it disappeared, apparently forever.

7

The Lord Tedesco returned to his apartments and to the current for plugging into the centers of pleasure in his brain. But as he arranged himself on the air-jet his hand stopped on its mission to press the button which would start the current. He realized, suddenly, that he had pleasure. The contemplation of the golden ship and of what he had accomplished—alone, deceptive, without the praise of all the worlds for his solitary daring—gave even greater pleasure than that of the electric current. And he sank back on the jet of air and thought of the golden ship, and his pleasure was greater than any he had ever experienced before.

8

On Earth, the lords of the Instrumentality gracefully acknowledged that the golden ship had destroyed all life on Raumsog's planet. Homage was paid to them by the many worlds of mankind. Lovaduck, his idiot, his little girl, and the monitor were taken to hospitals. Their minds were erased of all recollection of their accomplishments.

Lovaduck himself appeared before the lords of the Instrumentality. He felt that he had served on the golden ship and he did not remember what he had done. He knew nothing of a chronopathic idiot. And he remembered nothing of his little "vehicle." Tears poured down his face when the lords of the Instrumentality gave him their highest decorations and paid him an immense sum of money. They said: "You have served well and you are discharged. The blessings and the thanks of mankind will forever rest upon you . . ."

Lovaduck went back to his estates wondering that his service should have been so great. He wondered, too, in the centuries of the rest of his life, how any man—such as himself—could be so tremendous a hero and never quite remember how it was accomplished.

9

On a very remote planet, the survivors of a Raumsog cruiser were released from internment. By special orders, direct from Earth, their memories had been discoordinated so that they would not reveal the pattern of defeat. An obstinate reporter kept after one spaceman. After many hour of hard drinking the survivor's answer was still the same:

"Golden the ship was—oh! oh! oh! Golden the ship was—oh! oh! oh!"

The Dead Lady of Clown Town

Based on the seven generations of Jestocost, this story could have taken place two thousand years or more before the Rediscovery of Man, which it foreshadows. Parallels with the Joan of Arc legend are obvious, as are the allusions to the Old Strong Religion; not so some of the proper names. "An-fang" is literally "beginning" in German, while "Panc Ash-ash" is Hindi for "five-six." The style of the story is a Chinese-derived one Smith adopted for SF late in his career—yet he had used it in some unpublished historical stories as early as 1939.

1

YOU ALREADY KNOW the end—the immense drama of the Lord Jestocost, seventh of his line, and how the cat-girl C'mell initiated the vast conspiracy. But you do not know the beginning, how the first Lord Jestocost got his name, because of the terror and inspiration which his mother, Lady Goroke, obtained from the famous real-life drama of the dog-girl D'joan. It is even less likely that you know the other story—the one behind D'joan. This story is sometimes mentioned as the matter of the "nameless witch," which is absurd, because she really had a name. The name was "Elaine," an ancient and forbidden one.

Elaine was a mistake. Her birth, her life, her career were all mistakes. The ruby was wrong. How could that have happened?

Go back to An-fang, the Peace Square at An-fang, the Beginning Place at An-fang, where all things start. Bright it was. Red Square, dead square, clear square, under a yellow sun.

This was Earth Original, Manhome itself, where Earthport thrusts its way up through hurricane clouds that are higher than the mountains.

An-fang was near a city, the only living city with a pre-atomic name. The lovely meaningless name was Meeya Meefla, where the lines of ancient roadways, untouched by a wheel for thousands of years, forever paralleled the warm, bright, clear beaches of the Old South East.

The headquarters of the People Programmer was at An-fang, and there the mistake happened:

A ruby trembled. Two tourmaline nets failed to rectify the laser beam. A diamond noted the error. Both the error and the correction went into the general computer.

The error assigned, on the general account of births for Fomalhaut III, the profession of "lay therapist, female, intuitive capacity for correction of human physiology with local resources." On some of the early ships they used to call these people *witch-women*, because they worked unaccountable cures. For pioneer parties, these lay therapists were invaluable; in settled post-Riesmannian societies, they became an awful nuisance. Sickness disappeared with good conditions, accidents dwindled down to nothing, medical work became institutional.

Who wants a witch, even a good witch, when a thousand-bed hospital is waiting with its staff eager for clinical experience . . . and only seven out of its thousand beds filled with real people? (The remaining beds were filled with lifelike robots on which the staff could practice, lest they lose their morale. They could, of course, have worked on underpeople—animals in the shape of human beings, who did the heavy and the weary work which remained as the *caput mortuum* of a really perfected economy—but it was against the law for animals, even when they were underpeople, to go to a human hospital.

When underpeople got sick, the Instrumentality took care of them—in slaughterhouses. It was easier to breed new underpeople for the jobs than it was to repair sick ones. Furthermore, the tender, loving care of a hospital might give them ideas. Such as the idea that they were people. This would have been bad, from the prevailing point of view. Therefore the human hospitals remained almost empty while an underperson who sneezed four times or who vomited once was taken away, never to be ill again. The empty beds kept on with the robot patients, who went through endless repetitions of the human patterns of injury or disease.) This left no work for witches, bred and trained.

Yet the ruby had trembled; the program had indeed made a mistake; the birth-number for a "lay therapist, general, female, immediate use" had been ordered for Fomalhaut III.

Much later, when the story was all done down to its last historic detail, there was an investigation into the origins of Elaine. When the laser had trembled, both the original order and the correction were fed simultaneously into the machine. The machine recognized the contradiction and promptly referred both papers to the human supervisor, an actual man who had been working on the job for seven years.

He was studying music, and he was bored. He was so close to the end of his term that he was already counting the days to his own release. Meanwhile he was rearranging two popular songs. One was *The Big Bamboo*, a primitive piece which tried to evoke the original magic of man. The other was about a girl, *Elaine, Elaine*, whom the song asked to refrain from giving pain to her loving swain. Neither of the songs was important; but between them they influenced history, first a little bit and then very much.

The musician had plenty of time to practice. He had not had to meet a real emergency in all his seven years. From time to time the machine made reports to him, but the musician just told the machine to correct its own errors, and it infallibly did so.

On the day that the accident of Elaine happened, he

was trying to perfect his finger work on the guitar, a
very old instrument believed to date from the pre-space
period. He was playing *The Big Bamboo* for the hun-
dreth time.

The machine announced its mistake with an initial
musical chime. The supervisor had long since forgotten
all the instructions which he had so worrisomely memorized seven long years ago. The alert did not really and
truly matter, because the machine invariably corrected
its own mistakes whether the supervisor was on duty or
not.

The machine, not having its chime answered, moved
into a second-stage alarm. From a loudspeaker set in the
wall of the room, it shrieked in a high, clear human
voice, the voice of some employee who had died thousands of years earlier:

"Alert, alert! Emergency. Correction needed. Correction needed!"

The answer was one which the machine had never
had heard before, old though it was. The musician's fingers ran madly, gladly over the guitar strings and he
sang clearly, wildly back to the machine a message
strange beyond any machine's belief:

> *Beat, beat the Big Bamboo!*
> *Beat, beat, beat the Big Bamboo for me . . . !*

Hastily the machine set its memory banks and computers to work, looking for the code reference to "bamboo," trying to make that word fit the present context.
There was no reference at all. The machine pestered the
man some more.

"Instructions unclear. Instructions unclear. Please
correct."

"Shut up," said the man.

"Cannot comply," stated the machine. "Please state
and repeat, please state and repeat, please state and repeat."

"Do shut up," said the man, but he knew the machine
would not obey this. Without thinking, he turned to his
other tune and sang the first two lines twice over:

Elaine, Elaine,
  go cure the pain!
Elaine, Elaine,
  go cure the pain!

Repetition had been inserted as a safeguard into the machine, on the assumption that no real man would repeat an error. The name "Elaine" was not correct number code, but the fourfold emphasis seemed to confirm the need for a "lay therapist, female." The machine itself noted that a genuine man had corrected the situation card presented as a matter of emergency.

"Accepted," said the machine.

This word, too late, jolted the supervisor away from his music.

"Accepted what?" he asked.

There was no answering voice. There was no sound at all except for the whisper of slightly-moistened warm air through the ventilators.

The supervisor looked out the window. He could see a little of the blood-black red color of the Peace Square of An-fang; beyond lay the ocean, endlessly beautiful and endlessly tedious.

The supervisor sighed hopefully. He was young. "Guess it doesn't matter," he thought, picking up his guitar.

(Thirty-seven years later, he found out that it did matter. The Lady Goroke herself, one of the chiefs of the Instrumentality, sent a subchief of the Instrumentality to find out who had caused D'joan. When the man found that the witch Elaine was the source of the trouble she sent him on to find out how Elaine had gotten into a well-ordered universe. The supervisor was found. He was still a musician. He remembered nothing of the story. He was hypnotized. He still remembered nothing. The subchief invoked an emergency and Police Drug Four ("clear memory") was administered to the musician. He immediately remembered the whole silly scene, but insisted that it did not matter. The case was referred to Lady Goroke, who instructed the authorities that the musician be told the whole horrible, beautiful story of D'joan at Fomalhaut—the very story which you are now being told—and he wept. He was not punished otherwise, but the Lady Goroke commanded that those memories be left in his mind for so long as he might live.)

The man picked up his guitar, but the machine went on about its work.

It selected a fertilized human embryo, tagged it with the freakish name "Elaine," irradiated the genetic code with strong aptitudes for witchcraft and then marked the person's card for training in medicine, transportation by sail-ship to Fomalhaut III and release for service on the planet.

Elaine was born without being needed, without being wanted, without having a skill which could help or hurt any existing human being. She went into life doomed and useless.

It is not remarkable that she was misbegotten. Errors do happen. Remarkable was the fact that she managed to survive without being altered, corrected or killed by the safety devices which mankind has installed in society for its own protection.

Unwanted, unused, she wandered through the tedious months and useless years of her own existence. She was well fed, richly clothed, variously housed. She had machines and robots to serve her, underpeople to obey her, people to protect her against others or against herself, should the need arise. But she could never find work; without work, she had no time for love; without work or love, she had no hope at all.

If she had only stumbled into the right experts or the right authorities, they would have altered or re-trained her. This would have made her into an acceptable woman; but she did not find the police, nor did they find her. She was helpless to correct her own programming, utterly helpless. It had been imposed on her at An-fang, way back at An-fang, where all things begin.

The ruby had trembled, the tourmaline failed, the diamond passed unsupported. Thus, a woman was born doomed.

2

Much later, when people made songs about the strange case of the dog-girl D'joan, the minstrels and singers had tried to imagine what Elaine felt like, and they had made up *The Song of Elaine* for her. It is not authentic, but it shows how Elaine looked at her own life before the strange case of D'joan began to flow from Elaine's own actions:

> *Other women hate me.*
> *Men never touch me.*
> *I am too much me.*
> *I'll be a witch!*
>
> *Mama never towelled me.*
> *Daddy never growled me.*
> *Little kiddies grate me.*
> *I'll be a bitch!*
>
> *People never named me.*
> *Dogs never shamed me.*
> *Oh, I am a such me!*
> *I'll be a witch.*
>
> *I'll make them shun me.*
> *They'll never run me.*
> *Could they even stun me?*
> *I'll be a witch.*
>
> *Let them all attack me.*
> *They can only rack me.*
> *Me—I can hack me.*
> *I'll be a witch.*
>
> *Other women hate me.*
> *Men never touch me.*
> *I am too much me.*
> *I'll be a witch.*

The song overstates the case. Women did not hate Elaine; they did not look at her. Men did not shun

Elaine; they did not notice her either. There were no places on Fomalhaut III where she could have met human children, for the nurseries were far underground because of chancy radiation and fierce weather. The song pretends that Elaine began with the thought that she was not human, but underpeople, and had herself been born a dog. This did not happen at the beginning of the case, but only at the very end, when the story of D'joan was already being carried between the stars and developing with all the new twists of folklore and legend. She never went mad.

("Madness" is a rare condition, consisting of a human mind which does not engage its environment correctly. Elaine approached it before she met D'joan. Elaine was not the only case, but she was a rare and genuine one. Her life, thrust back from all attempts at growth, had turned back on itself and her mind had spiraled inward to the only safety she could really know, psychosis. Madness is always better than X, and X to each patient is individual, personal, secret and overwhelmingly important. Elaine had gone normally mad; her imprinted and destined career was the wrong one. "Lay therapists, female" were coded to work decisively, autonomously, on their own authority and with great rapidity. These working conditions were needed on new planets. They were not coded to consult other people; most places, there would be no one to consult. Elaine did what was set for her at An-fang, all the way down to the individual chemical conditions of her spinal fluid. She was herself the wrong and she never knew it. Madness was much kinder than the realization that she was not herself, should not have lived, and amounted at the most to a mistake committed between a trembling ruby and a young, careless man with a guitar.)

She found D'joan and the worlds reeled.

Their meeting occurred at a place nicknamed "the edge of the world," where the undercity met daylight. This was itself unusual; but Fomalhaut III was an unusual and uncomfortable planet, where wild weather and men's caprice drove architects to furious design and grotesque execution. Elaine walked through the city, secretly mad, looking for sick people whom she could help.

She had been stamped, imprinted, designed, born, bred and trained for this task. There was no task.

She was an intelligent woman. Bright brains serve madness as well as they serve sanity—namely, very well indeed. It never occurred to her to give up her mission.

The people of Fomalhaut III, like the people of Manhome Earth itself, are almost uniformly handsome; it is only in the far-out, half-unreachable worlds that the human stock, strained by the sheer effort to survive, becomes ugly, weary or varied. She did not look much different from the other intelligent, handsome people who flocked the streets. Her hair was black, and she was tall. Her arms and legs were long, the trunk of her body short. She wore her hair brushed straight back from a high, narrow, square forehead. Her eyes were an odd, deep blue. Her mouth might have been pretty, but it never smiled, so that no one could really tell whether it was beautiful or not. She stood erect and proud: but so did everyone else. Her mouth was strange in its very lack of communicativeness and her eyes swept back and forth, back and forth like ancient radar, looking for the sick, the needy, and stricken, whom she had a passion to serve.

How could she be unhappy? She had never had time to be happy. It was easy for her to think that happiness was something which disappeared at the end of childhood. Now and then, here and there, perhaps when a fountain murmured in sunlight or when leaves exploded in the startling Fomalhautian spring, she wondered that other people—people as responsible as herself by the doom of age, grade, sex, training and career number—should be happy when she alone seemed to have no time for happiness. But she always dismissed the thought and walked the ramps and streets until her arches ached, looking for work which did not yet exist.

Human flesh, older than history, more dogged than culture, has its own wisdom. The bodies of people are marked with the archaic ruses of survival, so that on Fomalhaut III, Elaine herself preserved the skills of ancestors she never even thought about—those ancestors who, in the incredible and remote past, had mastered terrible Earth itself. Elaine was mad. But there was a part of her which suspected that she was mad.

Perhaps this wisdom seized her as she walked from Waterrocky Road toward the bright esplanades of the Shopping Bar. She saw a forgotten door. The robots could clean near it but, because of the old, odd architectural shape, they could not sweep and polish right at the bottom line of the door. A thin hard line of old dust and caked polish lay like a sealant at the base of the doorline. It was obvious that no one had gone through for a long, long time.

The civilized rule was that prohibited areas were marked both telepathically and with symbols. The most dangerous of all had robot or underpeople guards. But everything which was not prohibited, was permitted. Thus Elaine had no right to open the door, but she had no obligation not to do so. She opened it—

By sheer caprice.

Or so she thought.

This was a far cry from the "I'll be a witch" motif attributed to her in the later ballad. She was not yet frantic, not yet desperate, she was not yet even noble.

That opening of a door changed her own world and changed life on thousands of planets for generations to come, but the opening was not itself strange. It was the tired caprice of a thoroughly frustrated and mildly unhappy woman. Nothing more. All the other descriptions of it have been improvements, embellishments, falsifications.

She did get a shock when she opened the door, but not for the reasons attributed backwards to her by balladists and historians.

She was shocked because the door opened on steps and the steps led down to landscape and sunlight—truly an unexpected sight on any world. She was looking from the New City to the Old City. The New City rose on its shell out over the old city, and when she looked "indoors" she saw the sunset in the city below. She gasped at the beauty and the unexpectedness of it.

There, the open door—*with another world beyond it.* Here, the old familiar street, clean, handsome, quiet, useless, where her own useless self had walked a thousand times.

There—something. Here, the world she knew. She did not know the words "fairyland" or "magic place," but if she had known them, she would have used them.

She glanced to the right, to the left.

The passersby noticed neither her nor the door. The sunset was just beginning to show in the upper city. In the lower city it was already blood-red with streamers of gold like enormous frozen flame. Elaine did not know that she sniffed the air; she did not know that she trembled on the edge of tears; she did not know that a tender smile, the first smile in years, relaxed her mouth and turned her tired tense face into a passing loveliness. She was too intent on looking around.

People walked about their business. Down the road, an underpeople type—female, possibly cat—detoured far around a true human who was walking at a slower pace. Far away, a police ornithopter flapped slowly around one of the towers; unless the robots used a telescope on her or unless they had one of the rare hawk-undermen who were sometimes used as police, they could not see her.

She stepped through the doorway and pulled the door itself back into the closed position.

She did not know it, but therewith unborn futures reeled out of existence, rebellion flamed into coming centuries, people and underpeople died in strange causes, mothers changed the names of unborn lords and starships whispered back from places which men had not even imagined before. Space$_3$, which had always been there, waiting for men's notice, would come the sooner —because of her, because of the door, because of her next few steps, what she would say and the child she would meet. (The ballad-writers told the whole story later on, but they told it backwards, from their own knowledge of D'joan and what Elaine had done to set the worlds afire. The simple truth is the fact that a lonely woman went through a mysterious door. That is all. Everything else happened later.)

At the top of the steps she stood, door closed behind her, the sunset gold of the unknown city streaming out in front of her. She could see where the great shell of the New City of Kalma arched out toward the sky; she could see that the buildings here were older, less harmonious than the ones she had left. She did not know the concept "picturesque," or she would have called it that. She knew no concept to describe the scene which lay peacefully at her feet.

There was not a person in sight.

Far in the distance, a fire-detector throbbed back and forth on top of an old tower. Outside of that there was nothing but the yellow-gold city beneath her, and a bird—was it a bird, or a large storm-swept leaf?—in the middle distance.

Filled with fear, hope, expectation and the surmisal of strange appetites, she walked downward with quiet, unknown purpose.

3

At the foot of the stairs, nine flights of them there had been, a child waited—a girl, about five. The child had a bright blue smock, wavy red-brown hair, and the daintiest hands which Elaine had ever seen.

Elaine's heart went out to her. The child looked up at her and shrank away. Elaine knew the meaning of those handsome brown eyes, of that muscular supplication of trust, that recoil from people. It was not a child at all— just some animal in the shape of a person, a dog perhaps, which would later be taught to speak, to work, to perform useful services.

The little girl rose, standing as though she were about to run. Elaine had the feeling that the little dog-girl had not decided whether to run toward her or from her. She did not wish to get involved with an underperson—what woman would?—but neither did she wish to frighten the little thing. After all, it was small, very young.

The two confronted each other for a moment, the little thing uncertain, Elaine relaxed. Then the little animal-girl spoke.

"Ask her," she said, and it was a command.

Elaine was surprised. Since when did animals command?

"Ask her!" repeated the little thing. She pointed at a window which had the words TRAVELERS' AID above it. Then the girl ran. A flash of blue from her dress, a twinkle of white from her running sandals, and she was gone.

Elaine stood quiet and puzzled in the forlorn and empty city.

The window spoke to her, "You might as well come on over. You will, you know."

It was the wise mature voice of an experienced woman—a voice with a bubble of laughter underneath its phonic edge, with a hint of sympathy and enthusiasm in its tone. The command was not merely a command. It was, even at its beginning, a happy private joke between two wise women.

Elaine was not surprised when a machine spoke to her. Recordings had been telling her things all her life. She was not sure of this situation, however.

"Is there somebody there?" she said.

"Yes and no," said the voice. "I'm 'Travelers' Aid' and I help everybody who comes through this way. You're lost or you wouldn't be here. Put your hand in my window."

"What I mean is," said Elaine, "are you a person or are you a machine?"

"Depends," said the voice. "I'm a machine, but I used to be a person, long, long ago. A lady, in fact, and one of the Instrumentality. But my time came and they said to me, 'Would you mind if we made a machine print of your whole personality? It would be very helpful for the information booths.' So of course I said yes, and they made this copy, and I died, and they shot my body into space with all the usual honors, but here I was. It felt pretty odd inside this contraption, me looking at things and talking to people and giving good advice and staying busy, until they built the new city. So what do you say? Am I me or aren't I?"

"I don't know, ma'am." Elaine stood back.

The warm voice lost its humor and became commanding. "Give me your hand, then, so I can identify you and tell you what to do."

"I think," said Elaine, "that I'll go back upstairs and go through the door into the upper city."

"And cheat me," said the voice in the window, "out of my first conversation with a real person in four years?" There was demand in the voice, but there was still the warmth and the humor; there was loneliness too. The loneliness decided Elaine. She stepped up to the window and put her hand flat on the ledge.

"You're Elaine," cried the window. "You're *Elaine!* The worlds wait for you. You're from An-fang, where all things begin, the Peace Square at An-fang, on Old Earth itself!"

"Yes," said Elaine.

The voice bubbled over with enthusiasm. "He is waiting for you. Oh, he has waited for you a long, long time. And the little girl you met. *That was D'joan herself.* The story has begun. 'The world's great age begins anew.' And I can die when it is over. So sorry, my dear. I don't mean to confuse you. I am the Lady Panc Ashash. You're Elaine. Your number originally ended 783 and you shouldn't even be on this planet. All the important people here end with the number 5 and 6. You're a lay therapist and you're in the wrong place, but your lover is already on his way, and you've never been in love yet, and it's all too exciting."

Elaine looked quickly around her. The old lower town was turning more red and less gold as the sunset progressed. The steps behind her seemed terribly high as she looked back, the door at the top very small. Perhaps it had locked on her when she closed it. Maybe she wouldn't ever be able to leave the old lower city.

The window must have been watching her in some way, because the voice of the Lady Panc Ashash became tender,

"Sit down my dear," said the voice from the window. "When I was me, I used to be much more polite. I haven't been me for a long, long time. I'm a machine, and still I feel like myself. Do sit down, and do forgive me."

Elaine looked around. There was the roadside marble bench behind her. She sat on it obediently. The happi-

ness which had been in her at the top of the steps bubbled forth anew. If this wise old machine knew so much
about her, perhaps it could tell her what to do. What did
the voice mean by "wrong planet"? By "lover"? By "he
is coming for you now," or was that what the voice had
actually said?

"Take a breath, my dear," said the voice of the Lady
Panc Ashash. She might have been dead for hundreds or
thousands of years, but still spoke with the authority
and kindness of a great lady.

Elaine breathed deep. She saw a huge red cloud, like
a pregnant whale, getting ready to butt the rim of the
upper city, far above her and far out over the sea. She
wondered if clouds could possibly have feelings.

The voice was speaking again. What had it said?

Apparently the question was repeated. "Did you
know you were coming?" said the voice from the window.

"Of course not." Elaine shrugged. "There was just
this door, and I didn't have anything special to do, so I
opened it. And here was a whole new world inside a
house. It looked strange and rather pretty, so I came
down. Wouldn't you have done the same thing?"

"I don't know," said the voice candidly. "I'm really a
machine. I haven't been me for a long, long time. Perhaps I would have, when I was alive. I don't know that,
but I know about things. Maybe I can see the future, or
perhaps the machine part of me computes such good
probabilities that it just seems like it. I know who you
are and what is going to happen to you. You had better
brush your hair."

"Whatever for?" said Elaine.

"He is coming," said the happy old voice of the Lady
Panc Ashash.

"*Who* is coming?" said Elaine, almost irritably.

"Do you have a mirror? I wish you would look at
your hair. It could be prettier, not that it isn't pretty
right now. You want to look your best. Your lover,
that's who is coming, of course."

"I haven't got a lover," said Elaine. "I haven't been
authorized one, not till I've done some of my lifework, and
I haven't even found my lifework yet. I'm not the kind of

girl who would go ask a subchief for the dreamies, not when I'm not entitled to the real thing. I may not be much of a person, but I have some self-respect." Elaine got so mad that she shifted her position on the bench and sat with her face turned away from the all-watching window.

The next words gave her gooseflesh down her arms, they were uttered with such real earnestness, such driving sincerity. *"Elaine, Elaine, do you really have no idea of who you are?"*

Elaine pivoted on the bench so that she looked toward the window. Her face was caught redly by the rays of the setting sun. She could only gasp.

"I don't know what you mean . . ."

The inexorable voice went on. "Think, Elaine, think. Does the name 'D'joan' mean nothing to you?"

"I suppose it's an underperson, a dog. That's what the D is for, isn't it?"

"That was the little girl you met, said the Lady Panc Ashash, as though the statement were something tremendous.

"Yes," said Elaine dutifully. She was a courteous woman, and never quarreled with strangers.

"Wait a minute," said the Lady Panc Ashash, "I'm going to get my body out. God knows when I wore it last, but it'll make you feel more at easy terms with me. Forgive the clothes. They're old stuff, but I think the body will work all right. This is the beginning of the story of D'joan, and I want that hair of yours brushed even if I have to brush it myself. Just wait right there, girl, wait right there. I'll just take a minute."

The clouds were turning from dark red to liver-black. What could Elaine do? She stayed on the bench. She kicked her shoe against the walk. She jumped a little when the old-fashioned street lights of the lower city went on with sharp geometrical suddenness; they did not have the subtle shading of the newer lights in the other city upstairs, where day phased into the bright clear night with no sudden shift in color.

The door beside the little window creaked open. Ancient plastic crumbled to the walk.

Elaine was astonished.

Elaine knew she must have been unconsciously expecting a monster, but this was a charming woman of about her own height, wearing weird, old-fashioned clothes. The strange woman had glossy black hair, no evidence of recent or current illness, no signs of severe lesions in the past, no impairment evident of sight, gait, reach or eyesight. (There was no way she could check on smell or taste right off, but this was the medical check-up she had had built into her from birth on—the checklist which she had run through with every adult person she had ever met. She had been designed as a "lay therapist, female" and she was a good one, even when there was no one at all to treat.)

Truly, the body was a rich one. It must have cost the landing charges of forty or fifty planetfalls. The human shape was perfectly rendered. The mouth moved over genuine teeth; the words were formed by throat, palate, tongue, teeth and lips, and not just by a microphone mounted in the head. The body was really a museum piece. It was probably a copy of the Lady Panc Ashash herself in time of life. When the face smiled, the effect was undescribably winning. The lady wore the costume of a bygone age—a stately frontal dress of heavy blue material, embroidered with a square pattern of gold at hem, waist and bodice. She had a matching cloak of dark, faded gold, embroidered in blue with the same pattern of squares. Her hair was upswept and set with jeweled combs. It seemed perfectly natural, but there was dust on one side of it.

The robot smiled, "I'm out of date. It's been a long time since I was me. But I thought, my dear, that you would find this old body easier to talk to than the window over there . . ."

Elaine nodded mutely.

"You know this is not me?" said the body, sharply.

Elaine shook her head. She didn't know; she felt that she didn't know anything at all.

The Lady Panc Ashash looked at her earnestly. "This is not me. It's a robot body. You looked at it as though it were a real person. And I'm not me, either. It hurts sometimes. Did you know a machine could hurt? I can. But—I'm not *me*."

"Who are you?" said Elaine to the pretty old woman.

"Before I died, I was the Lady Panc Ashash. Just as I told you. Now I am a machine, and a part of your destiny. We will help each other to change the destiny of worlds, perhaps even to bring mankind back to humanity."

Elaine stared at her in bewilderment. This was no common robot. It seemed like a real person and spoke with such warm authority. And this thing, whatever it was, this thing seemed to know so much about her. Nobody else had ever cared. The nurse-mothers at the Childhouse on earth had said, "Another witch-child, and pretty too, they're not much trouble," and had let her life go by.

At last Elaine could face the face which was not really a face. The charm, the humor, the expressiveness were still there.

"What—what," stammered Elaine, "do I do now?"

"Nothing," said the long-dead Lady Panc Ashash, "except to meet your destiny."

"You mean my lover?"

"So impatient!" laughed the dead woman's record in a very human way. "Such a hurry. Lover first and destiny later. I was like that myself when I was a girl."

"But what do I do?" persisted Elaine.

The night was now complete above them. The street lights glared on the empty and unswept streets. A few doorways, not one of them less than a full street-crossing away, were illuminated with rectangles of light or shadow—light if they were far from the street lights, so that their own interior lights shone brightly, shadow if they were so close under the big lights that they cut off the glare from overhead.

"Go through this door," said the old nice woman.

But she pointed at the undistinguished white of an uninterrupted wall. There was no door at all in that place.

"But there's no door there," said Elaine.

"If there were a door," said the Lady Panc Ashash, "you wouldn't need me to tell you to go through it. And you do need me."

"Why?" said Elaine.

"Because I've waited for you hundreds of years, that's why."

"That's no answer!" snapped Elaine.

"It is so an answer," smiled the woman, and her lack of hostility was not robotlike at all. It was the kindliness and composure of a mature human being. She looked up into Elaine's eyes and spoke emphatically and softly. "I know because I do know. Not because I'm a dead person—that doesn't matter any more—but because I am now a very old machine. You will go into the Brown and Yellow Corridor and you will think of your lover, and you will do your work, and men will hunt you. But you will come out happily in the end. Do you understand this?"

"No," said Elaine, "no, I don't." But she reached out her hand to the sweet old woman. The lady took her hand. The touch was warm and very human.

"You don't have to understand it. Just do it. And I know you will. So since you are going, go."

Elaine tried to smile at her, but she was troubled, more consciously worried than ever before in her life. Something real was happening to her, to her own individual self, at a very long last. "How will I get through the door?"

"I'll open it," smiled the lady, releasing Elaine's hand, "and you'll know your lover when he sings you the poem."

"Which poem?" said Elaine, stalling for time and frightened by a door which did not even exist.

"It starts, 'I knew you and loved you, and won you, in Kalma . . .' You'll know it. Go on in. It'll be bothersome at first, but when you meet the Hunter, it will all seem different."

"Have you ever been in there, yourself?"

"Of course not," said the dear old lady. "I'm a machine. That whole place is thoughtproof. Nobody can see, hear, think or talk in or out of it. It's a shelter left over from the ancient wars, when the slightest sign of a thought would have brought destruction on the whole place. That's why the Lord Englok built it, long before my time. But you can go in. And you will. Here's the door."

The old robot lady waited no longer. She gave Elaine

a strange friendly crooked smile, half proud and half apologetic. She took Elaine with firm fingertips holding Elaine's left elbow. They walked a few steps down toward the wall.

"Here, now," said the Lady Panc Ashash, and pushed.

Elaine flinched as she was thrust toward the wall. Before she knew it, she was through. Smells hit her like a roar of battle. The air was hot. The light was dim. It looked like a picture of the Pain Planet, hidden somewhere in space. Poets later tried to describe Elaine at the door with a verse which begins,

> *There were brown ones and blue ones*
> *And white ones and whiter,*
> *In the hidden and forbidden*
> *Downtown of Clown Town.*
> *There were horrid ones and horrider*
> *In the brown and yellow corridor.*

The truth was much simpler.

Trained witch, born witch that she was, she perceived the truth immediately. All these people, all she could see, at least, were sick. They needed help. They needed herself.

But the joke was on her, for she could not help a single one of them. Not one of them was a real person. They were just animals, things in the shape of man. Underpeople. Dirt.

And she was conditioned to the bone never to help *them*.

She did not know why the muscles of her legs made her walk forward, but they did.

There are many pictures of that scene.

The Lady Panc Ashash, only a few moments in her past, seemed very remote. And the city of Kalma itself, the new city, ten stories above her, almost seemed as though it had never existed at all. This, this was real.

She stared at the underpeople.

And this time, for the first time in her life, they stared right back at her. She had never seen anything like this before.

They did not frighten her; they surprised her. The fright, Elaine felt, was to come later. Soon, perhaps, but not here, not now.

4

Something which looked like a middle-aged woman walked right up to her and snapped at her.

"Are you death?"

Elaine stared. "Death? What do you mean? I'm Elaine."

"Be damned to that!" said the woman-thing. "Are you death?"

Elaine did not know the word "damned" but she was pretty sure that "death," even to these things, meant simply "termination of life."

"Of course not," said Elaine. "I'm just a person. A witch woman, ordinary people would call me. We don't have anything to do with you underpeople. Nothing at all." Elaine could see that the woman-thing had an enormous coiffure of soft brown sloppy hair, a sweat-reddened face and crooked teeth which showed when she grinned.

"They all say that. They never know that they're death. How do you think we die, if you people don't send contaminated robots in with diseases? We all die off when you do that, and then some more underpeople find this place again later on and make a shelter of it and live in it for a few generations until the death machines, things like you, come sweeping through the city and kill us off again. This is Clown Town, the underpeople place. Haven't you heard of it?"

Elaine tried to walk past the woman-thing, but she found her arm grabbed. This couldn't have happened before, not in the history of the world—an underperson seizing a real person!

"Let go!" she yelled.

The woman-thing let her arm go and faced toward the others. Her voice had changed. It was no longer shrill and excited, but low and puzzled instead. "I can't tell. Maybe it is a real person. Isn't that a joke? Lost, in here with us. Or maybe she *is* death. I can't tell. What do you think, Charley-is-my-darling?"

The man she spoke to stepped forward. Elaine thought, in another time, in some other place, that underperson might pass for an attractive human being. His face was illuminated by intelligence and alertness. He looked directly at Elaine as though he had never seen her before, which indeed he had not, but he continued looking with so sharp, so strange a stare that she became uneasy. His voice, when he spoke, was brisk, high, clear, friendly; set in this tragic place, it was the caricature of a voice, as though the animal had been programmed for speech from the habits of a human, persuader by profession, whom one saw in the storyboxes telling people messages which were neither good nor important, but merely clever. The handsomeness was itself deformity. Elaine wondered if he had come from goat stock.

"Welcome, young lady," said Charley-is-my-darling. "Now that you are here, how are you going to get out? If we turned her head around, Mabel," said he to the underwoman who had first greeted Elaine, "turned it around eight or ten times, it would come off. Then we could live a few weeks or months longer before our lords and creators found us and put us all to death. What do you say, young lady? Should we kill you?"

"Kill? You mean, terminate life? You cannot. It is against the law. Even the Instrumentality does not have the right to do that without trial. You can't. You're just underpeople."

"But we will die," said Charley-is-my-darling, flashing his quick intelligent smile, "if you go back out of that door. The police will read about the Brown and Yellow Corridor in your mind and they will flush us out with poison or they will spray disease in here so that we and our children will die."

Elaine stared at him.

The passionate anger did not disturb his smile or his persuasive tones, but the muscles of his eye-sockets and forehead showed the terrible strain. The result was an expression which Elaine had never seen before, a sort of self-control reaching out beyond the limits of insanity.

He stared back at her.

She was not really afraid of him. Underpeople could not twist the heads of real persons; it was contrary to all regulations.

A thought struck her. Perhaps regulations did not apply in a place like this, where illegal animals waited perpetually for sudden death. The being which faced her was strong enough to turn her head around ten times clockwise or counterclockwise. From her anatomy lessons, she was pretty sure that the head would come off somewhere during that process. She looked at him with interest. Animal-type fear had been conditioned out of her, but she had, she found, an extreme distaste for the termination of life under random circumstances. Perhaps her "witch" training would help. She tried to pretend that he was in fact a man. The diagnosis "hypertension: chronic aggression, now frustrated, leading to overstimulation and neurosis: poor nutritional record: hormone disorder probable" leapt into her mind.

She tried to speak in a new voice.

"I am smaller than you," she said, "and you can 'kill' me just as well later as now. We might as well get acquainted. I'm Elaine, assigned here from Manhome Earth."

The effect was spectacular.

Charley-is-my-darling stepped back. Mabel's mouth dropped open. The others gaped at her. One or two, more quick-witted than the rest, began whispering to their neighbors.

At last Charley-is-my-darling spoke to her. "Welcome, my lady. Can I call you my lady? I guess not. Welcome, Elaine. We are your people. We will do whatever you say. Of course you got in. The Lady Panc Ashash sent you. She has been telling us for a hundred years that somebody would come from Earth, a real person with an animal name, not a number, and that we should have a child named D'joan ready to take up the threads of destiny. Please, please sit down. Will you have a drink of water? We have no clean vessel here. We are all underpeople here and we have used everything in the place, so that it is contaminated for a real person." A thought struck him. "Baby-baby, do you have a new cup in the kiln?" Apparently he saw someone nod, because he went right on talking. "Get it out then, for our guest, with tongs. New tongs. Do not touch it. Fill it with water from the top of the little waterfall. That way our guest can have an uncontaminated drink. A clean drink." He beamed with a hospitality which was as ridiculous as it was genuine.

Elaine did not have the heart to say she did not want a drink of water.

She waited. They waited.

By now, her eyes had become accustomed to the darkness. She could see that the main corridor was painted a yellow, faded and stained, and a contrasting light brown. She wondered what possible human mind could have selected so ugly a combination. Cross-corridors seemed to open into it; at any rate, she saw illuminated archways further down and people walking out of them briskly. No one can walk briskly and naturally out of a shallow alcove, so she was pretty sure that the archways led to something.

The underpeople, too, she could see. They looked very much like people. Here and there, individuals reverted to the animal type—a horse-man whose muzzle had regrown to its ancestral size, a rat-woman with normal human features except for nylon-like white whiskers, twelve or fourteen on each side of her face, reaching twenty centimeters to either side. One looked very much like a person indeed—a beautiful young woman seated on a bench some eight or ten meters down the corridor, and paying no attention to the crowd, to Mabel, to Charley-is-my-darling or to herself.

"Who is that?" said Elaine, pointing with a nod at the beautiful young woman.

Mabel, relieved from the tension which had seized her when she had asked if Elaine were "death," babbled with a sociability which was outré in this environment. "That's Crawlie."

"What does she do?" asked Elaine.

"She has her pride," said Mabel, her grotesque red face now jolly and eager, her slack mouth spraying spittle as she spoke.

"But doesn't she *do* anything?" said Elaine.

Charley-is-my-darling intervened. "Nobody has to do anything here, Lady Elaine—"

"It's illegal to call me 'Lady,' " said Elaine.

"I'm sorry, human being Elaine. Nobody *has* to do anything at all here. The whole bunch of us are completely illegal. This corridor is a thought-shelter, so that no thoughts can escape or enter it. Wait a bit! Watch the ceiling . . . Now!"

A red glow moved across the ceiling and was gone.

"The ceiling glows," said Charley-is-my-darling, "whenever anything *thinks* against it. The whole tunnel registers 'sewage tank: organic waste' to the outside, so that dim perceptions of life which may escape here are not considered too unaccountable. People built it for their own use, a million years ago."

"They weren't here on Fomalhaut III a million years ago," snapped Elaine. Why, she wondered, did she snap at him? He wasn't a person, just a talking animal who had missed being dropped down the nearest incinerator.

"I'm sorry, Elaine," said Charley-is-my-darling. "I should have said, a long time ago. We underpeople don't get much chance to study real history. But we use this corridor. Somebody with a morbid sense of humor named this place Clown Town. We live along for ten or twenty or a hundred years, and then people or robots find us and kill us all. That's why Mabel was upset. She thought you were death for this time. But you're not. You're *Elaine*. That's wonderful, wonderful." His sly, too-clever face beamed with transparent sincerity. It must have been quite a shock to him to be honest.

"You were going to tell me what the undergirl is for," said Elaine.

"That's Crawlie," said he. "She doesn't do anything. None of us really have to. We're all doomed anyhow. She's a little more honest than the rest of us. She has her pride. She scorns the rest of us. She puts us in our place. She makes everybody feel inferior. We think she is a valuable member of the group. We all have our pride, which is hopeless anyway, but Crawlie has her pride all by herself, without doing anything whatever about it. She sort of reminds us. If we leave her alone, she leaves us alone."

Elaine thought, You're funny things, so much like people, but so inexpert about it, as though you all had to "die" before you really learned what it is to be alive. Aloud, she could only say, "I never met anybody like that."

Crawlie must have sensed that they were talking about her, because she looked at Elaine with a short quick stare of blazing hatred. Crawlie's pretty face locked itself into a glare of concentrated hostility and scorn; then her eyes wandered and Elaine felt that she, Elaine, no longer existed in the thing's mind, except as a rebuke which had been administered and forgotten. She had never seen privacy as impenetrable as Crawlie's. And yet the being, whatever she might have been made from, was very lovely in human terms.

A fierce old hag, covered with mouse-gray fur, rushed up to Elaine. The mouse-woman was the Baby-baby who had been sent on the errand. She held a ceramic cup in a pair of long tongs. Water was in it.

Elaine took the cup.

Sixty to seventy underpeople, including the little girl in the blue dress whom she had seen outside, watched her as she sipped. The water was good. She drank it all. There was a universal exhalation, as though everyone in the corridor had waited for this moment. Elaine started to put the cup down but the old mouse-woman was too quick for her. She took the cup from Elaine, stopping her in mid-gesture and using the tongs, so that the cup would not be contaminated by the touch of an underperson.

"That's right, Baby-baby," said Charley-is-my-darling, "we can talk. It is our custom not to talk with a newcomer until we have offered our hospitality. Let me be frank. We may have to kill you, if this whole business turns out to be a mistake, but let me assure you that if I do kill you, I will do it nicely and without the least bit of malice. Right?"

Elaine did not know what was so right about it, and said so. She visualized her head being twisted off. Apart from the pain and the degradation, it seemed so terribly messy—to terminate life in a sewer with things which did not even have a right to exist.

He gave her no chance to argue, but went on explaining, "Suppose things turn out just right. Suppose that you are the Esther-Elaine-or-Eleanor that we have all been waiting for—the person who will do something to D'joan and bring us all help and deliverance—give us life, in short, *real life*—then what do we do?"

"I don't know where you get all these ideas about me. Why am I Esther-Elaine-or-Eleanor? What do I do to D'joan? Why me?"

Charley-is-my-darling stared at her as though he could not believe her question. Mabel frowned as though she could not think of the right words to put forth her opinions. Baby-baby, who had glided back to the group with swift mouselike suddenness, looked around as though she expected someone from the rear to speak. She was right. Crawlie turned her face toward Elaine and said, with infinite condescension:

"I did not know that real people were ill-informed or stupid. You seem to be both. We have all our information from the Lady Panc Ashash. Since she is dead, she has no prejudices against us underpeople. Since she has not had much of anything to do, she has run through billions and billions of probabilities for us. All of us know what most probabilities come to—sudden death by disease or gas, or maybe being hauled off to the slaughterhouses in big police ornithopters. But Lady Panc Ashash found that perhaps a person with a name like yours would come, a human being with an old name and not a number name, that that person would meet the Hunter, that she and the Hunter would teach the underchild D'joan a message and that the message would change the worlds. We have kept one child after another named D'joan, waiting for a hundred years. Now you show up. Maybe you are the one. You don't look very competent to me. What are you good for?"

"I'm a witch," said Elaine.

Crawlie could not keep the surprise from showing in her face. "A witch? Really?"

"Yes," said Elaine, rather humbly.

"I wouldn't be one," said Crawlie. "I have my pride." She turned her face away and locked her features in their expression of perennial hurt and disdain.

Charley-is-my-darling whispered to the group nearby, not caring whether Elaine heard his words or not, "That's wonderful, wonderful. She is a witch. A human witch. Perhaps the great day is here! Elaine," said he humbly, "will you please look at us?"

Elaine looked. When she stopped to think about where she was, it was incredible that the empty old lower city of Kalma should be just outside, just beyond the wall, and the busy new city a mere thirty-five meters higher. This corridor was a world to itself. It felt like a world, with the ugly yellows and browns, the dim old lights, the stenches of man and animal mixed under intolerably bad ventilation. Baby-baby, Crawlie, Mabel and Charley-is-my-darling were part of this world. They were real; but they were outside, outside, so far as Elaine herself was concerned.

"Let me go," she said. "I'll come back some day."

Charley-is-my-darling, who was so plainly the leader, spoke as if in a trance: "You don't understand, Elaine. The only 'going' you are going to go is death. There is no other direction. We can't let the old you go out of this door, not when the Lady Panc Ashash has thrust you in to us. Either you go forward to your destiny, to our destiny too, either you do that, and all works out all right, so that you love us, and we love you," he added dreamily, "or else I kill you with my own hands. Right here. Right now. I could give you another clean drink of water first. But that is all. There isn't much choice for you, human being Elaine. What do you think would happen if you went outside?"

"Nothing, I hope," said Elaine.

"Nothing!" snorted Mabel, her face regaining its original indignation. "The police would come flapping by in their ornithopter—"

"And they'd pick your brains," said Baby-baby.

"And they'd know about us," said a tall pale man who had not spoken before.

"And we," said Crawlie from her chair, "would all of us die within an hour or two at the longest. Would that matter to you, Ma'am and Elaine?"

"And," added Charley-is-my-darling, "they would disconnect the Lady Panc Ashash, so that even the recording of that dear dead lady would be gone at last, and there would be no mercy at all left upon this world."

"What is 'mercy'?" asked Elaine.

"It's obvious you never heard of it," said Crawlie.

The old mouse-hag Baby-baby came close to Elaine. She looked up at her and whispered through yellow teeth. "Don't let them frighten you, girl. Death doesn't matter all that much, not even to you true humans with your four hundred years or to us animals with the slaughterhouse around the corner. Death is a *when*, not a *what*. It's the same for all of us. Don't be scared. Go straight ahead and you may find mercy and love. They're much richer than death, if you can only find them. Once you do find them, death won't be very important."

"I still don't know *mercy*," said Elaine, "but I thought I knew what *love* was, and I don't expect to find my lover in a dirty old corridor full of underpeople."

"I don't mean that kind of love," laughed Baby-baby, brushing aside Mabel's attempted interruption with a wave of her hand-paw. The old mouse face was on fire with sheer expressiveness. Elaine could suddenly imagine what Baby-baby had looked like to a mouse-under-man when she was young and sleek and gray. Enthusiasm flushed the old features with youth as Baby-baby went on, "I don't mean love for a lover, girl. I mean love for yourself. Love for life. Love for all things living. Love even for me. Your love for me. Can you imagine that?"

Elaine swam through fatigue but she tried to answer the question. She looked in the dim light at the wrinkled old mouse-hag with her filthy clothes and her little red eyes. The fleeting image of the beautiful young mouse-woman had faded away; there was only this cheap, useless old thing, with her inhuman demands and her senseless pleading. People never loved underpeople. They used them, like chairs or doorhandles. Since when did a doorhandle demand the Charter of Ancient Rights?

"No," said Elaine calmly and evenly, "I can't imagine ever loving you."

"I knew it," said Crawlie from her chair. There was triumph in the voice.

Charley-is-my-darling shook his head as if to clear his sight. "Don't you even know who controls Fomalhaut III?"

"The Instrumentality," said Elaine. "But do we have to go on talking? Let me go or kill me or something. This doesn't make sense. I was tired when I got here, and I'm a million years tireder now."

Mabel said, "Take her along."

"All right," said Charley-is-my-darling. "Is the Hunter there?"

The child D'joan spoke. She had stood at the back of the group. "He came in the other way when she came in the front."

Elaine said to Charley-is-my-darling, "You lied to me. You said there was only one way."

"I did not lie," said he. "There is only one way for you or me or for the friends of the Lady Panc Ashash. The way you came. The other way is death."

"What do you mean?"

"I mean," he said, "that it leads straight into the slaughterhouses of the men you do not know. The lords of the Instrumentality who are here on Fomalhaut III. There is the Lord Femtiosex, who is just and without pity. There is the Lord Limaono, who thinks that underpeople are a potential danger and should not have been started in the first place. There is the Lady Goroke, who does not know how to pray, but who tries to ponder the mystery of life and who has shown kindnesses to underpeople, as long as the kindnesses were lawful ones. And there is the Lady Arabella Underwood, whose justice no man can understand. Nor underpeople either," he added with a chuckle.

"Who is she? I mean, where did she get the funny name? It doesn't have a number in it. It's as bad as your names. Or my own," said Elaine.

"She's from Old North Australia, the stroon world, on loan to the Instrumentality, and she follows the laws she was born to. The Hunter can go through the rooms and the slaughterhouses of the Instrumentality, but could you? Could I?"

"No," said Elaine.

"Then forward," said Charley-is-my-darling, "to your death or to great wonders. May I lead the way, Elaine?"

Elaine nodded wordlessly.

The mouse-hag Baby-baby patted Elaine's sleeve, her eyes alive with strange hope. As Elaine passed Crawlie's chair, the proud, beautiful girl looked straight at her, expressionless, deadly and severe. The dog-girl D'joan followed the little procession as if she had been invited.

They walked down and down and down. Actually, it could not have been a full half-kilometer. But with the endless browns and yellows, the strange shapes of the lawless and untended underpeople, the stenches and the thick heavy air, Elaine felt as if she were leaving all known worlds behind.

In fact, she was doing precisely that, but it did not occur to her that her own suspicion might be true.

5

At the end of the corridor there was a round gate with a door of gold or brass.

Charley-is-my-darling stopped.

"I can't go further," he said. "You and D'joan will have to go on. This is the forgotten antechamber between the tunnel and the upper palace. The Hunter is there. Go on. You're a person. It is safe. Underpeople usually die in there. Go on." He nudged her elbow and pulled the sliding door apart.

"But the little girl," said Elaine.

"She's not a girl," said Charley-is-my-darling. "She's just a dog—as I'm not a man, just a goat brightened and cut and trimmed to look like a man. If you come back, Elaine, I will love you like god or I will kill you. It depends."

"Depends on what?" asked Elaine. "And what is 'god'?"

Charley-is-my-darling smiled the quick tricky smile which was wholly insincere and completely friendly, both at the same time. It was probably the trademark of his personality in ordinary times. "You'll find out about god somewhere else, if you do. Not from us. And the depending is something you'll know for yourself. You won't have to wait for me to tell you. Go along now. The whole thing will be over in the next few minutes."

"But D'joan?" persisted Elaine.

"If it doesn't work," said Charley-is-my-darling, "we can always raise another D'joan and wait for another you. The Lady Panc Ashash had promised us that. Go on in!"

He pushed her roughly, so that she stumbled through. Bright light dazzled her and the clean air tasted as good as fresh water on her first day out of the space-ship pod.

The little dog-girl had trotted in beside her.

The door, gold or brass, clanged to behind them.

Elaine and D'joan stood still, side by side, looking forward and upward.

There are many famous paintings of that scene. Most of the paintings show Elaine in rags with the distorted, suffering face of a witch. This is strictly unhistorical. She was wearing her everyday culottes, blouse and twin over-the-shoulder purses when she went in the other end of Clown Town. This was the usual dress on Fomalhaut III at that time. She had done nothing at all to spoil her clothes, so she must have looked the same when she came out. And D'joan—well, everyone knows what D'joan looked like.

The Hunter met them.

The Hunter met them, and new worlds began.

He was a shortish man, with black curly hair, black eyes that danced with laughter, broad shoulders and long legs. He walked with a quick sure step. He kept his hands quiet at his side, but the hands did not look tough and calloused, as though they had been terminating lives, even the lives of animals.

"Come up and sit down," he greeted them. "I've been waiting for you both."

Elaine stumbled upward and forward. "Waiting?" she gasped.

"Nothing mysterious," he said. "I had the viewscreen on. The one into the tunnel. Its connections are shielded, so the police could not have peeped it."

Elaine stopped dead still. The little dog-girl, one step behind her, stopped too. She tried to draw herself up to her full height. She was about the same tallness that he was. It was difficult, since he stood four or five steps above them. She managed to keep her voice even when she said:

"You know, then?"

"What?"

"All those things they said."

"Sure I know them," he smiled. "Why not?"

"But," stammered Elaine, "about you and me being lovers? That too?"

"That too," he smiled again. "I've been hearing it half my life. Come on up, sit down and have something to eat. We have a lot of things to do tonight, if history is to be fulfilled through us. What do you eat, little girl?" said he kindly to D'joan. "Raw meat or people food?"

"I'm a finished girl," said D'joan, "so I prefer chocolate cake with vanilla ice cream."

"That you shall have," said the Hunter. "Come, both of you, and sit down."

They had topped the steps. A luxurious table, already set, was waiting for them. There were three couches around it. Elaine looked for the third person who would join them. Only as she sat down did she realize that he meant to invite the dog-child.

He saw her surprise, but did not comment on it directly.

Instead, he spoke to D'joan.

"You know me, girl, don't you?"

The child smiled and relaxed for the first time since Elaine had seen her. The dog-girl was really strikingly beautiful when the tension went out of her. The wariness, the quietness, the potential disquiet—these were dog qualities. Now the child seemed wholly human and mature far beyond her years. Her white face had dark, dark brown eyes.

"I've seen you lots of times, Hunter. And you've told me what would happen if I turned out to be *the* D'joan. How I would spread the word and meet great trials. How I might die and might not, but people and under-people would remember my name for thousands of years. You've told me almost everything I know—except the things that I can't talk to you about. You know them too, but you won't talk, will you?" said the little girl imploringly.

"I know you've been to Earth," said the Hunter.

"Don't say it! Please don't say it!" pleaded the girl.

"Earth! Manhome itself?" cried Elaine. "How, by the stars, did you get there?"

The Hunter intervened. "Don't press her, Elaine. It's a big secret, and she wants to keep it. You'll find out more tonight than mortal woman was ever told before."

"What does 'mortal' mean?" asked Elaine, who disliked antique words.

"It just means having a termination of life."

"That's foolish," said Elaine. "Everything terminates. Look at those poor messy people who went on beyond the legal four hundred years." She looked around. Rich black-and-red curtains hung from ceiling to floor. On one side of the room there was a piece of furniture she had never seen before. It was like a table, but it had little broad flat doors on the front, reaching from side to side; it was richly ornamented with unfamiliar woods and metals. Nevertheless, she had more important things to talk about than furniture.

She looked directly at the Hunter (no organic disease; wounded in left arm at an earlier period; somewhat excessive exposure to sunlight; might need correction for near vision) and demanded of him:

"Am I captured by you, too?"

"Captured?"

"You're a Hunter. You hunt things. To kill them, I suppose. That underman back there, the goat who calls himself Charley-is-my-darling—"

"He never does!" cried the dog-girl, D'joan, interrupting.

"Never does what?" said Elaine, cross at being interrupted.

"He never calls himself that. Other people, underpeople I mean, call him that. His name is Balthasar, but nobody uses it."

"What does it matter, little girl?" said Elaine. "I'm

talking about my life. Your friend said he would take my life from me if something did not happen."

Neither D'joan nor the Hunter said anything.

Elaine heard a frantic edge go into her voice, "You heard it!" She turned to the Hunter, "You saw it on the viewscreen."

The Hunter's voice was serenity and assurance: "We three have things to do before this night is out. We won't get them done if you are frightened or worried. I know the underpeople, but I know the Lords of the Instrumentality as well—all four of them, right here. The Lords Limaono and Femtiosex and the Lady Goroke. And the Norstrilian, too. They will protect you. Charley-is-my-darling might want to take your life from you because he is worried, afraid that the tunnel of Englok, where you just were, will be discovered. I have ways of protecting him and yourself as well. Have confidence in me for a while. That's not so hard, is it?"

"But," protested Elaine, "the man—or the goat—or whatever he was, Charley-is-my-darling, he said it would all happen right away, as soon as I came up here with you."

"How can anything happen," said little D'joan, "if you keep talking all the time?"

The Hunter smiled.

"That's right," he said. "We've talked enough. Now we must become lovers."

Elaine jumped to her feet. "Not with me, you don't. Not with her here. Not when I haven't found my work to do. I'm a witch. I'm supposed to do something, but I've never really found out what it was."

"Look at this," said the Hunter calmly, walking over to the wall, and pointing with his finger at an intricate circular design.

Elaine and D'joan both looked at it.

The Hunter spoke again, his voice urgent. "Do you see it, D'joan? Do you really see it? The ages turn, waiting for this moment, little child. Do you see it? Do you see yourself in it?"

Elaine looked at the little dog-girl. D'joan had almost stopped breathing. She stared at the curious symmetrical pattern as though it were a window into enchanting worlds.

The Hunter roared, at the top of his voice, "D'joan! Joan! Joanie!"

The child made no response.

The Hunter stepped over to the child, slapped her gently on the cheek, shouted again. D'joan continued to stare at the intricate design.

"Now," said the Hunter, "you and I make love. The child is absent in a world of happy dreams. That design is a mandala, something left over from the unimaginable past. It locks the human consciousness in place. D'joan will not see us or hear us. We cannot help her go toward her destiny unless you and I make love first."

Elaine, her hand to her mouth, tried to inventory symptoms as a means of keeping her familiar thoughts in balance. It did not work. A relaxation spread over her, a happiness and quiet that she had not once felt since her childhood.

"Did you think," said the Hunter, "that I hunted with my body and killed with my hands? Didn't anyone ever tell you that the game comes to me rejoicing, that the animals die while they scream with pleasure? I'm a telepath, and I work under license. And I have my license now from the dead Lady Panc Ashash."

Elaine knew that they had come to the end of the talking. Trembling, happy, frightened, she fell into his arms and let him lead her over to the couch at the side of the black-and-gold room.

A thousand years later, she was kissing his ear and murmuring loving words at him, words that she did not even realize she knew. She must, she thought, have picked up more from the story-boxes than she ever realized.

"You're my love," she said, "my only one, my darling. Never, never leave me; never throw me away. Oh, Hunter, I love you so!"

"We part," he said, "before tomorrow is gone, but shall meet again. Do you realize that all this has only been a little more than an hour?"

Elaine blushed. "And I," she stammered, "I—I'm hungry."

"Natural enough," said the Hunter. "Pretty soon we can waken the little girl and eat together. And then history will happen, unless somebody walks in and stops us."

"But, darling," said Elaine, "can't we go on—at least for a while? A year? A month? A day? Put the little girl back in the tunnel for a while."

"Not really," said the Hunter, "but I'll sing you the song that came into my mind about you and me. I've been thinking bits of it for a long time, but now it has really happened. Listen."

He held her two hands in his two hands, looked easily and frankly into her eyes. There was no hint in him of telepathic power.

He sang to her the song which we know as *I Loved You and Lost You.*

> *I knew you, and loved you,*
>   *and won you, in Kalma.*
> *I loved you, and won you,*
>   *and lost you, my darling!*
> *The dark skies of Waterrock*
>   *swept down against us.*
> *Lightning-lit only*
>   *by our own love, my lovely!*
>
> *Our time was a short time,*
>   *a sharp hour of glory—*
> *We tasted delight*
>   *and we suffer denial.*
> *The tale of us two*
>   *is a bittersweet story,*
> *Short as a shot*
>   *but as long as death.*
>
> *We met and we loved,*
>   *and vainly we plotted*
> *To rescue beauty*
>   *from a smothering war.*
> *Time had no time for us,*
>   *the minutes, no mercy.*
> *We have loved and lost,*
>   *and the world goes on.*

We have lost and have kissed,
  and have parted, my darling!
All that we have,
  we must save in our hearts, love.
The memory of beauty
  and the beauty of memory . . .
I've loved you and won you
  and lost you, in Kalma.

His fingers, moving in the air, produced a soft organ-like music in the room. She had noticed music-beams before, but she had never had one played for herself.

By the time he was through singing, she was sobbing. It was all so true, so wonderful, so heartbreaking.

He had kept her right hand in his left hand. Now he released her suddenly. He stood up.

"Let's work first. Eat later. Someone is near us."

He walked briskly over to the little dog-girl, who was still seated on the chair looking at the mandala with open, sleeping eyes. He took her head firmly and gently between his two hands and turned her eyes away from the design. She struggled momentarily against his hands and then seemed to wake up fully.

She smiled. "That was nice. I rested. How long was it —five minutes?"

"More than that," said the Hunter gently. "I want you to take Elaine's hand."

A few hours ago, and Elaine would have protested at the grotesquerie of holding hands with an underperson. This time, she said nothing, but obeyed: she looked with much love toward the Hunter.

"You two don't have to know much," said the Hunter. "You, D'joan, are going to get everything that is in our minds and in our memories. You will become us, both of us. Forevermore. You will meet your glorious fate."

The little girl shivered. "Is this really the day?"

"It is," said the Hunter. "Future ages will remember this night."

"And you, Elaine," said he to her, "have nothing to do but to love me and to stand very still. Do you understand? You will see tremendous things, some of them frightening. But they won't be real. Just stand still."

Elaine nodded wordlessly.

"In the name," said the Hunter, "of the First Forgot-ten One, in the name of the Second Forgotten One, in the name of the Third Forgotten One. For the love of people, that will give them life. For the love that will give them a clean death and true . . ." His words were clear but Elaine could not understand them.

The day of days was here.

She knew it.

She did not know how she knew it, but she did.

The Lady Panc Ashash crawled up through the solid floor, wearing her friendly robot body. She came near to Elaine and murmured:

"Have no fear, no fear."

Fear? thought Elaine. This is no time for fear. It is much too interesting.

As if to answer Elaine, a clear, strong, masculine voice spoke out of nowhere:

This is the time for the daring sharing.

When these words were spoken, it was as if a bubble had been pricked. Elaine felt her personality and D'joan mingling. With ordinary telepathy, it would have been frightening. But this was not communication. It was being.

She had become Joan. She felt the clean little body in its tidy clothes. She became aware of the girl-shape again. It was oddly pleasant and familiar, in terribly far-away kinds of feeling, to remember that she had had that shape once—the smooth, innocent flat chest; the uncomplicated groin; the fingers which still felt as though they were separate and alive in extending from the palm of the hand. But the mind—*that* child's mind! It was like an enormous museum illuminated by rich stained-glass windows, cluttered with variegated heaps of beauty and treasure, scented by strange incense which moved slowly in unpropelled air. D'joan had a mind which reached all the way back to the color and glory of man's antiquity. D'joan had been a lord of the Instru-mentality, a monkey-man riding the ships of space, a friend of the dear dead Lady Panc Ashash, and Panc Ashash herself.

No wonder the child was rich and strange: she had been made the heir of all the ages.

This is the time for the glaring top of the truth at the wearing sharing, said the nameless, clear, loud voice in her mind. *This is the time for you and him.*

Elaine realized that she was responding to hypnotic suggestions which the Lady Panc Ashash had put into the mind of the little dog-girl—suggestions which were triggered into full potency the moment that the three of them came into telepathic contact.

For a fraction of a second, she perceived nothing but astonishment within herself. She saw nothing but herself —every detail, every secrecy, every thought and feeling and contour of flesh. She was curiously aware of how her breasts hung from her chest, the tension of her belly-muscles holding her female backbone straight and erect—

Female backbone?

Why had she thought that she had a female backbone?

And then she knew.

She was following the Hunter's mind as his awareness rushed through her body, drank it up, enjoyed it, loved it all over again, this time from the inside out.

She knew somehow that the little dog-girl watched everything quietly, wordlessly, drinking in from them both the full nuance of being truly human.

Even with the delirium, she sensed embarrassment. It might be a dream, but it was still too much. She began to close her mind and the thought had come to her that she should take her hands away from the hands of Hunter and the dog-child.

But then fire came . . .

6

Fire came up from the floor, burning about them intangibly. Elaine felt nothing . . . but she could sense the touch of the little girl's hand.

Flames around the dames, games, said an idiot voice from nowhere.

Fire around the pyre, sire, said another.

Hot is what we got, tot, said a third.

Suddenly Elaine remembered Earth, but it was not the Earth she knew. She was herself D'joan, and not D'joan. She was a tall, strong monkey-man, indistinguishable from a true human being. She/he had tremendous alertness in her/his heart as she/he walked across the Peace Square at An-fang, the Old Square at An-fang, where all things begin. She/he noticed a discrepancy. Some of the buildings were not there.

The real Elaine thought to herself, "So that's what they did with the child—printed her with the memories of other underpeople. Other ones, who dared things and went places."

The fire stopped.

Elaine saw the black-and-gold room clean and untroubled for a moment before the green white-topped ocean rushed in. The water poured over the three of them without getting them wet in the least. The greenness washed around them without pressure, without suffocation.

Elaine was the Hunter. Enormous dragons floated in the sky above Fomalhaut III. She felt herself wandering across a hill, singing with love and yearning. She had the Hunter's own mind, his own memory. The dragon sensed him, and flew down. The enormous reptilian wings were more beautiful than a sunset, more delicate than orchids. Their beat in the air was as gentle as the breath of a baby. She was not only Hunter but dragon too; she felt the minds meeting and the dragon dying in bliss, in joy.

Somehow the water was gone. So too were D'joan and the Hunter. She was not in the room. She was taut, tired, worried Elaine, looking down a nameless street for hopeless destinations. She had to do things which could never be done. The wrong me, the wrong time, the wrong place—and I'm alone, I'm alone, I'm alone, her mind screamed. The room was back again; so too were the hands of the Hunter and the little girl.

Mist began rising—

Another dream? thought Elaine. Aren't we done? But there was another voice somewhere, a voice which grated like the rasp of a saw cutting through bone, like the grind of a broken machine still working at ruinous top speed. It was an evil voice, a terror-filling voice.

Perhaps this really was the "death" which the tunnel underpeople had mistaken her for.

The Hunter's hand released hers. She let go of D'joan.

There was a strange woman in the room. She wore the baldric of authority and the leotards of a traveler. Elaine stared at her.

"You'll be punished," said the terrible voice, which now was coming out of the woman.

"Wh-wh-what?" stammered Elaine.

"You're conditioning an underperson without authority. I don't know who you are, but the Hunter should know better. The animal will have to die, of course," said the woman, looking at little D'joan.

Hunter muttered, half in greeting to the stranger, half in explanation to Elaine, as though he did not know what else to say:

"Lady Arabella Underwood."

Elaine could not bow to her, though she wanted to. The surprise came from the little dog girl.

I am your sister Joan, she said, *and no animal to you.*

The Lady Arabella seemed to have trouble hearing. (Elaine herself could not tell whether she was hearing spoken words or taking the message with her mind.)

I am Joan and I love you.

The Lady Arabella shook herself as though water had splashed on her. "Of course you're Joan. You love me. And I love you."

People and underpeople meet on the terms of love.

"Love. Love, of course. You're a good little girl. And so right." *You will forget me,* said Joan, *until we meet and love again.*

"Yes, darling. Good-by for now."

At last D'joan did use words. She spoke to the Hunter and Elaine, saying, "It is finished. I know who I am and what I must do. Elaine had better come with me. We will see you soon, Hunter—if we live."

Elaine looked at the Lady Arabella who stood stock

still, staring like a blind woman. The Hunter nodded at Elaine with his wise, kind, rueful smile.

The little girl led Elaine down, down, down to the door which led back to the tunnel of Englok. Just as they went through the brass door, Elaine heard the voice of the Lady Arabella say to the Hunter:

"What are you doing here all by yourself? The room smells funny. Have you had animals here? Have you killed something?"

"Yes, Ma'am," said the Hunter as D'joan and Elaine stepped through the door.

"What?" cried the Lady Arabella.

Hunter must have raised his voice to a point of penetrating emphasis because he wanted the other two to hear him, too:

"I have killed, Ma'am," he said, "as always—with love. This time it was a system."

They slipped through the door while the Lady Arabella's protesting voice, heavy with authority and inquiry, was still sweeping against the Hunter.

Joan led. Her body was the body of a pretty child, but her personality was the full awakening of all the underpeople who had been imprinted on her. Elaine could not understand it, because Joan was still the little doggirl, but Joan was now also Elaine, also Hunter. There was no doubt about their movement; the child, no longer an undergirl, led the way and Elaine, human or not, followed.

The door closed behind them. They were back in the Brown and Yellow Corridor. Most of the underpeople were awaiting them. Dozens stared at them. The heavy animal-human smells of the old tunnel rolled against them like thick, slow waves. Elaine felt the beginning of a headache at her temples, but she was much too alert to care.

For a moment, D'joan and Elaine confronted the underpeople.

Most of you have seen paintings or theatricals based upon this scene. The most famous of all is, beyond doubt, the fantastic "one-line drawing" of San Shigonanda—the board of the background almost uniformly gray, with a hint of brown and yellow on the left, a hint of black and red on the right, and in the center the strange white line, almost a smear of paint, which somehow suggests the bewildered girl Elaine and the doomblessed child Joan.

Charley-is-my-darling was, of course, the first to find his voice. (Elaine did not notice him as a goat-man any more. He seemed an earnest, friendly man of middle age, fighting poor health and an uncertain life with great courage. She now found his smile persuasive and charming. Why, thought Elaine, didn't I see him that way before? Have I changed?)

Charley-is-my-darling had spoken before Elaine found her wits. "He did it. Are you D'joan?"

"Am I D'joan?" said the child, asking the crowd of deformed, weird people in the tunnel. "Do you think I am D'joan?"

"No! No! You are the lady who was promised—you are the bridge-to-man," cried a tall yellow-haired old woman, whom Elaine could not remember seeing before. The woman flung herself to her knees in front of the child, and tried to get D'joan's hand. The child held her hands away, quietly, but firmly, so the woman buried her face in the child's skirt and wept.

"I am Joan," said the child, "and I am dog no more. You are people now, people, and if you die with me, you will die men. Isn't that better than it has ever been before? And you, Ruthie," said she to the woman at her feet, "stand up and stop crying. Be glad. These are the days that I shall be with you. I know your children were all taken away and killed, Ruthie, and I am sorry. I cannot bring them back. But I give you womanhood. I have even made a person out of Elaine."

"Who are you?" said Charley-is-my-darling. "Who are you?"

"I'm the little girl you put out to live or die an hour ago. But now I am Joan, not D'joan, and I bring you a weapon. You are women. You are men. You are people. You can use the weapon."

"What weapon?" The voice was Crawlie's, from about the third row of spectators.

"Life and life-with," said the child Joan.

"Don't be a fool," said Crawlie. "What's the weapon?

Don't give us words. We've had words and death ever since the world of underpeople began. That's what *people* give us—good words, fine principles and cold murder, year after year, generation after generation. Don't tell me I'm a person—I'm not. I'm a bison and I know it. An animal fixed up to look like a person. Give me a something to kill with. Let me die fighting."

Little Joan looked incongruous in her young body and short stature, still wearing the little blue smock in which Elaine had first seen her. She commanded the room. She lifted her hand and the buzz of low voices, which had started while Crawlie was yelling, dropped off to silence again.

"Crawlie," she said, in a voice that carried all the way down the hall, "peace be with you in the everlasting now."

Crawlie scowled. She did have the grace to look puzzled at Joan's message to her, but she did not speak.

"Don't talk to me, dear people," said little Joan. "Get used to me first. I bring you life-with. It's more than love. Love's a hard, sad, dirty word, a cold word, an old word. It says too much and it promises too little. I bring you something much bigger than love. If you're alive, you're alive. If you're alive-with, then you know the other life is there too—both of you, any of you, all of you. Don't do anything. Don't grab, don't clench, don't possess. Just *be*. That's the weapon. There's not a flame or a gun or a poison that can stop it."

"I want to believe you," said Mabel, "but I don't know how to."

"Don't believe me," said little Joan. "Just wait and let things happen. Let me through, good people. I have to sleep for a while. Elaine will watch me while I sleep and when I get up, I will tell you why you are underpeople no longer."

Joan started to move forward—

A wild ululating screech split the corridor.

Everyone looked around to see where it came from.

It was almost like the shriek of a fighting bird, but the sound came from among them.

Elaine saw it first.

Crawlie had a knife and just as the cry ended, she flung herself on Joan.

Child and woman fell on the floor, their dresses a tangle. The large hand rose up twice with the knife, and the second time it came up red.

From the hot shocking burn in her side, Elaine knew that she must herself have taken one of the stabs. She could not tell whether Joan was still living.

The undermen pulled Crawlie off the child.

Crawlie was white with rage, "Words, words, words. She'll kill us all with her words."

A large, fat man with the muzzle of a bear on the front of an otherwise human-looking head and body, stepped around the man who held Crawlie. He gave her one tremendous slap. She dropped to the floor unconscious. The knife, stained with blood, fell on the old worn carpet. (Elaine thought automatically: restorative for her later; check neck vertebrae; no problem of bleeding.)

For the first time in her life, Elaine functioned as a wholly efficient witch. She helped the people pull the clothing from little Joan. The tiny body, with the heavy purple-dark blood pumping out from just below the ribcage, looked hurt and fragile. Elaine reached in her left handbag. She had a surgical radar pen. She held it to her eye and looked through the flesh, up and down the wound. The peritoneum was punctured, the liver cut, the upper folds of the large intestine were perforated in two places. When she saw this, she knew what to do. She brushed the bystanders aside and got to work.

First she glued the cuts from the inside out, starting with the damage to the liver. Each touch of the organic adhesive was preceded by a tiny spray of re-coding powder, designed to reinforce the capacity of the injured organ to restore itself. The probing, pressing, squeezing, took eleven minutes. Before it was finished, Joan had awakened, and was murmuring:

"Am I dying?"

"Not at all," said Elaine, "unless these human medicines poison your dog blood."

"Who did it?"

"Crawlie?"

"Why?" said the child. "Why? Is she hurt too? Where is she?"

"Not as hurt as she is going to be," said the goat-man, Charley-is-my-darling. "If she lives, we'll fix her up and try her and put her to death."

"No, you won't," said Joan. "You're going to love her. You must."

The goat-man looked bewildered.

He turned in his perplexity to Elaine. "Better have a look at Crawlie," said he. "Maybe Orson killed her with that slap. He's a bear, you know."

"So I saw," said Elaine, drily. What did the man think that thing looked like, a hummingbird?

She walked over to the body of Crawlie. As soon as she touched the shoulders, she knew that she was in for trouble. The outer appearances were human, but the musculature beneath was not. She suspected that the laboratories had left Crawlie terribly strong, keeping the buffalo strength and obstinacy for some remote industrial reason of their own. She took out a brainlink, a close-range telepathic hookup which worked only briefly and slightly, to see if the mind still functioned. As she reached for Crawlie's head to attach it, the unconscious girl sprang suddenly to life, jumped to her feet and said:

"No, you don't! you don't peep me, you dirty human!"

"Crawlie, stand still."

"Don't boss me, you monster!"

"Crawlie, that's a bad thing to say." It was eerie to hear such a commanding voice coming from the throat and mouth of a small child. Small she might have been, but Joan commanded the scene.

"I don't care what I say. You all hate me."

"That's not true, Crawlie."

"You're a dog and now you're a person. You're born a traitor. Dogs have always sided with people. You hated me even before you went into that room and changed into something else. Now you are going to kill us all."

"We may die, Crawlie, but I won't do it."

"Well, you hate me, anyhow. You've always hated me."

"You may not believe it," said Joan, "but I've always

loved you. You were the prettiest woman in our whole corridor."

Crawlie laughed. The sound gave Elaine gooseflesh. "Suppose I believed it. How could I live if I thought that people loved me? If I believed you, I would have to tear myself to pieces, to break my brains on the wall, to do—" The laughter changed to sobs, but Crawlie managed to resume talking: "You things are so stupid that you don't even know that you're monsters. You're not people. You never will be people. I'm one of you myself. I'm honest enough to admit what I am. We're dirt, we're nothing, we're things that are less than machines. We hide in the earth like dirt and when people kill us they do not weep. At least we were hiding. Now you come along, you and your tame human woman—" Crawlie glared briefly at Elaine—"and you try to change even that. I'll kill you again if I can, you dirt, you slut, you dog! What are you doing with that child's body? We don't even know who you are now. Can you tell us?"

The bear-man had moved up close to Crawlie, unnoticed by her, and was ready to slap her down again if she moved against little Joan.

Joan looked straight at him and with a mere movement of her eyes she commanded him not to strike.

"I'm tired," she said, "I'm tired, Crawlie. I'm a thousand years old when I am not even five. And I am Elaine now, and I am Hunter too, and I am the Lady Panc Ashash, and I know a great many more things than I thought I would ever know. I have work to do, Crawlie, because I love you, and I think I will die soon. But please, good people, first let me rest."

The bear-man was on Crawlie's right. On her left, there had moved up a snake-woman. The face was pretty and human, except for the thin forked tongue which ran in and out of the mouth like a dying flame. She had good shoulders and hips but no breasts at all. She wore empty golden brassiere cups which swung against her chest. Her hands looked as though they might be stronger than steel. Crawlie started to move toward Joan, and the snake-woman hissed.

It was the snake hiss of Old Earth.

For a second, every animal-person in the corridor

stopped breathing. They all stared at the snake-woman. She hissed again, looking straight at Crawlie. The sound was an abomination in that narrow space. Elaine saw that Joan tightened up like a little dog, Charley-is-my-darling looked as though he was ready to leap twenty meters in one jump, and Elaine herself felt an impulse to strike, to kill, to destroy. Ths hiss was a challenge to them all.

The snake-woman looked around calmly, fully aware of the attention she had obtained.

"Don't worry, dear people. See, I'm using Joan's name for all of us. I'm not going to hurt Crawlie, not unless she hurts Joan. But if she hurts Joan, if anybody hurts Joan, they will have me to deal with. You have a good idea who I am. We S-people have great strength, high intelligence and no fear at all. You know we cannot breed. People have to make us one by one, out of ordinary snakes. Do not cross me, dear people. I want to learn about this new love which Joan is bringing, and nobody is going to hurt Joan while I am here. Do you hear me, people? Nobody. Try it, and you die. I think I could kill almost all of you before I died, even if you all attacked me at once. Do you hear me, people? *Leave Joan alone.* That goes for you, too, you soft human woman. I am not afraid of you either. You there," said she to the bear-man, "pick little Joan up and carry her to a quiet bed. She must rest. She must be quiet for a while. You be quiet too, all you people, or you will meet me. Me." Her black eyes roved across their faces. The snake-woman moved forward and they parted in front of her, as though she were the only solid being in a throng of ghosts.

Her eyes rested a moment on Elaine. Elaine met the gaze, but it was an uncomfortable thing to do. The black eyes with neither eyebrows nor lashes seemed full of intelligence and devoid of emotion. Orson, the bear-man, followed obediently behind. He carried little Joan.

As the child passed Elaine she tried to stay awake. She murmured, "Make me bigger. Please make me bigger. Right away."

"I don't know how . . ." said Elaine.

The child struggled to full awakening. "I'll have work

to do. Work . . . and maybe my death to die. It will all
be wasted if I am this little. Make me bigger."

"But—" protested Elaine again.

"If you don't know, ask the lady."

"What lady?"

The S-woman had paused, listening to the conversation. She cut in.

"The Lady Panc Ashash, of course. The dead one.
Do you think that a living lady of the Instrumentality
would do anything but kill us all?"

As the snake-woman and Orson carried Joan away,
Charley-is-my-darling came up to Elaine and said, "Do
you want to go?"

"Where?"

"To the Lady Panc Ashash, of course."

"Me?" said Elaine. "Now?" said Elaine, even more
emphatically. "Of course not," said Elaine, pronouncing
each word as though it were a law. "What do you think
I am? A few hours ago I did not even know that you existed. I wasn't sure about the word 'death.' I just assumed that everything terminated at four hundred years,
the way it should. It's been hours of danger, and everybody has been threatening everybody else for all that
time. I'm tired and I'm sleepy and I'm dirty, and I've
got to take care of myself, and besides—"

She stopped suddenly and bit her lip. She had started
to say, and besides, my body is all worn out with that
dreamlike love-making which the Hunter and I had together. That was not the business of Charley-is-my-darling: he was goat enough as he was. His mind was goat-
ish and would not see the dignity of it all.

The goat-man said, very gently, "You are making history, Elaine, and when you make history you cannot always take care of all the little things too. Are you hap-
pier and more important than you ever were before?
Yes? Aren't you a different you from the person who
met Balthasar just a few hours ago?"

Elaine was taken aback by the seriousness. She nodded.

"Stay hungry and tired. Stay dirty. Just a little longer.
Time must not be wasted. You can talk to the Lady
Panc Ashash. Find out what we must do about little

Joan. When you come back with further instructions, I will take care of you myself. This tunnel is not as bad a town as it looks. We will have everything you could need, in the Room of Englok. Englok himself built it, long ago. Work just a little longer, and then you can eat and rest. We have everything here. 'I am the citizen of no mean city.' But first you must help Joan. You love Joan, don't you?"

"Oh, yes, I do," she said.

"Then help us just a little bit more."

With death? she thought. With murder? With violation of law? But—but it was all for Joan.

It was thus that Elaine went to the camouflaged door, went out under the open sky again, saw the great saucer of Upper Kalma reaching out over the Old Lower City. She talked to the voice of the Lady Panc Ashash, and obtained certain instructions, together with other messages. Later, she was able to repeat them, but she was too tired to make out their real sense.

She staggered back to the place in the wall where she thought the door to be, leaned against it, and nothing happened.

"Further down, Elaine, further down. Hurry! When I used to be me, I too got tired," came the strong whisper of the Lady Panc Ashash, "but do hurry!"

Elaine stepped away from the wall, looking at it.

A beam of light struck her.

The Instrumentality had found her.

She rushed wildly at the wall.

The door gaped briefly. The strong welcome hand of Charley-is-my-darling helped her in.

"The light! The light!" cried Elaine. "I've killed us all. They saw me."

"Not yet," smiled the goat-man, with his quick crooked intelligent smile. "I may not be educated, but I am pretty smart."

He reached toward the inner gate, glanced back at Elaine appraisingly, and then shoved a man-sized robot through the door.

"There it goes, a sweeper about your size. No memory bank. A worn-out brain. Just simple motivations. If they come down to see what they thought they saw, they will see this instead. We keep a bunch of these at the door. We don't go out much, but when we do, it's handy to have these to cover up with."

He took her by the arm. "While you eat, you can tell me. Can we make her bigger . . . ?"

"Who?"

"Joan, of course. Our Joan. That's what you went to find out for us."

Elaine had to inventory her own mind to see what the Lady Panc Ashash had said on that subject. In a moment she remembered.

"You need a pod. And a jelly bath. And narcotics, because it will hurt. Four hours."

"Wonderful," said Charley-is-my-darling, leading her deeper and deeper into the tunnel.

"But what's the use of it," said Elaine, "if I've ruined us all? The Instrumentality saw me coming in. They will follow. They will kill all of you, even Joan. Where is the Hunter? Shouldn't I sleep first?" She felt her lips go thick with fatigue; she had not rested or eaten since she took that chance on the strange little door between Waterrocky Road and the Shopping Bar.

"You're safe, Elaine, you're safe," said Charley-is-my-darling, his sly smile very warm and his smooth voice carrying the ring of sincere conviction. For himself, he did not believe a word of it. He thought they were all in danger, but there was no point in terrifying Elaine. Elaine was the only real person on their side, except for the Hunter, who was a strange one, almost like an animal himself, and for the Lady Panc Ashash, who was very benign, but who was, after all, a dead person. He was frightened himself, but he was afraid of fear. Perhaps they were all doomed.

In a way, he was right.

7

The Lady Arabella Underwood had called the Lady Goroke.

"Something has tampered with my mind."

The Lady Goroke felt very shocked. She threw back the inquiry. Put a probe on it.

"I did. Nothing."

Nothing?

More shock for the Lady Goroke. Sound the alert, then.

"Oh, no. Oh, no, no. It was a friendly, nice tampering." The Lady Arabella Underwood, being an Old North Australian, was rather formal: she always thought full words at her friends, even in telepathic contact. She never sent mere raw ideas.

But that's utterly unlawful. You're part of the Instrumentality. It's a crime! thought the Lady Goroke.

She got a giggle for reply.

You laugh . . . ? she inquired.

"I just thought a new lord might be here. From the Instrumentality. Having a look at me."

The Lady Goroke was very proper and easily shocked. We wouldn't do that!

The Lady Arabella thought to herself but did not transmit, "Not to you, my dear. You're a blooming prude." To the other she transmitted, "Forget it then."

Puzzled and worried, the Lady Goroke thought: Well, all right. Break?

"Right-ho. Break."

The Lady Goroke frowned to herself. She slapped her wall. Planet Central, she thought at it.

A mere man sat at a desk.

"I am the Lady Goroke," she said.

"Of course, my Lady," he replied.

"Police fever, one degree. One degree only. Till rescinded. Clear?"

"Clear, my lady. The entire planet?"

"Yes," she said.

"Do you wish to give a reason?" his voice was respectful and routine.

"Must I?"

"Of course not, my Lady."

"None given, then. Close."

He saluted and his image faded from the wall.

She raised her mind to the level of a light clear call. Instrumentality Only—Instrumentality Only. I have raised the police fever level one degree by command. Reason, personal disquiet. You know my voice. You know me. Goroke.

Far across the city—a police ornithopter flapped slowly down the street.

The police robot was photographing a sweeper, the most elaborately malfunctioning sweeper he had ever seen.

The sweeper raced down the road at unlawful speeds, approaching three hundred kilometers an hour, stopped with a sizzle of plastic on stone, and began picking dust-motes off the pavement.

When the ornithopter reached it, the sweeper took off again, rounded two or three corners at tremendous speed and then settled down to its idiot job.

The third time this happened, the robot in the ornithopter put a disabling slug through it, flew down and picked it up with the claws of his machine.

He saw it in close view.

"Birdbrain. Old model. Birdbrain. Good they don't use those any more. The thing could have hurt A Man. Now, I'm printed from a mouse, a real mouse with lots and lots of brains."

He flew toward the central junkyard with the worn-out sweeper. The sweeper, crippled but still conscious, was trying to pick dust off the iron claws which held it.

Below them, the Old City twisted out of sight with its odd geometrical lights. The New City, bathed in its soft perpetual glow, shone out against the night of Fomalhaut III. Beyond them, the everlasting ocean boiled in its private storms.

On the actual stage the actors cannot do much with the scene of the interlude, where Joan was cooked in a single night from the size of a child five years old to the tallness of a miss fifteen or sixteen. The biological machine did work well, though at the risk of her life. It made her into a vital, robust young person, without changing her mind at all. This is hard for any actress to portray. The storyboxes have the advantage. They can show the machine with all sorts of improvements—flashing lights, bits of lightning, mysterious rays. Actually, it looked like a bathtub full of boiling brown jelly, completely covering Joan.

Elaine, meanwhile, ate hungrily in the palatial room of Englok himself. The food was very, very old, and she had doubts, as a witch, about its nutritional value, but it stilled her hunger. The denizens of Clown Town had declared this room "off limits" to themselves, for reasons which Charley-is-my-darling could not make plain. He stood in the doorway and told her what to do to find food, to activate the bed out of the floor, to open the bathroom. Everything was very old-fashioned and nothing responded to a simple thought or to a mere slap.

A curious thing happened.

Elaine had washed her hands, had eaten and was preparing for her bath. She had taken most of her clothes off, thinking only that Charley-is-my-darling was an animal, not a man, so that it did not matter.

Suddenly she knew it did matter.

He might be an underperson but he was a man to her. Blushing deeply all the way down to her neck, she ran into the bathroom and called back to him:

"Go away. I will bathe and then sleep. Wake me when you have to, not before."

"Yes, Elaine."

"And—and—"

"Yes?"

"Thank you," she said. "Thank you very much. Do you know, I never said 'thank you' to an underperson before."

"That's all right," said Charley-is-my-darling with a smile. "Most real people don't. Sleep well, my dear Elaine. When you awaken, be ready for great things. We shall take a star out of the skies and shall set thousands of worlds on fire . . ."

"What's that?" she said, putting her head around the corner of the bathroom.

"Just a figure of speech," he smiled. "Just meaning that you won't have much time. Rest well. Don't forget to put your clothes in the ladysmaid machine. The ones in Clown Town are all worn out. But since we haven't used this room, yours ought to work."

"Which is it?" she said.

"The red lid with the gold handle. Just lift it." On that domestic note he left her to rest, while he went off and plotted the destiny of a hundred billion lives.

They told her it was mid-morning when she came out of the room of Englok. How could she have known it? The brown-and-yellow corridor, with its gloomy old yellow lights, was just as dim and stench-ridden as ever. The people all seemed to have changed.

Baby-baby was no longer a mouse-hag, but a woman of considerable force and much tenderness. Crawlie was as dangerous as a human enemy, staring at Elaine, her beautiful face gone bland with hidden hate. Charley-is-my-darling was gay, friendly and persuasive. She thought she could read expressions on the faces of Orson and the S-woman, odd though their features were.

After she had gotten through some singularly polite greetings, she demanded, "What's happening now?"

A new voice spoke up—a voice she knew and did not know.

Elaine glanced over at a niche in the wall.

The Lady Panc Ashash! And who was that with her?

Even as she asked herself the question, Elaine knew the answer. It was Joan, grown, only half a head less tall than the Lady Panc Ashash or herself. It was a new Joan, powerful, happy, and quiet; but it was all the dear little old D'joan too.

"Welcome," said the Lady Panc Ashash, "to our revolution."

"What's a revolution?" asked Elaine. "And I thought you couldn't come in here with all the thought shielding?"

The Lady Panc Ashash lifted a wire which trailed back from her robot body, "I rigged this up so that I could use the body. Precautions are no use any more. It's the other side which will need the precautions now. A revolution is a way of changing systems and people. This is one. You go first, Elaine. This way."

"To die? Is that what you mean?"

The Lady Panc Ashash laughed warmly. "You know me by now. You know my friends here. You know what your own life has been down to now, a useless witch in a world which did not want you. We may die, but it's what we do before we die that counts. This is Joan going to meet her destiny. You lead as far as the Upper City. Then Joan will lead. And then we shall see."

"You mean, all these people are going too?" Elaine looked at the ranks of the underpeople, who were beginning to form into two queues down the corridor. The queues bulged wherever mothers led their children by the hand or carried small ones in their arms. Here and there the line was punctuated by a giant underperson.

They have been nothing, thought Elaine, and I was nothing too. Now we are all going to do something, even though we may be terminated for it. "May be" thought she: "shall be" is the word. But it is worth it if Joan can change the worlds, even a little bit, even for other people.

Joan spoke up. Her voice had grown with her body, but it was the same dear voice which the little dog-girl had had sixteen hours (they seem sixteen years, thought Elaine) ago, when Elaine first met her at the door to the tunnel of Englok.

Joan said, "Love is not something special, reserved for men alone.

"Love is not proud. Love has no real name. Love is for life itself, and we have life.

"We cannot win by fighting. People outnumber us, outgun us, outrun us, outfight us. But people did not create us. Whatever made people, made us too. You all know that, but will we say the name?"

There was a murmur of *no* and *never* from the crowd.

"You have waited for me. I have waited too. It is time to die, perhaps, but we will die the way people did in the beginning, before things became easy and cruel for them. They live in a stupor and they die in a dream. It is not a good dream and if they awaken, they will know that we are people too. Are you with me?" They murmured yes. "Do you love me?" Again they murmured agreement. "Shall we go out and meet the day?" They shouted their acclaim.

Joan turned to the Lady Panc Ashash. "Is everything as you wished and ordered?"

"Yes," said the dear dead woman in the robot body. "Joan first, to lead you. Elaine preceding her, to drive away robots or ordinary underpeople. When you meet real people, you will love them. That is all. You will love them. If they kill you, you will love them. Joan will show you how. Pay no further attention to me. Ready?"

Joan lifted her right hand and said words to herself. The people bowed their heads before her, faces and muzzles and snouts of all sizes and colors. A baby of some kind mewed in a tiny falsetto to the rear.

Just before she turned to lead the procession, Joan turned back to the people and said, "Crawlie, where are you?"

"Here, in the middle," said a clear, calm voice far back.

"Do you love me now, Crawlie?"

"No, D'joan. I like you less than when you were a little dog. But these are my people too, as well as yours. I am brave. I can walk. I won't make trouble."

"Crawlie," said Joan, "will you love people if we meet them?"

All faces turned toward the beautiful bison-girl. Elaine could just see her, way down the murky corridor. Elaine could see that the girl's face had turned utter, dead white with emotion. Whether rage or fear, she could not tell.

At last Crawlie spoke, "No, I won't love people. And I won't love you. I have my pride."

Softly, softly, like death itself at a quiet bedside, Joan spoke. "You *can* stay behind, Crawlie. You can stay here. It isn't much of a chance, but it's a chance."

Crawlie looked at her, "Bad luck to you, dog-woman, and bad luck to the rotten human being up there beside you."

Elaine stood on tiptoe to see what would happen. Crawlie's face suddenly disappeared, dropping downward.

The snake woman elbowed her way to the front, stood close to Joan where the others could see her, and sang out in a voice as clear as metal itself:

"Sing 'poor, poor, Crawlie,' dear people. Sing 'I love Crawlie,' dear people. She is dead. I just killed her so that we would all be full of love. I love you too," said the S-woman, on whose reptilian features no sign of love or hate could be seen.

Joan spoke up, apparently prompted by the Lady Panc Ashash. "We do love Crawlie, dear people. Think of her and then let us move forward."

Charley-is-my-darling gave Elaine a little shove. "Here, you lead."

In a dream, in a bewilderment, Elaine led.

She felt warm, happy, brave when she passed close to the strange Joan, so tall and yet so familiar. Joan gave her a full smile and whispered, "Tell me I'm doing well, human woman. I'm a dog and dogs have lived a million years for the praise of man."

"You're right, Joan, you're completely right! I'm with you. Shall I go now?" responded Elaine.

Joan nodded, her eyes brimming with tears.

Elaine led.

Joan and the Lady Panc Ashash followed, dog and dead woman championing the procession.

The rest of the underpeople followed them in turn, in a double line.

When they made the secret door open, daylight flooded the corridor. Elaine could almost feel the stale odor-ridden air pouring out with them. When she glanced back into the tunnel for the last time, she saw the body of Crawlie lying all alone on the floor.

Elaine herself turned to the steps and began going up them.

No one had yet noticed the procession.

Elaine could hear the wire of the Lady Panc Ashash dragging on the stone and metal of the steps as they climbed.

When she reached the top door, Elaine had a moment of indecision and panic. "This is my life, my life," she thought. "I have no other. What have I done? Oh, Hunter, Hunter, where are you? Have you betrayed me?"

Said Joan softly behind her, "Go on! Go on! This is a war of love. Keep going."

Elaine opened the door to the upper street. The roadway was full of people. Three police ornithopters flapped slowly overhead. This was an unusual number. Elaine stopped again.

"Keep walking," said Joan, "and warn the robots off."

Elaine advanced and the revolution began.

8

The revolution lasted six minutes and covered one hundred and twelve meters.

The police flew over as soon as the underpeople began pouring out of the doorway.

The first one glided in like a big bird, his voice asking, "Identify! Who are you?"

Elaine said, "Go away. That is a command."

"Identify yourself," said the bird-like machine, banking steeply with the lens-eyed robot peering at Elaine out of its middle.

"Go away," said Elaine. "I am a true human and I command."

The first police ornithopter apparently called to the others by radio. Together they flapped their way down the corridor between the big buildings.

A lot of people had stopped. Most of their faces were blank, a few showing animation or amusement or horror at the sight of so many underpeople all crowded in one place.

Joan's voice sang out, in the clearest possible enunciation of the Old Common Tongue:

"Dear people, we are people. We love you. We love you."

The underpeople began to chant *love, love, love* in a weird plainsong full of sharps and halftones. The true humans shrank back. Joan herself set the example by embracing a young woman of about her own height. Charley-is-my-darling took a human man by the shoulders and shouted at him:

"I love you, my dear fellow! Believe me, I do love you. It's wonderful meeting you." The human man was startled by the contact and even more startled by the glowing warmth of the goat-man's voice. He stood mouth slack and body relaxed with sheer, utter and accepted surprise.

Somewhere to the rear a person screamed.

A police ornithopter came flapping back. Elaine could not tell if it was one of the three she had sent away, or a new one altogether. She waited for it to get close enough to hail, so that she could tell it to go away. For the first time, she wondered about the actual physical character of danger. Could the police machine put a slug through her? Or shoot flame at her? Or lift her screaming, carrying her away with its iron claws to some place where she would be pretty and clean and never herself again? "Oh, Hunter, Hunter, where are you now? Have you forgotten me? Have you betrayed me?"

The underpeople were still surging forward and mingling with the real people, clutching them by their hands or their garments and repeating in the queer medley of voices:

"I love you. Oh, please, I love you! We are people. We are your sisters and brothers . . ."

The snake-woman wasn't making much progress. She had seized a human man with her more-than-iron hand. Elaine hadn't seen her saying anything, but the man had fainted dead away. The snake-woman had him draped over her arm like an empty overcoat and was looking for somebody else to love.

Behind Elaine a low voice said, "He's coming soon."

"Who?" said Elaine to the Lady Panc Ashash, knowing perfectly well whom she meant, but not wanting to admit it, and busy with watching the circling ornithopter at the same time.

"The Hunter, of course," said the robot with the dear dead lady's voice. "He'll come for you. You'll be all right. I'm at the end of my wire. Look away, my dear. They are about to kill me again and I am afraid that the sight would distress you."

Fourteen robots, foot models, marched with military decision into the crowd. The true humans took heart from this and some of them began to slip away into doorways. Most of the real people were still so surprised that they stood around with the underpeople pawing at them, babbling the accents of love over and over again, the animal origin of their voices showing plainly.

The robot sergeant took no note of this. He approached the Lady Panc Ashash only to find Elaine standing in his way.

"I command you," she said, with all the passion of a working witch, "I *command* you to leave this place."

His eye-lenses were like dark-blue marbles floating in milk. They seemed swimmy and poorly focused as he looked her over. He did not reply but stepped around her, faster than her own body could intercept him. He made for the dear, dead Lady Panc Ashash.

Elaine, bewildered, realized that the Lady's robot body seemed more human than ever. The robot-sergeant confronted her.

This is the scene which we all remember, the first authentic picture tape of the entire incident:

The gold and black sergeant, his milky eyes staring at the Lady Panc Ashash.

The Lady herself, in the pleasant old robot body, lifting a commanding hand.

Elaine, distraught, half-turning as though she would grab the robot by his right arm. Her head is moving so rapidly that her black hair swings as she turns.

Charley-is-my-darling shouting, "I love, love, love!" at a small handsome man with mouse-colored hair. The man is gulping and saying nothing.

All this we know.

Then comes the unbelievable, which we now believe, the event for which the stars and worlds were unprepared.

Mutiny.

Robot mutiny.

Disobedience in open daylight.

The words are hard to hear on the tape, but we can still make them out. The recording device on the police ornithopter had gotten a square fix on the face of the Lady Panc Ashash. Lip-readers can see the words plainly; non-lip-readers can hear the words the third or fourth time the tape is run through the eyebox.

Said the Lady, "Overridden."

Said the sergeant, "No, you're a robot."

"See for yourself. Read my brain. I am a robot. I am also a woman. You cannot disobey people. I am people. I love you. Furthermore, you are people. You think. We love each other. Try. Try to attack."

"I—I cannot," said the robot sergeant, his milky eyes seeming to spin with excitement. "You love me? You mean I'm *alive? I exist?*"

"With love, you do," said the Lady Panc Ashash. "Look at her," said the Lady, pointing to Joan, "because she has brought you love."

The robot looked and disobeyed the law. His squad looked with him.

He turned back to the Lady and bowed to her: "Then you know what we must do, if we cannot obey you and cannot disobey the others."

"Do it," she said sadly, "but know what you are doing. You are not really escaping two human commands. You are making a choice. You. That makes you men."

The sergeant turned to his squad of man-sized robots: "You hear that? She says we are *men*. I believe her. Do you believe her?"

"We do," they cried almost unanimously.

This is where the picture-tape ends, but we can imagine how the scene was concluded. Elaine had stopped short, just behind the sergeant-robot. The other robots had come up behind her. Charley-is-my-darling had stopped talking. Joan was in the act of lifting her hands in blessing, her warm brown dog eyes gone wide with pity and understanding.

People wrote down the things that we cannot see.

Apparently the robot-sergeant said, "Our love, dear people, and good-by. We disobey and die." He waved his hand to Joan. It is not certain whether he did or did not say, "Good-by, our lady and our liberator." Maybe some poet made up the second saying; the first one, we are sure about. And we are sure about the next word, the one which historians and poets all agree on. He turned to his men and said,

"Destruct."

Fourteen robots, the black-and-gold sergeant and his

thirteen silver-blue foot soldiers, suddenly spurted white
fire in the street of Kalma. They detonated their suicide
buttons, thermite caps in their own heads. They had
done something with no human command at all, on an
order from another robot, the body of the Lady Panc
Ashash, and she in turn had no human authority, but
merely the word of the little dog-girl Joan, who had
been made an adult in a single night.

Fourteen white flames made people and underpeople
turn their eyes aside. Into the light there dropped a special police ornithopter. Out of it came the two ladies,
Arabella Underwood and Goroke. They lifted their fore-
arms to shield their eyes from the blazing dying robots. They did not see the Hunter, who had moved mys-
teriously into an open window above the street and
who watched the scene by putting his hands over his
eyes and peeking through the slits between his fingers.
While the people still stood blinded, they felt the fierce
telepathic shock of the mind of the Lady Goroke taking
command of the situation. That was her right, as a chief
of the Instrumentality. Some of the people, but not all of
them, felt the outré countershock of Joan's mind reaching out to meet the Lady Goroke.

"I command," thought the Lady Goroke, her mind
kept open to all beings.

"Indeed you do, but I love, I love you," thought
Joan.

The first-order forces met.

They engaged.

The revolution was over. Nothing had really happened, but Joan had forced people to meet her. This
was nothing like the poem about people and underpeople getting all mixed up. The mixup came much later,
even after the time of C'mell. The poem is pretty, but it
is dead wrong, as you can see for yourself:

> *You should ask me,*
>   *Me, me, me*
> *Because I know—*
> *I used to live*
>   *On the Eastern Shore.*

Men aren't men,
And women aren't women,
And people aren't people any more.

There is no Eastern Shore on Fomalhaut III anyhow;
the people/underpeople crisis came much later than
this. The revolution had failed, but history had reached
its new turning-point, the quarrel of the two ladies. They
left their minds open out of sheer surprise. Suicidal robots and world-loving dogs were unheard-of. It was bad
enough to have illegal underpeople on the prowl, but
these new things—ah!

Destroy them all, said the Lady Goroke.

"Why?" thought the Lady Arabella Underwood.

Malfunction, replied Goroke.

"But they're not machines!"

Then they're animals—underpeople. Destroy! Destroy!

Then came the answer which has created our own
time. It came from the Lady Arabella Underwood, and
all Kalma heard it:

Perhaps they are people. They must have a trial.

The dog-girl Joan dropped to her knees. "I have succeeded. I have succeeded, I have succeeded! You can
kill me, dear people, but I love, love, you!"

The Lady Panc Ashash said quietly to Elaine, "I
thought I would be dead by now. Really dead, at last.
But I am not. I have seen the worlds turn, Elaine, and
you have seen them turn with me."

The underpeople had fallen quiet as they heard the
high-volume telepathic exchange between the two great
Ladies.

The real soldiers dropped out of the sky, their ornithopters whistling as they hawked down to the ground.
They ran up to the underpeople and began binding them
with cord.

One soldier took a single look at the robot body of
the Lady Panc Ashash. He touched it with his staff, and
the staff turned cherry-red with heat. The robot-body,
its heat suddenly drained, fell to the ground in a heap of
icy crystals.

Elaine walked between the frigid rubbish and the red-hot staff. She had seen Hunter.

She missed seeing the soldier who came up to Joan, started to bind her and then fell back weeping, babbling, "She loves me! She loves me!"

The Lord Femtiosex, who commanded the inflying soldiers, bound Joan with cord despite her talking.

Grimly he answered her: "Of course you love me. You're a good dog. You'll die soon, doggy, but till then, you'll obey."

"I'm obeying," said Joan, "but I'm a dog *and* a person. Open your mind, man, and you'll feel it."

Apparently he did open his mind and felt the ocean of love riptiding into him. It shocked him. His arm swung up and back, the edge of the hand striking at Joan's neck for the ancient kill.

"No, you don't," thought the Lady Arabella Underwood. "That child is going to get a proper trial."

He looked at her and glared, chief doesn't strike chief, my Lady. Let go my arm.

Thought the Lady Arabella at him, openly and in public: "A trial, then."

In his anger he nodded at her. He would not think or speak to her in the presence of all the other people.

A soldier brought Elaine and Hunter before him.

"Sir and master, these are people, not underpeople. But they have dog-thoughts, cat-thoughts, goat-thoughts and robot-ideas in their heads. Do you wish to look?"

"Why look?" said the Lord Femtiosex, who was as blond as the ancient pictures of Baldur, and oftentimes that arrogant as well. "The Lord Limaono is arriving. That's all of us. We can have the trial here and now."

Elaine felt cords bite into her wrists; she heard the Hunter murmur comforting words to her, words which she did not quite understand.

"They will not kill us," he murmured, "though we will wish they had, before this day is out. Everything is happening as she said it would, and—"

"Who is that she?" interrupted Elaine.

"She? The lady, of course. The dear dead Lady Panc Ashash, who has worked wonders after her own death, merely with the print of her personality on the machine.

Who do you think told me what to do? Why did we wait for you to condition Joan to greatness? Why did the people way down in Clown Town keep on raising one D'joan after another, hoping that hope and a great wonder would occur?"

"You knew?" said Elaine. "You knew . . . before it happened?"

"Of course," said the Hunter, "not exactly, but more or less. She had had hundreds of years after death inside that computer. She had time for billions of thoughts. She saw how it would be if it had to be, and I—"

"Shut up, you people!" roared the Lord Femtiosex. "You are making the animals restless with your babble. Shut up, or I will stun you!"

Elaine fell silent.

The Lord Femtiosex glanced around at her, ashamed at having made his anger naked before another person. He added quietly:

"The trial is about to begin. The one that the tall lady ordered."

9

You all know about the trial, so there is no need to linger over it. There is another picture of San Shigonanda, the one from his conventional period, which shows it very plainly.

The street had filled full of real people, crowding together to see something which would ease the boredom of perfection and time. They all had numbers or number-codes instead of names. They were handsome, well, dully happy. They even looked a great deal alike, similar in their handsomeness, their health and their underlying boredom. Each of them had a total of four hundred years to live. None of them knew real war, even though the extreme readiness of the soldiers showed vain practice of hundreds of years. The people were beautiful, but they felt themselves useless, and they were quietly desperate without knowing it themselves. This is all clear from the painting, and from the wonderful way that San Shigonanda has of forming them in informal ranks and letting the calm blue light of day shine down on their handsome, hopeless features.

With the underpeople, the artist performs real wonders.

Joan herself is bathed in light. Her light brown hair and her doggy brown eyes express softness and tenderness. He even conveys the idea that her new body is terribly new and strong, that she is virginal and ready to die, that she is a mere girl and yet completely fearless. The posture of love shows in her legs: she stands lightly. Love shows in her hands: they are turned outward toward the judges. Love shows in her smile: it is confident.

And the judges!

The artist has them, too. The Lord Femtiosex, calm again, his narrow sharp lips expressing perpetual rage against a universe which has grown too small for him. The Lord Limaono, wise, twice-reborn, sluggardly, but alert as a snake behind the sleepy eyes and the slow smile. The Lady Arabella Underwood, the tallest true-human present, with her Norstrilian pride and the arrogance of great wealth, along with the capricious tenderness of great wealth, showing in the way that she sat, judging her fellow-judges instead of the prisoners. The Lady Goroke, bewildered at last, frowning at a play of fortune which she does not understand. The artist has it all.

And you have the real view-tapes, too, if you want to go to a museum. The reality is not as dramatic as the famous painting, but it has value of its own. The voice of Joan, dead these many centuries, is still strangely moving. It is the voice of a dog-carved-into-man, but it is also the voice of a great lady. The image of the Lady Panc Ashash must have taught her that, along with what she had learned from Elaine and Hunter in the antechamber above the Brown and Yellow Corridor of Englok.

The words of the trial, they too have survived. Many of them have became famous, all across the worlds.

Joan said, during inquiry, "But it is the duty of life to find more than life, and to exchange itself for that higher goodness."

Joan commented, upon sentence. "My body is your property, but my love is not. My love is my own, and I shall love you fiercely while you kill me."

When the soldiers had killed Charley-is-my-darling and were trying to hack off the head of the S-woman until one of them thought to freeze her into crystals, Joan said:

"Should we be strange to you, we animals of earth that you have brought to the stars? We shared the same sun, the same oceans, the same sky. We are all from Manhome. How do you know that we would not have caught up with you if we had all stayed at home together? My people were dogs. They loved you before you made a woman-shaped thing out of my mother. Should I not love you still? The miracle is not that you have made people out of us. The miracle is that it took us so long to understand it. We are people now, and so are you. You will be sorry for what you are going to do to me, but remember that I shall love your sorrow, too, because great and good things will come out of it."

The Lord Limaono slyly asked, "What is a 'miracle'?"

And her words were, "There is knowledge from Earth which you have not yet found again. There is the name of the nameless one. There are secrets hidden in time from you. Only the dead and the unborn can know them right now: I am both."

The scene is familiar, and yet we will never understand it.

We know what the Lords Femtiosex and Limaono thought they were doing. They were maintaining established order and they were putting it on tape. The minds of men can live together only if the basic ideas are communicated. Nobody has, even now, found out a way of recording telepathy directly into an instrument. We get pieces and snatches and wild jumbles, but we never get a satisfactory record of what one of the great ones was transmitting to another. The two male chiefs were trying to put on record all those things about the episode which would teach careless people not to play with the lives of the underpeople. They were even trying to make underpeople understand the rules and designs by virtue of which they had been transformed from animals into the highest servants of man. This would have been hard to do, given the bewildering events of the last few hours, even from one chief of the Instrumentality to another; for the general public, it was almost impossible. The outpouring from the Brown and Yellow Corridor was wholly unexpected, even though the Lady Goroke had surprised D'joan; the mutiny of the robot police posed problems which would have to be discussed halfway across the galaxy. Furthermore, the dog-girl was making points which had some verbal validity. If they were left in the form of mere words without proper context, they might affect heedless or impressionable minds. A bad idea can spread like a mutated germ. If it is at all interesting, it can leap from one mind to another halfway across the universe before it has a stop put to it. Look at the ruinous fads and foolish fashions which have nuisanced mankind even in the ages of the highest orderliness. We today know that variety, flexibility, danger and the seasoning of a little hate can make love and life bloom as they never bloomed before; we know it is better to live with the complications of thirteen thousand old languages resurrected from the dead ancient past than it is to live with the cold blind-alley perfection of the Old Common Tongue. We know a lot of things which the Lords Femtiosex and Limaono did not, and before we consider them stupid or cruel, we must remember that centuries passed before mankind finally came to grips with the problem of the underpeople and decided what "life" was within the limits of the human community.

Finally, we have the testimony of the two lords themselves. They both lived to very advanced ages, and toward the end of their lives they were worried and annoyed to find that the episode of D'joan overshadowed all the bad things which had not happened during their long careers—bad things which they had labored to forestall for the protection of the planet Fomalhaut III —and they were distressed to see themselves portrayed as casual, cruel men when in fact they were nothing of the sort. If they had seen that the story of Joan on Fomalhaut III would get to be what it is today—one of the great romances of mankind, along with the story of C'mell or the romance of the lady who sailed *The Soul* —they would not only have been disappointed, but they would have been justifiably angry at the fickleness of mankind as well. Their roles are clear, because they made them clear. The Lord Femtiosex accepts the responsibility for the notion of fire; the Lord Limaono agrees that he concurred in the decision. Both of them, many years later, reviewed the tapes of the scene and agreed that something which the Lady Arabella Underwood had said or thought—

Something had made them do it.

But even with the tapes to refresh and clarify their memories, they could not say what.

We have even put computers on the job of cataloguing every word and every inflection of the whole trial, but they have not pinpointed the critical point either.

And the Lady Arabella—nobody ever questioned her. They didn't dare. She went back to her own planet of Old North Australia, surrounded by the immense treasure of the santaclara drug, and no planet is going to pay at the rate of two thousand million credits a day for the privilege of sending an investigator to talk to a lot of obstinate, simple, wealthy Norstrilian peasants who will not talk to offworlders anyhow. The Norstrilians charge that sum for the admission of any guest not selected by their own invitation; so we will never know what the Lady Arabella Underwood said or did after she went home. The Norstrilians said they did not wish to discuss the matter, and if we do not wish to go back to living a mere seventy years we had better not anger the only planet which produces stroon.

And the Lady Goroke—she, poor thing, went mad.

Mad, for a period of years.

People did not know it till later, but there was no word to be gotten out of her. She performed the odd actions which we now know to be a part of the dynasty of Lords Jestocost, who forced themselves by diligence and merit upon the Instrumentality for two hundred and more years. But on the case of Joan she had nothing to say.

The trial is therefore a scene about which we know everything—and nothing.

We think that we know the physical facts of the life of D'joan who became Joan. We know about the Lady Panc Ashash who whispered endlessly to the underpeople about a justice yet to come. We know the whole life of the unfortunate Elaine and of her involvement with the case. We know that there were in those centuries, when underpeople first developed, many warrens in which illegal underpeople used their near-human wits, their animal cunning and their gift of speech to survive even when mankind had declared them surplus. The Brown and Yellow Corridor was not by any means the only one of its kind. We even know what happened to the Hunter.

For the other underpeople—Charley-is-my-darling, Baby-baby, Mabel, the S-woman, Orson and all the others—we have the tapes of the trial itself. They were not tried by anybody. They were put to death by the soldiers on the spot, as soon as it was plain that their testimony would not be needed. As witnesses, they could live a few minutes or an hour; as animals, they were already outside the regulations.

Ah, we know all about that now, and yet know nothing. Dying is simple, though we tend to hide it away. The *how* of dying is a minor scientific matter; the *when* of dying is a problem to each of us, whether he lives on the old-fashioned 400-year-life planets or on the radical new ones where the freedoms of disease and accident have been reintroduced; the *why* of it is still as shocking to us as it was to pre-atomic man, who used to cover farmland with the boxed bodies of his dead. These underpeople died as no animals had ever died before. Joyfully.

One mother held her children up for the soldier to kill them all.

She must have been of rat origin, because she had septuplets in closely matching form.

The tape shows us the picture of the soldier getting ready.

The rat-woman greets him with a smile and holds up her seven babies. Little blondes they are, wearing pink or blue bonnets, all of them with glowing cheeks and bright little eyes.

"Put them on the ground," said the soldier. "I'm going to kill you and them too." On the tape, we can hear the nervous peremptory edge of his voice. He added one word, as though he had already begun to think that he had to justify himself to these underpeople. "Orders," he added.

"It doesn't matter if I hold them, soldier. I'm their mother. They'll feel better if they die easily with their mother near. I love you, soldier. I love all people. You are my brother, even though my blood is rat blood and yours is human. Go ahead and kill them, soldier. I can't even hurt you. Can't you understand it? *I love you, soldier*. We share a common speech, common hopes, common fears, and a common death. That is what Joan has taught us all. Death is not bad, soldier. It just comes badly, sometimes, but you will remember me after you have killed me and my babies. You will remember that I love you now—"

The soldier, we see on the tape, can stand it no longer. He clubs his weapon, knocks the woman down; the babies scatter on the ground. We see his booted heel rise up and crush down against their heads. We hear the wet popping sound of the little heads breaking, the sharp cut-off of the baby wails as they die. We get one last view of the rat-woman herself. She has stood up again by the time the seventh baby is killed. She offers her hand to the soldier to shake. Her face is dirty and bruised, a trickle of blood running down her left cheek. Even now, we know she is a rat, an underperson, a modified animal, a nothing. And yet we, even we across the centuries, feel that she has somehow become more of a person than we are—that she dies human and fulfilled. We know that she has triumphed over death: we have not.

We see the soldier looking straight at her with eerie horror, as though her simple love were some unfathomable device from an alien source.

We hear her next words on the tape:

"Soldier, I love all of you—"

His weapon could have killed her in a fraction of a

second, if he had used it properly. But he didn't. He clubbed it and hit her, as though his heat-remover had been a wooden club and himself a wild man instead of part of the elite guard of Kalma.

We know what happens then.

She falls under his blows. She points. Points straight at Joan, wrapped in fire and smoke.

The rat-woman screams one last time, screams into the lens of the robot camera as though she were talking not to the soldier but to all mankind:

"You can't kill *her*. You can't kill love. I love you, soldier, love you. You can't kill *that*. Remember—"

His last blow catches her in the face.

She falls back on the pavement. He thrusts his foot, as we can see by the tape, directly on her throat. He leaps forward in an odd little jig, bringing his full weight down on her fragile neck. He swings while stamping downward, and we then see his face, full on in the camera.

It is the face of a weeping child, bewildered by hurt and shocked by the prospect of more hurt to come.

He had started to do his duty, and duty had gone wrong, all wrong.

Poor man. He must have been one of the first men in the new world who tried to use weapons against love. Love is a sour and powerful ingredient to meet in the excitement of battle.

All the underpeople died that way. Most of them died smiling, saying the word "love" or the name "Joan."

The bear-man Orson had been kept to the very end.

He died very oddly. He died laughing.

The soldier lifted his pellet-thrower and aimed it straight at Orson's forehead. The pellets were 22 millimeters in diameter and had a muzzle velocity of only 125 meters per second. In that manner, they could stop recalcitrant robots or evil underpeople, without any risk of penetrating buildings and hurting the true people who might be inside, out of sight.

Orson looks, on the tape the robots made, as though he knows perfectly well what the weapon is. (He probably did. Underpeople used to live with the danger of a violent death hanging over them from birth until removal.) He shows no fear of it, in the pictures we have; he begins to laugh. His laughter is warm, generous, relaxed —like the friendly laughter of a happy foster-father who has found a guilty and embarrassed child, knowing full well that the child expects punishment but will not get it.

"Shoot, man. You can't kill me, man. I'm in your mind. I love you. Joan taught us. Listen, man. There is no death. Not for love. Ho, ho, ho, poor fellow, don't be afraid of me. Shoot! You're the unlucky one. You're going to live. And remember. And remember. And remember. I've made you human, fellow."

The soldier croaks, "What did you say?"

"I'm saving you, man. I'm turning you into a real human being. With the power of Joan. The power of love. Poor guy! Go ahead and shoot me if it makes you uncomfortable to wait. You'll do it anyhow."

This time we do not see the soldier's face but the tightness of his back and neck betray his own internal stress.

We see the big broad bear face blossom forth in an immense splash of red as the soft heavy pellets plow into it.

Then the camera turns to something else.

A little boy, probably a fox, but very finished in his human shape.

He was bigger than a baby, but not big enough, like the larger underchildren, to have understood the deathless importance of Joan's teaching.

He was the only one of the group who behaved like an ordinary underperson. He broke and ran.

He was clever: He ran among the spectators, so that the soldier could not use pellets or heat-reducers on him without hurting an actual human being. He ran and jumped and dodged, fighting passively but desperately for his life.

At last one of the spectators—a tall man with a silver hat—tripped him up. The fox-boy fell to the pavement, skinning his palms and knees. Just as he looked up to see who might be coming at him, a bullet caught him neatly in the head. He fell a little way forward, dead.

People die. We know how they die. We have seen them die shy and quiet in the Dying Houses. We have seen others go into the 400-year-rooms, which have no door knobs and no cameras on the inside. We have seen pictures of many dying in natural disasters, where the robot crews took picture-tapes for the record and the investigation later on. Death is not uncommon, and it is very unpleasant.

But this time, death itself was different. All the fear of death—except for the one little fox-boy, too young to understand and too old to wait for death in his mother's arms—had gone out of the underpeople. They met death willingly, with love and calmness in their bodies, their voices, their demeanor. It did not matter whether they lived long enough to know what happened to Joan herself: they had perfect confidence in her, anyway.

This indeed was the new weapon, love and the good death.

Crawlie, with her pride, had missed it all.

The investigators later found the body of Crawlie in the corridor. It was possible to reconstruct who she had been and what had happened to her. The computer in which the bodiless image of the Lady Panc Ashash survived for a few days after the trial was, of course, found and disassembled. Nobody thought at the time to get her opinions and last words. A lot of historians have gnashed their teeth over that.

The details are therefore clear. The archives even preserve the long interrogation and responses concerning Elaine, when she was processed and made clear after the trial. But we do not know how the idea of "fire" came in.

Somewhere, beyond sight of the tape-scanner, the word must have been passed between the four chiefs of the Instrumentality who were conducting the trial. There is the protest of the chief of birds (robot), or police chief of Kalma, a subchief named Fisi.

The records show his appearance. He comes in at the right side of the scene, bows respectfully to the four Chiefs and lifts his right hand in the traditional sign for "beg to interrupt," an odd twist of the elevated hand which the actors had found it very difficult to copy when they tried to put the whole story of Joan and Elaine into a single drama. (In fact, he had no more idea that future ages would be studying his casual appearance than did the others. The whole episode was characterized by haste and precipitateness, in the light of what we now know.) The Lord Limaono says:

"Interruption refused. We are making a decision."

The chief of birds spoke up anyhow.

"My words are for your decision, my Lords and my Ladies."

"Say it, then," commanded the Lady Goroke, "but be brief."

"Shut down the viewers. Destroy that animal. Brainwash the spectators. Get amnesia yourselves, for this one hour. This whole scene is dangerous. I am nothing but a supervisor of ornithopters, keeping perfect order, but I—"

"We have heard enough," said the Lord Femtiosex. "You manage your birds and we'll run the worlds. How do you dare to think 'like a chief'? We have responsibilities which you can't even guess at. Stand back."

Fisi, in the pictures, stands back, his face sullen. In that particular frame of scenes, one can see some of the spectators going away. It was time for lunch and they had become hungry; they had no idea that they were going to miss the greatest atrocity in history, about which a thousand and more grand operas would be written.

Femtiosex then moved to the climax. "More knowledge, not less, is the answer to this problem. I have heard about something which is not as bad as the Planet Shayol, but which can do just as well for an exhibit on a civilized world. You there," said he to Fisi, the Chief of Birds, "bring oil and a spray. Immediately."

Joan looked at him with compassion and longing, but she said nothing. She suspected what he was going to do. As a girl, as a dog, she hated it; as a revolutionary, she welcomed it as the consummation of her mission.

The Lord Femtiosex lifted his right hand. He curled the ring finger and the little finger, putting his thumb over them. That left the first two fingers extended straight out. At that time, the sign from one chief to another, meaning, "private channels, telepathic, immediate." It has since been adopted by underpeople as their emblem for political unity.

The four chiefs went into a trancelike state and shared the judgment.

Joan began to sing in a soft, protesting, doglike wail, using the off-key plainsong which the underpeople had sung just before their hour of decision when they left the Brown and Yellow Corridor. Her words were nothing special, repetitions of the "people, dear people, I love you" which she had been communicating ever since she came to the surface of Kalma. But the way she did it has defied imitation across the centuries. There are thousands of lyrics and melodies which call themselves, one way and another, *The Song of Joan,* but none of them come near to the heart-wrenching pathos of the original tapes. The singing, like her own personality, was unique.

The appeal was deep. Even the real people tried to listen, shifting their eyes from the four immobile chiefs of the Instrumentality to the brown-eyed singing girl. Some of them just could not stand it. In true human fashion, they forgot why they were there and went absent-mindedly home to lunch.

Suddenly Joan stopped.

Her voice ringing clearly across the crowd, she cried out:

"The end is near, dear people. The end is near."

Eyes all shifted to the two lords and the two ladies of the Instrumentality. The Lady Arabella Underwood looked grim after the telepathic conference. The Lady Goroke was haggard with wordless grief. The two Lords looked severe and resolved.

It was the Lord Femtiosex who spoke.

"We have tried you, animal. Your offense is great. You have lived illegally. For that the penalty is death. You have interfered with robots in some manner which we do not understand. For that brand-new crime, the penalty should be more than death; and I have recommended a punishment which was applied on a planet of the Violet Star. You have also said many unlawful and improper things, detracting from the happiness and security of mankind. For that the penalty is re-education, but since you have two death sentences already, this does not matter. Do you have anything to say before I pronounce sentence?"

"If you light a fire today, my Lord, it will never be put out in the hearts of men. You can destroy me. You can reject my love. You cannot destroy the goodness in yourselves, no matter how much goodness may anger you—"

"Shut up!" he roared. "I asked for a plea, not a speech. You will die by fire, here and now. What do you say to that?"

"I love you, dear people."

Femtiosex nodded to the men of the chief of birds, who had dragged a barrel and a spray into the street in front of Joan.

"Tie her to that post," he commanded. "Spray her. Light her. Are the tape-makers in focus? We want this to be recorded and known. If the underpeople try this again, they will see that mankind controls the worlds." He looked at Joan and his eyes seemed to go out of focus. In an unaccustomed voice he said, "I am not a bad man, little dog-girl, but you are a bad animal and we must make an example of you. Do you understand that?"

"Femtiosex," she cried, leaving out his title, "I am very sorry for you. I love you too."

With these words of hers, his face became clouded and angry again. He brought his right hand down in a chopping gesture.

Fisi copied the gesture and the men operating the barrel and spray began to squirt a hissing stream of oil on Joan. Two guards had already chained her to the lamp post, using an improvised chain of handcuffs to make sure that she stood upright and remained in plain sight of the crowd.

"Fire," said Femtiosex.

Elaine felt the Hunter's body, beside her, cramp sharply. He seemed to strain intensely. For herself, she felt the way she had felt when she was defrozen and taken out of the adiabatic pod in which she had made the trip from earth—sick to her stomach, confused in her mind, emotions rocking back and forth inside her.

Hunter whispered to her, "I tried to reach her mind

so that she would die easy. Somebody else got there first. I . . . don't know who it is."

Elaine stared.

The fire was being brought. Suddenly it touched the oil and Joan flamed up like a human torch.

10

The burning of D'joan at Fomalhaut took very little time, but the ages will not forget it.

Femtiosex had taken the cruelest step of all.

By telepathic invasion he had suppressed her human mind, so that only the primitive canine remained.

Joan did not stand still like a martyred queen.

She struggled against the flames which licked her and climbed her. She howled and shrieked like a dog in pain, like an animal whose brain—good though it is—cannot comprehend the senselessness of human cruelty.

The result was directly contrary to what the Lord Femtiosex had planned.

The crowd of people stirred forward, not with curiosity but because of compassion. They had avoided the broad areas of the street on which the dead underpeople lay as they had been killed, some pooled in their own blood, some broken by the hands of robots, some reduced to piles of frozen crystal. They walked over the dead to watch the dying, but their watching was not the witless boredom of people who never see a spectacle; it was the movement of living things, instinctive and deep, toward the sight of another living thing in a position of danger and ruin.

Even the guard who had held Elaine and Hunter by gripping Hunter's arm—even he moved forward a few unthinking steps. Elaine found herself in the first row of the spectators, the acrid, unfamiliar smell of burning oil making her nose twitch, the howls of the dying dog-girl tearing through her eardrums into her brain. Joan was turning and twisting in the fire now, trying to avoid the flames which wrapped her tighter than clothing. The odor of something sickening and strange reached the crowd. Few of them had ever smelled the stink of burning meat before.

Joan gasped.

In the ensuing seconds of silence, Elaine heard something she had never expected to hear before—the weeping of grown human beings. Men and women stood there sobbing and not knowing why they sobbed.

Femtiosex loomed over the crowd, obsessed by the failure of his demonstration. He did not know that the Hunter, with a thousand kills behind him, was committing the legal outrage of peeping the mind of a chief of the Instrumentality.

The Hunter whispered to Elaine, "In a minute I'll try it. She deserves something better than that . . ."

Elaine did not ask what. She too was weeping.

The whole crowd became aware that a soldier was calling. It took them several seconds to look away from the burning, dying Joan.

The soldier was an ordinary one. Perhaps he was the one who had been unable to tie Joan with bonds a few minutes ago, when the lords decreed that she be taken into custody.

He was shouting now, shouting frantically and wildly, shaking his fist at the Lord Femtiosex.

"You're a liar, you're a coward, you're a fool, and I challenge you—"

The Lord Femtiosex became aware of the man and of what he was yelling. He came out of his deep concentration and said, mildly for so wild a time:

"What do you mean?"

"This is a crazy show. There is no girl here. No fire. Nothing. You are hallucinating the whole lot of us for some horrible reason of your own, and I'm challenging you for it, you animal, you fool, you coward."

In normal times even a lord had to accept a challenge or adjust the matter with clear talk.

This was no normal time.

The Lord Femtiosex said, "All this is real. I deceive no one."

"If it's real, Joan, I'm with you!" shrieked the young soldier. He jumped in front of the jet of oil before the

other soldiers could turn it off and then he leapt into the
fire beside Joan.

Her hair had burned away but her features were still
clear. She had stopped the doglike whining shriek. Femtiosex had been interrupted. She gave the soldier, who
had begun to burn as he stood voluntarily beside her the
gentlest and most feminine of smiles. Then she frowned,
as though there were something which she should remember to do, despite the pain and terror which surrounded her.

"Now!" whispered the Hunter. He began to hunt the
Lord Femtiosex as sharply as he had ever sought the alien, native minds of Fomalhaut III.

The crowd could not tell what had happened to the
Lord Femtiosex. Had he turned coward? Had he gone
mad? (Actually, the Hunter, by using every gram of the
power of his mind, had momentarily taken Femtiosex
courting in the skies; he and Femtiosex were both male
birdlike beasts, singing wildly for the beautiful female
who lay hidden in the landscape far, far below.)

Joan was free, and she knew she was free.

She sent out her message. It knocked both Hunter
and Femtiosex out of thinking; it flooded Elaine; it
made even Fisi, the chief of birds, breathe quietly. She
called so loudly that within the hour messages were
pouring in from the other cities to Kalma, asking what
had happened. She thought a single message, not words.
But in words it came to this:

"Loved ones, you kill me. This is my fate. I bring
love, and love must die to live on. Love asks nothing,
does nothing. Love thinks nothing. Love is knowing
yourself and knowing all other people and things. Know
—and rejoice. I die for all of you now, dear ones—"

She opened her eyes for a last time, opened her
mouth, sucked in the raw flame and slumped forward.
The soldier, who had kept his nerve while his clothing
and body burned, ran out of the fire, afire himself, toward his squad. A shot stopped him and he pitched flat
forward.

The weeping of the people was audible throughout
the streets. Underpeople, tame and licensed ones, stood
shamelessly among them and wept too.

The Lord Femtiosex turned wearily back to his colleagues.

The face of Lady Goroke was a sculptured, frozen caricature of sorrow.

He turned to the Lady Arabella Underwood. "I seem to have done something wrong, my lady. Take over, please."

The Lady Arabella stood up. She called to Fisi, "Put out that fire."

She looked out over the crowd. Her hard, honest Norstrilian features were unreadable. Elaine, watching her, shivered at the thought of a whole planet full of people as tough, obstinate and clever as these.

"It's over," said the Lady Arabella. "People, go away. Robots, clean up. Underpeople, to your jobs."

She looked at Elaine and the Hunter. "I know who you are and I suspect what you have been doing. Soldiers, take them away."

The body of Joan was fire-blackened. The face did not look particularly human anymore; the last burst of fire had caught her in the nose and eyes. Her young, girlish breasts showed with heart-wrenching immodesty that she had been young and female once. Now she was dead, just dead.

The soldiers would have shoveled her into a box if she had been an underperson. Instead, they paid her the honors of war that they would have given to one of their own comrades or to an important civilian in time of disaster. They unslung a litter, put the little blackened body on it and covered the body with their own flag. No one had told them to do so.

As their own soldier led them up the road toward the Waterrock, where the houses and offices of the military were located, Elaine saw that he too had been crying.

She started to ask him what he thought of it, but Hunter stopped her with a shake of the head. He later told her that the soldier might be punished for talking with them.

When they got to the office they found the Lady Goroke already there.

The Lady Goroke already there . . . It became a nightmare in the weeks that followed. She had gotten over her grief and was conducting an inquiry into the case of Elaine and D'joan.

The Lady Goroke already there . . . She was waiting when they slept. Her image, or perhaps herself, sat in on all the endless interrogations. She was particularly interested in the chance meeting of the dead Lady Panc Ashash, the misplaced witch Elaine, and the non-adjusted man, the Hunter.

The Lady Goroke already there . . . She asked them everything, but she told them nothing.

Except for once.

Once she burst out, violently personal after endless hours of formal, official work, "Your minds will be cleansed when we get through, so it wouldn't matter how much else you know. Do you know that this has hurt me—me!—all the way to the depths of everything I believe in?"

They shook their heads.

"I'm going to have a child, and I'm going back to Manhome to have it. And I'm going to do the genetic coding myself. I'm going to call him Jestocost. That's one of the Ancient Tongues, the Paroskii one, for 'cruelty,' to remind him where he comes from, and why. And he, or his son, or *his* son will bring justice back into the world and solve the puzzle of the underpeople. What do you think of that? On second thought, don't think. It's none of your business, and I am going to do it anyway."

They stared at her sympathetically, but they were too wound up in the problems of their own survival to extend her much sympathy or advice. The body of Joan had been pulverized and blown into the air, because the Lady Goroke was afraid that the underpeople would make a *goodplace* out of it; she felt that way herself, and she knew that if she herself were tempted, the underpeople would be even more tempted.

Elaine never knew what happened to the bodies of all the other people who had turned themselves, under Joan's leadership, from animals into mankind, and who had followed the wild, foolish march out of the Tunnel of Englok into the Upper City of Kalma. Was it really wild? Was it really foolish? If they had stayed where they were, they might have had a few days or months or years of life, but sooner or later the robots would have found them and they would have been exterminated like the vermin which they were. Perhaps the death they had chosen was better. Joan *did* say, "It's the mission of life always to look for something better than itself, and then to try to trade life itself for meaning."

At last, the Lady Goroke called them in and said, "Goodbye, you two. It's foolish, saying goodbye, when an hour from now you will remember neither me nor Joan. You've finished your work here. I've set up a lovely job for you. You won't have to live in a city. You will be weather-watchers, roaming the hills and watching for all the little changes which the machines can't interpret fast enough. You will have whole lifetimes of marching and picnicking and camping together. I've told the technicians to be very careful, because you two are very much in love with each other. When they re-route your synapses, I want that love to be there with you."

They each knelt and kissed her hand. They never wittingly saw her again. In later years they sometimes saw a fashionable ornithopter soaring gently over their camp, with an elegant woman peering out of the side of it; they had no memories to know that it was the Lady Goroke, recovered from madness, watching over them.

Their new life was their final life.

Of Joan and the Brown and Yellow Corridor, nothing remained.

They were both very sympathetic toward animals, but they might have been this way even if they had never shared in the wild political gamble of the dear dead Lady Panc Ashash.

One time a strange thing happened. An underman from an elephant was working in a small valley, creating an exquisite rock garden for some important official of the Instrumentality who might later glimpse the garden once or twice a year. Elaine was busy watching the weather, and the Hunter had forgotten that he had ever hunted, so that neither of them tried to peep the underman's mind. He was a huge fellow, right at the maximum permissible size—five times the gross stature of a man. He had smiled at them friendlily in the past.

One evening he brought them fruit. Such fruit! Rare

offworld items which a year of requests would not have obtained for ordinary people like them. He smiled his big, shy, elephant smile, put the fruit down and prepared to lumber off.

"Wait a minute," cried Elaine, "why are you giving us this? Why us?"

"For the sake of Joan," said the elephant-man.

"Who's Joan?" said the Hunter.

The elephant-man looked sympathetically at them. "That's all right. You don't remember her, but I do."

"But what did Joan do?" said Elaine.

"She loved you. She loved us all," said the elephant-man. He turned quickly, so as to say no more. With incredible deftness for so heavy a person, he climbed speedily into the fierce lovely rocks above them and was gone.

"I wish we had known her," said Elaine. "She sounds very nice."

In that year there was born the man who was to be the first Lord Jestocost.

Under Old Earth

This was the last story Smith wrote, and perhaps the strangest. No reference is made to the Douglas-Ouyang planets elsewhere in the Smith canon, and it is hard to judge which events are "real" and which "legendary" in this tale that explores one of the roots of the Rediscovery of Man. Sto Odin by the way, is Russian for one-Hundred and one."

> *I need a temporary dog*
> *For a temporary job*
> *On a temporary place*
> *Like Earth!*

—Song from *The Merchant of Menace*

1

THERE WERE THE Douglas-Ouyang planets, which circled their sun in a single cluster, riding around and around the same orbit unlike any other planets known. There were the gentlemen-suicides back on Earth, who gambled their lives—even more horribly, gambled sometimes for things worse than their lives—against different kinds of geophysics which real men had never ex-

perienced. There were girls who fell in love with such
men, however stark and dreadful their personal fates
might be. There was the Instrumentality, with its un-
ceasing labor to keep man man. And there were the citizens who walked in the boulevards before the Rediscovery of Man. The citizens were happy. They had to be
happy. If they were found sad, they were calmed and
drugged and changed until they were happy again.

This story concerns three of them: the gambler who
took the name Sun-boy, who dared to go down to the
Gebiet, who confronted himself before he died; the girl
Santuna, who was fulfilled in a thousand ways before
she died; and the Lord Sto Odin, a most ancient of days,
who knew it all and never dreamed of preventing any of
it.

Music runs through this story. The soft sweet music
of the Earth Government and the Instrumentality, bland
as honey and sickening in the end. The wild illegal pul-
sations of the Gebiet, where most men were forbidden to
enter. Worst of all, the crazy fugues and improper melodies of the Bezirk, closed to men for fifty-seven centuries—opened by accident, found, trespassed in! And
with it our story begins.

2

The Lady Ru had said, a few centuries before:
"Scraps of knowledge have been found. In the ultimate
beginning of man, even before there were aircraft, the
wise man Laodz declared, 'Water does nothing but it
penetrates everything. Inaction finds the road.' Later an
ancient lord said this: 'There is a music which underlies
all things. We dance to the tunes all our lives, though
our living ears never hear the music which guides us and
moves us. Happiness can kill people as softly as shadows seen in dreams.' We must be people first and happy
later, lest we live and die in vain."

The Lord Sto Odin was more direct. He declared the
truth to a few private friends: "Our population is dropping on most worlds, including the Earth. People have
children, but they don't want them very much. I myself

have been a three-father to twelve children, a two-father to four, and a one-father, I suppose, to many others. I have had zeal for work and I have mistaken it for zeal in living. They are not the same.

"Most people want happiness. Good: we have given them happiness.

"Dreary useless centuries of happiness, in which all the unhappy were corrected or adjusted or killed. Unbearable desolate happiness without the sting of grief, the wine of rage, the hot fumes of fear. How many of us have ever tasted the acid, icy taste of old resentment? That's what people really lived for in the Ancient Days, when they pretended to be happy and were actually alive with grief, rage, fury, hate, malice and hope! Those people bred like mad. They populated the stars while they dreamed of killing each other, secretly or openly. Their plays concerned murder or betrayal or illegal love. Now we have no murder. We cannot imagine any kind of love which is illegal. Can you imagine the Murkins with their highway net? Who can fly anywhere today without seeing that net of enormous highways? Those roads are ruined, but they're still here. You can see the abominable things quite clearly from the moon. Don't think about the roads. Think of the millions of vehicles that ran on those roads, the people filled with greed and rage and hate, rushing past each other with their engines on fire. They say that fifty thousand a year were killed on the roads alone. We would call that a war. What people they must have been, to rush day and night and to build things which would help other people to rush even more! They were different from us. They must have been wild, dirty, free. Lusting for life, perhaps, in a way that we do not. We can easily go a thousand times faster than they ever went, but who, nowadays, bothers to go? Why go? It's the same there as here, except for a few fighters or technicians." He smiled at his friends and added, " . . . and Lords of the Instrumentality, like ourselves. We go for the reasons of the Instrumentality. Not ordinary people reasons. Ordinary people don't have much reason to do anything. They work at the jobs which we think up for them, to keep them happy while the robots and the underpeople do the real work. They walk. They make love. But they are never unhappy.

"They can't be!"

The Lady Mmona disagreed, "Life can't be as bad as you say. We don't just think they are happy. We *know* they are happy. We look right into their brains with telepathy. We monitor their emotional patterns with robots and scanners. It's not as though we didn't have samples. People are always turning unhappy. We're correcting them all the time. And now and then there are bad accidents, which even we cannot correct. When people are very unhappy, they scream and weep. Sometimes they even stop talking and just die, despite everything we can do for them. You can't say that isn't real!"

"But I do," said the Lord Sto Odin.

"You do what?" cried Mmona.

"I do say this happiness is not real," he insisted.

"How can you," she shouted at him, "in the face of the evidence? *Our* evidence, which we of the Instrumentality decided on a long time ago. We collect it ourselves. Can we, the Instrumentality, be wrong?"

"Yes," said the Lord Sto Odin.

This time it was the entire circle who went silent.

Sto Odin pleaded with them. "Look at *my* evidence. People don't care whether they are one-fathers or one-mothers or not. They don't know which children are theirs, anyhow. Nobody dares to commit suicide. We keep them too happy. But do we spend any time keeping the talking animals, the underpeople, as happy as men? And do underpeople commit suicide?"

"Certainly," said Mmona. "They are preconditioned to commit suicide if they are hurt too badly for easy repair or if they fail in their appointed work."

"I don't mean that. Do they ever commit suicide for *their* reasons, not ours?"

"No," said the Lord Nuru-or, a wise young Lord of the Instrumentality. "They are too desperately busy doing their jobs and staying alive."

"How long does an underperson live?" said Sto Odin, with deceptive mildness.

"Who knows?" said Nuru-or. "Half a year, a hundred years, maybe several hundred years."

"What happens if he does not work?" said the Lord Sto Odin, with a friendly-crafty smile.

"We kill him," said Mmona, "or our robot-police do."

"And does the animal know it?"

"Know he will be killed if he does not work?" said Mmona. "Of course. We tell all of them the same thing. Work or die. What's that got to do with people?"

The Lord Nuru-or had fallen silent and a wise, sad smile had begun to show on his face. He had begun to suspect the shrewd, dreadful conclusion toward which the Lord Sto Odin was driving.

But Mmona did not see it and she pressed the point. "My Lord," said she, "you are insisting that people are happy. You admit they do not like to be unhappy. You seem to want to bring up a problem which has no solution. Why complain of happiness? Isn't it the best which the Instrumentality can do for mankind? That's our mission. Are you saying that we are failing in it?"

"Yes. We are failing." The Lord Sto Odin looked blindly at the room as though alone.

He was the oldest and wisest, so they waited for him to talk.

He breathed lightly and smiled at them again. "You know when I am going to die?"

"Of course," said Mmona, thinking for half a second. "Seventy-seven days from now. But you posted the time yourself. And it is not our custom, my Lord, as you well know, to bring intimate things into meetings of the Instrumentality."

"Sorry," said Sto Odin, "but I'm not violating a law. I'm making a point. We are sworn to uphold the dignity of man. Yet we are killing mankind with a bland hopeless happiness which has prohibited news, which has suppressed religion, which has made all history an official secret. I say that the evidence is that we are failing and that mankind, whom we've sworn to cherish, is failing too. Failing in vitality, strength, numbers, energy. I have a little while to live. I am going to try to find out."

The Lord Nuru-or asked with sorrowful wisdom, as

though he guessed the answer: "And where will you go to find out?"

"I shall go," said the Lord Sto Odin, "down into the Gebiet."

"The Gebiet—oh, no!" cried several. And one voice added, "You're immune."

"I shall waive immunity and I shall go," said the Lord Sto Odin. "Who can do anything to a man who is already almost a thousand years old and who has chosen only seventy-seven more days to live?"

"But you can't!" said Mmona. "Some criminal might capture you and duplicate you, and then we would all of us be in peril."

"When did you last hear of a criminal among mankind?" said Sto Odin.

"There are plenty of them, here and there in the off-worlds."

"But on Old Earth itself?" asked Sto Odin.

She stammered. "I don't know. There must have been a criminal once." She looked around the room. "Don't any of the rest of you know?"

There was silence.

The Lord Sto Odin stared at them all. In his eyes was the brightness and fierceness which had made whole generations of lords plead with him to live just a few more years, so that he could help them with their work. He had agreed, but within the last quarter-year he had overridden them all and had picked his day of death. He had lost none of his powers in doing this. They shrank from his stare while they waited with respect for his decision.

The Lord Sto Odin looked at the Lord Nuru-or and said, "I think you have guessed what I am going to do in the Gebiet and why I have to go there."

"The Gebiet is a preserve where no rules apply and no punishments are inflicted. Ordinary people can do what *they* want down there, not what we think they should want. From all I hear, it is pretty nasty and pointless, the things that they find out. But you, perhaps, may sense the inwardness of these things. You may find a cure for the weary happiness of mankind."

"That is right," said Sto Odin. "And that is why I am going, after I make the appropriate official preparations."

3

Go he did. He used one of the most peculiar conveyances ever seen on Earth, since his own legs were too weak to carry him far. With only two-ninths of a year to live, he did not want to waste time getting his legs regrafted.

He rode in an open sedan-chair carried by two Roman legionaries.

The legionaries were actually robots, without a trace of blood or living tissue in them. They were the most compact and difficult kind to create, since their brains had to be located in their chests—several million sheets of incredibly fine laminations, imprinted with the whole life experience of an important, useful and long-dead person. They were clothed as legionaries, down to cuirasses, swords, kilts, greaves, sandals and shields, merely because it was the whim of the Lord Sto Odin to go behind the rim of history for his companions. Their bodies, all metal, were very strong. They could batter walls, jump chasms, crush any man or underperson with their mere fingers, or throw their swords with the accuracy of guided projectiles.

The forward legionary, Flavius, had been head of Fourteen-B in the Instrumentality—an espionage division so secret that even among lords, few knew exactly of its location or its function. He was (or had been, till he was imprinted on a robot-mind as he lay dying) the director of historical research for the whole human race. Now he was a dull, pleasant machine carrying two poles until his master chose to bring his powerful mind into bright, furious alert by speaking the simple Latin phrase, understood by no other person living, *Summa nulla est.*

The rear legionary, Livius, had been a psychiatrist who turned into a general. He had won many battles until he chose to die, somewhat before his time, because he perceived that battle itself was a struggle for the defeat of himself.

Together, and added to the immense brainpower of the Lord Sto Odin himself, they represented an unsurpassable team.

"The Gebiet," commanded the Lord Sto Odin.

"The Gebiet," said both of them heavily, picking up the chair with its supporting poles.

"And then the Bezirk," he added.

"The Bezirk," they chimed in toneless voices.

Sto Odin felt his chair tilt back as Livius put his two ends of the poles carefully on the ground, came up beside Sto Odin and saluted with open palm.

"May I awaken?" said Livius in an even, mechanical voice.

"Summa nulla est," said the Lord Sto Odin.

Livius' face sprang into full animation. "You must not go there, my Lord! You would have to waive immunity and meet all dangers. There is nothing there yet. Not yet. Some day they will come pouring out of that underground Hades and give you men a real fight. Now, no. They are just miserable beings, cooking away in their weird unhappiness, making love in manners which you never thought of—"

"Never mind what you think I've thought. What's your objection in real terms?"

"It's pointless, my Lord! You have only bits of a year to live. Do something noble and great for man before you die. They may turn us off. We would like to share your work before you go away."

"Is that all?" said Sto Odin.

"My Lord," said Flavius, "you have awakened me too. I say, go forward. History is being respun down there. Things are loose which you great ones of the Instrumentality have never even suspected. Go now and look, before you die. You may do nothing, but I disagree with my companion. It is as dangerous as space$_3$ might be, if we ever were to find it, but it is *interesting*. And in this world where all things have been done, where all thoughts have been thought, it is hard to find things which still prompt the human mind with raw curiosity. I'm dead, as you perfectly well know, but even I, inside this machine brain, feel the tug of adventure, the pull of danger, the magnetism of the unknown. For one thing, they are committing crimes down there. And you Lords are overlooking them."

"We chose to overlook them. We are not stupid. We wanted to see what might happen," said the Lord Sto Odin, "and we have to give those people time before we find out just how far they might go if they are cut off from controls."

"They are having babies!" said Flavius excitedly.

"I know that."

"They have hooked in two illegal instant-message machines," shouted Flavius.

Sto Odin was calm. "So that's why the Earth's credit structure has appeared to be leaking in its balance of trade."

"They have a piece of the congohelium!" shouted Flavius.

"The congohelium!" shouted the Lord Sto Odin. "Impossible! It's unstable. They could kill themselves. They could hurt Earth! What are they doing with it?"

"Making music," said Flavius, more quietly.

"Making *what*?"

"Music. Songs. Nice noise to dance to."

The Lord Sto Odin sputtered. "Take me there right now. This is ridiculous. Having a piece of the congohelium down there is as bad as wiping out inhabited planets to play checkers."

"My Lord," said Livius.

"Yes?" said Sto Odin.

"I withdraw my objections," said Livius.

Sto Odin said, very drily, "Thank you."

"They have something else down there. When I did not want you to go, I did not mention it. It might have aroused your curiosity. They have a god."

The Lord Sto Odin said, "If this is going to be a historical lecture, save it for another time. Go back to sleep and carry me down."

Livius did not move. "I mean what I said."

"A god? What do you call a god?"

"A person or an idea capable of starting wholly new cultural patterns in motion."

The Lord Sto Odin leaned forward, "You *know* this?"

"We both do," said Flavius and Livius.

"We saw him," said Livius. "You told us, a tenth-year ago to walk around freely for thirty hours, so we put on ordinary robot bodies and happened to get into the Gebiet. When we sensed the congohelium operating, we had to go on down to find out what it was doing. Usually, it is employed to keep the stars in their place—"

"Don't tell me that. I know it. Was it a man?"

"A man," said Flavius, "who is re-living the life of Akhnaton."

"Who's that?" said the Lord Sto Odin, who knew history, but wanted to see how much his robots knew.

"A king, tall, long-faced, thick lipped, who ruled the human world of Egypt long, long before atomic power. Akhnaton invented the best of the early gods. This man is re-enacting Akhnaton's life step by step. He has already made a religion out of the sun. He mocks at happiness. People listen to him. They joke about the Instrumentality."

Livius added, "We saw the girl who loves him. She herself was young, but beautiful. And I think she has powers which will make the Instrumentality promote her or destroy her some day in the future."

"They both made music," said Flavius, "with that piece of the congohelium. And this man or god—this new kind of Akhnaton, whatever you may want to call him, my Lord—he was dancing a strange kind of dance. It was like a corpse being tied with rope and dancing like a marionette. The effect on the people around him was as good as the best hypnotism you ever saw. I'm a robot now, but it bothered even me."

"Did the dance have a name?" said Sto Odin.

"I don't know the name," said Flavius, "but I memorized the song, since I have total recall. Do you wish to hear it?"

"Certainly," said the Lord Sto Odin.

Flavius stood on one leg, threw his arms out at weird, improbable angles and began to sing in a high, insulting tenor voice which was both fascinating and repugnant:

Jump, dear people, and I'll howl for you.
Jump and howl and I'll weep for you.
I weep because I'm a weeping man.
I'm a weeping man because I weep.
I weep because the day is done,
> *Sun is gone,*
> *Home is lost,*
> *Time killed dad.*
> *I killed time.*
> *World is round.*
> *Day is run,*
> *Clouds are shot,*
> *Stars are out,*
> *Mountain's fire,*
> *Rain is hot,*
> *Hot is blue.*
> *I am done.*
> *So are you.*
Jump, dear people, for the howling man.
Leap, dear people, for the weeping man.
> *I'm a weeping man because I weep for*
> *you!*

"Enough," said the Lord Sto Odin.

Flavius saluted. His face went back to amiable stolidity. Just before he took the front ends of the shaft he glanced back and brought forth one last comment:

"The verse is skeltonic."

"Tell me nothing more of your history. Take me there."

The robots obeyed. Soon the chair was jogging comfortably down the ramps of the ancient left-over city which sprawled beneath Earthport, that miraculous tower which seemed to touch the stratocumulus clouds in the blue, clear nothingness above mankind. Sto Odin went to sleep in his strange vehicle and did not notice that the human passers-by often stared at him.

The Lord Sto Odin woke fitfully in strange places as the legionaries carried him further and further into the depths below the city, where sweet pressures and warm, sick smells made the air itself feel dirty to his nose.

"Stop!" whispered the Lord Sto Odin, and the robots stopped.

"Whom am I?" he said to them.

"You have announced your will to die, my lord," said Flavius, "seventy-seven days from now, but so far your name is still the Lord Sto Odin."

"I am alive?" the Lord asked.

"Yes," said both the robots.

"You are dead?"

"We are not dead. We are machines, printed with the minds of men who once lived. Do you wish to turn back, my lord?"

"No. No. Now I remember. You are the robots. Livius, the psychiatrist and general. Flavius, the secret historian. You have the minds of men, and are not men?"

"That is right, my Lord," said Flavius.

"Then how can *I* be alive—I, Sto Odin?"

"You should feel it yourself, sir," said Livius, "though the mind of the old is sometimes very strange."

"How can I be alive?" asked Sto Odin, staring around the city. "How can I be alive when the people who knew me are dead? They have whipped through the corridors like wraiths of smoke, like traces of cloud; they were here, and they loved me, and they knew me, and now they are dead. Take my wife, Eileen. She was a pretty thing, a brown-eyed child who came out of her learning chamber all perfect and all young. Time touched her and she danced to the cadence of time. Her body grew full, grew old. We repaired it. But at last she cramped in death and she went to that place to which I am going. If you are dead, you ought to be able to tell me what death is like, where the bodies and minds and voices and music of men and women whip past these enormous corridors, these hardy pavements, and are then gone. How can passing ghosts like me and my kind, each with just a few dozen or a few hundred years to go before the great blind winds of time whip us away—how can phantoms like me have built this solid city, these wonderful engines, these brilliant lights which never go dim? How did we do it, when we pass so swiftly, each of us, all of us? Do you know?"

The robots did not answer. Pity had not been pro-

grammed into their systems. The Lord Sto Odin ha-
rangued them nonetheless:

"You are taking me to a wild place, a free place, an
evil place, perhaps. They are dying there too, as all men
die, as I shall die, so soon, so brightly and simply. I
should have died a long time ago. I was the people who
knew me, I was the brothers and comrades who trusted
me, I was the women who comforted me, I was the children whom I loved so bitterly and so sweetly many ages
ago. Now they are gone. Time touched them, and they
were not. I can see everyone that I ever knew racing
through these corridors, see them young as toddlers, see
them proud and wise and full with business and maturi-
ty, see them old and contorted as time reached out for
them and they passed hastily away. Why did they do it?
How can I live on? When I am dead, will I know that I
once lived? I know that some of my friends have cheat-
ed and lie in the icy sleep, hoping for something which
they do not know. I've had life, and I know it. What is
life? A bit of play, a bit of learning, some words well-
chosen, some love, a trace of pain, more work, memories, and then dirt rushing up to meet sunlight. That's all
we've made of it—we, who have conquered the stars!
Where are my friends? Where is my *me* that I once was
so sure of, when the people who knew me were time-
swept like storm-driven rags toward darkness and oblivi-
on? You tell me. You ought to know! You are machines and you were given the minds of men. You ought
to know what we amount to, from the outside in."

"We were built," said Livius, "by men and we have
whatever men put into us, nothing more. How can we
answer talk like yours? It is rejected by our minds, good
though our minds may be. We have no grief, no fear, no
fury. We know the names of these feelings but not the
feelings themselves. We hear your words but we do not
know what you are talking about. Are you trying to tell
us what life feels like? If so, we already know. Not
much. Nothing special. Birds have life too, and so do
fishes. It is you people who can talk and who can knot
life into spasms and puzzles. You muss things up.
Screaming never made the truth truthful, at least, not to
us."

"Take me down," said Sto Odin. "Take me down to the Gebiet, where no well-mannered man has gone in many years. I am going to judge that place before I die."

They lifted the sedan-chair and resumed their gentle dog-trot down the immense ramps down toward the warm steaming secrets of the Earth itself. The human pedestrians became more scarce, but undermen—most often of gorilla or ape origin—passed them, toiling their way upward while dragging shrouded treasures which they had filched from the uncatalogued storehouses of Man's most ancient past. At other times there was a wild whirr of metal wheels on stone roadway; the undermen, having offloaded their treasures at some intermediate point high above, sat on their wagons and rolled back downhill, like grotesque enlargements of the ancient human children who were once reported to have played with wagons in this way.

A command, scarcely a whisper, stopped the two legionaries again. Flavius turned. Sto Odin was indeed calling both of them. They stepped out of the shafts and came around to him, one on each side.

"I may be dying right now," he whispered, "and that would be most inconvenient at this time. Get out my manikin meee!"

"My Lord," said Flavius, "it is strictly forbidden for us robots to touch any human manikin, and if we do touch one, we are commanded to destroy ourselves immediately thereafter! Do you wish us to try, nevertheless? If so, which one of us? You have the command, my Lord."

4

He waited so long that even the robots began to wonder if he died amid the thick wet air and the nearby stench of steam and oil.

The Lord Sto Odin finally roused himself and said: "I need no help. Just put the bag with my manikin meee on my lap."

"This one?" asked Flavius, lifting a small brown suitcase and handling it with a very gingerly touch indeed.

The Lord Sto Odin gave a barely perceptible nod and whispered, "Open it carefully for me. But do not touch the manikin, if those are your orders."

Flavius twisted at the catch of the bag. It was hard to manage. Robots did not feel fear, but they were intellectually attuned to the avoidance of danger; Flavius found his mind racing with wild choices as he tried to get the bag open. Sto Odin tried to help him, but the ancient hand, palsied and weak, could not even reach the top of the case. Flavius labored on, thinking that the Gebiet and Bezirk had their dangers, but that this meddling with manikins was the riskiest thing which he had ever encountered while in robot form, though in his human life he had handled many of them, including his own. They were "manikin, electro-encephalographic and endocrine" in model form, and they showed in miniaturized replica the entire diagnostic position of the patient for whom they were fashioned.

Sto Odin whispered to them. "There's no helping it. Turn me up. If I die, take my body back and tell the people that I misjudged my time."

Just as he spoke, the case sprang open. Inside it there lay a little naked human man, a direct copy of Sto Odin himself.

"We have it, my Lord," cried Livius, from the other side. "Let me guide your hand to it, so that you can see what to do."

Though it was forbidden for robots to touch manikins meee, it was legal for them to touch a human person with the person's consent. Livius's strong cupro-plastic fingers, with a reserve of many tons of gripping power in their human-like design, pulled the hands of the Lord Sto Odin forward until they rested on the manikin meee. Flavius, quick, smooth, agile, held the Lord's head upright on his weary old neck, so that the ancient Lord could see what the hands were doing.

"Is any part dead?" said the old Lord to the manikin, his voice clearer for the moment.

The manikin shimmered and two spots of solid black showed along the outside upper right thigh and the right buttock.

"Organic reserve?" said the Lord to his own manikin

meee, and again the machine responded to his command. The whole miniature body shimmered to a violent purple and then subsided to an even pink.

"I still have some all-around strength left in this body, prosthetics and all," said Sto Odin to the two robots. "Set me up, I tell you! Set me up."

"Are you sure, my Lord," said Livius, "that we should do a thing like that here where the three of us are alone in a deep tunnel? In less than half an hour we could take you to a real hospital, where actual doctors could examine you."

"I said," repeated the Lord Sto Odin, "set me up. I'll watch the manikin while you do it."

"Your control is in the usual place, my Lord?" asked Livius.

"How much of a turn?" asked Flavius.

"Nape of my neck, of course. The skin over it is artificial and self-sealing. One twelfth of a turn will be enough. Do you have a knife with you?"

Flavius nodded. He took a small sharp knife from his belt, probed gently around the old Lord's neck and then brought the knife down with a quick, sure turn.

"That did it!" said Sto Odin, in a voice so hearty that both of them stepped back a little. Flavius put the knife back in his belt. Sto Odin, who had almost been comatose a moment before, now held the manikin mee in his unaided hands. "See, gentlemen!" he cried. "You may be robots, but you can still see the truth and report it."

They both looked at the manikin meee, which Sto Odin now held in front of himself, his thumb and fingertip in the armpits of the medical doll.

"Watch what it reads," he said to them with a clear, ringing voice.

"Prosthetics!" he shouted at the manikin.

The tiny body changed from its pink color to a mixture. Both legs turned the color of a deep bruised blue. The legs, the left arm, one eye, one ear and the skullcap stayed blue, showing the prostheses in place.

"Felt pain!" shouted Sto Odin at the manikin. The little doll returned to its light pink color. All the details were there, even to genitals, toenails and eyelashes.

There was no trace of the black color of pain in any part of the little body.

"Potential pain!" shouted Sto Odin. The doll shimmered. Most of it settled to the color of dark walnut wood, with some areas of intense brown showing more clearly then the rest.

"Potential breakdown—one day!" shouted Sto Odin. The little body went back to its normal color of pink. Small lightnings showed at the base of the brain, but nowhere else.

"I'm all right," said Sto Odin. "I can continue as I have done for the last several hundred years. Leave me set up on this high life-output. I can stand it for a few hours, and if I cannot, there's little lost." He put the manikin back in its bag, hung the bag on the doorhandle of the sedan-chair and commanded the legionaries, "Proceed!"

The legionaries stared at him as if they could not see him.

He followed the lines of glance and saw that they were gazing rigidly at his manikin meee. It had turned black.

"Are you dead?" asked Livius, speaking as hoarsely as a robot could.

"Not dead at all!" cried Sto Odin. "I have been death in fractions of a moment, but for the time I am still life. That was just the pain-sum of my living body which showed on the manikin meee. The fire of life still burns within me. Watch as I put the manikin away . . ." The doll flared into a swirl of pastel orange as the Lord Sto Odin pulled the cover down.

They looked away as though they had seen an evil or an explosion.

"Down men, down," he cried, calling them wrong names as they stepped back between their carrying shafts to take him deeper under the vitals of the earth.

5

He dreamed brown dreams while they trotted down endless ramps. He woke a little to see the yellow walls passing. He looked at his dry old hand and it seemed to him that in this atmosphere, he had himself become more reptilian than human.

"I am caught by the dry, drab enturtlement of old, old age," he murmured, but the voice was weak and the robots did not hear him. They were running downward on a long meaningless concrete ramp which had become filmed by a leak of ancient oil, and they were taking care that they did not stumble and drop their precious master.

At a deep, hidden point the downward ramp divided, the left into a broad arena of steps which could have seated thousands of spectators for some never-to-occur event, and right into a narrow ramp which bore upward and then curved, yellow lights and all.

"Stop!" called Sto Odin. "Do you see her? Do you hear it?"

"Hear what?" said Flavius.

"The beat and the cadence of the congohelium rising out of the Gebiet. The whirl and the skirl of impossible music coming at us through miles of solid rock? That girl whom I can already see, waiting at a door which should never have been opened? The sound of the star-borne music, not designed for the proper human ear?" He shouted, "Can't you hear it? That cadence. The unlawful metal of congohelium so terrible far underground? Dah, dah. Dah, dah. Dah. Music which nobody has ever understood before?"

Said Flavius, "I hear nothing, saving the pulse of air in this corridor, and your own heartbeat, my Lord. And something else, a little like machinery, very far away."

"There, that!" cried Sto Odin, "which you call 'a little like machinery,' does it come in a beat of five separate sounds, each one distinct?"

"No. No, sir. Not five."

"And you, Livius, when you were a man, you were very telepathic? Is there any of that left in the robot which is you?"

"No, my Lord, nothing. I have good senses, and I am also cut into the subsurface radio of the Instrumentality. Nothing unusual."

"No five-beat? Each note separate, short of prolonged, given meaning and shape by the terrible music of the congohelium, imprisoned with us inside this much-too-solid rock? You hear nothing?"

The two robots, shaped like Roman legionaries, shook their heads.

"But I can see her, through this stone. She has breasts like ripe pears and dark brown eyes that are like the stones of fresh-cut peaches. And I can hear what they are singing, their weird silly words of a pentapaul, made into something majestic by the awful music of the congohelium. Listen to the words. When I repeat them, they sound just silly, because the dread-inspiring music does not come with them. Her name is Santuna and she stares at him. No wonder she stares. He is much more tall than most men, yet he makes this foolish song into something frightening and strange.

> Slim Jim.
> Dim him.
> Grim.

And his name is Yebayee, but now he is Sun-boy. He has the long face and the thick lips of the first man to talk about one god and one only. Akhnaton."

"Akhnaton the pharaoh," said Flavius. "That name was known in my office when I was a man. It was a secret. One of the first and greatest of the more-than-ancient kings. You see him, my Lord?"

"Through this rock I see him. Through this rock I hear the delirium engendered by the congohelium. I go to him." The Lord Sto Odin stepped out of the sedan chair and beat softly and weakly against the solid stone wall of the corridor. The yellow lamps gleamed. The legionaries were helpless. Here was something which their sharp swords could not pierce. Their once-human personalities, engraved on their micro-miniaturized brains, could not make sense out of the all-too-human situation of an old, old man dreaming wild dreams in a remote tunnel.

Sto Odin leaned against the wall, breathing heavily, and said to them with a sibilant rasp:

"These are no whispers which can be missed. Can't you hear the five-beat of the congohelium, making its crazy music again? Listen to the words of this one. It's another pentapaul. Silly, bony words given flesh and blood and entrails by the music which carries them. Here, listen.

> *Try. Vie.*
> *Cry. Die.*
> *Bye.*

This one you did not hear either?"

"May I use my radio to ask the surface of Earth for advice?" said one of the robots.

"Advice! Advice! What advice do we need? This *is* the Gebiet and one more hour of running and you will be in the heart of the Bezirk."

He climbed back into the sedan chair and commanded, "Run, men, run! It can't be more than three or four kilometers somewhere in this warren of stone. I will guide you. If I stop guiding you, you may take my body back to the surface, so that I can be given a wonderful funeral and be shot with a rocket-coffin into space with an orbit of no return. You have nothing to worry about. You are machines, nothing more, are you not? Are you not?" His voice shrilled at the end.

Said Flavius, "Nothing more."

Said Livius, "Nothing more. And yet—"

"And yet what?" demanded the Lord Sto Odin.

"And yet," said Livius, "I know I am a machine, and I know that I have known feelings only when I was once a living man. I sometimes wonder if you people might go too far. Too far, with us robots. Too far, perhaps, with the underpeople too. Things were once simple, when everything that talked was a human being and everything which did not talk was not. You may be coming to an ending of the ways."

"If you had said that on the surface," said the Lord

Sto Odin grimly, "your head might have been burned off by its automatic magnesium flare. You know that there you are monitored against having illegal thoughts."

"Too well do I know it," said Livius, "and I know that I must have died once as a man, if I exist here in robot form. Dying didn't seem to hurt me then and it probably won't hurt next time. But nothing really matters much when we get down this far into the Earth. When we get this far down, everything changes. I never really understood that the inside of the world was this big and this sick."

"It's not how far down we are," said the lord crossly, "it's *where* we are. This is the Gebiet, where all laws have been lifted, and down below and over yonder is the Bezirk, where laws have never been. Carry me rapidly now. I want to look on this strange musician with the face of Akhnaton and I want to talk to the girl who worships him, Santuna. Run carefully now. Up a little, to the left a little. If I sleep, do not worry. Keep going. I will waken myself when we come anywhere near the music of the congohelium. If I can hear it now, so far away, think of what it will be like when you yourselves approach it!"

He leaned back in his seat. They picked up the shafts of the sedan-chair and ran in the direction which they had been told.

6

They had run for more than an hour, with occasional delays when they had tricky footwork over leaking pipes or damaged walkways, when the light became so bright that they had to reach in their pouches and put on sunglasses, which looked very odd indeed underneath the Roman helmets of two fully armed legionaries. (It was even more odd, of course, that the eyes were not eyes at all; robot eyes were like white marbles swimming in little bowls of glittering ink, producing a grimly milky stare.) They looked at their master and he had not yet stirred, so they took a corner of his robe and twisted it firmly into a bandage to protect his eyes against the bright light.

The new light made the yellow bulbs of the corridor fade out of notice. The light was like a whole aurora borealis compressed and projected through the basement corridor of a hotel left over from long ago. Neither of the robots knew the nature of the light, but it pulsed in beats of five.

The music and the lights became obtrusive even to the two robots as they walked or trotted downward toward the center of the world. The air-forcing system must have been very strong, because the inner heat of the earth had not reached them, even at this great depth. Flavius had no idea of how many kilometers below the surface they had come. He knew that it was not much in planetary distance, but it was very far indeed for an ordinary walk.

The Lord Sto Odin sat up in the litter quite suddenly. When the two robots slowed, he said crossly at them:

"Keep going. Keep going. I am going to set myself up. I'm strong enough to do it."

He took out the manikin meee and studied it in the light of the minor aurora borealis which repeated itself in the corridor. The manikin ran through its changes of diagnoses and colors. The Lord was satisfied. With firm old fingers he put the knifetip to the back of his neck and set his output of vital energies at an even higher level.

The robots did what they had been told.

The lights had been bewildering. Sometimes they made walking itself difficult. It was hard to believe that dozens or hundreds, perhaps thousands, of human beings had found their way through these uncharted corridors in order to discover the inmost precincts of Bezirk, where all things were allowed. Yet the robots had to believe it. They themselves had been here before and they scarcely remembered how they had found their way the other time.

And the music! It beat at them harder than ever before. It came in beats of five, ringing out the tones of the pentapaul, the five-word verse which the mad cat-minstrel C'paul had developed while playing his c'lute some

centuries before. The form itself confirmed and rein-
forced the poignancy of cats combined with the heart-
breaking intelligence of the human being. No wonder
people had found their way down here.

In all the history of man, there was no act which
could not be produced by any one of the three bitterest
forces in the human spirit—religious faith, vengeful
vainglory or sheer vice. Here, for the sake of vice, men
had found the undiscoverable deep and had put it to
wild, filthy uses. The music called them on.

This was very special music. It came at Sto Odin and
his legionaries in two utterly different ways by now, re-
verberating at them through solid rock and echoing, re-
echoing through the maze of corridors, carried by the
dark heavy air. The corridor lights were still yellow, but
the electromagnetic illuminations, which kept time to
the music, made the ordinary lighting seem wan. The
music controlled all things, paced all time, called all life
to itself. It was song of a kind which the two robots had
not noticed with such intensity on their previous visit.

Even the Lord Sto Odin, for all his travels and experiences, had never heard it before.

It was all of this:

The beat and the heat and the neat repeat of the notes
which poured from the congohelium—metal never made
for music, matter and anti-matter locked in a fine magnetic grid to ward off the outermost perils of space.
Now a piece of it was deep in the body of Old Earth,
counting out strange cadences. The churn and the burn
and the hot return of music riding the living rock, ac-
companying itself in an air-carried echo. The surge and
the urge of an erotic dirge which moaned, groaned
through the heavy stone.

Sto Odin woke and stared sharply forward, seeing
nothing but experiencing everything.

"Soon we shall see the gate and the girl," said he.

"You know this, man? *You* who have never been
here before?" Livius had spoken.

"I know it," said the Lord Sto Odin, "because I know
it."

"You wear the feathers of immunity."

"I wear the feathers of immunity."

"Does that mean that we, your robots, are free too, down in this Bezirk?"

"Free as you like," said the Lord Sto Odin, "provided that you do my wishes. Otherwise I shall kill you."

"If we keep going," said Flavius, "may we sing the underpeople song? It might keep some of that terrible music out of our brains. The music has all feelings and we have none. Nevertheless it disturbs us. I do not know why."

"My radio contact with the surface has lapsed," said Livius irrelevantly. "I need to sing too."

"Go ahead, both of you," said the Lord Sto Odin. "But keep on going, or you die."

The robots lifted their voice in song:

> *I eat my rage.*
> *I swallow my grief.*
> *There's no relief*
> *From pain or age.*
> > *Our time comes.*
> *I work my life.*
> *I breathe my breath.*
> *I face my death*
> *Without a wife.*
> > *Our time comes.*

> *We undermen*
> *Shove, crush and crash.*
> *There'll be a clash*
> *And thunder when*
> > *Our time comes.*

Though the song had the barbarous, ancient thrill of bagpipes in it, the melody could not counter or cancel the sane, wild rhythm of the congohelium beating at them, now, from all directions at once.

"Nice piece of sedition, that," said the Lord Sto Odin drily, "but I like it better as music than I do this noise which is tearing its way through the depths of the world. Keep going. Keep going. I must meet this mystery before I die."

"We find it hard to endure that music coming at us through the rock," said Livius.

"It seems to us that it is much stronger than it was when we came here some months ago. Could it have changed?" asked Flavius.

"*That* is the mystery. We let them have the Gebiet, beyond our own jurisdiction. We gave them the Bezirk, to do with as they please. But these ordinary people have created or encountered some extraordinary power. They have brought new things into the Earth. It may be necessary for all three of us to die before we settle the matter."

"We can't die the way you do," said Livius. "We're already robots, and the people from whom we were imprinted have been dead a long time. Do you mean you would turn us off?"

"I would, perhaps, or else some other force. Would you mind?"

"Mind? You mean, have emotions about it? I don't know," said Flavius. "I used to think that I had real, full experience when you used the phrase *summa nulla est* and brought us up to full capacity, but that music which we have been hearing has the effect of a thousand passwords all said at once. I am beginning to care about my life and I think that I am becoming what your reference explained by the word 'afraid'."

"I too feel it," said Livius. "This is not a power which we knew to exist on Earth before. When I was a strategist someone told me about the really indescribable dangers connected with the Douglas-Ouyang planets, and it seems to me now that a danger of that kind is already with us, here inside the tunnel. Something which Earth never made. Something which man never developed. Something which no robot could out-compute. Something wild and very strong brought into being by the use of the congohelium. Look around us."

He did not need to say that. The corridor itself had becoming a living, pulsing rainbow.

They turned one last loop in the corridor and they were there—

The very last limit of the realm of distress.

The source of evil music.

The end of the Bezirk.

They knew it because the music blinded them, the lights deafened them, their senses ran into one another and became confused. This was the immediate presence of the congohelium.

There was a door, immensely large, carved with elaborate Gothic ornament. It was much too big for any human man to have had need of it. In the door a single figure stood, her breasts accented into vivid brights and darks by the brilliant light which poured from one side of the door only, the right.

They could see through the door, into an immense hall wherein the floor was covered by hundreds of limp bundles of ragged clothing. These were the people, unconscious. Above them and between them there danced the high figure of a male, holding a glittering something in his hands. He prowled and leaped and twisted and turned to the pulsation of the music which he himself produced.

"*Summa nulla est,*" said the Lord Sto Odin. "I want you two robots to be keyed to maximum. Are you now to top alert?"

"We are, sir," chorused Livius and Flavius.

"You have your weapons?"

"We cannot use them," said Livius, "since it is contrary to our programming, but *you* can use them, sir."

"I'm not sure," said Flavius. "I'm not at all sure. We are equipped with surface weapons. This music, these hypnotics, these lights—who knows what they may have done to us and to our weapons, which were never designed to operate this far underground?"

"No fear," said Sto Odin, "I'll take care of all of it."

He took out a small knife.

When the knife gleamed under the dancing lights, the girl in the doorway finally took notice of the Lord Sto Odin and his strange companions.

She spoke to him, and her voice rode through the heavy air with the accents of clarity and death.

7

"Who are you," she said, "that you should bring weapons to the last uttermost limits of the Bezirk?"

"This is just a small knife, lady," said the Lord Sto Odin, "and with this I can do no harm to anyone. I am an old man and I am setting my own vitality button higher."

She watched incuriously as he brought the point of the knife to the nape of his own neck and then gave it three full, deliberate turns.

Then she stared and said, "You are strange, my Lord. Perhaps you are dangerous to my friends and me."

"I am dangerous to no one." The robots looked at him, surprised, because of the fullness and the richness of his voice. He had set his vitality very high indeed, giving himself, at that rate, perhaps no more than an hour or two of life, but he had regained the physical power and the emotional force of his own prime years. They looked at the girl. She had taken Sto Odin's statement at full face value, almost as though it were an incontrovertible canon of faith.

"I wear," Sto Odin went on, "these feathers. Do you know what they signify?"

"I can see," she said, "that you are a lord of the Instrumentality, but I do not know what the feathers mean . . ."

"Waiver of immunity. Anyone who can manage it is allowed to kill me or to hurt me without danger of punishment." He smiled, a little grimly. "Of course, I have the right to fight back, and I do know how to fight. My name is the Lord Sto Odin. Why are you here, girl?"

"I love that man in there—if he is a man any more."

She stopped and pursed her lips in bewilderment. It was strange to see those girlish lips compressed in a momentary stammer of the soul. She stood there, more nude than a newborn infant, her face covered with provocative, off-beat cosmetics. She lived for a mission of love in the depths of the nothing and nowhere: yet she remained a girl, a person, a human being capable, as she was now, of an immediate relationship to another human being.

"He *was* a man, my Lord, even when he came back from the surface with that piece of congohelium. Only a few weeks ago, those people were dancing too. Now they just lie on the ground. They do not even die. I myself held the congohelium too, and I made music with it. Now the power of the music is eating him up and he dances without resting. He won't come out to me and I do not dare go into that place with him. Perhaps I too would end up as one more heap on the floor."

A crescendo of the intolerable music made speech intolerable for her. She waited for it to pass while the room beyond blazed a pulsing violet at them.

When the music of the congohelium subsided a little, Sto Odin spoke: "How long has it been that he has danced alone with this strange power coursing through him?"

"One year. Two years. Who can tell? I came down here and lost time when I arrived. You Lords don't even let us have clocks and calendars up on the surface."

"We ourselves saw you dancing just a tenth-year ago," said Livius, interrupting.

She glanced at them, quickly, incuriously. "Are you the same two robots who were here a while back? You look very different now. You look like ancient soldiers. I can't imagine why . . . All right, maybe it was a week, maybe it was a year."

"What were you doing down here?" asked Sto Odin, gently.

"What do you think?" she said. "Why do all the other people come down here? I was running away from the timeless time, the lifeless life, the hopeless hope that you Lords apply to all mankind on the surface. You let the robots and the underpeople work, but you freeze the real people in a happiness which has no hope and no escape."

"I'm right," cried Sto Odin. "I'm right, though I die for it!"

"I don't understand you," said the girl. "Do you mean that you too, a lord, have come down here to escape from the useless hope that wraps up all of us?"

"No, no, no," he said, as the shifting lights of the congohelium music made improbable traceries across his features. "I just meant that I told the other lords that something like this was happening to you ordinary people on the surface. Now you are telling me exactly what I told them. Who were you, anyhow?"

The girl glanced down at her unclothed body as though she were aware, for the first time, of her nakedness. Sto Odin could see the blush pour from her face down across her neck and chest. She said, very quietly:

"Don't you know? We never answer that question down here."

"You have rules?" he said. "You people have rules, even here in the Bezirk?"

She brightened up when she realized that he had not meant the indecent question as an impropriety. Eagerly she explained. "There aren't any rules. They are just understandings. Somebody told me when I left the ordinary world and crossed the line of Gebiet. I suppose they did not tell you because you were a lord, or because they hid from your strange war-robots."

"I met no one, coming down."

"Then they were hiding from you, my Lord."

Sto Odin looked around at his legionaries to see if they would confirm that statement but neither Flavius nor Livius said anything at all.

He turned back to the girl. "I didn't mean to pry. Can you tell me what kind of person you are? I don't need the particulars."

"When I was alive, I was a once-born," she said. "I did not live long enough to be renewed. The robots and a subcommissioner of the Instrumentality took a look at me to see if I could be trained for the Instrumentality. More than enough brains, they said, but no character at all. I thought about that a long time. 'No character at all.' I knew I couldn't kill myself, and I didn't want to live, so I looked happy every time I thought a monitor might be scanning me and I found my way to the Gebiet. It wasn't death, and it wasn't life, but it was an escape from endless fun. I hadn't been down here long—" she pointed at the Gebiet above them—"before I met him. We loved each other very soon and he said that the Gebiet was not much improvement on the surface. He said he had already been down here, in the Bezirk looking for a fun-death."

"A what?" said Sto Odin, as if he could not believe the words.

"A fun-death. Those were his words and his idea. I followed him around and we loved each other. I waited for him when he went to the surface to get the congohelium. I thought that his love for me would put the fun-death out of his mind."

"Are you telling me the whole truth?" said Sto Odin. "Or is this just your part of the story?"

She stammered protests but he did not ask again.

The Lord Sto Odin said nothing but he looked heavily at her.

She winced, bit her lip, and finally said, through all the music and the lights, very clearly indeed, "Stop it. You are hurting me."

The Lord Sto Odin stared at her, said innocently, "I am doing nothing," and stared on. There was much to stare at. She was a girl the color of honey. Even through these lights and shadows he could see that she had no clothing at all. Nor did she have a single hair left on her body—no head of hair, no eyebrows, probably no eyelashes, though he could not tell at that distance. She had traced golden eyebrows far up on her forehead, giving her the look of endless mocking inquiry. She had painted her mouth gold, so that when she spoke, her words cascaded from a golden source. She had painted her upper eyelids golden too, but the lower were black as carbon itself. The total effect was alien to all the previous experiences of mankind: it was lascivious grief to the thousandth power, dry wantonness perpetually unfulfilled, femaleness in the service of remote purposes, humanity enraptured by strange planets.

He stood and stared. If she were still human at all, this would sooner or later force her to take the initiative. It did.

She spoke again, "Who are you? You are living too fast, too fiercely. Why don't you go in and dance, like all the others?" She gestured past the open door, where the ragged unconscious shapes of all the people lay strewn about the floor.

"You call that dancing?" said the Lord Sto Odin. "I do not. There is one man who dances. Those others lie on the floor. Let me ask you the same question. Why don't you dance yourself?"

"I want *him*, not the dance. I am Santuna and he seized me once in human, mortal, ordinary love. But he becomes Sun-boy, more so every day, and he dances with those people who lie on the floor—"

"You call that dancing?" snapped the Lord Sto Odin. He shook his head and added grimly, "I see no dance."

"You don't see it? You really don't see it?" she cried. He shook his head obstinately and grimly.

She turned so that she looked into the room beyond her and she brought her high, clear penetrating wail which even cut through the five-beat pulse of the congo-helium. She cried:

"Sun-boy, Sun-boy, hear me!"

There was no break in the quick escape of the feet which pattered in the figure eight, no slowing down the fingers which beat against the shimmering non-focus of the metal which was carried in the dancer's arms.

"My lover, my beloved, my man!" she cried again, her voice even more shrill and demanding than before.

There was a break in the cadence of the music and the dance. The dancer sheered toward them with a perceptible slowing down of his cadence. The lights of the inner room, the great door and the outer hall all became more steady. Sto Odin could see the girl more clearly; she really didn't have a single hair on her body. He could see the dancer too; the young man was tall, thin beyond the ordinary suffering of man, and the metal which he carried shimmered like water reflecting a thousand lights. The dancer spoke, quickly and angrily:

"You called me. You have called me thousands of times. Come on in, if you wish. But don't call me."

As he spoke, the music faded out completely, the bundles on the floor began to stir and to groan and to awaken.

Santuna stammered hastily, "This time it wasn't me. It was these people. One of them is very strong. He cannot see the dancers."

The Sun-boy turned to the Lord Sto Odin. "Come in

and dance then, if you wish. You are already here. You might as well. Those machines of yours—" he nodded at the robot-legionaries—"they couldn't dance anyhow. Turn them off." The dancer started to turn away.

"I shall not dance, but I would like to see it," said Sto Odin, with enforced mildness. He did not like this young man at all—not the phosphorescence of his skin, the dangerous metal cradled in his arm, the suicidal recklessness of his prancing walk. Anyhow, there was too much light this far underground and too few explanations of what was being done.

"Man, you're a peeper. That's real nasty, for an old man like you. Or do you just want to be a *man*?"

The Lord Sto Odin felt his temper flare up. "Who are you, man, that you should call man *man* in such a tone? Aren't you still human, yourself?"

"Who knows? Who cares? I have tapped the music of the universe. I have piped all imaginable happiness into this room. I am generous. I share it with these friends of mine." Sun-boy gestured at the ragged heaps on the floor, who had begun to squirm in their misery without the music. As Sto Odin saw into the room more clearly, he could see that the bundles on the floor were young people, mostly young men, though there were a few girls among them. They all of them looked sick and weak and pale.

Sto Odin retorted. "I don't like the looks of this. I have half a mind to seize you and to take that metal."

The dancer spun on the ball of his right foot, as though to leap away in a wild prance.

The Lord Sto Odin stepped into the room after Sun-boy.

Sun-boy turned full circle, so that he faced Sto Odin once again. He pushed the lord out of the door, marching him firmly but irresistibly three steps backward.

"Flavius, seize the metal. Livius, take the man," spat Sto Odin.

Neither robot moved.

Sto Odin, his senses and his strength set high by the severe twist upward which he had given his vitality button, stepped forward to seize the congohelium himself.

Made one step and no more: he froze in the doorway, immobile.

He had not felt like that since the last time the doctors put him in a surgery machine, when they found that part of his skull had developed bone-cancer from old, old radiation in space and from the subsequent effects of sheer age. They had given him a prosthetic half-skull and for the time of the operation he had been immobilized by straps and drugs. This time there were no straps, no drugs, but the forces which Sun-boy had invoked were equally strong.

The dancer danced in an enormous figure-eight among the clothed bodies lying on the floor. He had been singing the song which the robot Flavius had repeated far up above, on the surface of the Earth—the song about the weeping man.

But Sun-boy did not weep.

His ascetic, thin face was twisted in a broad grin of mockery. When he sang about sorrow it was not sorrow which he really expressed, but derision, laughter, contempt for ordinary human sorrow. The congohelium shimmered and the aurora borealis almost blinded Sto Odin. There were two other drums in the middle of the room, one with high notes and the other with even higher ones.

The conghohelium resonated: *boom—boom—doom—doom—room!*

The large ordinary drum rattled out, when Sun-boy passed it and reached out his fingers: *ritiplin, ritiplin, rataplan, ritiplin!*

The small, strange drum emitted only two notes, and it almost croaked them: *kid-nork, kid-nork, kid-nork!*

As Sun-boy danced back the Lord Sto Odin thought that he could hear the voice of the girl Santuna, calling to Sun-boy, but he could not turn his head to see if she were speaking.

Sun-boy stood in front of Sto Odin, his feet still weaving as he danced, his thumbs and his palms torturing hypnotic dissonances from the gleaming congohelium.

"Old man, you tried to trick me. You failed."

The Lord Sto Odin tried to speak, but the muscles of his mouth and throat would not respond. He wondered what force this was, which could stop all unusual effort but still leave his heart free to beat, his lungs to breathe, his brain (both natural and prosthetic) to think.

The boy danced on. He danced away a few steps, turned and danced back to Sto Odin.

"You wear the feather of immunity. I am free to kill you. If I did the Lady Mmona and the Lord Nuru-or and your other friends would never know what happened."

If Sto Odin could have moved his eyelids that much, he would have opened his eyes in astonishment at the discovery that a superstitious dancer, far underground, knew the secret business of the Instrumentality.

"You can't believe what you are looking at, even though you see it plainly," said Sun-boy more seriously. "You think that a lunatic has found a way to work wonders with a piece of the congohelium taken far underground. Foolish old man! No ordinary lunatic would have carried this metal down here without blowing up the fragment and himself with it. No man could have done what I have done. You are thinking, If the gambler who took the name Sun-boy is not a man, what is he? What brings the power and music of the Sun so far down underground? Who makes the wretched ones of the world dream in a crazy, happy sleep while their life spills and leaks into a thousand kinds of times, a thousand kinds of worlds? Who does it, if it is not mere me? You don't have to ask. I can tell perfectly well what you are thinking. I'll dance it for you. I am a very kind man, even though you do not like me."

The dancer's feet had been moving in the same place while he spoke.

Suddenly he whirled away, leaping and vaulting over the wretched human figures on the floor.

He passed the big drum and touched it: *ritiplin, rataplan!*

Left hand brushed the little drum: *kid-nork, kidnork!*

Both hands seized the congohelium, as though the strong wrists were going to tear it apart.

The whole room blazed with music, gleamed with thunder as the human senses interpenetrated each other.

The Lord Sto Odin felt the air pass his skin like cool, wet oil. Sun-boy the dancer became transparent and through him the Lord Sto Odin could see a landscape which was not earth and never would be.

"Fluminescent, luminescent, incandescent, fluorescent," sang the dancer. "Those are the worlds of the Douglas-Ouyang planets, seven planets in a close group, all travelling together around a single sun. Worlds of wild magnetism and perpetual dustfall, where the surfaces of the planets are changed by the forever-shifting magnetism of their erratic orbits! Strange worlds, where stars dance dances wilder than any dance ever conceived by man—planets which have a consciousness in common, but perhaps not intelligence—planets which called across all space and all time for companionship until *I*, me the gambler, came down to this cavern and found them. Where you had left them, my Lord Sto Odin, when you said to a robot:

"'I do not like the looks of those planets,' said you, Sto Odin, speaking to a robot a long time ago. 'People might get sick or crazy, just looking at them,' said you, Sto Odin, long, long ago. 'Hide the knowledge in some out of the way computer,' you commanded, Sto Odin, before I was born. But the computer was that one, that one in the corner behind you, which you cannot turn to see. I came down to this room, looking for a fun-suicide, something really unusual which would bang the noddies when they found I had gotten away. I danced here in the darkness, almost the way I am dancing now, and I had taken about twelve different kinds of drugs, so that I was wild and free and very very receptive. That computer spoke to me, Sto Odin. *Your* computer, not mine. It spoke to me, and you know what it said?

"You might as well know, Sto Odin, because you are dying. You set your vitality high in order to fight me. I have made you stand still. Could I do that if I were a mere man? Look. I will turn solid again."

With a rainbow-like scream of chords and sounds, Sun-boy twisted the congohelium again until both the inner chamber and the outer bloomed with lights of a thousand colors and the deep underground air became drenched with music which seemed psychotic, because no human mind had ever invented it. The Lord Sto Odin, imprisoned in his own body with his two legionary-robots frozen half a pace behind him, wondered if he really were dying in vain and tried to guess whether he would be blinded and deafened by this dancer before he died. The congohelium twisted and shone before him.

Sun-boy danced backward over the bodies on the floor, danced backward with an odd cadenced run which looked as though he were plunging forward in a wild, competitive foot-race when the music and his own foot-steps carried him back, toward the center of the inner room. The figure jumped in an odd stance, face looking so far downward that Sun-boy might have been studying his own steps on the floor, the congohelium held above and behind his neck, legs lifting high in the cruel high-kneed prance.

The Lord Sto Odin thought he could hear the girl calling again, but he could not distinguish words.

The drums spoke again: *ritiplin, ritiplin, rataplan!* and then *kid-nork, kid-nork, kid-nork!*

The dancer spoke as the pandemonium subsided. He spoke, as his voice was high, strange, like a bad record-ing played on the wrong machine:

"The something is talking to you. You can talk."

The Lord Sto Odin found that his throat and lips moved. Quietly, secretly, like an old soldier, he tried his feet and fingers: these did not move. Only his voice could be used. He spoke, and he said the obvious:

"Who are you, *something?*"

Sun-boy looked across at Sto Odin. He stood erect and calm. Only his feet moved, and they did a wild, ag-ile little jig which did not affect the rest of his body. Ap-parently some kind of dance was necessary to keep the connection going between the unexplained reach of the Douglas-Ouyang planets, the piece of the congohelium, the more than human dancer and the tortured blissful fig-ures on the floor. The face, the face itself was quite com-posed and almost sad.

"I have been told," said Sun-boy, "to show you who I am."

He danced around the drums *rataplan, rataplan! kid-nork-nork, kid-nork, kid-nork-nork!*

He held the congohelium high and wrenched it so that a great moan came out. Sto Odin felt sure that a sound as wild and forlorn as that would be sure to reach the surface of the Earth many kilometers above, but his prudent judgment assured him that this was a fanciful thought gestated by his personal situation, and that any real sound strong enough to reach all the way to the surface would also be strong enough to bring the bruised and shattered rock of the ceiling pouring down upon their heads.

The congohelium ran down the colors of the spectrum until it stopped at a dark, wet liver-red, very close to black.

The Lord Sto Odin, in that momentary near silence, found that the entire story had been thrust into his mind without being strung out and articulated with words. The true history of this chamber had entered his memory sidewise, as it were. In one moment he knew nothing of it; in the next instance it was as if he had remembered the whole narrative for most of his life.

He also felt himself set free.

He stumbled backward three or four steps.

To his immense relief, his robots turned around, themselves free, and accompanied him. He let them put their hands in his armpits.

His face was suddenly covered with kisses.

His plastic cheek felt, thinly and dimly, the imprint, real and living, of female human lips. It was the odd girl —beautiful, bald, naked and golden-lipped—who had waited and shouted from the door.

Despite physical fatigue and the sudden shock of intruded knowledge, the Lord Sto Odin knew what he had to say.

"Girl, you shouted for me."

"Yes, my Lord."

"You have had the strength to watch the congohelium and not to give in to it?"

She nodded but said nothing.

"You have been strong-willed enough not to go into that room?"

"Not strong-willed, my Lord. I just love him, my man in there."

"You have waited, girl, for many months?"

"Not all the time. I go up the corridor when I have to eat or drink or sleep or do my personals. I even have mirrors and combs and tweezers and paint there, to make myself beautiful, the way that Sun-boy might want me."

The Lord Sto Odin looked over his shoulder. The music was low and keening with some emotions other than grief. The dancer was doing a long, slow dance, full of creeping and reaches, as he passed the congohelium from one hand to the other. "Do you hear me, dancer?" called the Lord Sto Odin, the Instrumentality once more coursing through his veins.

The dancer did not speak nor seem to change his course. But *kid-nork, kid-nork* said the little drum, quite unexpectedly.

"He, and the face behind him—they will let the girl leave if she really forgets him and this place in the act of leaving. Won't you?" said Sto Odin to the dancer.

Ritiplin, rataplan said the big drum, which had not sounded since Sto Odin was let free.

"But I don't want to go," said the girl.

"I know you don't want to go. You will go to please me. You can come back as soon as I have done my work." She stood mute so he continued.

"One of my robots, Livius, the one imprinted by a psychiatrist general, will run with you, but I command him to forget this place and all things connected with it. *Summa nulla est.* Have you heard me, Livius? You will run with this girl and you will forget. You will run and forget. You too will run and forget, Santuna my dear, but two Earthnychtherons from now you will remember just enough to come back here, should you wish to, should you need to. Otherwise you will go to the Lady Mmona and learn from her what you should do for the rest of your life."

"You are promising, my lord, that in two days and nights I can come back if I even feel like it."

"Now run, my girl, run. Run to the surface. Livius, carry her if you must. But run! run! run! More than she depends upon it."

Santuna looked at him very earnestly. Her nakedness

was innocence. The gold upper eyelids met the black lower eyelids as she blinked and then brushed away wet tears.

"Kiss me," she said, "and I will run."

He leaned down and kissed her.

She turned, looked back one last time at her dancer-lover, and then ran long-legged into the corridor. Livius ran after her, gracefully, untiringly. In twenty minutes they would be reaching the upper limits of the Gebiet.

"You know what I am doing?" said Sto Odin to the dancer.

This time the dancer and the force behind him did not deign to answer.

Said Sto Odin, "Water. There is water in a jug in my litter. Take me there, Flavius."

The robot-legionary took the aged and trembling Sto Odin to the litter.

8

The Lord Sto Odin then performed the trick which changed human history for many centuries to come and, in so doing, exploded an enormous cavern in the vitals of the Earth.

He used one of the most secret ruses of the Instrumentality.

He triple-thought.

Only a few very adept persons could triple-think, when they were given every possible chance of training. Fortunately for mankind, the Lord Sto Odin had been one of the successful ones.

He set three systems of thought into action. At the top level be behaved rationally as he explored the old room; at a lower level of his mind he planned a wild surprise for the dancer with the congohelium. But at the third, lowest level, he decided what he must do in the time of a single blink and trusted his autonomic nervous system to carry out the rest.

These are the commands he gave:

Flavius should be set on the wild-alert and readied for attack.

The computer should be reached and told to record the whole episode, everything which Sto Odin had learned, and should be shown how to take counter-measures while Sto Odin gave the matter no further conscious thought. The gestalt of action—the general frame of retaliation—was clear for thousandths of a second in Sto Odin's mind and then it dropped from sight.

The music rose to a roar.

White light covered Sto Odin.

"You meant me harm!" called Sun-boy from beyond the Gothic door.

"I meant you harm," Sto Odin acknowledged, "but it was a passing thought. I did nothing. You are watching me."

"I am watching you," said the dancer grimly. *Kid-nork, kid-nork* went the little drum. "Do not go out of my sight. When you are ready to come through my door, call me or just think of it. I will meet you and help you in."

"Good enough," said Lord Sto Odin.

Flavius still held him. Sto Odin concentrated on the melody which Sun-boy was creating, a wild new song never before suspected in the history of the world. He wondered if he could surprise the dancer by throwing his own song back at him. At the same instant, his fingers were performing a third set of actions which Sto Odin's mind no longer had to heed. Sto Odin's hand opened a lid in the robot's chest, right into the laminated controls of the brain. The hand itself changed certain adjustments, commanding that the robot should within the quarter-hour, kill all forms of life within reach other than the command-transmitter. Flavius did not know what had been done to him; Sto Odin did not even notice what his own hand had done.

"Take me over to the old computer," said Sto Odin to the robot Flavius. "I want to discover how the strange story which I have just learned may be true." Sto Odin kept thinking of music which would even startle the user of the congohelium.

He stood at the computer.

His hand, responding to the triple-think command which it had been given, turned the computer up and pressed the button, *Record this scene.* The computer's old relays almost grunted as they came to the alert and complied.

"Let me see the map," said Sto Odin to the computer.

Far behind him, the dancer had changed his pace into a fast jog-trot of hot suspicion.

The map appeared on the computer.

"Beautiful," said Sto Odin.

The entire labyrinth had become plain. Just above them was one of the ancient, sealed-off anti-seismic shafts—a straight, empty tubular shaft, two hundred meters wide, kilometers high. At the top, it had a lid which kept out the mud and water of the ocean floor. At the bottom, since there was no pressure other than air to worry about, it had been covered with a plastic which looked like rock, so that neither people nor robots which might be passing would try to climb into it.

"Watch what I am doing!" cried Sto Odin to the dancer.

"I am watching," said Sun-boy and there was almost a growl of perplexity in his sung-forth response.

Sto Odin shook the computer and ran the fingers of his right hand over it and coded a very specific request. His left hand—preconditioned by the triple-think—coded the emergency panel at the side of the computer with two simple, clear engineering instructions.

Sun-boy's laughter rang out behind him. "You are asking that a piece of the congohelium be sent down to you. Stop! Stop, before you sign it with your name and your authority as a lord of the Instrumentality. Your unsigned request will do no harm. The central computer up top will just think that it is some of the crazy people in the Bezirk making senseless demands." The voice rose to a note of urgency, "Why did the machine signal 'received and complied with' to you just now?"

The Lord Sto Odin lied blandly, "I don't know. Maybe they will send me a piece of the congohelium to match the one that you have there."

"You're lying," cried the dancer. "Come over here to the door."

Flavius led the Lord Sto Odin to the ridiculous-beautiful Gothic archway.

The dancer was leaping from foot to foot. The congo-helium shone a dull alert red. The music wept as though all the anger and suspicion of mankind had been incorporated into a new unforgettable fugue, like a delirious atonal counterpoint to Johann Sebastian Bach's *Third Brandenburg Concerto.*

"I am here." The Lord Sto Odin spoke easily.

"You are dying!" cried the dancer.

"I was dying before you first noticed me. I set my vitality control to maximum after I entered the Bezirk."

"Come on in, then," said Sun-boy, "and you will never die."

Sto Odin took the edge of the door and let himself down to the stone floor. Only when he was comfortably seated did he speak:

"I am dying, that is true. But I would rather not come in. I will just watch you dance as I die."

"What are you doing? What have you done?" cried Sun-boy. He stopped dancing and walked over to the door.

"Search me if you wish," said the Lord Sto Odin.

"I am searching you," said the dancer, "but I see nothing but your desire to get a piece of the congohelium for yourself and to out-dance me."

At this point Flavius went berserk. He ran back to the litter, leaned over, and ran toward the door. In each hand he carried an enormous solid-steel bearing.

"What's that robot doing?" cried the dancer. "I can see your mind but you are not telling him anything! He uses those steel balls to break obstructions—"

He gasped as the attack came.

Quicker than the eye could follow the movement, Flavius' sixty-ton-capacity arm whistled through the air as he flung the first steel missile directly at Sun-boy. Sun-boy, or the power within him, leapt aside with insect speed. The ball plowed through two of the rag-clothed human bodies on the floor. One body said *whoof!* as it died, but the other body let out no sound at all: the head had been torn off in first impact. Before the dancer could speak, Flavius flung the second ball.

This time the doorway caught it. The powers which had immobilized Sto Odin and his robots were back in operation. The ball sang as it plunged into the doorway, stopped in mid-air, sang again as the door flung it back at Flavius.

The returning ball missed Flavius' head but crushed his chest utterly. That was where his real brain was. There was a flicker of light as the robot went out, but even in dying Flavius seized the ball one last time and flung it at Sun-boy. The robot terminated operation and the heavy ball, flung wild, caught the Lord Sto Odin in the right shoulder. The Lord Sto Odin felt pain until he dragged over his manikin meee and turned all pain off. Then he looked at the shoulder. It was almost totally demolished. Blood from his organic body and hydraulic fluid from his prosthetics joined in a slow, heavy stream as the liquids met, merged and poured down his side.

The dancer almost forgot to dance.

Sto Odin wondered how far the girl had gone.

The air pressure changed.

"What is happening to the air? Why did you think about the girl? What is happening?"

"Read me," said the Lord Sto Odin.

"I will dance and get my powers first," said Sun-boy.

For a few brief minutes it seemed that the dancer with the congohelium would cause a rock-fall.

The Lord Sto Odin, dying, closed his eyes and found that it was restful to die. The blaze and noise of the world around him remained interesting, but had become unimportant.

The congohelium with a thousand shifting rainbows and the dancer had attained near-transparency when Sun-boy came back to read Sto Odin's mind.

"I see nothing," said Sun-boy worriedly. "Your vitality button is too high and you will die soon. Where is all that air coming from? I seem to hear a faraway roar. But you are not causing it. Your robot went wild. All you do is to look at me contentedly and die. That is very strange. You want to die your way when you could live unimaginable lives in here with us!"

"That is right," said the Lord Sto Odin. "I am dying my way. But dance for me, do dance for me with the congohelium, while I tell you your own story as you told it to me. It would be a pleasure to get the story straight before I die."

The dancer looked irresolute, started to dance, and then turned back to the Lord Sto Odin.

"Are you sure you want to die right away? With the power of what you call the Douglas-Ouyang planets, which I receive right here with the help of the congohelium, you could be comfortable enough while I danced and you could still die whenever you wished. Vitality buttons are much weaker than the powers which I command. I could even help to lift you across the threshold of my door . . ."

"No," said the Lord Sto Odin. "Just dance for me while I die. My way."

9

Thus the world turned. Millions of tons of water were rushing toward them.

Within minutes the Gebiet and the Bezirk would drown as the air whistled upward. Sto Odin noted contentedly that there was an air-shaft at the top of the dancer's room. He did not allow himself to third-think of what would happen when the matter and anti-matter of the congohelium were immersed in rushing salt water. Something like forty megatons, he supposed, with the tired feeling of a man who has thought a problem through long, long ago and remembers it briefly only after the situation has long passed.

Sun-boy was acting out religion before the age of space. He chorused hymns, he lifted his eyes and his hands and his piece of the congohelium to the sun; he played the rattle of whirling dervishes, the temple bells of the Man on the Two Pieces of Wood and the other temple bells of that saint who had escaped time simply by seeing it and stepping out of it. Buddha, was that his name? And he went on to the severe profanities which afflicted mankind after the Old World fell.

The music kept measure.

And the lights, too.

Whole processions of ghostly shadows followed Sun-boy as he showed how old mankind had found the gods, and the Sun, and then other gods. He pantomimed man's most ancient mystery—that man pretended to be afraid of death, when it was life that never understood it.

And as he danced, the Lord Sto Odin repeated his own story to him:

"You fled the surface, Sun-boy, because the people were stupid clods, happy and dull in their miserable happiness. You fled because you could not stand being a chicken in a poultry house, antiseptically bred, safely housed and frozen when dead. You joined the other miserable, bright restless people who sought freedom in the Gebiet. You learned about their drugs and their liquors and their smokes. You knew their women, and their parties, and their games. It wasn't enough. You became a gentleman-suicide, a hero seeking a fun-death which would stamp you with your individuality. You came on down to the Bezirk, the most forgotten and loathesome place of all. You found nothing. Just the old machines and the empty corridors. Here and there a few mummies or bones. Just the silent lights and the faint murmur of air through the corridors."

"I hear water now," said the dancer, still dancing, "rushing water. Don't you hear it, my dying Lord?"

"If I did hear it, I wouldn't care. Let's get on with your story. You came to this room. The weird door made it look like a good place for a fun-death, such as you poor castaways liked to seek, except that there was not much sport in dying unless other people know that you did it intentionally, and know how you did it. Anyway, it was a long climb back up into the Gebiet, where your friends were, so you slept by this computer.

"In the night, while you slept, as you dreamed, the computer sang to you:

> *I need a temporary dog*
> *For a temporary job*
> *On a temporary place*
> *Like Earth!*

When you woke up you were surprised to find that you had dreamed an entire new kind of music. Really wild music which made people shudder with its delicious evil. And with the music, you had a job. To steal a piece of the congohelium.

"You were a clever man, Sun-boy, before the trip down here. The Douglas-Ouyang planets caught you and made you a thousand times cleverer. You and your friends, this is what you told me—or what the presence behind you told me, just a half hour ago—you and your friends stole a subspace communicator console, got a fix on the Douglas-Ouyang planets, and got drunk at the sight. Iridescent, luminescent. Waterfalls uphill. All that kind of thing.

"And you did get the congohelium. The congohelium is made of matter and antimatter laminated apart by a dual magnetic grid. With that the presence of the Douglas-Ouyang planets made you independent of organic processes. You did not need food or rest or even air or drink any more. The Douglas-Ouyang planets are very old. They kept you as a link. I have no idea of what they intended to do with Earth and with mankind. If this story gets out, future generations will call you the merchant of menace, because you used the normal human appetitiousness for danger to trap other people with hypnotics and with music."

"I hear water," interrupted Sun-boy. "I *do* hear water!"

"Never mind," said the Lord Sto Odin, "your story is more important. Anyhow, what could you and I do about it? I am dying, sitting in a pool of blood and effluvium. You can't leave this room with the congohelium. Let me go on. Or perhaps the Douglas-Ouyang entity, whatever it was—"

"*Is*," said Sun-boy.

"—whatever it is, may just have been longing for sensuous companionship. Dance on, man, dance on."

Sun-boy danced and the drums talked with him, *rataplan, rataplan! kid-nork, kid-nork, nork!* while the congohelium made music scream through the solid rock.

The other sound persisted.

Sun-boy stopped and stared.

"It is water. It *is*."

"Who knows?" said the Lord Sto Odin.

"Look," screamed Sun-boy, holding the congohelium high. "Look!"

The Lord Sto Odin did not need to look. He knew full well that the first few tons of water, mud-laden and heavy, had come frothing down the corridor and into their rooms.

"But what do *I* do?" screamed the voice of Sun-boy. Sto Odin felt that it was not Sun-boy speaking, but some relay speaking from the power of the Douglas-Ouyang planets. A power which had tried to find friendship with man, but had found the wrong man and the wrong friendship.

Sun-boy took control of himself. His feet splashed in the water as he danced. The colors shone on the water as it rose. *Ritiplin, tiplin!* said the big drum. *Kid-nork, kid-nork,* said the little drum. *Boom, boom, doom, doom, room,* said the congohelium.

The Lord Sto Odin felt his old eyes blur but he could still see the blazing image of the wild dancer.

"This is a good way to die," thought he, as he died.

10

Far above, on the surface of the planet, Santuna felt the continent itself heave beneath her feet and saw the eastern horizon grow dark as a volcano of muddy steam shot up from the calm blue sunlit ocean.

"This must not, must *not* happen again!" she said, thinking of Sun-boy and the congohelium and the death of the Lord Sto Odin.

"Something must be done about it," she added to herself.

And she did it.

In later centuries she brought disease, risk and misery back to increase the happiness of man. She was one of the principal architects of the Rediscovery of Man, and at her most famous she was known as the Lady Alice More.

Mother Hitton's Littul Kittons

A rather oblique look at Old North Australia, source of the stroon by which men live four hundred years or more—a fabulously wealthy, and therefore well-defended world. The plot is taken partly from "Ali Baba and the Forty Thieves," and the action apparently occurs about a generation before that of Norstrilia—wherein Viola Siderea is still trying to recover from Bozart's escapade.

> *Poor communications deter theft;*
> *good communications promote theft;*
> *perfect communications stop theft.*
> Van Braam

1

THE MOON SPUN. The woman watched. Twenty-one facets had been polished at the moon's equator. Her function was to arm it. She was Mother Hitton, the weapons mistress of Old North Australia.

She was a ruddy-faced, cheerful blonde of indeterminate age. Her eyes were blue, her bosom heavy, her arms strong. She looked like a mother, but the only child she had ever had died many generations ago. Now she acted as mother to a planet, not to a person; the

Norstrilians slept well because they knew she was watching. The weapons slept their long, sick sleep.

This night she glanced for the two-hundredth time at the warning bank. The bank was quiet. No danger lights shone. Yet she felt an enemy out somewhere in the universe—an enemy waiting to strike at her and her world, to snatch at the immeasurable wealth of the Norstrilians —and she snorted with impatience. *Come along, little man,* she thought. *Come along, little man, and die. Don't keep me waiting.*

She smiled when she recognized the absurdity of her own thought.

She waited for him.

And he did not know it.

He, the robber, was relaxed enough. He was Benjacomin Bozart, and was highly trained in the arts of relaxation.

No one at Sunvale, here on Ttiollé, could suspect that he was a senior warden of the Guild of Thieves, reared under the light of the starry-violet star. No one could smell the odor of Viola Siderea upon him. "Viola Siderea," the Lady Ru had said, "was once the most beautiful of worlds and it is now the most rotten. Its people were once models for mankind, and now they are thieves, liars and killers. You can smell their souls in the open day." The Lady Ru had died a long time ago. She was much respected, but she was wrong. The robber did not smell to others at all. He knew it. He was no more "wrong" than a shark approaching a school of cod. Life's nature is to live, and he had been nurtured to live as he had to live—by seeking prey.

How else could he live? Viola Siderea had gone bankrupt a long time ago, when the photonic sails had disappeared from space and the planoforming ships began to whisper their way between the stars. His ancestors had been left to die on an off-trail planet. They refused to die. Their ecology shifted and they became predators upon man, adapted by time and genetics to their deadly tasks. And he, the robber, was champion of all his people—the best of their best.

He was Benjacomin Bozart.

He had sworn to rob Old North Australia or to die in the attempt, and he had no intention of dying.

The beach at Sunvale was warm and lovely. Ttiollé was a free and casual transit planet. His weapons were luck and himself: he planned to play both well.

The Norstrilians could kill.

So could he.

At this moment, in this place, he was a happy tourist at a lovely beach. Elsewhere, elsewhen, he could become a ferret among conies, a hawk among doves.

Benjacomin Bozart, thief and warden. He did not know that someone was waiting for him. Someone who did not know his name was prepared to waken death, just for him. He was still serene.

Mother Hitton was not serene. She sensed him dimly but could not yet spot him.

One of her weapons snored. She turned it over.

A thousand stars away, Benjacomin Bozart smiled as he walked toward the beach.

2

Benjacomin felt like a tourist. His tanned face was tranquil. His proud, hooded eyes were calm. His handsome mouth, even without its charming smile, kept a suggestion of pleasantness at its corners. He looked attractive without seeming odd in the least. He looked much younger than he actually was. He walked with springy, happy steps along the beach of Sunvale.

The waves rolled in, white-crested, like the breakers of Mother Earth. The Sunvale people were proud of the way their world resembled Manhome itself. Few of them had ever seen Manhome, but they had all heard a bit of history and most of them had a passing anxiety when they thought of the ancient government still wielding political power across the depth of space. They did not like the old Instrumentality of Earth, but they respected and feared it. The waves might remind them of the pretty side of Earth; they did not want to remember the not-so-pretty side.

This man was like the pretty side of old Earth. They could not sense the power within him. The Sunvale people smiled absently at him as he walked past them along the shoreline.

The atmosphere was quiet and everything around him serene. He turned his face to the sun. He closed his eyes. He let the warm sunlight beat through his eyelids, illuminating him with its comfort and its reassuring touch.

Benjacomin dreamed of the greatest theft that any man had ever planned. He dreamed of stealing a huge load of the wealth from the richest world that mankind had ever built. He thought of what would happen when he would finally bring riches back to the planet of Viola Siderea where he had been reared. Benjacomin turned his face away from the sun and languidly looked over the other people on the beach.

There were no Norstrilians in sight yet. They were easy enough to recognize. Big people with red complexions; superb athletes and yet, in their own way, innocent, young and very tough. He had trained for this theft for two hundred years, his life prolonged for the purpose by the Guild of Thieves on Viola Siderea. He himself embodied the dreams of his own planet, a poor planet once a crossroads of commerce, now sunken to being a minor outpost for spoliation and pilferage.

He saw a Norstrilian woman come out from the hotel and go down to the beach. He waited, and he looked, and he dreamed. He had a question to ask and no adult Australian would answer it.

"Funny," thought he, "that I call them 'Australians' even now. That's the old, old Earth name for them—rich, brave, tough people. Fighting children standing on half the world . . . and now they are the tyrants of all mankind. They hold the wealth. They have the santa-clara, and other people live or die depending upon the commerce they have with the Norstrilians. But I won't. And my people won't. We're men who are wolves to man."

Benjacomin waited gracefully. Tanned by the light of many suns, he looked forty though he was two hundred. He dressed casually, by the standards of a vacationer.

He might have been an intercultural salesman, a senior gambler, an assistant starport manager. He might even have been a detective working along the commerce lanes. He wasn't. He was a thief. And he was so good a thief that people turned to him and put their property in his hands because he was reassuring, calm, gray-eyed, blond-haired. Benjacomin waited. The woman glanced at him, a quick glance full of open suspicion.

What she saw must have calmed her. She went on past. She called back over the dune, "Come on, Johnny, we can swim out here." A little boy, who looked eight or ten years old, came over the dune top, running toward his mother.

Benjacomin tensed like a cobra. His eyes became sharp, his eyelids narrowed.

This was the prey. Not too young, not too old. If the victim had been too young he wouldn't know the answer; if the victim were too old it was no use taking him on. Norstrilians were famed in combat; adults were mentally and physically too strong to warrant attack.

Benjacomin knew that every thief who had approached the planet of the Norstrilians—who had tried to raid the dream world of Old North Australia—had gotten out of contact with his people and had died. There was no word of any of them.

And yet he knew that hundreds of thousands of Norstrilians must know *the* secret. They now and then made jokes about it. He had heard these jokes when he was a young man, and now he was more than an old man without once coming near the answer. Life was expensive. He was well into his third lifetime and the lifetimes had been purchased honestly by his people. Good thieves all of them, paying out hard-stolen money to obtain the medicine to let their greatest thief remain living. Benjacomin didn't like violence. But when violence prepared the way to the greatest theft of all time, he was willing to use it.

The woman looked at him again. The mask of evil which had flashed across his face faded into benignity; he calmed. She caught him in that moment of relaxation. She liked him.

She smiled and, with that awkward hesitation so characteristic of the Norstrilians, she said, "Could you mind my boy a bit while I go in the water? I think we've seen each other here at the hotel."

"I don't mind," said he. "I'd be glad to. Come here, son."

Johnny walked across the sunlight dunes to his own death. He came within reach of his mother's enemy.

But the mother had already turned.

The trained hand of Benjacomin Bozart reached out. He seized the child by the shoulder. He turned the boy toward him, forcing him down. Before the child could cry out, Benjacomin had the needle into him with the truth drug.

All Johnny reacted to was pain, and then a hammer-blow inside his own skull as the powerful drug took force.

Benjacomin looked out over the water. The mother was swimming. She seemed to be looking back at them. She was obviously unworried. To her, the child seemed to be looking at something the stranger was showing him in a relaxed, easy way.

"Now, sonny," said Benjacomin, "tell me, what's the outside defense?"

The boy didn't answer.

"What is the outer defense, sonny? What is the outer defense?" repeated Benjacomin. The boy still didn't answer.

Something close to horror ran over the skin of Benjacomin Bozart as he realized that he had gambled his safety on this planet, gambled the plans themselves for a chance to break the secret of the Norstrilians.

He had been stopped by simple, easy devices. The child had already been conditioned against attack. Any attempt to force knowledge out of the child brought on a conditioned reflex of total muteness. The boy was literally unable to talk.

Sunlight gleaming on her wet hair, the mother turned around and called back, "Are you all right, Johnny?"

Benjacomin waved to her instead. "I'm showing him my pictures, ma'am. He likes 'em. Take your time." The mother hesitated and then turned back to the water and swam slowly away.

Johnny, taken by the drug, sat lightly, like an invalid, on Benjacomin's lap.

Benjacomin said, "Johnny, you're going to die now and you will hurt terribly if you don't tell me what I want to know." The boy struggled weakly against his grasp. Benjacomin repeated. "I'm going to hurt you if you don't tell me what I want to know. What are the outer defenses? What are the outer defenses?"

The child struggled and Benjacomin realized that the boy was putting up a fight to comply with the orders, not a fight to get away. He let the child slip through his hands and the boy put out a finger and began writing on the wet sand. The letters stood out.

A man's shadow loomed behind them.

Benjacomin, alert, ready to spin, kill or run, slipped to the ground beside the child and said, "That's a jolly puzzle. That is a good one. Show me some more." He smiled up at the passing adult. The man was a stranger. The stranger gave him a very curious glance which became casual when he saw the pleasant face of Benjacomin, so tenderly and so agreeably playing with the child.

The fingers were still making the letters in the sand.

There stood the riddle in letters: MOTHER HITTON'S LITTUL KITTONS.

The woman was coming back from the sea, the mother with questions. Benjacomin stroked the sleeve of his coat and brought out his second needle, a shallow poison which it would take days or weeks of laboratory work to detect. He thrust it directly into the boy's brain, slipping the needle up behind the skin at the edge of the hairline. The hair shadowed the tiny prick. The incredibly hard needle slipped under the edge of the skull. The child was dead.

Murder was accomplished. Benjacomin casually erased the secret from the sand. The woman came nearer. He called to her, his voice full of pleasant concern, "Ma'am, you'd better come here, I think your son has fainted from the heat."

He gave the mother the body of her son. Her face changed to alarm. She looked frightened and alert. She didn't know how to meet this.

For a dreadful moment she looked into his eyes.

Two hundred years of training took effect . . . She saw nothing. The murderer did not shine with murder. The hawk was hidden beneath the dove. The heart was masked by the trained face.

Benjacomin relaxed in professional assurance. He had been prepared to kill her too, although he was not sure that he could kill an adult, female Norstrilian. Very helpfully said he, "You stay here with him. I'll run to the hotel and get help. I'll hurry."

He turned and ran. A beach attendant saw him and ran toward him. "The child's sick," he shouted. He came to the mother in time to see blunt, puzzled tragedy on her face and with it, something more than tragedy: doubt.

"He's not sick," said she. "He's dead."

"He can't be." Benjacomin looked attentive. He felt attentive. He forced the sympathy to pour out of his posture, out of all the little muscles of his face. "He can't be. I was talking to him just a minute ago. We were doing little puzzles in the sand."

The mother spoke with a hollow, broken voice that sounded as though it would never find the right chords for human speech again, but would go on forever with the ill-attuned flats of unexpected grief. "He's dead," she said. "You saw him die and I guess I saw him die, too. I can't tell what's happened. The child was full of santaclara. He had a thousand years to live but now he's dead. What's your name?"

Benjacomin said, "Eldon. Eldon the salesman, ma'am. I live here lots of times."

3

"Mother Hitton's littul kittons. Mother Hitton's littul kittons."

The silly phrase ran in his mind. Who was Mother Hitton? Who was she the mother of? What were *kittons?* Were they a misspelling for "kittens?" Little cats? Or were they something else?

Had he killed a fool to get a fool's answer?

How many more days did he have to stay there with the doubtful, staggered woman? How many days did he have to watch and wait? He wanted to get back to Viola Siderea; to take the secret, bad as it was, for his people to study. Who was Mother Hitton?

He forced himself out of his room and went downstairs.

The pleasant monotony of a big hotel was such that the other guests looked interestedly at him. He was the man who had watched while the child died on the beach.

Some lobby-living scandalmongers that stayed there had made up fantastic stories that he had killed the child. Others attacked the stories, saying they knew perfectly well who Eldon was. He was Eldon the salesman. It was ridiculous.

People hadn't changed much, even though the ships with the Go-captains sitting at their hearts whispered between the stars, even though people shuffled between worlds—when they had the money to pay their passage back and forth—like leaves falling in soft, playful winds. Benjacomin faced a tragic dilemma. He knew very well that any attempt to decode the answer would run directly into the protective devices set up by the Norstrilians.

Old North Australia was immensely wealthy. It was known the length and breadth of all the stars that they had hired mercenaries, defensive spies, hidden agents and alerting devices.

Even Manhome—Mother Earth herself, whom no money could buy—was bribed by the drug of life. An ounce of the santaclara drug, reduced, crystallized and called "stroon," could give forty to sixty years of life. Stroon entered the rest of the Earth by ounces and pounds, but it was refined back on North Australia by the ton. With treasure like this, the Norstrilians owned an unimaginable world whose resources overreached all conceivable limits of money. They could buy anything. They could pay with other peoples' lives.

For hundreds of years they had given secret funds to buying foreigners' services to safeguard their own security.

Benjacomin stood there in the lobby: "Mother Hitton's littul kittons."

He had all the wisdom and wealth of a thousand worlds stuck in his mind but he didn't dare ask anywhere as to what it meant.

Suddenly he brightened.

He looked like a man who had thought of a good game to play, a pleasant diversion to be welcomed, a companion to be remembered, a new food to be tasted. He had had a very happy thought.

There was one source that wouldn't talk. The library. He could at least check the obvious, simple things, and find out what there was already in the realm of public knowledge concerning the secret he had taken from the dying boy.

His own safety had not been wasted, Johnny's life had not been thrown away, if he could find any one of the four words as a key. *Mother* or *Hitton* or *Littul*, in its special meaning, or *Kitton*. He might yet break through to the loot of Norstrilia.

He swung jubilantly, turning on the ball of his right foot. He moved lightly and pleasantly toward the billiard room, beyond which lay the library. He went in.

This was a very expensive hotel and very old-fashioned. It even had books made out of paper, with genuine bindings. Benjacomin crossed the room. He saw that they had the *Galactic Encyclopedia* in two hundred volumes. He took down the volume headed "Hi-Hi." He opened it from the rear, looking for the name "Hitton" and there it was. "Hitton, Benjamin—pioneer of old North Australia. Said to be originator of part of the defense system. Lived A.D. 10719-17213." That was all. Benjacomin moved among the books. The word "kittons" in that peculiar spelling did not occur anywhere, neither in the encyclopedia nor in any other list maintained by the library. He walked out and upstairs, back to his room.

"Littul" had not appeared at all. It was probably the boy's own childish mistake.

He took a chance. The mother, half blind with bewilderment and worry, sat in a stiff-backed chair on the edge of the porch. The other women talked to her. They knew her husband was coming. Benjacomin went up to her and tried to pay his respects. She didn't see him.

"I'm leaving now, ma'am. I'm going on to the next planet, but I'll be back in two or three subjective weeks. And if you need me for urgent questions, I'll leave my addresses with the police here."

Benjacomin left the weeping mother.

Benjacomin left the quiet hotel. He obtained a priority passage.

The easy-going Sunvale Police made no resistance to his demand for a sudden departure visa. After all, he had an identity, he had his own funds, and it was not the custom of Sunvale to contradict its guests. Benjacomin went on the ship and as he moved toward the cabin in which he could rest for a few hours, a man stepped up beside him. A youngish man, hair parted in the middle, short of stature, gray of eyes.

This man was the local agent of the Norstrilian secret police.

Benjacomin, trained thief that he was, did not recognize the policeman. It never occurred to him that the library itself had been attuned and that the word "kittons" in the peculiar Norstrilian spelling was itself an alert. Looking for that spelling had set off a minor alarm. He had touched the trip-wire.

The stranger nodded. Benjacomin nodded back. "I'm a traveling man, waiting over between assignments. I haven't been doing very well. How are you making out?"

"Doesn't matter to me. I don't earn money; I'm a technician. Liverant is the name."

Benjacomin sized him up. The man was a technician all right. They shook hands perfunctorily. Liverant said, "I'll join you in the bar a little later. I think I'll rest a bit first."

They both lay down then and said very little while the momentary flash of planoform went through the ship. The flash passed. From books and lessons they knew that the ship was leaping forward in two dimensions while, somehow or other, the fury of space itself was fed into the computers—and that these in turn were managed by the Go-captain who controlled the ship.

They knew these things but they could not feel them.
All they felt was the sting of a slight pain.

The sedative was in the air itself, sprayed in the ventilating system. They both expected to become a little drunk.

The thief Benjacomin Bozart was trained to resist intoxication and bewilderment. Any sign whatever that a telepath had tried to read his mind would have been met with fierce animal resistance, implanted in his unconscious during early years of training. Bozart was not trained against deception by a technician; it never occurred to the Thieves' Guild back on Viola Siderea that it would be necessary for their own people to resist deceivers. Liverant had already been in touch with Norstrilia—Norstrilia whose money reached across the stars, Norstrilia who had alerted a hundred thousand worlds against the mere thought of trespass.

Liverant began to chatter. "I wish I could go further than this trip. I wish that I could go to Olympia. You can buy anything in Olympia."

"I've heard of it," said Bozart. "It's sort of a funny trading planet with not much chance for businessmen, isn't it?"

Liverant laughed and his laughter was merry and genuine. "Trading? They don't trade. They swap. They take all the stolen loot of a thousand worlds and sell it over again and they change and they paint it and they mark it. That's their business there. The people are blind. It's a strange world, and all you have to do is to go in there and you can have anything you want. Man," said Liverant, "what I could do in a year in that place! Everybody is blind except me and a couple of tourists. And there's all the wealth that everybody thought he's mislaid, half the wrecked ships, the forgotten colonies (they've all been cleaned out) and bang! it all goes to Olympia."

Olympia wasn't really that good and Liverant didn't know why it was his business to guide the killer there. All he knew was that he had a duty and the duty was to direct the trespasser.

Many years before either man was born the code word had been planted in directories, in books, in packing cases and invoices: *Kittons* misspelled. This was the

cover name for the outer moon of Norstrilian defense.
The use of the cover name brought a raging alert ready
into action, with systemic nerves as hot and quick as incandescent tungsten wire.

By the time that they were ready to go to the bar and
have refreshments, Benjacomin had half forgotten that it
was his new acquaintance who had suggested Olympia
rather than another place. He had to go to Viola Siderea
to get the credits to make the flight to take the wealth, to
win the world of Olympia.

4

At home on his native planet Bozart was a subject of
a gentle but very sincere celebration.

The elders of the Guild of Thieves welcomed him.
They congratulated him. "Who else could have done
what you've done, boy? You've made the opening move
in a brand new game of chess. There has never been a
gambit like this before. We have a name; we have an
animal. We'll try it right here." The Thieves' Council
turned to their own encyclopedia. They turned through
the name "Hitton" and then found the reference "kitton." None of them knew that a false lead had been
planted there—by an agent in their world.

The agent, in his turn, had been seduced years before,
debauched in the middle of his career, forced into temporary honesty, blackmailed and sent home. In all the
years that he had waited for a dreaded countersign—a
countersign which he himself never knew to be an ex-
tension of Norstrilian intelligence—he never dreamed
that he could pay his debt to the outside world so simply. All they had done was to send him one page to add
to the encyclopedia. He added it and then went home,
weak with exhaustion. The years of fear and waiting
were almost too much for the thief. He drank heavily
for fear that he might otherwise kill himself. Meanwhile,
the pages remained in order, including the new one,
slightly altered for his colleagues. The encyclopedia in-
dicated the change like any normal revision, though the
whole entry was new and falsified:

Beneath this passage one revision ready. Dated 24th year of second issue.

The reported "Kittons" of Norstrilia are nothing more than the use of organic means to induce the disease in Earth-mutated sheep which produces a virus in its turn, refinable as the santaclara drug. The term "Kittons" enjoyed a temporary vogue as a reference term both to the disease and to the destructibility of the disease in the event of external attack. This is believed to have been connected with the career of Benjamin Hitton, one of the original pioneers of Norstrilia.

The Council of Thieves read it and the Chairman of the Council said, "I've got your papers ready. You can go try them now. Where do you want to go? Through Neuhamburg?"

"No," said Benjacomin. "I thought I'd try Olympia."

"Olympia's all right," said the chairman. "Go easy. There's only one chance in a thousand you'll fail. But if you do, we might have to pay for it."

He smiled wryly and handed Benjacomin a blank mortgage against all the labor and all the property of Viola Siderea.

The Chairman laughed with a sort of snort. "It'd be pretty rough on us if you had to borrow enough on the trading planet to force us to become honest—and then lost out anyhow."

"No fear," said Benjacomin. "I can cover that."

There are some worlds where all dreams die, but square-clouded Olympia is not one of them. The eyes of men and women are bright on Olympia, for they see nothing.

"Brightness was the color of pain," said Nachtigall, "when we could see. If thine eye offend thee, pluck thyself out, for the fault lies not in the eye but in the soul."

Such talk was common in Olympia, where the settlers went blind a long time ago and now think themselves superior to sighted people. Radar wires tickle their living brains; they can perceive radiation as well as can an animal-type man with little aquariums hung in the middle of his face. Their pictures are sharp, and they demand sharpness. Their buildings soar at impossible angles. Their blind children sing songs as the tailored climate proceeds according to the numbers, geometrical as a kaleidoscope.

There went the man, Bozart himself. Among the blind his dreams soared, and he paid money for information which no living person had ever seen.

Sharp-clouded and aqua-skied, Olympia swam past him like another man's dream. He did not mean to tarry there, because he had a rendezvous with death in the sticky, sparky space around Norstrilia.

Once in Olympia, Benjacomin went about his arrangements for the attack on Old North Australia. On his second day on the planet he had been very lucky. He met a man named Lavender and he was sure he had heard the name before. Not a member of his own Guild of Thieves, but a daring rascal with a bad reputation among the stars.

It was no wonder that he had found Lavender. His pillow had told him Lavender's story fifteen times during his sleep in the past week. And, whenever he dreamed, he dreamed dreams which had been planted in his mind by the Norstrilian counterintelligence. They had beaten him in getting to Olympia first and they were prepared to let him have only that which he deserved. The Norstrilian Police were not cruel, but they were out to defend their world. And they were also out to avenge the murder of a child.

The last interview which Benjacomin had with Lavender in striking a bargain before Lavender agreed was a dramatic one.

Lavender refused to move forward.

"I'm not going to jump off anywhere. I'm not going to raid anything. I'm not going to steal anything. I've been rough, of course I have. But I don't get myself killed and that's what you're bloody well asking for."

"Think of what we'll have. The wealth. I tell you, there's more money here than anything else anybody's ever tried."

Lavender laughed. "You think I haven't heard that before? You're a crook and I'm a crook. I don't do anything that's speculation. I want my hard cash down. I'm a fighting man and you're a thief and I'm not going to ask you what you're up to . . . but I want my money first."

"I haven't got it," said Benjacomin.

Lavender stood up.

"Then you shouldn't have talked to me. Because it's going to cost you money to keep me quiet whether you hire me or not."

The bargaining process started.

Lavender looked ugly indeed. He was a soft, ordinary man who had gone to a lot of trouble to become evil. Sin is a lot of work. The sheer effort it requires often shows in the human face.

Bozart stared him down, smiling easily, not even contemptuously.

"Cover me while I get something from my pocket," said Bozart.

Lavender did not even acknowledge the comment. He did not show a weapon. His left thumb moved slowly across the outer edge of his hand. Benjacomin recognized the sign, but did not flinch.

"See," he said. "A planetary credit."

Lavender laughed. "I've heard that, too."

"Take it," said Bozart.

The adventurer took the laminated card. His eyes widened. "It's real," he breathed. "It is real." He looked up, incalculably more friendly. "I never even saw one of these before. What are your terms?"

Meanwhile the bright, vivid Olympians walked back and forth past them, their clothing all white and black in dramatic contrast. Unbelievable geometric designs shone on their cloaks and their hats. The two bargainers ignored the natives. They concentrated on their own negotiations.

Benjacomin felt fairly safe. He placed a pledge of one year's service of the entire planet of Viola Siderea in exchange for the full and unqualified services of Captain Lavender, once of the Imperial Marines Internal Space Patrol. He handed over the mortgage. The year's guarantee was written in. Even on Olympia there were accounting machines which relayed the bargain back to

Earth itself, making the mortgage a valid and binding commitment against the whole planet of thieves.

"This," thought Lavender, "was the first step of revenge." After the killer had disappeared his people would have to pay with sheer honesty. Lavender looked at Banjacomin with a clinical sort of concern.

Benjacomin mistook his look for friendliness and Benjacomin smiled his slow, charming, easy smile. Momentarily happy, he reached out his right hand to give Lavender a brotherly solemnification of the bargain. The men shook hands, and Bozart never knew with what he shook hands.

5

"Gray lay the land oh. Gray grass from sky to sky. Not near the weir, dear. Not a mountain, low or high—only hills and gray gray. Watch the dappled, dimpled twinkles blooming on the star bar.

"That is Norstrilia.

"All the muddy gubbery is gone—all the work and the waiting and the pain.

"Beige-brown sheep lie on blue-gray grass while the clouds rush past, low overhead, like iron pipes ceilinging the world.

"Take your pick of sick sheep, man, it's the sick that pays. Sneeze me a planet, man, or cough me up a spot of immortality. If it's barmy there, where the noddies and the trolls like you live, it's too right here.

"That's the book, boy.

"If you haven't seen Norstrilia, you haven't seen it. If you did see it, you wouldn't believe it.

"Charts call it Old North Australia."

Here in the heart of the world was the farm which guarded the world. This was the Hitton place.

Towers surrounded it, and wires hung between the towers, some of them drooping crazily and some gleaming with the sheen not shown by any other metal made by men from Earth. Within the towers there was open land. And within the open land there were twelve thousand hectares of concrete. Radar reached down to within millimeter smoothness of the surface of the concrete and the other radar threw patterns back and forth, down through molecular thinness. The farm went on. In its center there was a group of buildings. That was where Katherine Hitton worked on the task which her family had accepted for the defense of her world.

No germ came in, no germ went out. All the food came in by space transmitter. Within this, there lived animals. The animals depended on her alone. Were she to die suddenly, by mischance or as a result of an attack by one of the animals, the authorities of her world had complete facsimiles of herself with which to train new animal tenders under hypnosis.

This was a place where the gray wind leapt forward released from the hills, where it raced across the gray concrete, where it blew past the radar towers. The polished, faceted, captive moon always hung due overhead. The wind hit the buildings, themselves gray, with the impact of a blow, before it raced over the open concrete beyond and whistled away into the hills.

Outside the buildings, the valley had not needed much camouflage. It looked like the rest of Norstrilia. The concrete itself was tinted very slightly to give the impression of poor, starved, natural soil. This was the farm, and this the woman. Together they were the outer defense of the richest world mankind had ever built.

Katherine Hitton looked out the window and thought to herself, "Forty-two days before I go to market and it's a welcome day that I get there and hear the jig of a music.

> Oh, to walk on market day,
> And see my people proud and gay!

She breathed deeply of the air. She loved the gray hills—though in her youth she had seen many other worlds. And then she turned back into the building to the animals and the duties which awaited her. She was the only Mother Hitton and these were her littul kittons.

She moved among them. She and her father had bred them from Earth mink, from the fiercest, smallest, craziest little minks that had ever been shipped out from

Manhome. Out of these minks they had made their lives to keep away other predators who might bother the sheep on whom the stroon grew. But these minks were born mad.

Generations of them had been bred psychotic to the bone. They lived only to die and they died so that they could stay alive. These were the kittons of Norstrilia. Animals in whom fear, rage, hunger and sex were utterly intermixed; who could eat themselves or each other; who could eat their young, or people, or anything organic; animals who screamed with murder-lust when they felt love; animals born to loathe themselves with a fierce and livid hate and who survived only because their waking moments were spent on couches, strapped tight, claw by claw, so that they could not hurt each other or themselves. Mother Hitton let them waken only a few moments in each lifetime. They bred and killed. She wakened them only two at a time.

All that afternoon she moved from cage to cage. The sleeping animals slept well. The nourishment ran into their blood streams; they lived sometimes for years without awaking. She bred them when the males were only partly awakened and the females aroused only enough to accept her veterinary treatments. She herself had to pluck the young away from their mothers as the sleeping mothers begot them. Then she nourished the young through a few happy weeks of kittonhood, until their adult natures began to take, their eyes ran red with madness and heat and their emotions sounded in the sharp, hideous, little cries they uttered through the building; and the twisting of their neat, furry faces, the rolling of their crazy, bright eyes and the tightening of their sharp, sharp claws.

She woke none of them this time. Instead, she tightened them in their straps. She removed the nutrients. She gave them delayed stimulus medicine which would, when they were awakened, bring them suddenly full waking with no lulled stupor first.

Finally, she gave herself a heavy sedative, leaned back in a chair and waited for the call which would come.

When the shock came and the call came through, she

would have to do what she had done thousands of times before.

She would ring an intolerable noise through the whole laboratory.

Hundreds of the mutated minks would awaken. In awakening, they would plunge into life with hunger, with hate, with rage and with sex; plunge against their straps; strive to kill each other, their young, themselves, her. They would fight everything and everywhere, and do everything they could to keep going.

She knew this.

In the middle of the room there was a tuner. The tuner was a direct, empathic relay, capable of picking up the simpler range of telepathic communications. Into this tuner went the concentrated emotions of Mother Hitton's littul kittons.

The rage, the hate, the hunger, the sex were all carried far beyond the limits of the tolerable, and then all were thereupon amplified. And then the waveband on which this telepathic control went out was amplified, right there beyond the studio, on the high towers that swept the mountain ridge, up and beyond the valley in which the laboratory lay. And Mother Hitton's moon, spinning geometrically, bounced the relay into a hollow englobement.

From the faceted moon, it went to the satellites—sixteen of them, apparently part of the weather control system. These blanketed not only space, but nearby subspace. The Nostrilians had thought of everything.

The short shocks of an alert came from Mother Hitton's transmitter bank.

A call came. Her thumb went numb.

The noise shrieked.

The mink awakened.

Immediately, the room was full of chattering, scraping, hissing, growling and howling.

Under the sound of the animal voices, there was the other sound: a scratchy, snapping sound like hail falling on a frozen lake. It was the individual claws of hundreds of mink trying to tear their way through metal panels.

Mother Hitton heard a gurgle. One of the minks had succeeded in tearing its paw loose and had obviously started to work on its own throat. She recognized the tearing fur, the ripping of veins.

She listened for the cessation of that individual voice, but she couldn't be sure. The others were making too much noise. One mink less.

Where she sat, she was partly shielded from the telepathic relay, but not altogether. She herself, old as she was, felt queer wild dreams go through her. She thrilled with hate as she thought of beings suffering out beyond her—suffering terribly, since they were not masked by the built-in defenses of the Norstrilian communications system.

She felt the wild throb of long-forgotten lust.

She hungered for things she had not known she remembered. She went through the spasms of fear that the hundreds of animals expressed.

Underneath this, her sane mind kept asking, "How much longer can I take it? How much longer must I take it? Lord God, be good to your people here on this world! Be good to poor old me."

The green light went on.

She pressed a button on the other side of her chair. The gas hissed in. As she passed into unconsciousness, she knew that her kittons passed into instant unconsciousness too.

She would waken before they did and then her duties would begin: checking the living ones, taking out the one that had clawed out its own throat, taking out those who had died of heart attacks, re-arranging them, dressing their wounds, treating them alive and asleep—asleep and happy—breeding, living in their sleep—until the next call should come to waken them for the defense of the treasures which blessed and cursed her native world.

6

Everything had gone exactly right. Lavender had found an illegal planoform ship. This was no inconsequential accomplishment, since planoform ships were very strictly licensed and obtaining an illegal one was a chore on which a planet full of crooks could easily have worked a lifetime.

Lavender had been lavished with money—Benjacomin's money.

The honest wealth of the thieves' planet had gone in and had paid the falsifications and great debts, imaginary transactions that were fed to the computers for ships and cargoes and passengers that would be almost untraceably commingled in the commerce of ten thousand worlds.

"Let him pay for it," said Lavender, to one of his confederates, an apparent criminal who was also a Norstrilian agent. "This is paying good money for bad. You better spend a lot of it."

Just before Benjacomin took off Lavender sent on an additional message.

He sent it direstly through the Go-captain, who usually did not carry messages. The Go-captain was a relay commander of the Norstrilian fleet, but he had been carefully ordered not to look like it.

The message concerned the planoform license—another twenty-odd tablets of stroon which could mortgage Viola Siderea for hundreds upon hundreds of years. The captain said: "I don't have to send that through. The answer is yes."

Benjacomin came into the control room. This was contrary to regulations, but he had hired the ship to violate regulations.

The captain looked at him sharply. "You're a passenger, get out."

Benjacomin said: "You have my little yacht on board. I am the only man here outside of your people."

"Get out. There's a fine if you're caught here."

"It does not matter," Benjacomin said. "I'll pay it."

"You will, will you?" said the Captain. "You would not be paying twenty tablets of stroon. That's ridiculous. Nobody could get that much stroon."

Benjacomin laughed, thinking of the thousands of tablets he would soon have. All he had to do was to leave the planoform ship behind, strike once, go past the kittons and come back.

His power and his wealth came from the fact that he

knew he could now reach it. The mortgage of twenty tablets of stroon against this planet was a low price to pay if it would pay off at thousands to one. The Captain replied: "It's not worth it, it just is not worth risking twenty tablets for your being here. But I can tell you how to get inside the Norstrilian communications net if that is worth twenty-seven tablets."

Benjacomin went tense.

For a moment he thought he might die. All this work, all this training—the dead boy on the beach, the gamble with the credit, and now this unsuspected antagonist!

He decided to face it out. "What do you know?" said Benjacomin.

"Nothing," said the Captain.

"You said 'Norstrilia.'"

"That I did," said the Captain.

"If you said Norstrilia, you must have guessed it. Who told you?"

"Where else would a man go if you look for infinite riches? If you get away with it. Twenty tablets is nothing to a man like you."

"It's two hundred years' worth of work from three hundred thousand people," said Benjacomin grimly.

"When you get away with it, you will have more than twenty tablets, and so will your people."

And Benjacomin thought of the thousands and thousands of tablets. "Yes, that I know."

"If you don't get away with it, you've got the card."

"That's right. All right. Get me inside the net. I'll pay the twenty-seven tablets."

"Give me the card."

Benjacomin refused. He was a trained thief, and he was alert to thievery. Then he thought again. This was the crisis of his life. He had to gamble a little on somebody.

He had to wager the card. "I'll mark it and then I'll give it back to you." Such was his excitement that Benjacomin did not notice that the card went into a duplicator, that the transaction was recorded, that the message went back to Olympic Center, that the loss and the mortgage against the planet of Viola Siderea should be credited to certain commercial agencies in Earth for three hundred years to come.

Benjacomin got the card back. He felt like an honest thief.

If he did die, the card would be lost and his people would not have to pay. If he won, he could pay that little bit out of his own pocket.

Benjacomin sat down. The Go-captain signalled to his pinlighters. The ship lurched.

For half a subjective hour they moved, the Captain wearing a helmet of space upon his head, sensing and grasping and guessing his way, stepping stone to stepping stone, right back to his home. He had to fumble the passage, or else Benjacomin might guess that he was in the hands of double agents.

But the captain was well trained. Just as well trained as Benjacomin.

Agents and thieves, they rode together.

They planoformed inside the communications net. Benjacomin shook hands with them. "You are allowed to materialize as soon as I call."

"Good luck, Sir," said the Captain.

"Good luck to me," said Benjacomin.

He climbed into his space yacht. For less than a second in real space, the gray expanse of Norstrilia loomed up. The ship which looked like a simple warehouse disappeared into planoform, and the yacht was on its own.

The yacht dropped.

As it dropped, Benjacomin had a hideous moment of confusion and terror.

He never knew the woman down below but she sensed him plainly as he received the wrath of the much-amplified kittons. His conscious mind quivered under the blow. With a prolongation of subjective experience which made one or two seconds seem like months of hurt drunken bewilderment, Benjacomin Bozart swept beneath the tide of his own personality. The moon relay threw minkish minds against him. The synapses of his brain re-formed to conjure up might-have-beens, terrible things that never happened to any man. Then his knowing mind whited out in an overload of stress.

His subcortical personality lived on a little longer.

His body fought for several minutes. Mad with lust and hunger, the body arched in the pilot's seat, the mouth bit deep into his own arm. Driven by lust, the left hand tore at his face, ripping out his left eyeball. He screeched with animal lust as he tried to devour himself . . . not entirely without success.

The overwhelming telepathic message of Mother Hitton's littul kittons ground into his brain.

The mutated minks were fully awake.

The relay satellites had poisoned all the space around him with the craziness to which the minks were bred.

Bozart's body did not live long. After a few minutes, the arteries were open, the head slumped forward and the yacht was dropping helplessly toward the warehouses which it had meant to raid. Norstrilian police picked it up.

The police themselves were ill. All of them were ill. All of them were white-faced. Some of them had vomited. They had gone through the edge of the mink defense. They had passed through the telepathic band at its thinnest and weakest point. This was enough to hurt them badly.

They did not want to know.

They wanted to forget.

One of the younger policemen looked at the body and said, "What on earth could do that to a man?"

"He picked the wrong job," said the police captain.

The young policeman said: "What's the wrong job?"

"The wrong job is trying to rob us, boy. We are defended, and we don't want to know how."

The young policeman, humiliated and on the verge of anger, looked almost as if he would defy his superior, while keeping his eyes away from the body of Benjacomin Bozart.

The older man said: "It's all right. He did not take long to die and this is the man who killed the boy Johnny, not very long ago."

"Oh, him? So soon?"

"We brought him." The old police officer nodded. "We let him find his death. That's how we live. Tough, isn't it?"

The ventilators whispered softly, gently. The animals slept again. A jet of air poured down on Mother Hitton. The telepathic relay was still on. She could feel herself, the sheds, the faceted moon, the little satellites. Of the robber there was no sign.

She stumbled to her feet. Her raiment was moist with perspiration. She needed a shower and fresh clothes . . .

Back at Manhome, the Commercial Credit Circuit called shrilly for human attention. A junior subchief of the Instrumentality walked over to the machine and held out his hand.

The machine dropped a card neatly into his fingers. He looked at the card.

"Debit Viola Siderea—credit Earth Contingency—subcredit Norstrilian account—four hundred million man megayears."

Though all alone, he whistled to himself in the empty room. "We'll all be dead, stroon or no stroon, before they finish paying that!" He went off to tell his friends the odd news.

The machine, not getting its card back, made another one.

Alpha Ralpha Boulevard

Here we see the very beginning of the Rediscovery of Man—the great undertaking of Lord Jestocost and Lady Alice More—to restore man's right to freedom: to risk, to uncertainty and even to death. The Storm, a painting by Pierre-Auguste Côt inspired the scene on Alpha Ralpha Boulevard—Macht is, perhaps, one of the evil Vomacts; but perhaps not. And the Abbadingo, perplexingly, may be a bastardized Semitic-cum-Aussie slang for "Father of Lies . . ."

WE WERE DRUNK with happiness in those early years. Everybody was, especially the young people. These were the first years of the Rediscovery of Man, when the Instrumentality dug deep in the treasury, reconstructing the old cultures, the old languages, and even the old troubles. The nightmare of perfection had taken our forefathers to the edge of suicide. Now under the leadership of the Lord Jestocost and the Lady Alice More, the ancient civilizations were rising like great land masses out of the sea of the past.

I myself was the first man to put a postage stamp on a letter, after fourteen thousand years. I took Virginia to hear the first piano recital. We watched at the eye-machine when cholera was released in Tasmania, and we saw the Tasmanians dancing in the streets, now that they did not have to be protected any more. Everywhere, things became exciting. Everywhere, men and women worked with a wild will to build a more imperfect world.

I myself went into a hospital and came out French. Of course I remembered my early life; I remembered it, but it did not matter. Viginia was French, too, and we had the years of our future lying ahead of us like ripe fruit hanging in an orchard of perpetual summers. We had no idea when we would die. Formerly, I would be able to go to bed and think, "The government has given me four hundred years. Three hundred and seventy-four years from now, they will stop the stroon injections and I will then die." Now I knew anything could happen. The safety devices had been turned off. The diseases ran free. With luck, and hope, and love, I might live a thousand years. Or I might die tomorrow. I was free.

We revelled in every moment of the day.

Virginia and I brought the first French newspaper to appear since the Most Ancient World fell. We found delight in the news, even in the advertisements. Some parts of the culture were hard to reconstruct. It was difficult to talk about foods of which only the names survived, but the homunculi and the machines, working tirelessly in Downdeep-downdeep, kept the surface of the world filled with enough novelties to fill anyone's heart with hope. We knew that all of this was make-believe, and yet it was not. We knew that when the diseases had killed the statistically correct number of people, they would be turned off; when the accident rate rose too high, it would stop without our knowing why. We knew that over us all, the Instrumentality watched. We had confidence that the Lord Jestocost and the Lady Alice More would play with us as friends and not use us as victims of a game.

Take, for example, Virginia. She had been called Menerima, which represented the coded sounds of her birth number. She was small, verging on chubby; she was compact; her head was covered with tight brown curls; her eyes were a brown so deep and so rich that it took sunlight, with her squinting against it, to bring forth the treasures of her irises. I had known her well, but never known her. I had seen her often, but never seen her with my heart, until we met just outside the hospital, after becoming French.

I was pleased to see an old friend and started to speak in the Old Common Tongue, but the words jammed, and as I tried to speak it was not Menerima any longer, but someone of ancient beauty, rare and strange—someone who had wandered into these latter days from the treasure worlds of time past. All I could do was to stammer:

"What do you call yourself now?" And I said it in ancient French.

She answered in the same language, "Je m'appelle Virginie."

Looking at her and falling in love was a single process. There was something strong, something wild in her, wrapped and hidden by the tenderness and youth of her girlish body. It was as though destiny spoke to me out of the certain brown eyes, eyes which questioned me surely and wonderingly, just as we both questioned the fresh new world which lay about us.

"May I?" said I, offering her my arm, as I had learned in the hours of hypnopedia. She took my arm and we walked away from the hospital.

I hummed a tune which had come into my mind, along with the ancient French language.

She tugged gently on my arm, and smiled up at me.

"What is it," she asked, "or don't you know?"

The words came soft and unbidden to my lips and I sang it very quietly, muting my voice in her curly hair, half-singing half-whispering the popular song which had poured into my mind with all the other things which the Rediscovery of Man had given me:

> She wasn't the woman I went to seek.
> I met her by the merest chance.
> She did not speak the French of France,
> But the surded French of Martinique.
>
> She wasn't rich. She wasn't chic.
> She had a most entrancing glance,
> And that was all . . .

Suddenly I ran out of words, "I seem to have forgotten the rest of it. It's called 'Macouba' and it has something to do with a wonderful island which the ancient French called Martinique."

"I know where that is," she cried. She had been given the same memories that I had. "You can see it from Earthport!"

This was a sudden return to the world we had known. Earthport stood on its single pedestal, twelve miles high, at the eastern edge of the small continent. At the top of it, the lords worked amid machines which had no meaning any more. There the ships whispered their way in from the stars. I had seen pictures of it, but I had never been there. As a matter of fact, I had never known anyone who had actually been up Earthport. Why should we have gone? We might not have been welcome, and we could always see it just as well through the pictures on the eye-machine. For Menerima—familiar, dully pleasant, dear little Menerima—to have gone there was uncanny. It made me think that in the Old Perfect World things had not been as plain or forthright as they seemed.

Virginia, the new Menerima, tried to speak in the Old Common Tongue, but she gave up and used French instead:

"My aunt," she said, meaning a kindred lady, since no one had had aunts for thousands of years, "was a Believer. She took me to the Abba-dingo. To get holiness and luck."

The old me was a little shocked; the French me was disquieted by the fact that this girl had done something unusual even before mankind itself turned to the unusual. The Abba-dingo was a long-obsolete computer set part way up the column of Earthport. The homunculi treated it as a god, and occasionally people went to it. To do so was tedious and vulgar.

Or had been. Till all things became new again.

Keeping the annoyance out of my voice, I asked her: "What was it like?"

She laughed lightly, yet there was a trill to her laughter which gave me a shiver. If the old Menerima had had secrets, what might the new Virginia do? I almost hated the fate which made me love her, which made me feel that the touch of her hand on my arm was a link between me and time-forever.

She smiled at me instead of answering my question. The surfaceway was under repair; we followed a ramp down to the level of the top underground, where it was legal for true persons and hominids and homunculi to walk.

I did not like the feeling; I had never gone more than twenty minutes' trip from my birthplace. This ramp looked safe enough. There were few hominids around these days, men from the stars who (though of true human stock) had been changed to fit the conditions of a thousand worlds. The homunculi were morally repulsive, though many of them looked like very handsome people; bred from animals into the shape of men, they took over the tedious chores of working with machines where no real man would wish to go. It was whispered that some of them had even bred with actual people, and I would not want my Virginia to be exposed to the presence of such a creature.

She had been holding my arm. When we walked down the ramp to the busy passage, I slipped my arm free and put it over her shoulders, drawing her closer to me. It was light enough, bright enough to be clearer than the daylight which we had left behind, but it was strange and full of danger. In the old days, I would have turned around and gone home rather than to expose myself to the presence of such dreadful beings. At this time, in this moment, I could not bear to part from my new-found love, and I was afraid that if I went back to my own apartment in the tower, she might go to hers. Anyhow, being French gave a spice to danger.

Actually, the people in the traffic looked commonplace enough. There were many busy machines, some in human form and some not. I did not see a single hominid. Other people, whom I knew to be homunculi because they yielded the right of way to us, looked no different from the real human beings on the surface. A brilliantly beautiful girl gave me a look which I did not like—saucy, intelligent, provocative beyond all limits of flirtation. I suspected her of being a dog by origin. Among the homunculi, d'persons are the ones most apt to take liberties. They even have a dog-man philosopher who once produced a tape arguing that since dogs are the most ancient of men's allies, they have the right to be closer to man than any other form of life. When I saw the tape, I thought it amusing that a dog should be bred into the form of a Socrates; here, in the top underground, I was not so sure at all. What would I do if one of them became insolent? Kill him? That meant a brush with the law and a talk with the subcommissioners of the Instrumentality.

Virginia noticed none of this.

She had not answered my question, but was asking me questions about the top underground instead. I had been there only once before, when I was small, but it was flattering to have her wondering, husky voice murmuring in my ear.

Then it happened.

At first I thought he was a man, foreshortened by some trick of the underground light. When he came closer, I saw that it was not. He must have been five feet across the shoulders. Ugly red scars on his forehead showed where the horns had been dug out of his skull. He was a humunculus, obviously derived from cattle stock. Frankly, I had never known that they left them that ill-formed.

And he was drunk.

As he came closer I could pick up the buzz of his mind. . . . *they're not people, they're not hominids, and they're not Us—what are they doing here? The words they think confuse me.* He had never telepathed French before.

This was bad. For him to talk was common enough, but only a few of the humunculi were telepathic—those with special jobs, such as in the Downdeep-downdeep, where only telepathy could relay instructions.

Virginia clung to me.

Thought I, in clear Common Tongue: *True men are we. You must let us pass.*

There was no answer but a roar. I do not know where he got drunk, or on what, but he did not get my message.

I could see his thoughts forming up into panic, help-lessness, hate. Then he charged, almost dancing toward us, as though he could crush our bodies.

My mind focused and I threw the stop order at him. It did not work.

Horror-stricken, I realized that I had thought French at him.

Virginia screamed.

The bull-man was upon us.

At the last moment he swerved, passed us blindly, and let out a roar which filled the enormous passage. He had raced beyond us.

Still holding Virginia, I turned around to see what had made him pass us.

What I beheld was odd in the extreme.

Our figures ran down the corridor away from us—my black-purple cloak flying in the still air as my image ran, Virginia's golden dress swimming out behind her as she ran with me. The images were perfect and the bull-man pursued them.

I stared around in bewilderment. We had been told that the safeguards no longer protected us.

A girl stood quietly next to the wall. I had almost mistaken her for a statue. Then she spoke,

"Come no closer. I am a cat. It was easy enough to fool him. You had better get back to the surface."

"Thank you," I said, "thank you. What is your name?"

"Does it matter?" said the girl. "I'm not a person."

A little offended, I insisted, "I just wanted to thank you." As I spoke to her I saw that she was as beautiful and as bright as a flame. Her skin was clear, the color of cream, and her hair—finer than any human hair could possibly be—was the wild golden orange of a Persian cat.

"I'm C'mell," said the girl, "and I work at Earth-port."

That stopped both Virginia and me. Cat-people were below us, and should be shunned, but Earthport was above us, and had to be respected. Which was C'mell?

She smiled, and her smile was better suited for my eyes than for Virginia's. It spoke a whole world of vo-

luptous knowledge. I knew she wasn't trying to do anything to me; the rest of her manner showed that. Perhaps it was the only smile she knew.

"Don't worry," she said, "about the formalities.
You'd better take these steps here. I hear him coming
back."

I spun around, looking for the drunken bull-man. He
was not to be seen.

"Go up here," urged C'mell, "They are emergency
steps and you will be back on the surface. I can keep
him from following. Was that French you were speaking?"

"Yes," said I. "How did you—?"

"Get along," she said. "Sorry I asked. Hurry!"

I entered the small door. A spiral staircase went to
the surface. It was below our dignity as true people to
use steps, but with C'mell urging me, there was nothing
else I could do. I nodded goodbye to C'mell and drew
Virginia after me up the stairs.

At the surface we stopped.

Virginia gasped, "Wasn't it horrible?"

"We're safe now," said I.

"It's not safety," she said. "It's the dirtiness of it. Imagine having to talk to her!"

Virginia meant that C'mell was worse than the drunken bull-man. She sensed my reserve because she said,

"The sad thing is, you'll see her again . . ."

"What! How do you know that?"

"I don't know it," said Virginia. "I guess it. But I
guess good, very good. After all, I went to the Abba-
dingo."

"I asked you, darling, to tell me what happened
there."

She shook her head mutely and began walking down
the streetway. I had no choice but to follow her. It made
me a little irritable.

I asked again, more crossly, "What was it like?"

With hurt girlish dignity she said, "Nothing, nothing.
It was a long climb. The old woman made me go with
her. It turned out that the machine was not talking that
day, anyhow, so we got permission to drop down a shaft

and to come back on the rolling road. It was just a wasted day."

She had been talking straight ahead, not to me, as though the memory were a little ugly.

Then she turned her face to me. The brown eyes looked into my eyes as though she were searching for my soul. (Soul. There's a word we have in French, and there is nothing quite like it in the Old Common Tongue.) She brightened and pleaded with me:

"Let's not be dull on the new day. Let's be good to the new us, Paul. Let's do something really French, if that's what we are to be."

"A café," I cried. "We need a café. And I know where one is."

"Where?"

"Two undergrounds over. Where the machines come out and where they permit the homunculi to peer in the window." The thought of homunculi peering at us struck the new me as amusing, though the old me had taken them as much for granted as windows or tables. The old me never met any, but knew that they weren't exactly people, since they were bred from animals, but they looked just about like people, and they could talk. It took a Frenchman like the new me to realize that they could be ugly, or beautiful, or picturesque. More than picturesque: romantic.

Evidently Virginia now thought the same, for she said, "But they're *nette,* just adorable. What is the café called?"

"The Greasy Cat," said I.

The Greasy Cat. How was I to know that this led to a nightmare between high waters, and to the winds which cried? How was I to suppose that this had anything to do with Alpha Ralpha Boulevard?

No force in the world could have taken me there, if I had known.

Other new-French people had gotten to the café before us.

A waiter with a big brown moustache took our order. I looked closely at him to see if he might be a licensed homunculus, allowed to work among people because his services were indispensable; but he was not. He was pure machine, though his voice rang out with old-Parisian heartiness, and the designers had even built into him the nervous habit of mopping the back of his hand against his big moustache, and had fixed him so that little beads of sweat showed high up on his brow, just below the hairline.

"Mamselle? M'sieu? Beer? Coffee? Red wine next month. The sun will shine in the quarter after the hour and after the half-hour. At twenty minutes to the hour it will rain for five minutes so that you can enjoy these umbrellas. I am a native of Alsace. You may speak French or German to me."

"Anything," said Virginia. "You decide, Paul."

"Beer, please," said I. "Blonde beer for both of us."

"But certainly, M'sieu," said the waiter.

He left, waving his cloth wildly over his arm.

Virginia puckered up her eyes against the sun and said, "I wish it would rain now. I've never seen real rain."

"Be patient, honey."

She turned earnestly to me. "What is 'German,' Paul?"

"Another language, another culture. I read they will bring it to life next year. But don't you like being French?"

"I like it fine," she said. "Much better than being a number. But Paul—" And then she stopped, her eyes blurred with perplexity.

"Yes, darling?"

"Paul," she said, and the statement of my name was a cry of hope from some depth of her mind beyond new me, beyond old me, beyond even the contrivances of the lords who moulded us. I reached for her hand.

Said I, "You can tell me, darling."

"Paul," she said, and it was almost weeping, "Paul, why does it all happen so fast? This is our first day, and we both feel that we may spend the rest of our lives together. There's something about marriage, whatever that is, and we're supposed to find a priest, and I don't understand that, either. Paul, Paul, Paul, why does it happen so fast? I want to love you. I do love you. But I don't want to be *made* to love you. I want it to be the

real me," and as she spoke, tears poured from her eyes
though her voice remained steady enough.

Then it was that I said the wrong thing.

"You don't have to worry, honey. I'm sure that the
lords of the Instrumentality have programmed everything well."

At that, she burst into tears, loudly and uncontrollably. I had never seen an adult weep before. It was strange
and frightening.

A man from the next table came over and stood beside me, but I did not so much as glance at him.

"Darling," said I, reasonably, "darling, we can work
it out—"

"Paul, let me leave you, so that I may be yours. Let
me go away for a few days or a few weeks or a few
years. Then, if—if—if I *do* come back, you'll know it's
me and not some program ordered by a machine. For
God's sake, Paul—for God's sake!" In a different voice
she said, "What is God, Paul? They gave us the words
to speak, but I do not know what they mean."

The man beside me spoke. "I can take you to God,"
he said.

"Who are you?" said I. "And who asked you to interfere?" This was not the kind of language that we had
ever used when speaking the Old Common Tongue—
when they had given us a new language they had built in
temperament as well.

The stranger kept his politeness—he was as French as
we but he kept his temper well.

"My name," he said, "is Maximilien Macht, and I
used to be a Believer."

Virginia's eyes lit up. She wiped her face absent-
mindedly while staring at the man. He was tall, lean, sunburned. (How could he have gotten sunburned so
soon?) He had reddish hair and a moustache almost like
that of the robot waiter.

"You asked about God, Mamselle," said the stranger.
"God is where he has always been—around us, near us,
in us."

This was strange talk from a man who looked world-
ly. I rose to my feet to bid him goodbye. Virginia
guessed what I was doing and she said:

"That's nice of you, Paul. Give him a chair."

There was warmth in her voice.

The machine waiter came back with two conical beakers made of glass. They had a golden fluid in them with a cap of foam on top. I had never seen or heard of beer before, but I knew exactly how it would taste. I put imaginary money on the tray, received imaginary change, paid the waiter an imaginary tip. The Instrumentality had not yet figured out how to have separate kinds of money for all the new cultures, and of course you could not use real money to pay for food or drink. Food and drink are free.

The machine wiped his moustache, used his serviette (checked red and white) to dab the sweat off his brow, and then looked inquiringly at Monsieur Macht.

"M'sieu, you will sit here?"

"Indeed," said Macht.

"Shall I serve you here?"

"But why not?" said Macht. "If these good people permit."

"Very well," said the machine, wiping his moustache with the back of his hand. He fled to the dark recesses of the bar.

All this time Virginia had not taken her eyes off Macht.

"You are a Believer?" she asked. "You are still a Believer, when you have been made French like us? How do you know you're you? Why do I love Paul? Are the lords and their machines controlling everything in us? I want to be *me*. Do you know how to be *me?*"

"Not you, Mamselle," said Macht, "that would be too great an honor. But I am learning how to be myself. You see," he added, turning to me, "I have been French for two weeks now, and I know how much of me is myself, and how much has been added by this new process of giving us language and danger again."

The waiter came back with a small beaker. It stood on a stem, so that it looked like an evil little miniature of Earthport. The fluid it contained was milky white.

Macht lifted his glass to us. "Your health!"

Virginia stared at him as if she were going to cry again. When he and I sipped, she blew her nose and put her handkerchief away. It was the first time I had ever seen a person perform that act of blowing the nose, but it seemed to go well with our new culture.

Macht smiled at both of us, as if he were going to begin a speech. The sun came out, right on time. It gave him a halo, and made him look like a devil or a saint.

But it was Virginia who spoke first.

"You have been there?"

Macht raised his eyebrows a little, frowned, and said, "Yes," very quietly.

"Did you get a word?" she persisted.

"Yes." He looked glum, and a little troubled.

"What did it say?"

For answer, he shook his head at her, as if there were things which should never be mentioned in public.

I wanted to break in, to find out what this was all about.

Virginia went on, heeding me not at all: "But it did say something!"

"Yes," said Macht.

"Was it important?"

"Mamselle, let us not talk about it."

"We must," she cried. "It's life or death." Her hands were clenched so tightly together that her knuckles showed white. Her beer stood in front of her, untouched, growing warm in the sunlight.

"Very well," said Macht, "you may ask . . . I cannot guarantee to answer."

I controlled myself no longer. "What's all this about?"

Virginia looked at me with scorn, but even her scorn was the scorn of a lover, not the cold remoteness of the past. "Please, Paul, you wouldn't know. Wait a while. What did it say to you, M'sieu Macht?"

"That I, Maximilien Macht, would live or die with a brown-haired girl who was already betrothed." He smiled wrily, "And I do not even quite know what 'betrothed' means."

"We'll find out," said Virginia. "When did it say this?"

"Who is 'it'?" I shouted at them. "For God's sake, what is this all about?"

Macht looked at me and dropped his voice when he spoke: "The Abba-dingo." To her he said, "Last week."

Virginia turned white. "So it does work, it does, it does. Paul darling, it said nothing to me. But it said to my aunt something which I can't ever forget!"

I held her arm firmly and tenderly and tried to look into her eyes, but she looked away. Said I, "What did it say?"

"Paul and Virginia."

"So what?" said I.

I scarcely knew her. Her lips were tense and compressed. She was not angry. It was something different, worse. She was in the grip of tension. I suppose we had not seen that for thousands of years, either. "Paul, seize this simple fact, if you can grasp it. The machine gave that woman our names—but it gave them to her twelve years ago."

Macht stood up so suddenly that his chair fell over, and the waiter began running toward us.

"That settles it," he said. "We're all going back."

"Going where?" I said.

"To the Abba-dingo."

"But why now?" said I; and, "Will it work?" said Virginia, both at the same time.

"It always works," said Macht, "if you go on the northern side."

"How do you get there?" said Virginia.

Macht frowned sadly, "There's only one way. By Alpha Ralpha Boulevard." Virginia stood up. And so did I.

Then, as I rose, I remembered. Alpha Ralpha Boulevard. It was a ruined street hanging in the sky, faint as a vapor trail. It had been a processional highway once, where conquerors came down and tribute went up. But it was ruined, lost in the clouds, closed to mankind for a hundred centuries.

"I know it," said I. "It's ruined."

Macht said nothing, but he stared at me as if I were an outsider . . .

Virginia, very quiet and white of countenance, said, "Come along."

"But why?" said I. "Why?"

"You fool," she said, "if we don't have a God, at least

we have a machine. This is the only thing left on or off the world which the Instrumentality doesn't understand. Maybe it tells the future. Maybe it's an un-machine. It certainly comes from a different time. Can't you use it, darling? If it says we're us, we're *us*."

"And if it doesn't?"

"Then we're not." Her face was sullen with grief.

"What do you mean?"

"If we're not us," she said, "we're just toys, dolls, puppets that the lords have written on. You're not you and I'm not me. But if the Abba-dingo, which knew the names Paul and Virginia twelve years before it happened—if the Abba-dingo says that we are us, I don't care if it's a predicting machine or a god or a devil or a what. I don't care, but I'll have the truth."

What could I have answered to that? Macht led, she followed, and I walked third in single file. He left the sunlight of The Greasy Cat; just as we left, a light rain began to fall. The waiter, looking momentarily like the machine that he was, stared straight ahead. We crossed the lip of the underground and went down to the fast expressway.

When we came out, we were in a region of fine homes. All were in ruins. The trees had thrust their way into the buildings. Flowers rioted across the lawn, through the open doors, and blazed in the roofless rooms. Who needed a house in the open, when the population of Earth had dropped so that the cities were commodious and empty?

Once I thought I saw a family of homunculi, including little ones, peering at me as we trudged along the soft gravel road. Maybe the faces I had seen at the edge of the house were fantasies.

Macht said nothing.

Virginia and I held hands as we walked beside him. I could have been happy at this odd excursion, but her hand was tightly clenched in mine. She bit her lower lip from time to time. I knew it mattered to her—she was on a pilgrimage. (A pilgrimage was an ancient walk to some powerful place, very good for body and soul.) I didn't mind going along. In fact, they could not have kept me from coming, once she and Macht decided to leave the café. But I didn't have to take it seriously. Did I?

What did Macht want?

Who was Macht? What thoughts had that mind learned in two short weeks? How had he preceded us into a new world of danger and adventure? I did not trust him. For the first time in my life I felt alone. Always, always, up to now, I had only to think about the Instrumentality and some protector leaped fully armed into my mind. Telepathy guarded against all dangers, healed all hurts, carried each of us forward to the one hundred and forty-six thousand and ninety-seven days which had been allotted us. Now it was different. I did not know this man, and it was on him that I relied, not on the powers which had shielded and protected us.

We turned from the ruined road into an immense boulevard. The pavement was so smooth and unbroken that nothing grew on it, save where the wind and dust had deposited random little pockets of earth.

Macht stopped.

"This is it," he said. "Alpha Ralpha Boulevard."

We fell silent and looked at the causeway of forgotten empires.

To our left the boulevard disappeared in a gentle curve. It led far north of the city in which I had been reared. I knew that there was another city to the north, but I had forgotten its name. Why should I have remembered it? It was sure to be just like my own.

But to the right—

To the right the boulevard rose sharply, like a ramp. It disappeared into the clouds. Just at the edge of the cloud-line there was a hint of disaster. I could not see for sure, but it looked to me as though the whole boulevard had been sheared off by unimaginable forces. Somewhere beyond the clouds there stood the Abbadingo, the place where all questions were answered . . .

Or so they thought.

Virginia cuddled close to me.

"Let's turn back," said I. "We are city people. We don't know anything about ruins."

"You can if you want to," said Macht. "I was just trying to do you a favor."

We both looked at Virginia.

She looked up at me with those brown eyes. From the eyes there came a plea older than woman or man, older than the human race. I knew what she was going to say before she said it. She was going to say that she *had* to know.

Macht was idly crushing some soft rocks near his foot.

At last Virginia spoke up: "Paul, I don't want danger for its own sake. But I meant what I said back there. Isn't there a chance that we were *told* to love each other? What sort of a life would it be if our happiness, our own selves, depended on a thread in a machine or on a mechanical voice which spoke to us when we were asleep and learning French? It may be fun to go back to the old world. I guess it is. I know that you give me a kind of happiness which I never even suspected before this day. If it's really us, we have something wonderful, and we ought to know it. But if it isn't—" She burst into sobs.

I wanted to say, "If it isn't, it will seem just the same," but the ominous sulky face of Macht looked at me over Virginia's shoulder as I drew her to me. There was nothing to say.

I held her close.

From beneath Macht's foot there flowed a trickle of blood. The dust drank it up."

"Macht," said I, "are you hurt?"

Virginia turned around, too.

Macht raised his eyebrows at me and said with unconcern, "No. Why?"

"The blood. At your feet."

He glanced down. "Oh, those," he said, "they're nothing. Just the eggs of some kind of an un-bird which does not even fly."

"Stop it!" I shouted telepathically, using the Old Common Tongue. I did not even try to think in our new-learned French.

He stepped back a pace in surprise.

Out of nothing there came to me a message: *thankyou thankyou goodgreat gohomeplease thankyou goodgreat goaway manbad manbad manbad* . . . Somewhere an animal or bird was warning me against Macht. I thought a casual *thanks* to it and turned my attention to Macht.

He and I stared at each other. Was this what *culture* was? Were we now men? Did freedom always include the freedom to mistrust, to fear, to hate?

I liked him not at all. The words of forgotten crimes came into my mind: *assassination, murder, abduction, insanity, rape, robbery* . . .

We had known none of these things and yet I felt them all.

He spoke evenly to me. We had both been careful to guard our minds against being read telepathically, so that our only means of communication were empathy and French. "It's your idea," he said, most untruthfully, "or at least your lady's . . ."

"Has lying already come into the world," said I, "so that we walk into the clouds for no reason at all?"

"There is a reason," said Macht.

I pushed Virginia gently aside and capped my mind so tightly that the anti-telepathy felt like a headache.

"Macht," said I, and I myself could hear the snarl of an animal in my own voice, "tell me why you have brought us here or I will kill you."

He did not retreat. He faced me, ready for a fight. He said, "Kill? You mean, to make me dead?" but his words did not carry conviction. Neither one of us knew how to fight, but he readied for defense and I for attack.

Underneath my thought shield an animal thought crept in: *goodman goodman take him by the neck no-air he-aaah no-air he-aaah like broken egg* . . .

I took the advice without worrying where it came from. It was simple. I walked over to Macht, reached my hands around his throat and squeezed. He tried to push my hands away. Then he tried to kick me. All I did was hang on to his throat. If I had been a lord or a Go-captain, I might have known about fighting. But I did not, and neither did he.

It ended when a sudden weight dragged at my hands. Out of surprise, I let go.

Macht had become unconscious. Was that *dead?*

It could not have been, because he sat up. Virginia

ran to him. He rubbed his throat and said with a rough voice:

"You should not have done that."

This gave me courage. "Tell me," I spat at him, "tell me why you wanted us to come, or I will do it again."

Macht grinned weakly. He leaned his head against Virginia's arm. "It's fear," he said. "Fear."

"Fear?" I knew the word—*peur*—but not the meaning. Was it some kind of disquiet or animal alarm?

I had been thinking with my mind open; he thought back *yes*.

"But why do you like it?" I asked.

It is delicious, he thought. *It makes me sick and thrilly and alive. It is like strong medicine, almost as good as stroon. I went there before. High up, I had much fear. It was wonderful and bad and good, all at the same time. I lived a thousand years in a single hour. I wanted more of it, but I thought it would be even more exciting with other people.*

"Now I will kill you," said I in French. "You are very —very . . ." I had to look for the word. "You are very evil."

"No," said Virginia, "let him talk."

He thought at me, not bothering with words. *This is what the lords of the Instrumentality never let us have. Fear. Reality. We were born in a stupor and we died in a dream. Even the underpeople, the animals, had more life than we did. The machines did not have fear. That's what we were. Machines who thought they were men. And now we are free.*

He saw the edge of raw, red anger in my mind, and he changed the subject. *I did not lie to you. This is the way to the Abba-dingo. I have been there. It works. On this side, it always works.*

"It works," cried Virginia. "You see he says so. It works! He is telling the truth. Oh, Paul, do let's go on!"

"All right," said I, "we'll go."

I helped him rise. He looked embarrassed, like a man who has shown something of which he is ashamed.

We walked onto the surface of the indestructible boulevard. It was comfortable to the feet.

At the bottom of my mind the little unseen bird or

animal babbled its thoughts at me: *goodman goodman make him dead take water take water . . .*

I paid no attention as I walked forward with her and him, Virginia between us. I paid no attention.

I wish I had.

We walked for a long time.

The process was new to us. There was something exhilarating in knowing that no one guarded us, that the air was free air, moving without benefit of weather machines. We saw many birds, and when I thought at them I found their minds startled and opaque; they were natural birds, the like of which I had never seen before. Virginia asked me their names, and I outrageously applied all the bird-names which we had learned in French without knowing whether they were historically right or not.

Maximilien Macht cheered up, too, and he even sang us a song, rather off key, to the effect that we would take the high road and he the low one, but that he would be in Scotland before us. It did not make sense, but the lilt was pleasant. Whenever he got a certain distance ahead of Virginia and me, I made up variations on "Macouba" and sang-whispered the phrases into her pretty ear:

> *She wasn't the woman I went to seek.*
> *I met her by the merest chance.*
> *She did not speak the French of France,*
> *But the surded French of Martinique.*

We were happy in adventure and freedom, until we became hungry. Then our troubles began.

Virginia stepped up to a lamp-post, struck it lightly with her fist and said, "Feed me." The post should either have opened, serving us a dinner, or else told us where, within the next few hundred yards, food was to be had. It did neither. It did nothing. It must have been broken.

With that, we began to make a game of hitting every single post.

Alpha Ralpha Boulevard had risen about half a kilometer above the surrounding countryside. The wild birds wheeled below us. There was less dust on the pavement, and fewer patches of weeds. The immense road, with no pylons below it, curved like an unsupported ribbon into the clouds.

We wearied of beating posts and there was neither food nor water.

Virginia became fretful: "It won't do any good to go back now. Food is even farther the other way. I do wish you'd brought something."

How should I have thought to carry food? Who ever carries food? Why would they carry it, when it is everywhere? My darling was unreasonable, but she was my darling and I loved her all the more for the sweet imperfections of her temper.

Macht kept tapping pillars, partly to keep out of our fight, and obtained an unexpected result.

At one moment I saw him leaning over to give the pillar of a large lamp the usual hearty but guarded *whop* —in the next instant he yelped like a dog and was sliding uphill at a high rate of speed. I heard him shout something, but could not make out the words, before he disappeared into the clouds ahead.

Virginia looked at me. "Do you want to go back now? Macht is gone. We can say that I got tired."

"Are you serious?"

"Of course, darling."

I laughed, a little angrily. She had insisted that we come, and now she was ready to turn around and give it up, just to please me.

"Never mind," said I. "It can't be far now. Let's go on."

"Paul . . ." She stood close to me. Her brown eyes were troubled, as though she were trying to see all the way into my mind through my eyes. I thought to her, *Do you want to talk this way?*

"No," said she, in French. "I want to say things one at a time. Paul, I do want to go to the Abba-dingo. I need to go. It's the biggest need in my life. But at the same time. I don't want to go. There is something wrong up there. I would rather have you on the wrong terms than not have you at all. Something could happen."

Edgily, I demanded, "Are you getting this 'fear' that Macht was talking about?"

"Oh, no, Paul, not at all. This feeling isn't exciting. It feels like something broken in a machine—"

"Listen!" I interrupted her.

From far ahead, from within the clouds, there came a sound like an animal wailing. There were words in it. It must have been Macht. I thought I heard "take care." When I sought him with my mind, the distance made circles and I got dizzy.

"Let's follow, darling," said I.

"Yes, Paul," said she, and in her voice there was an unfathomable mixture of happiness, resignation, and despair . . .

Before we moved on, I looked carefully at her. She *was* my girl. The sky had turned yellow and the lights were not yet on. In the yellow rich sky her brown curls were tinted with gold, her brown eyes approached the black in their irises, her young and fate-haunted face seemed more meaningful than any other human face I had ever seen.

"You *are* mine," I said.

"Yes, Paul," She answered me and then smiled brightly. "*You* said it! That is doubly nice."

A bird on the railing looked sharply at us and then left. Perhaps he did not approve of human nonsense, so flung himself downward into dark air. I saw him catch himself, far below, and ride lazily on his wings.

"We're not as free as birds, darling," I told Virginia, "but we are freer than people have been for a hundred centuries."

For answer she hugged my arm and smiled at me.

"And now," I added, "to follow Macht. Put your arms around me and hold me tight. I'll try hitting that post. If we don't get dinner we may get a ride."

I felt her take hold tightly and then I struck the post.

Which post? An instant later the posts were sailing by us in a blur. The ground beneath our feet seemed steady, but we were moving at a fast rate. Even in the service underground I had never seen a roadway as fast as this. Virginia's dress was blowing so hard that it made snapping sounds like the snap of fingers. In no time at all we were in the cloud and out of it again.

A new world surrounded us. The clouds lay below

and above. Here and there blue sky shone through. We were steady. The ancient engineers must have devised the walkway cleverly. We rode up, up, up without getting dizzy.

Another cloud.

Then things happened so fast that the telling of them takes longer than the event.

Something dark rushed at me from up ahead. A violent blow hit me in the chest. Only much later did I realize that this was Macht's arm trying to grab me before we went over the edge. Then we went into another cloud. Before I could even speak to Virginia a second blow struck me. The pain was terrible. I had never felt anything like that in all my life. For some reason, Virginia had fallen over me and beyond me. She was pulling at my hands.

I tried to tell her to stop pulling me, because it hurt, but I had no breath. Rather than argue, I tried to do what she wanted. I struggled toward her. Only then did I realize that there was nothing below my feet—no bridge, no jetway, nothing.

I was on the edge of the boulevard, the broken edge of the upper side. There was nothing below me except for some looped cables, and, far underneath them, a tiny ribbon which was either a river or a road.

We had jumped blindly across the great gap and I had fallen just far enough to catch the upper edge of the roadway on my chest.

It did not matter, the pain.

In a moment the doctor-robot would be there to repair me.

A look at Virginia's face reminded me there was no doctor-robot, no world, no Instrumentality, nothing but wind and pain. She was crying. It took a moment for me to hear what she was saying.

"I did it, I did it, darling, are you dead?"

Neither one of us was sure what "dead" meant, because people always went away at their appointed time, but we knew that it meant a cessation of life. I tried to tell her that I was living, but she fluttered over me and kept dragging me farther from the edge of the drop.

I used my hands to push myself into a sitting position.

She knelt beside me and covered my face with kisses. At last I was able to gasp, "Where's Macht?"

She looked back. "I don't see him."

I tried to look too. Rather than have me struggle, she said, "You stay quiet. I'll look again."

Bravely she walked to the edge of the sheared-off boulevard. She looked over toward the lower side of the gap, peering through the clouds which drifted past us as rapidly as smoke sucked by a ventilator. Then she cried out:

"I see him. He looks so funny. Like an insect in the museum. He is crawling across on the cables."

Struggling to my hands and knees, I neared her and looked too. There he was, a dot moving along a thread, with the birds soaring by beneath him. It looked very unsafe. Perhaps he was getting all the "fear" that he needed to keep himself happy. I did not want that "fear," whatever it was. I wanted food, water, and a doctor-robot.

None of these were here.

I struggled to my feet. Virginia tried to help me but I was standing before she could do more than touch my sleeve.

"Let's go on."

"On?" she said.

"On to the Abba-dingo. There may be friendly machines up there. Here there is nothing but cold and wind, and the lights have not yet gone on."

She frowned. "But Macht . . . ?"

"It will be hours before he gets here. We can come back."

She obeyed.

Once again we went to the left of the boulevard. I told her to squeeze my waist while I struck the pillars, one by one. Surely there must have been a reactivating device for the passengers on the road.

The fourth time, it worked.

Once again the wind whipped our clothing as we raced upward on Alpha Ralpha Boulevard.

We almost fell as the road veered to the left. I caught my balance, only to have it veer the other way.

And then we stopped.

This was the Abba-dingo.

A walkway littered with white objects—knobs and rods and imperfectly formed balls about the size of my head.

Virginia stood beside me, silent.

About the size of my head? I kicked one of the objects aside and then knew, knew for sure, what it was. It was people. The inside parts. I had never seen such things before. And that, that on the ground, must once have been a hand. There were hundreds of such things along the walk.

"Come, Virginia," said I, keeping my voice even, and my thoughts hidden.

She followed without saying a word. She was curious about the things on the ground, but she did not seem to recognize them.

For my part, I was watching the wall.

At last I found them—the little doors of Abba-dingo.

One said METEOROLOGICAL. It was not Old Common Tongue, nor was it French, but it was so close that I knew it had something to do with the behavior of air. I put my hand against the panel of the door. The panel became translucent and ancient writing showed through. There were numbers which meant nothing, words which meant nothing, and then:

Typhoon coming.

My French had not taught me what a "coming" was, but "typhoon" was plainly *typhon,* a major air disturbance. Thought I, *let the weather machines take care of the matter*. It had nothing to do with us.

"That's no help," said I.

"What does it mean?" she said.

"The air will be disturbed."

"Oh," said she. "That couldn't matter to us, could it?"

"Of course not."

I tried the next panel, which said FOOD. When my hand touched the little door, there was an aching creak inside the wall, as though the whole tower retched. The door opened a little bit and a horrible odor came out of it. Then the door closed again.

The third door said HELP and when I touched it nothing happened. Perhaps it was some kind of tax-collecting device from the ancient days. It yielded nothing to my touch. The fourth door was larger and already partly open at the bottom. At the top, the name of the door was PREDICTIONS. Plain enough, that one was, to anyone who knew Old French. The name at the bottom was more mysterious: PUT PAPER HERE it said, and I could not guess what it meant.

I tried telepathy. Nothing happened. The wind whistled past us. Some of the calcium balls and knobs rolled on the pavement. I tried again, trying my utmost for the imprint of long-departed thoughts. A scream entered my mind, a thin long scream which did not sound much like people. That was all.

Perhaps it did upset me. I did not feel "fear," but I was worried about Virginia.

She was staring at the ground.

"Paul," she said, "isn't that a man's coat on the ground among those funny things?"

Once I had seen an ancient X-ray in the museum, so I knew that the coat still surrounded the material which had provided the inner structure of the man. There was no ball there, so that I was quite sure he was *dead*. How could that have happened in the old days? Why did the Instrumentality let it happen? But then, the Instrumentality had always forbidden this side of the tower. Perhaps the violators had met their own punishment in some way I could not fathom.

"Look, Paul," said Virginia. "I can put my hand in."

Before I could stop her, she had thrust her hand into the flat open slot which said PUT PAPER HERE.

She screamed.

Her hand was caught.

I tried to pull at her arm, but it did not move. She began gasping with pain. Suddenly her hand came free.

Clear words were cut into the living skin. I tore my cloak off and wrapped her hand.

As she sobbed beside me I unbandaged her hand. As I did so she saw the words on her skin.

The words said, in clear French: *You will love Paul all your life.*

Virginia let me bandage her hand with my cloak and

then she lifted her face to be kissed. "It was worth it," she said; "it was worth all the trouble, Paul. Let's see if we can get down. Now I know."

I kissed her again and said, reassuringly, "You do know, don't you?"

"Of course," she smiled through her tears. "The Instrumentality could not have contrived this. What a clever old machine! Is it a god or a devil, Paul?"

I had not studied those words at that time, so I patted her instead of answering. We turned to leave.

At the last minute I realized that I had not tried PRE-DICTIONS myself.

"Just a moment, darling. Let me tear a little piece off the bandage."

She waited patiently. I tore a piece the size of my hand, and then I picked up one of the ex-person units on the ground. It may have been the front of an arm. I returned to push the cloth into the slot, but when I turned to the door, an enormous bird was sitting there.

I used my hand to push the bird aside, and he cawed at me. He even seemed to threaten me with his cries and his sharp beak. I could not dislodge him.

Then I tried telepathy. *I am a true man. Go away!*

The bird's dim mind flashed back at me nothing but *no-no-no-no-no!*

With that I struck him so hard with my fist that he fluttered to the ground. He righted himself amid the white litter on the pavement and then, opening his wings, he let the wind carry him away.

I pushed in the scrap of cloth, counted to twenty in my mind, and pulled the scrap out.

The words were plain, but they meant nothing: *You will love Virginia twenty-one more minutes.*

Her happy voice, reassured by the prediction but still unsteady from the pain in her written-on hand, came to me as though it were far away. "What does it say, darling?"

Accidentally on purpose, I let the wind take the scrap. It fluttered away like a bird. Virginia saw it go.

"Oh," she cried disappointedly. "We've lost it! What did it say?"

"Just what yours did."

"But what words, Paul? How did it say it?"

With love and heartbreak and perhaps a little "fear," I lied to her and whispered gently,

"It said, 'Paul will always love Virginia.'"

She smiled at me radiantly. Her stocky, full figure stood firmly and happily against the wind. Once again she was the chubby, pretty Menerima whom I had noticed in our block when we both were children. And she was more than that. She was my new-found love in our new-found world. She was my mademoiselle from Martinique. The message was foolish. We had seen from the food-slot that the machine was broken.

"There's no food or water here," said I. Actually, there was a puddle of water near the railing, but it had been blown over the human structural elements on the ground, and I had no heart to drink it.

Virginia was so happy that, despite her wounded hand, her lack of water and her lack of food, she walked vigorously and cheerfully.

Thought I to myself, *Twenty-one minutes. About six hours have passed. If we stay here we face unknown dangers.*

Vigorously we walked downward, down Alpha Ralpha Boulevard. We had met the Abba-dingo and were still "alive." I did not think that I was "dead," but the words had been meaningless so long that it was hard to think them.

The ramp was so steep going down that we pranced like horses. The wind blew into our faces with incredible force. That's what it was, wind, but I looked up the word *vent* only after it was all over.

We never did see the whole tower—just the wall at which the ancient jetway had deposited us. The rest of the tower was hidden by clouds which fluttered like torn rags as they raced past the heavy material.

The sky was red on one side and a dirty yellow on the other.

Big drops of water began to strike at us.

"The weather machines are broken," I shouted to Virginia.

She tried to shout back to me but the wind carried her words away. I repeated what I had said about the weather machines. She nodded happily and warmly, though the wind was by now whipping her hair past her face and the pieces of water which fell from up above were spotting her flame-golden gown. It did not matter. She clung to my arm. Her happy face smiled at me as we stamped downward, bracing ourselves against the decline in the ramp. Her brown eyes were full of confidence and life. She saw me looking at her and she kissed me on the upper arm without losing step. She was my own girl forever, and she knew it.

The water-from-above, which I later knew was actual "rain," came in increasing volume. Suddenly it included birds. A large bird flapped his way vigorously against the whistling air and managed to stand still in front of my face, though his air speed was many leagues per hour. He cawed in my face and then was carried away by the wind. No sooner had that one gone than another bird struck me in the body. I looked down at it but it too was carried away by the racing current of air. All I got was a telepathic echo from its bright blank mind: *no-no-no-no!*

Now what? thought I. A bird's advice is not much to go upon.

Virginia grabbed my arm and stopped.

I too stopped.

The broken edge of Alpha Ralpha Boulevard was just ahead. Ugly yellow clouds swam through the break like poisonous fish hastening on an inexplicable errand.

Virginia was shouting.

I could not hear her, so I leaned down. That way her mouth could almost touch my ear.

"Where is Macht?" she shouted.

Carefully I took her to the left side of the road, where the railing gave us some protection against the heavy racing air, and against the water commingled with it. By now neither of us could see very far. I made her drop to her knees. I got down beside her. The falling water pelted our backs. The light around us had turned to a dark dirty yellow.

We could still see, but we could not see much.

I was willing to sit in the shelter of the railing, but she nudged me. She wanted us to do something about

Macht. What anyone could do, that was beyond me. If he had found shelter, he was safe, but if he was out on those cables, the wild pushing air would soon carry him off and then there would be no more Maximilien Macht. He would be "dead" and his interior parts would bleach somewhere on the open ground.

Virginia insisted.

We crept to the edge.

A bird swept in, true as a bullet, aiming for my face. I flinched. A wing touched me. It stung against my cheek like fire. I did not know that feathers were so tough. The birds must all have damaged mental mechanisms, thought I, if they hit people on Alpha Ralpha. That is not the right way to behave toward true people.

At last we reached the edge, crawling on our bellies. I tried to dig the fingernails of my left hand into the stone-like material of the railing, but it was flat, and there was nothing much to hold to, save for the ornamental fluting. My right arm was around Virginia. It hurt me badly to crawl forward that way, because my body was still damaged from the blow against the edge of the road, on the way coming up. When I hesitated, Virginia thrust herself forward.

We saw nothing.

The gloom was around us.

The wind and the water beat at us like fists.

Her gown pulled at her like a dog worrying its master. I wanted to get her back into the shelter of the railing, where we could wait for the air-disturbance to end.

Abruptly, the light shone all around us. It was wild electricity, which the ancients called *lightning*. Later I found that it occurs quite frequently in the areas beyond the reach of the weather machines.

The bright quick light showed us a white face staring at us. He hung on the cables below us. His mouth was open, so he must have been shouting. I shall never know whether the expression on his face showed "fear" or great happiness. It was full of excitement. The bright light went out and I thought that I heard the echo of a call. I reached for his mind telepathically and there was nothing there. Just some dim, obstinate bird thinking at me, *no-no-no-no-no!*

Virginia tightened in my arms. She squirmed around.
I shouted at her in French. She could not hear.

Then I called with my mind.

Someone else was there.

Virginia's mind blazed at me, full of revulsion, *The
cat girl. She is going to touch me!*

She twisted. My right arm was suddenly empty. I saw
the gleam of a golden gown flash over the edge, even in
the dim light. I reached with my mind, and I caught her
cry:

"Paul, Paul, I love you. Paul . . . help me!"

The thoughts faded as her body dropped.

The someone else was C'mell, whom we had first met
in the corridor.

I came to get you both, she thought at me; *not that
the birds cared about her.*

What have the birds got to do with it?

*You saved them. You saved their young, when the
red-topped man was killing them all. All of us have
been worried about what you true people would do to us
when you were free. We found out. Some of you are bad
and kill other kinds of life. Others of you are good and
protect life.*

Thought I, is that all there is to *good* and *bad?*

Perhaps I should not have left myself off guard. People did not have to understand fighting, but the homunculi did. They were bred amidst battle and they served
through troubles. C'mell, cat-girl that she was, caught
me on the chin with a pistonlike fist. She had no anes-
thesia and the only way—cat or no cat—that she could
carry me across the cables in the "typhoon" was to have
me unconscious and relaxed.

I awakened in my own room. I felt very well indeed.
The robot-doctor was there. Said he:

"You've had a shock. I've already reached the subcommissioner of the Instrumentality, and I can erase the
memories of the last full day, if you want me to."

His expression was pleasant.

Where was the racing wind? The air falling like stone
around us? The water driving where no weather machines controlled it? Where was the golden gown and
the wild fear-hungry face of Maximilien Macht?

I thought these things, but the robot-doctor, not being telepathic, caught none of it. I stared hard at him.

"Where," I cried, "is my own true love?"

Robots cannot sneer, but this one attempted to do so. "The naked cat-girl with the blazing hair? She left to get some clothing."

I stared at him.

His fuddy-duddy little machine mind cooked up its own nasty little thoughts, "I must say, sir, you 'free people' change very fast indeed . . ."

Who argues with a machine? It wasn't worth answering him.

But that other machine? Twenty-one minutes. How could that work out? How could it have known? I did not want to argue with that other machine either. It must have been a very powerful left-over machine—perhaps something used in ancient wars. I had no intention of finding out. Some people might call it a god. I call it nothing. I do not need "fear" and I do not propose to go back to Alpha Ralpha Boulevard again.

But hear, oh heart of mine!—how can you ever visit the café again?

C'mell came in and the robot-doctor left.

The Ballad of Lost C'mell

"Rather loosely inspired by some of the magical and conspiratorial scenes of The Romance of Three Kingdoms," a 14th-century work by Lo Kuan-chung, according to Smith himself. C'mell herself was inspired by Cat Melanie, one of the felines in Smith's household. She and Lord Jestocost, of course, both figure later in the events of his novel Norstrilia . . .

> *She got the which of the what-she-did,*
> *Hid the bell with a blot, she did,*
> *But she fell in love with a hominid.*
> *Where is the which of the what-she-did?*
> from THE BALLAD OF LOST C'MELL

SHE WAS A girlygirl and they were true men, the lords of creation, but she pitted her wits against them and she won. It had never happened before, and it is sure never to happen again, but she did win. She was not even of human extraction. She was cat-derived, though human in outward shape, which explains the C in front of her name. Her father's name was C'mackintosh and her name C'mell. She won her tricks against the lawful and assembled lords of the Instrumentality.

It all happened at Earthport, greatest of buildings,

315

smallest of cities, standing twenty-five kilometers high at the western edge of the Smaller Sea of Earth.

Jestocost had an office outside the fourth valve.

1

Jestocost liked the morning sunshine, while most of the other lords of Instrumentality did not, so that he had no trouble in keeping the office and the apartments which he had selected. His main office was ninety meters deep, twenty meters high, twenty meters broad. Behind it was the 'fourth valve,' almost a thousand hectares in extent. It was shaped helically, like an enormous snail. Jestocost's apartment, big as it was, was merely one of the pigeonholes in the muffler of the rim of Earthport. Earthport stood like an enormous wineglass, reaching from the magma to the high atmosphere.

Earthport had been built during mankind's biggest mechanical splurge. Though men had had nuclear rockets since the beginning of consecutive history, they had used chemical rockets to load the interplanetary ion-drive and nuclear-drive vehicles or to assemble the photonic sail-ships for interstellar cruises. Impatient with the troubles of taking things bit by bit into the sky, they had worked out a billion-ton rocket, only to find that it ruined whatever countryside it touched in landing. The Daimoni—people of Earth extraction, who came back from somewhere beyond the stars—had helped men build it of weatherproof, rustproof, timeproof, stressproof material. Then they had gone away and had never come back.

Jestocost often looked around his apartment and wondered what it might have been like when white-hot gas, muted to a whisper, surged out of the valve into his own chamber and the sixty-three other chambers like it. Now he had a back wall of heavy timber, and the valve itself was a great hollow cave where a few wild things lived. Nobody needed that much space any more. The chambers were useful, but the valve did nothing. Planoforming ships whispered in from the stars; they landed at Earthport as a matter of legal convenience, but they made no noise and they certainly had no hot gases.

Jestocost looked at the high clouds far below him and talked to himself,

"Nice day. Good air. No trouble. Better eat.

Jestocost often talked like that to himself. He was an individual, almost an eccentric. One of the top council of mankind, he had problems, but they were not personal problems. He had a Rembrandt hanging above his bed—the only Rembrandt known in the world, just as he was possibly the only person who could appreciate a Rembrandt. He had the tapestries of a forgotten empire hanging from his back wall. Every morning the sun played a grand opera for him, muting and lighting and shifting the colors so that he could almost imagine that the old days of quarrel, murder and high drama had come back to Earth again. He had a copy of Shakespeare, a copy of Colegrove and two pages of the Book of Ecclesiastes in a locked box beside his bed. Only forty-two people in the universe could read Ancient English, and he was one of them. He drank wine, which he had made by his own robots in his own vineyards on the Sunset coast. He was a man, in short, who had arranged his own life to live comfortably, selfishly and well on the personal side, so that he could give generously and impartially of his talents on the official side.

When he awoke on this particular morning, he had no idea that a beautiful girl was about to fall hopelessly in love with him—that he would find, after a hundred years and more of experience in government, another government on Earth just as strong and almost as ancient as his own—that he would willingly fling himself into conspiracy and danger for a cause which he only half understood. All these things were mercifully hidden from him by time, so that his only question on arising was, should he or should he not have a small cup of white wine with his breakfast. On the one hundred seventy-third day of each year, he always made a point of eating eggs. They were a rare treat, and he did not want to spoil himself by having too many, nor to deprive himself and forget a treat by having none at all. He puttered around the room, muttering, "White wine? White wine?"

C'mell was coming into his life, but he did not know

it. She was fated to win; that part, she herself did not know.

Ever since mankind had gone through the Rediscovery of Man, bringing back governments, money, newspapers, national languages, sickness and occasional death, there had been the problem of the underpeople —people who were not human, but merely humanly shaped from the stock of Earth animals. They could speak, sing, read, write, work, love and die; but they were not covered by human law, which simply defined them as "homunculi" and gave them a legal status close to animals or robots. Real people from off-world were always called "hominids."

Most of the underpeople did their jobs and accepted their half-slave status without question. Some became famous—C'mackintosh had been the first Earth-being to manage a fifty-meter broad-jump under normal gravity. His picture was seen in a thousand worlds. His daughter, C'mell, was a girlygirl, earning her living by welcoming human beings and hominids from the outworlds and making them feel at home when they reached Earth. She had the privilege of working at Earthport, but she had the duty of working very hard for a living which did not pay well. Human beings and hominids had lived so long in an affluent society that they did not know what it meant to be poor. But the lords of the Instrumentality had decreed that underpeople—derived from animal stock—should live under the economics of the Ancient World; they had to have their own kind of money to pay for their rooms, their food, their possessions and the education of their children. If they became bankrupt, they went to the Peorhouse, where they were killed painlessly by mean of gas.

It was evident that humanity, having settled all of its own basic problems, was not quite ready to let Earth animals, no matter how much they might be changed, assume a full equality with man.

The Lord Jestocost, seventh of that name, opposed the policy. He was a man who had little love, no fear, freedom from ambition and a dedication to his job: but there are passions of government as deep and challenging as the emotions of love. Two hundred years of

thinking himself right and of being outvoted had in-
stilled in Jestocost a furious desire to get things done his
own way.

Jestocost was one of the few true men who believed
in the rights of the underpeople. He did not think that
mankind would ever get around to correcting ancient
wrongs unless the underpeople themselves had some of
the tools of power—weapons, conspiracy, wealth and
(above all) organization with which to challenge man.
He was not afraid of revolt, but he thirsted for justice
with an obsessive yearning which overrode all other considerations.

When the lords of the Instrumentality heard that
there was the rumor of a conspiracy among the underpeople, they left it to the robot police to ferret it out.

Jestocost did not.

He set up his own police, using underpeople themselves for the purpose, hoping to recruit enemies who
would realize that he was a friendly enemy and who
would in course of time bring him into touch with the
leaders of the underpeople.

If those leaders existed, they were clever. What sign
did a girlygirl like C'mell ever give that she was the
spearhead of a crisscross of agents who had penetrated
Earthport itself? They must, if they existed, be very,
very careful. The telepathic monitors, both robotic and
human, kept every thought-band under surveillance by
random sampling. Even the computers showed nothing
more significant than improbable amounts of happiness
in minds which had no objective reason for being happy.

The death of her father, the most famous cat-athlete
which the underpeople had ever produced, gave Jestocost his first definite clue.

He went to the funeral himself, where the body was
packed in an ice-rocket to be shot into space. The mour-
ners were thoroughly mixed with the curiosity-seekers.
Sport is international, inter-race, inter-world, inter-spe-
cies. Hominids were there: true men, one hundred percent
human, they looked weird and horrible because they or
their ancestors had undergone bodily modifications to
meet the life conditions of a thousand worlds.

Underpeople, the animal-derived "homunculi," were

there, most of them in their work clothes, and they looked more human than did the human beings from the outer worlds. None were allowed to grow up if they were less than half the size of man, or more than six times the size of man. They all had to have human features and acceptable human voices. The punishment for failure in their elementary schools was death. Jestocost looked over the crowd and wondered to himself, "We have set up the standards of the toughest kind of survival for these people and we give them the most terrible incentive, life itself, as the condition of absolute progress. What fools we are to think that they will not overtake us!" The true people in the group did not seem to think as he did. They tapped the underpeople peremptorily with their canes, even though this was an underperson's funeral, and the bear-men, bull-men, cat-men and others yielded immediately and with a babble of apology.

C'mell was close to her father's icy coffin.

Jestocost not only watched her; she was pretty to watch. He committed an act which was an indecency in an ordinary citizen but lawful for a lord of the Instrumentality: he peeped her mind.

And then he found something which he did not expect.

As the coffin left, she cried, "Ee-telly-kelly, help me! help me!"

She had thought phonetically, not in script, and he had only the raw sound on which to base a search.

Jestocost had not become a lord of the Instrumentality without applying daring. His mind was quick, too quick to be deeply intelligent. He thought by gestalt, not by logic. He determined to force his friendship on the girl.

He decided to await a propitious occasion, and then changed his mind about the time.

As she went home from the funeral, he intruded upon the circle of her grim-faced friends, underpeople who were trying to shield her from the condolences of ill-mannered but well-meaning sports enthusiasts.

She recognized him, and showed him the proper respect.

"My Lord, I did not expect you here. You knew my father?"

He nodded gravely and addressed sonorous words of consolation and sorrow, words which brought a murmur of approval from humans and underpeople alike.

But with his left hand hanging slack at his side, he made the perpetual signal of *alarm! alarm!* used with the Earthport staff—a repeated tapping of the thumb against the third finger—when they had to set one another on guard without alerting the offworld transients.

She was so upset that she almost spoiled it all. While he was still doing his pious doubletalk, she cried in a loud clear voice:

"You mean *me?*"

And he went on with his condolences: ". . . and I do mean *you*, C'mell, to be the worthiest carrier of your father's name. *You* are the one to whom we turn in this time of common sorrow. *Who could I mean but you* if I say that C'mackintosh never did things by halves, and died young as a result of his own zealous conscience? Good-by, C'mell, I go back to my office."

She arrived forty minutes after he did.

2

He faced her straightaway, studying her face.

"This is an important day in your life."

"Yes, my Lord, a sad one."

"I do not," he said, "mean your father's death and burial. I speak of the future to which we all must turn. Right now, it's you and me."

Her eyes widened. She had not thought that he was that kind of man at all. He was an official who moved freely around Earthport, often greeting important offworld visitors and keeping an eye on the bureau of ceremonies. She was a part of the reception team, when a girlygirl was needed to calm down a frustrated arrival or to postpone a quarrel. Like the geisha of ancient Japan, she had an honorable profession; she was not a bad girl but a professionally flirtatious hostess. She stared at the Lord Jestocost. He did not *look* as though he meant anything improperly personal. But, thought she, you can never tell about men.

"You know men," he said, passing the initiative to her.

"I guess so," she said. Her face looked odd. She started to give him smile No. 3 (extremely adhesive) which she had learned in the girlygirl school. Realizing it was wrong, she tried to give him an ordinary smile. She felt she had made a face at him.

"Look at me," he said, "and see if you can trust me. I am going to take both our lives in my hands."

She looked at him. What imaginable subject could involve him, a lord of the Instrumentality, with herself, an undergirl? They never had anything in common. They never would.

But she stared at him.

"I want to help the underpeople."

He made her blink. That was a crude approach, usually followed by a very raw kind of pass indeed. But his face was illuminated by seriousness. She waited.

"Your people do not have enough political power even to talk to us. I will not commit treason to the true human race, but I am willing to give your side an advantage. If you bargain better with us, it will make all forms of life safer in the long run."

C'mell stared at the floor, her red hair soft as the fur of a Persian cat. It made her head seem bathed in flames. Her eyes looked human, except that they had the capacity of reflecting when light struck them; the irises were the rich green of the ancient cat. When she looked right at him, looking up from the floor, her glance had the impact of a blow. "What do you want from me?"

He stared right back. "Watch me. Look at my face. Are you sure, *sure* that I want nothing from you personally?"

She looked bewildered. "What else is there to want from me except personal things? I am a girlygirl. I'm not a person of any importance at all, and I do not have much of an education. You know more, sir, than I will ever know."

"Possibly," he said, watching her.

She stopped feeling like a girlygirl and felt like a citizen. It made her uncomfortable.

"Who," he said, in a voice of great solemnity, "is your own leader?"

"Commissioner Teadrinker, sir. He's in charge of all outworld visitors." She watched Jestocost carefully; he still did not look as if he were playing tricks.

He looked a little cross. "I don't mean him. He's part of my own staff. Who's your leader among the underpeople?"

"My father was, but he died."

Jestocost said. "Forgive me. Please have a seat. But I don't mean that."

She was so tired that she sat down into the chair with an innocent voluptuousness which would have disorganized any ordinary man's day. She wore girlygirl clothes, which were close enough to the everyday fashion to seem agreeably modish when she stood up. In line with her profession, her clothes were designed to be unexpectedly and provocatively revealing when she sat down— not revealing enough to shock the man with their brazenness, but so slit, tripped and cut that he got far more visual stimulation than he expected.

"I must ask you to pull your clothing together a little," said Jestocost in a clinical turn of voice. "I am a man, even if I am an official, and this interview is more important to you and to me than any distraction would be."

She was a little frightened by his tone. She had meant no challenge. With the funeral that day, she meant nothing at all; these clothes were the only kind she had.

He read all this in her face.

Relentlessly, he pursued the subject.

"Young lady, I asked about your leader. You name your boss and you name your father. I want your leader."

"I don't understand," she said, on the edge of a sob, "I don't understand."

Then, he thought to himself, I've got to take a gamble. He thrust the mental dagger home, almost drove his words like steel straight into her face. "Who . . ." he said slowly and icily, "is . . . Ee . . . telly . . . kelly?"

The girl's face had been cream-colored, pale with sorrow. Now she went white. She twisted away from him.
Her eyes glowed like twin fires.

Her eyes . . . like twin fires.

(No undergirl, thought Jestocost as he reeled, could
hypnotize me.)

Her eyes . . . were like cold fires.

The room faded around him. The girl disappeared.
Her eyes became a single white, cold fire.

Within this fire stood the figure of a man. His arms
were wings, but he had human hands growing at the el-
bows of his wings. His face was clear, white, cold as the
marble of an ancient statue; his eyes were opaque white.
"I am the E'telekeli. You will believe in me. You may
speak to my daughter C'mell."

The image faded.

Jestocost saw the girl staring as she sat awkwardly on
the chair, looking blindly through him. He was on the
edge of making a joke about her hypnotic capacity when
he saw that she was still deeply hypnotized even after
he had been released. She had stiffened and again her
clothing had fallen into its planned disarray. The effect was not stimulating; it was pathetic beyond words,
as though an accident had happened to a pretty child.
He spoke to her.

He spoke to her, not really expecting an answer.

"Who are you?" he said to her, testing her hypnosis.

"I am he whose name is never said aloud," said the
girl in a sharp whisper, "I am he whose secret you have
penetrated. I have printed my image and my name in
your mind."

Jestocost did not quarrel with ghosts like this. He
snapped out a decision. "If I open my mind, will you
search it while I watch you? Are you good enough to do
that?"

"I am very good," hissed the voice in the girl's mouth.

C'mell arose and put her two hands on his shoulders.
She looked into his eyes. He looked back. A strong telepath himself, Jestocost was not prepared for the enormous thought-voltage which poured out of her.

Look in my mind, he commanded, for the subject of
underpeople only.

I see it, thought the mind behind C'mell.

Do you see what I mean to do for the underpeople?

Jestocost heard the girl breathing hard as her mind served as a relay to his. He tried to remain calm so that he could see which part of his mind was being searched. Very good so far, he thought to himself. An intelligence like that on Earth itself, he thought—and we of the lords not knowing it!

The girl hacked out a dry little laugh.

Jestocost thought at the mind, Sorry. Go ahead.

This plan of yours—thought the strange mind—may I see more of it?

That's all there is.

Oh, said the strange mind, you want me to think for you. Can you give me the keys in the Bell and Bank which pertain to destroying underpeople?

You can have the information keys if I can ever get them, thought Jestocost, but not the control keys and not the master switch of the Bell.

Fair enough, thought the other mind, and what do I pay for them?

You support me in my policies before the Instrumentality. You keep the underpeople reasonable, if you can, when the time comes to negotiate. You maintain honor and good faith in all subsequent agreements. But how can I get the keys? It would take me a year to figure them out myself.

Let the girl look once, thought the strange mind, and I will be behind her. Fair?

Fair, thought Jestocost.

Break? thought the mind.

How do we re-connect? thought Jestocost back.

As before. Through the girl. Never say my name. Don't think it if you can help it. Break?

Break! thought Jestocost.

The girl, who had been holding his shoulders, drew his face down and kissed him firmly and warmly. He had never touched an underperson before, and it never had occured to him that he might kiss one. It was pleasant, but he took her arms away from his neck, half-turned her around, and let her lean against him.

"Daddy!" she sighed happily.

Suddenly she stiffened, looked at his face, and sprang for the door. "Jestocost!" she cried. "Lord Jestocost! What am I doing here?"

"Your duty is done, my girl. You may go."

She staggered back into the room. "I'm going to be sick," she said. She vomited on his floor.

He pushed a button for a cleaning robot and slapped his desk-top for coffee.

She relaxed and talked about his hopes for the under-people. She stayed an hour. By the time she left they had a plan. Neither of them had mentioned E'telekeli, neither had put purposes in the open. If the monitors had been listening, they would have found no single sentence or paragraph which was suspicious.

When she had gone, Jestocost looked out of his window. He saw the clouds far below and he knew the world below him was in twilight. He had planned to help the underpeople, and he had met powers of which organized mankind had no conception or perception. He was righter than he had thought. He had to go on through.

But as partner—C'mell herself!

Was there ever an odder diplomat in the history of worlds?

3

In less than a week they had decided what to do. It was the Council of the lords of the Instrumentality at which they would work—the brain center itself. The risk was high, but the entire job could be done in a few minutes if it were done at the Bell itself.

This is the sort of thing which interested Jestocost.

He did not know that C'mell watched him with two different facets of her mind. One side of her was alertly and wholeheartedly his fellow-conspirator, utterly in sympathy with the revolutionary aims to which they were both committed. The other side of her—was feminine.

She had a womanliness which was truer than that of any hominid woman. She knew the value of her trained smile, her splendidly kept red hair with its unimaginably soft texture, her lithe young figure with firm breasts and persuasive hips. She knew down to the last millimeter the effect which her legs had on hominid men. True humans kept few secrets from her. The men betrayed themselves by their unfulfillable desires, the women by their irrepressible jealousies. But she knew people best of all by not being one herself. She had to learn by imitation, and imitation is conscious. A thousand little things which ordinary women took for granted, or thought about just once in a whole lifetime, were subjects of acute and intelligent study to her. She was a girl by profession; she was a human by assimilation: she was an inquisitive cat in her genetic nature. Now she was falling in love with Jestocost, and she knew it.

Even she did not realize that the romance would sometime leak out into rumor, be magnified into legend, distilled into romance. She had no idea of the ballad about herself that would open with the lines which became famous much later:

> *She got the which of the what-she-did,*
> *Hid the bell with a blot, she did,*
> *But she fell in love with a hominid.*
> *Where is the which of the what-she-did?*

All this lay in the future, and she did not know it. She knew her own past.

She remembered the off-Earth prince who had rested his head in her lap and had said, sipping his glass of mott by way of farewell:

"Funny, C'mell, you're not even a person and you're the most intelligent human being I've met in this place. Do you know it made my planet poor to send me here? And what did I get out of them? Nothing, nothing, and a thousand times nothing. But you, now. If you'd been running the government of Earth, I'd have gotten what my people need, and this world would be richer too. Manhome, they call it. Manhome, my eye! The only smart person on it is a female cat."

He ran his fingers around her ankle. She did not stir. That was part of hospitality, and she had her own ways of making sure that hospitality did not go too far. Earth police were watching her; to them, she was a convenience maintained for outworld people, something like a soft chair in the Earthport lobbies or a drinking fountain with acid-tasting water for strangers who could not tolerate the insipid water of Earth. She was not expected to have feelings or to get involved. If she had ever caused an incident, they would have punished her fiercely, as they often punished animals or underpeople, or else (after a short formal hearing with no appeal) they would have destroyed her, as the law allowed and custom encouraged.

She had kissed a thousand men, maybe fifteen hundred. She had made them feel welcome and she had gotten their complaints or their secrets out of them as they left. It was a living, emotionally tiring but intellectually very stimulating. Sometimes it made her laugh to look at human women with their pointed-up noses and their proud airs, and to realize that she knew more about the men who belonged to the human women than the human women themselves ever did.

Once a policewoman had had to read over the record of two pioneers from New Mars. C'mell had been given the job of keeping in very close touch with them. When the policewoman got through reading the report she looked at C'mell and her face was distorted with jealousy and prudish rage.

"Cat, you call yourself. Cat! You're a pig, you're a dog, you're an animal. You may be working for Earth but don't ever get the idea that you're as good as a person. I think it's a crime that the Instrumentality lets monsters like you greet real human beings from outside! I can't stop it. But may the Bell help you, girl, if you ever touch a real Earth man! If you ever get near one! If you ever try tricks here! Do you understand me?"

"Yes, Ma'am," C'mell had said. To herself she thought, "That poor thing doesn't know how to select her own clothes or how to do her own hair. No wonder she resents somebody who manages to be pretty."

Perhaps the policewoman thought that raw hatred would be shocking to C'mell. It wasn't. Underpeople were used to hatred, and it was not any worse raw than it was when cooked with politeness and served like poison. They had to live with it.

But now, it was all changed.

She had fallen in love with Jestocost.

Did he love her?

Impossible. No, not impossible. Unlawful, unlikely, indecent—yes, all these, but not impossible. Surely he felt something of her love.

If he did, he gave no sign of it.

People and underpeople had fallen in love many times before. The underpeople were always destroyed and the real people brainwashed. There were laws against that kind of thing. The scientists among people had created the underpeople, had given them capacities which real people did not have (the fifty-meter jump, the telepath two miles underground, the turtle-man waiting a thousand years next to an emergency door, the cow-man guarding a gate without reward), and the scientists had also given many of the underpeople the human shape. It was handier that way. The human eye, the five-fingered hand, the human size—these were convenient for engineering reasons. By making underpeople the same size and shape as people, more or less, the scientists eliminated the need for two or three or a dozen different sets of furniture. The human form was good enough for all of them.

But they had forgotten the human heart.

And now she, C'mell had fallen in love with a man, a true man old enough to have been her own father's grandfather.

But she didn't feel daughterly about him at all. She remembered that with her own father there was an easy comradeship, an innocent and forthcoming affection, which masked the fact that he was considerably more catlike than she was. Between them there was an aching void of forever-unspoken words—things that couldn't quite be said by either of them, perhaps things that couldn't be said at all. They were so close to each other that they could get no closer. This created enormous distance, which was heart-breaking but unutterable. Her father had died, and now this true man was here with all the kindness—

"That's it," she whispered to herself, "with all the kindness that none of these passing men have ever really shown. With all the depth which my poor underpeople can never get. Not that it's not in them. But they're born like dirt, treated like dirt, put away like dirt when they die. How can any of my own men develop real kindness? There's a special sort of majesty to kindness. It's the best part there is to being people. And he has whole oceans of it in him. And it's strange, strange, strange that he's never given his real love to any human woman."

She stopped, cold.

Then she consoled herself and whispered on, "Or if he did, it's so long ago that it doesn't matter now. He's got *me*. Does he know it?"

4

The Lord Jestocost did know, and yet he didn't. He was used to getting loyalty from people, because he offered loyalty and honor in his daily work. He was even familiar with loyalty becoming obsessive and seeking physical form, particularly from women, children and underpeople. He had always coped with it before. He was gambling on the fact that C'mell was a wonderfully intelligent person, and that as a girlygirl, working on the hospitality staff of the Earthport police, she must have learned to control her personal feelings.

"We're born in the wrong age," he thought, "when I meet the most intelligent and beautiful female I've ever met, and then have to put business first. But this stuff about people and underpeople is sticky. Sticky. We've got to keep personalities out of it."

So he thought. Perhaps he was right.

If the nameless one, whom he did not dare to remember, commanded an attack on the Bell itself, that was worth their lives. Their emotions could not come into it. The Bell mattered; justice mattered; the perpetual return of mankind to progress mattered. He did not matter, because he had already done most of his work. C'mell did not matter, because their failure would leave her with mere underpeople forever. The Bell did count.

The price of what he proposed to do was high, but the entire job could be done in a few minutes if it were done at the Bell itself.

The Bell, of course, was not a Bell. It was a three-dimensional situation table, three times the height of a man. It was set one story below the meeting room, and shaped roughly like an ancient bell. The meeting table of the lords of the Instrumentality had a circle cut out of it, so that the lords could look down into the Bell at whatever situation one of them called up either manually or telepathically. The Bank below it, hidden by the floor, was the key memory-bank of the entire system. Duplicates existed at thirty-odd other places on Earth. Two duplicates lay hidden in interstellar space, one of them beside the ninety-million-mile gold-colored ship left over from the war against Raumsog and the other masked as an asteroid.

Most of the lords were off-world on the business of the Instrumentality.

Only three besides Jestocost were present—the Lady Johanna Gnade, the Lord Issan Olascoaga and the Lord William Not-from-here. (The Not-from-heres were a great Norstrilian family which had migrated back to Earth many generations before.)

The E'telekeli told Jestocost the rudiments of a plan.

He was to bring C'mell into the chambers on a summons.

The summons was to be serious.

They should avoid her summary death by automatic justice, if the relays began to trip.

C'mell would go into partial trance in the chamber.

He was then to call the items in the Bell which E'telekeli wanted traced. A single call would be enough. E'telekeli would take the responsibility for tracing them. The other lords would be distracted by him, E'telekeli.

It was simple in appearance.

The complication came in action.

The plan seemed flimsy, but there was nothing which Jestocost could do at this time. He began to curse himself for letting his passion for policy involve him in the intrigue. It was too late to back out with honor; besides, he had given his word; besides, he liked C'mell—as a being, not as a girlygirl—and he would hate to see her marked with disappointment for life. He knew how the underpeople cherished their identities and their status.

With heavy heart but quick mind he went to the council chamber. A dog-girl, one of the routine messengers whom he had seen many months outside the door, gave him the minutes.

He wondered how C'mell or E'telekeli would reach him, once he was inside the chamber with its tight net of telepathic intercepts.

He sat wearily at the table—

And almost jumped out of his chair.

The conspirators had forged the minutes themselves and the top item was: "C'mell daughter to C'mackintosh, cat stock (pure), lot 1138, confession of. Subject: conspiracy to export homuncular material. Reference: planet De Prinsensmacht."

The Lady Johanna Gnade had already pushed the buttons for the planet concerned. The people there, Earth by origin, were enormously strong but they had gone to great pains to maintain the original Earth appearance. One of their first-men was at the moment on Earth. He bore the title of the Twilight Prince (Prins van de Schemering) and he was on a mixed diplomatic and trading mission.

Since Jestocost was a little late, C'mell was being brought into the room as he glanced over the minutes.

The Lord Not-from-here asked Jestocost if he would preside.

"I beg you, Sir and Scholar," he said, "to join me in asking the Lord Issan to preside this time."

The presidency was a formality. Jestocost could watch the Bell and Bank better if he did not have to chair the meeting too.

C'mell wore the clothing of a prisoner. On her it looked good. He had never seen her wearing anything but girlygirl clothes before. The pale-blue prison tunic made her look very young, very human, very tender and very frightened. The cat family showed only in the fiery cascade of her hair and the lithe power of her body as she sat, demure and erect.

Lord Issan asked her: "You have confessed. Confess again."

"This man," and she pointed at a picture of the Twilight Prince, "wanted to go to the place where they torment human children for a show."

"What!" cried three of the Lords together.

"What place?" said the Lady Johanna, who was bitterly in favor of kindness.

"It's run by a man who looks like this gentleman here," said C'mell, pointing at Jestocost. Quickly, so that nobody could stop her, but modestly, so that none of them thought to doubt her, she circled the room and touched Jestocost's shoulder. He felt a thrill of contact-telepathy and heard bird-cackle in her brain. Then he knew that the E'telekeli was in touch with her.

"The man who has the place," said C'mell, "is five pounds lighter than this gentleman, two inches shorter, and he has red hair. His place is at the Cold Sunset corner of Earthport, down the boulevard and under the boulevard. Underpeople, some of them with bad reputations, live in that neighborhood."

The Bell went milky, flashing through hundreds of combinations of bad underpeople in that part of the city. Jestocost felt himself staring at the casual milkiness with unwanted concentration.

The Bell cleared.

It showed the vague image of a room in which children were playing Hallowe'en tricks.

The Lady Johanna laughed, "Those aren't people. They're robots. It's just a dull old play."

"Then," added C'mell, "he wanted a dollar and a shilling to take home. Real ones. There was a robot who had found some."

"What are those?" said Lord Issan.

"Ancient money—the real money of old America and old Australia," cried Lord William. "I have copies, but there are no originals outside the state museum." He was an ardent, passionate collector of coins.

"The robot found them in an old hiding place right under Earthport."

Lord William almost shouted at the Bell. "Run through every hiding place and get me that money."

The Bell clouded. In finding the bad neighborhoods it had flashed every police point in the northwest sector of the tower. Now it scanned all the police points under the tower, and ran dizzily through thousands of combinations before it settled on an old toolroom. A robot was polishing circular pieces of metal.

When Lord William saw the polishing, he was furious. "Get that here," he shouted. "I want to buy those myself!"

"All right," said Lord Issan. "It's a little irregular, but all right."

The machine showed the key search devices and brought the robot to the escalator.

The Lord Issan said, "This isn't much of a case."

C'mell sniveled. She was a good actress. "Then he wanted me to get a homunculus egg. One of the E-type, derived from birds, for him to take home."

Issan put on the search device.

"Maybe," said C'mell, "somebody has already put it in the disposal series."

The Bell and Bank ran through all the disposal devices at high speed. Jestocost felt his nerves go on edge. No human being could have memorized these thousands of patterns as they flashed across the Bell too fast for human eyes, but the brain reading the Bell through his eyes was not human. It might even be locked into a computer of its own. It was, thought Jestocost, an indignity for a lord of the Instrumentality to be used as a human spy-glass.

The machine blotted up.

"You're a fraud," cried the Lord Issan. "There's no evidence."

"Maybe the offworlder tried," said the Lady Johanna.

"Shadow him," said Lord William. "If he would steal ancient coins he would steal anything."

The Lady Johanna turned to C'mell. "You're a silly thing. You have wasted our time and you have kept us from serious inter-world business."

"It *is* inter-world business," wept C'mell. She let her

hand slip from Jestocost's shoulder, where it had rested all the time. The body-to-body relay broke and the telepathic link broke with it.

"We should judge that," said Lord Issan.

"You might have been punished," said Lady Johanna.

The Lord Jestocost had said nothing, but there was a glow of happiness in him. If the E'telekeli was half as good as he seemed, the underpeople had a list of checkpoints and escape routes which would make it easier to hide from the capricious sentence of painless death which human authorities meted out.

5

There was singing in the corridors that night.

Underpeople burst into happiness for no visible reason.

C'mell danced a wild cat dance for the next customer who came in from outworld stations, that very evening. When she got home to bed, she knelt before the picture of her father C'mackintosh and thanked the E'telekeli for what Jestocost had done.

But the story became known a few generations later, when the Lord Jestocost had won acclaim for being the champion of the underpeople and when the authorities, still unaware of E'telekeli, accepted the elected representatives of the underpeople as negotiators for better terms of life; and C'mell had died long since.

She had first had a long, good life.

She became a female chef when she was too old to be a girlygirl. Her food was famous. Jestocost once visited her. At the end of the meal he had asked, "There's a silly rhyme among the underpeople. No human beings know it except me."

"I don't care about rhymes," she said.

"This is called 'The what-she-did.' "

C'mell blushed all the way down to the neckline of her capacious blouse. She had filled out a lot in middle age. Running the restaurant had helped.

"Oh, that rhyme!" she said. "It's silly."

"It says you were in love with a hominid."

"No," she said. "I wasn't." Her green eyes, as beautiful as ever, stared deeply into his. Jestocost felt uncomfortable. This was getting personal. He liked political relationships; personal things made him uncomfortable.

The light in the room shifted and her cat eyes blazed at him, she looked like the magical fire-haired girl he had known.

"I wasn't in love. You couldn't call it that . . ."

Her heart cried out, *It was you, it was you, it was you.*

"But the rhyme," insisted Jestocost, "says it was a hominid. It wasn't that Prins van de Schemering?"

"Who was he?" C'mell asked the question quietly, but her emotions cried out, *Darling, will you never, never know?*

"The strong man."

"Oh, him. I've forgotten him."

Jestocost rose from the table. "You've had a good life, C'mell. You've been a citizen, a committeewoman, a leader. And do you even know how many children you have had?"

"Seventy-three," she snapped at him. "Just because they're multiple doesn't mean we don't know them."

His playfulness left him. His face was grave, his voice kindly. "I meant no harm, C'mell."

He never knew that when he left she went back to the kitchen and cried for a while. It was Jestocost whom she had vainly loved ever since they had been comrades, many long years ago.

Even after she died, at the full age of five-score and three, he kept seeing her about the corridors and shafts of Earthport. Many of her great-granddaughters looked just like her and several of them practiced the girlygirl business with huge success.

They were not half-slaves. They were citizens (reserved grade) and they had photopasses which protected their property, their identity and their rights. Jestocost was the godfather to them all; he was often embarrassed when the most voluptuous creatures in the universe threw playful kisses at him. All he asked was fulfillment of his political passions, not his personal ones. He had always been in love, madly in love—

With justice itself.

At last, his own time came, and he knew that he was dying, and he was not sorry. He had had a wife, hundreds of years ago, and had loved her well; their children had passed into the generations of man.

In the ending, he wanted to know something, and he called to a nameless one (or to his successor) far beneath the ground. He called with his mind till it was a scream.

I have helped your people.

"Yes," came back the faintest of faraway whispers, inside his head.

I am dying. I must know. Did she love me?

"She went on without you, so much did she love you. She let you go, for your sake, not for hers. She really loved you. More than death. More than life. More than time. You will never be apart."

Never apart?

"Not, not in the memory of man," said the voice, and was then still.

Jestocost lay back on his pillow and waited for the day to end.

A Planet Named Shayol

Smith acknowledged his debt to Dante in this story, which retells parts of the Inferno in science-fiction form—but with a twist distinctly Smith's own. The action apparently takes place even after that of Nostrilia, for banishment to Shayol is still used as a threat in the novel. At the end of this collection, as at the beginning, a member of the Vomact family appears—and we even meet Suzdal again. But Smith never shed any more light on the origin of the Go-Captain Alvarez . . .

1

THERE WAS A tremendous difference between the liner and the ferry in Mercer's treatment. On the liner, the attendants made gibes when they brought him his food.

"Scream good and loud," said one rat-faced steward, "and then we'll know it's you when they broadcast the sounds of punishment on the Emperor's birthday."

The other, fat steward ran the tip of his wet, red tongue over his thick, purple-red lips one time and said, "Stands to reason, man. If you hurt all the time, the whole lot of you would die. Something pretty good must happen, along with the—whatchamacallit. Maybe you turn into a woman. Maybe you turn into two people.

338

Listen, cousin, if it's real crazy fun, let me know . . ."

Mercer said nothing. Mercer had enough troubles of his own not to wonder about the daydreams of nasty men.

At the ferry it was different. The biopharmaceutical staff was deft, impersonal, quick in removing his shackles. They took off all his prison clothes and left them on the liner. When he boarded the ferry, naked, they looked him over as if he were a rare plant or a body on the operating table. They were almost kind in the clinical deftness of their touch. They did not treat him as a criminal, but as a specimen.

Men and women, clad in their medical smocks, they looked at him as though he were already dead.

He tried to speak. A man, older and more authoritative than the others, said firmly and clearly, "Do not worry about talking. I will talk to you myself in a very little time. What we are having now are the preliminaries, to determine your physical condition. Turn around, please."

Mercer turned around. An orderly rubbed his back with a very strong antiseptic.

"This is going to sting," said one of the technicians, "but it is nothing serious or painful. We are determining the toughness of the different layers of your skin."

Mercer, annoyed by this impersonal approach, spoke up just as a sharp little sting burned him above the sixth lumbar vertebra. "Don't you know who I am?"

"Of course we know who you are," said a woman's voice. "We have it all in a file in the corner. The chief doctor will talk about your crime later, if you want to talk about it. Keep quiet now. We are making a skin test, and you will feel much better if you do not make us prolong it."

Honesty forced her to add another sentence: "And we will get better results as well."

They had lost no time at all in getting to work.

He peered at them sidewise to look at them. There was nothing about them to indicate that they were human devils in the antechambers of hell itself. Nothing was there to indicate that this was the satellite of Shayol, the final and uttermost place of chastisement and shame.

They looked like medical people from his life before he committed the crime without a name.

They changed from one routine to another. A woman, wearing a surgical mask, waved her hand at a white table.

"Climb up on that, please."

No one had said "please" to Mercer since the guards had seized him at the edge of the palace. He started to obey her and then he saw that there padded handcuffs at the head of the table. He stopped.

"Get along, please," she demanded. Two or three of the others turned around to look at both of them.

The second "please" shook him. He had to speak. These were people, and he was a person again. He felt his voice rising, almost cracking into shrillness as he asked her, "Please, Ma'am, is the punishment going to begin?"

"There's no punishment here," said the woman. "This is the satellite. Get on the table. We're going to give you your first skin-toughening before you talk to the head doctor. Then you can tell him all about your crime—"

"You know my crime?" he said, greeting it almost like a neighbor.

"Of course not," said she, "but all the people who come through here are believed to have committed crimes. Somebody thinks so or they wouldn't be here. Most of them want to talk about their personal crimes. But don't slow me down. I'm a skin technician, and down on the surface of Shayol you're going to need the very best work that any of us can do for you. Now get on that table. And when you are ready to talk to the chief you'll have something to talk about besides your crime."

He complied.

Another masked person, probably a girl, took his hands in cool, gentle fingers and fitted them to the padded cuffs in a way he had never sensed before. By now he thought he knew every interrogation machine in the whole empire, but this was nothing like any of them.

The orderly stepped back. "All clear, Sir and Doctor."

"Which do you prefer?" said the skin technician. "A

great deal of pain or a couple of hours' unconsciousness?"

"Why should I want pain?" said Mercer.

"Some specimens do," said the technician, "by the
time they arrive here. I suppose it depends on what people have done to them before they got here. I take it you
did not get any of the dream-punishments."

"No," said Mercer. "I missed those." He thought to
himself, I didn't know that I missed anything at all.

He remembered his last trial, himself wired and
plugged in to the witness stand. The room had been high
and dark. Bright blue light shone on the panel of judges,
their judicial caps a fantastic parody of the episcopal
mitres of long, long ago. The judges were talking, but he
could not hear them. Momentarily the insulation slipped
and he heard one of them say, "Look at that white, devil-
ish face. A man like that is guilty of everything. I vote
for Pain Terminal." "Not Planet Shayol?" said a second
voice. "The dromozoa place," said a third voice. "That
should suit him," said the first voice. One of the judicial
engineers must then have noticed that the prisoner was
listening illegally. He was cut off. Mercer then thought
that he had gone through everything which the cruelty
and intelligence of mankind could devise.

But this woman said he had missed the dream-punishments. Could there be people in the universe even worse
off than himself? There must be a lot of people down on
Shayol. They never came back.

He was going to be one of them; would they boast to
him of what they had done, before they were made to
come to this place?

"You asked for it," said the woman technician. "It is
just an ordinary anesthetic. Don't panic when you awaken.
Your skin is going to be thickened and strengthened
chemically and biologically."

"Does it hurt?".

"Of course," said she. "But get this out of your head.
We're not punishing you. The pain here is just ordinary
medical pain. Anybody might get it if they needed a lot
of surgery. The punishment, if that's what you want to
call it, is down on Shayol. Our only job is to make sure
that you are fit to survive after you are landed. In a way,

we are saving your life ahead of time. You can be grateful for that if you want to be. Meanwhile, you will save
yourself a lot of trouble if you realize that your nerve
endings will respond to the change in the skin. You had
better expect to be very uncomfortable when you recover. But then, we can help that, too." She brought
down an enormous lever and Mercer blacked out.

When he came to, he was in an ordinary hospital
room, but he did not notice it. He seemed bedded in
fire. He lifted his hand to see if there were flames on it.
It looked the way it always had, except that it was a little red and a little swollen. He tried to turn in the bed.
The fire became a scorching blast which stopped him in
mid-turn. Uncontrollably, he moaned.

A voice spoke, "You are ready for some pain-killer."

It was a girl nurse. "Hold your head still," she said,
"and I will give you half an amp of pleasure. Your skin
won't bother you then."

She slipped a soft cap on his head. It looked like metal but it felt like silk.

He had to dig his fingernails into his palms to keep
from threshing about on the bed.

"Scream if you want to," she said. "A lot of them do.
It will just be a minute or two before the cap finds the
right lobe in your brain."

She stepped to the corner and did something which
he could not see.

There was the flick of a switch.

The fire did not vanish from his skin. He still felt it;
but suddenly it did not matter. His mind was full of delicious pleasure which throbbed outward from his head
and seemed to pulse down through his nerves. He had
visited the pleasure palaces, but he had never felt anything like this before.

He wanted to thank the girl, and he twisted around in
the bed to see her. He could feel his whole body flash
with pain as he did so, but the pain was far away. And
the pulsating pleasure which coursed out of his head,
down his spinal cord and into his nerves was so intense
that the pain got through only as a remote, unimportant
signal.

She was standing very still in the corner.

"Thank you, nurse," said he.

She said nothing.

He looked more closely, though it was hard to look while enormous pleasure pulsed through his body like a symphony written in nerve-messages. He focused his eyes on her and saw that she too wore a soft metallic cap.

He pointed at it.

She blushed all the way down to her throat.

She spoke dreamily, "You looked like a nice man to me. I didn't think you'd tell on me . . ."

He gave her what he thought was a friendly smile, but with the pain in his skin and the pleasure bursting out of his head, he really had no idea of what his actual expression might be. "It's against the law," he said. "It's terribly against the law. But it is nice."

"How do you think we stand it here?" said the nurse. "You specimens come in here talking like ordinary people and then you go down to Shayol. Terrible things happen to you on Shayol. Then the surface station sends up parts of you, over and over again. I may see your head ten times, quick-frozen and ready for cutting up, before my two years are up. You prisoners ought to know how we suffer," she crooned, the pleasure-charge still keeping her relaxed and happy, "you ought to die as soon as you get down there and not pester us with your torments. We can hear you screaming, you know. You keep on sounding like people even after Shayol begins to work on you. Why do you do it, Mr. Specimen?" She giggled sillily. "You hurt our feelings so. No wonder a girl like me has to have a little jolt now and then. It's real, real dreamy and I don't mind getting you ready to go down on Shayol." She staggered over to his bed. "Pull this cap off me, will you? I haven't got enough will power left to raise my hands."

Mercer saw his hand tremble as he reached for the cap.

His fingers touched the girl's soft hair through the cap. As he tried to get his thumb under the edge of the cap, in order to pull it off, he realized this was the loveliest girl he had ever touched. He felt that he had always loved her, that he always would. Her cap came off. She stood erect, staggering a little before she found a chair to hold to. She closed her eyes and breathed deeply.

"Just a minute," she said in her normal voice. "I'll be with you in just a minute. The only time I can get a jolt of this is when one of you visitors gets a dose to get over the skin trouble."

She turned to the room mirror to adjust her hair. Speaking with her back to him, she said, "I hope I didn't say anything about downstairs."

Mercer still had the cap on. He loved this beautiful girl who had put it on him. He was ready to weep at the thought that she had had the same kind of pleasure which he still enjoyed. Not for the world would he say anything which could hurt her feelings. He was sure she wanted to be told that she had not said anything about "downstairs"—probably shop talk for the surface of Shayol—so he assured her warmly, "You said nothing. Nothing at all."

She came over to the bed, leaned, kissed him on the lips. The kiss was as far away as the pain; he felt nothing; the Niagara of throbbing pleasure which poured through his head left no room for more sensation. But he liked the friendliness of it. A grim, sane corner of his mind whispered to him that this was probably the last time he would ever kiss a woman, but it did not seem to matter.

With skilled fingers she adjusted the cap on his head. "There, now. You're a sweet guy. I'm going to pretend-forget and leave the cap on you till the doctor comes."

With a bright smile she squeezed his shoulder.

She hastened out of the room.

The white of her skirt flashed prettily as she went out the door. He saw that she had very shapely legs indeed.

She was nice, but the cap . . . ah, it was the cap that mattered! He closed his eyes and let the cap go on stimulating the pleasure centers of his brain. The pain in his skin was still there, but it did not matter any more than did the chair standing in the corner. The pain was just something that happened to be in the room.

A firm touch on his arm made him open his eyes. The older, authoritative-looking man was standing beside the bed, looking down at him with a quizzical smile.

"She did it again," said the old man.

Mercer shook his head, trying to indicate that the young nurse had done nothing wrong.

"I'm Doctor Vomact," said the older man, "and I am going to take this cap off you. You will then experience the pain again, but I think it will not be so bad. You can have the cap several more times before you leave here."

With a swift, firm gesture he snatched the cap off Mercer's head.

Mercer promptly doubled up with the inrush of fire from his skin. He started to scream and then saw that Doctor Vomact was watching him calmly.

Mercer gasped, "It is—easier now."

"I knew it would be," said the doctor. "I had to take the cap off to talk to you. You have a few choices to make."

"Yes, Doctor," gasped Mercer.

"You have committed a serious crime and you are going down to the surface of Shayol."

"Yes," said Mercer.

"Do you want to tell me your crime?"

Mercer thought of the white palace walls in perpetual sunlight, and the soft mewing of the little things when he reached them. He tightened his arms, legs, back and jaw. "No," he said, "I don't want to talk about it. It's the crime without a name. Against the Imperial family . . ."

"Fine," said the doctor, "that's a healthy attitude. The crime is past. Your future is ahead. Now, I can destroy your mind before you go down—if you want me to."

"That's against the law," said Mercer.

Doctor Vomact smiled warmly and confidently. "Of course it is. A lot of things are against human law. But there are laws of science, too. Your body, down on Shayol, is going to serve science. It doesn't matter to me whether the body has Mercer's mind or the mind of a low-grade shellfish. I have to leave enough mind in you to keep the body going, but I can wipe out the historic you and give your body a better chance of being happy.

It's your choice, Mercer. Do you want to be you or not?"

Mercer shook his head back and forth, "I don't know."

"I'm taking a chance," said Doctor Vomact, "in giving you this much leeway. I'd have it done if I were in your position. It's pretty bad down there."

Mercer looked at the full, broad face. He did not trust the comfortable smile. Perhaps this was a trick to increase his punishment. The cruelty of the Emperor was proverbial. Look at what he had done to the widow of his predecessor, the Dowager Lady Da. She was younger than the Emperor himself, and he had sent her to a place worse than death. If he had been sentenced to Shayol, why was this doctor trying to interfere with the rules? Maybe the doctor himself had been conditioned, and did not know what he was offering.

Doctor Vomact read Mercer's face. "All right. You refuse. You want to take your mind down with you. It's all right with me. I don't have you on my conscience. I suppose you'll refuse the next offer too. Do you want me to take your eyes out before you go down? You'll be much more comfortable without vision. I *know* that, from the voices that we record for the warning broadcasts. I can sear the optic nerves so that there will be no chance of your getting vision again."

Mercer rocked back and forth. The fiery pain had become a universal itch, but the soreness of his spirit was greater than the discomfort of his skin.

"You refuse that, too?" said the doctor.

"I suppose so," said Mercer.

"Then all I have to do is to get ready. You can have the cap for a while, if you want."

Mercer said, "Before I put the cap on, can you tell me what happens down there?"

"Some of it," said the doctor. "There is an attendant. He is a man, but not a human being. He is a homunculus fashioned out of cattle material. He is intelligent and very conscientious. You specimens are turned loose on the surface of Shayol. The dromozoa are a special lifeform there. When they settle in your body, B'dikkat—that's the attendant—carves them out with an anesthetic and sends them up here. We freeze the tissue cultures, and they are compatible with almost any kind of oxygen-based life. Half the surgical repair you see in the whole universe comes out of buds that we ship from here. Shayol is a very healthy place, so far as survival is concerned. You won't die."

"You mean," said Mercer, "that I am getting perpetual punishment."

"I didn't say that," said Doctor Vomact. "Or if I did, I was wrong. You won't die soon. I don't know how long you will live down there. Remember, no matter how uncomfortable you get, the samples which B'dikkat sends up will help thousands of people in all the inhabited worlds. Now take the cap."

"I'd rather talk," said Mercer. "It may be my last chance."

The doctor looked at him strangely. "If you can stand that pain, go ahead and talk."

"Can I commit suicide down there?"

"I don't know," said the doctor. "It's never happened. And to judge by the voices, you'd think they wanted to."

"Has anybody ever come back from Shayol?"

"Not since it was put off limits about four hundred years ago."

"Can I talk to other people down there?"

"Yes," said the doctor.

"Who punishes me down there?"

"Nobody does, you fool," cried Doctor Vomact. "It's not punishment. People don't like it down on Shayol, and it's better, I guess, to get convicts instead of volunteers. But there isn't anybody *against* you at all."

"No jailers?" asked Mercer, with a whine in his voice.

"No jailers, no rules, no prohibitions. Just Shayol, and B'dikkat to take care of you. Do you still want your mind and your eyes?"

"I'll keep them," said Mercer. "I've gone this far and I might as well go the rest of the way."

"Then let me put the cap on you for your second dose," said Doctor Vomact.

The doctor adjusted the cap just as lightly and delicately as had the nurse; he was quicker about it. There was no sign of his picking out another cap for himself.

The inrush of pleasure was like a wild intoxication. His burning skin receded into distance. The doctor was near in space, but even the doctor did not matter. Mercer was not afraid of Shayol. The pulsation of happiness out of his brain was too great to leave room for fear or pain.

Doctor Vomact was holding out his hand.

Mercer wondered why, and then realized that the wonderful, kindly cap-giving man was offering to shake hands. He lifted his own. It was heavy, but his arm was happy, too.

They shook hands. It was curious, thought Mercer, to feel the handshake beyond the double level of cerebral pleasure and dermal pain.

"Goodbye, Mr. Mercer," said the doctor. "Goodbye and a good night . . ."

2

The ferry satellite was a hospitable place. The hundreds of hours that followed were like a long, weird dream.

Twice again the young nurse sneaked into his bedroom with him when he was being given the cap and had a cap with him. There were baths which calloused his whole body. Under strong local anesthetics, his teeth were taken out and stainless steel took their place. There were irradiations under blazing lights which took away the pain of his skin. There were special treatments for his fingernails and toenails. Gradually they changed into formidable claws; he found himself stropping them on the aluminum bed one night and saw that they left deep marks.

His mind never became completely clear.

Sometimes he thought he was home with his mother, that he was little again, and in pain. Other times, under the cap, he laughed in his bed to think that people were sent to this place for punishment when it was all so terribly much fun. There were no trials, no questions, no judges. Food was good, but he did not think about it much; the cap was better. Even when he was awake, he was drowsy.

At last, with the cap on him, they put him into an adiabatic pod—a one-body missile which could be dropped from the ferry to the planet below. He was all closed in, except for his face.

Doctor Vomact seemed to swim into the room. "You are strong, Mercer," the doctor shouted, "you are very strong! Can you hear me?"

Mercer nodded.

"We wish you well, Mercer. No matter what happens, remember you are helping other people up here."

"Can I take the cap with me?" said Mercer.

For an answer, Doctor Vomact removed the cap himself. Two men closed the lid of the pod, leaving Mercer in total darkness. His mind started to clear, and he panicked against his wrappings.

There was the roar of thunder and the taste of blood.

The next thing that Mercer knew, he was in a cool, cool room, much chillier than the bedrooms and operating rooms of the satellite. Someone was lifting him gently onto a table.

He opened his eyes.

An enormous face, four times the size of any human face Mercer had ever seen, was looking down at him. Huge brown eyes, cowlike in their gentle inoffensiveness, moved back and forth as the big face examined Mercer's wrappings. The face was that of a handsome man of middle years, clean-shaven, hair chestnut-brown, with sensual, full lips and gigantic but healthy yellow teeth exposed in a half-smile. The face saw Mercer's eyes open, and spoke with a deep friendly roar.

"I'm your best friend. My name is B'dikkat, but you don't have to use that here. Just call me Friend, and I will always help you."

"I hurt," said Mercer.

"Of course you do. You hurt all over. That's a big drop," said B'dikkat.

"Can I have a cap, please," begged Mercer. It was not a question; it was a demand; Mercer felt that his private inward eternity depended on it.

B'dikkat laughed. "I haven't any caps down here. I

might use them myself. Or so they think. I have other things, much better. No fear, fellow, I'll fix you up."

Mercer looked doubtful. If the cap had brought him happiness on the ferry, it would take at least electrical stimulation of the brain to undo whatever torments the surface of Shayol had to offer.

B'dikkat's laughter filled the room like a bursting pillow.

"Have you ever heard of condamine?"

"No," said Mercer.

"It's a narcotic so powerful that the pharmacopoeias are not allowed to mention it."

"You have that?" said Mercer hopefully.

"Something better. I have super-condamine. It's named after the New French town where they developed it. The chemists hooked in one more hydrogen molecule. That gave it a real jolt. If you took it in your present shape, you'd be dead in three minutes, but those three minutes would seem like ten thousand years of happiness to the inside of your mind." B'dikkat rolled his brown cow eyes expressively and smacked his rich red lips with a tongue of enormous extent.

"What's the use of it, then?"

"*You* can take it," said B'dikkat. "You can take it after you have been exposed to the dromozoa outside this cabin. You get all the good effects and none of the bad. You want to see something?"

What answer is there except *yes,* thought Mercer grimly; does he think I have an urgent invitation to a tea party?

"Look out the window," said B'dikkat, "and tell me what you see."

The atmosphere was clear. The surface was like a desert, ginger-yellow with streaks of green where lichen and low shrubs grew, obviously stunted and tormented by high, dry winds. The landscape was monotonous. Two or three hundred yards away there was a herd of bright pink objects which seemed alive, but Mercer could not see them well enough to describe them clearly. Further away, on the extreme right of his frame of vision, there was the statue of an enormous human foot, the height of a six-story building. Mercer could not see what the foot was connected to. "I see a big foot," said he, "but—"

"But what?" said B'dikkat, like an enormous child hiding the denouement of a hugely private joke. Large as he was, he would have been dwarfed by any one of the toes on that tremendous foot.

"But it can't be a real foot," said Mercer.

"It is," said B'dikkat. "That's Go-Captain Alvarez, the man who found this planet. After six hundred years he's still in fine shape. Of course, he's mostly dromozootic by now, but I think there is some human consciousness inside him. You know what I do?"

"What?" said Mercer.

"I give him six cubic centimeters of super-condamine and he snorts for me. Real happy little snorts. A stranger might think it was a volcano. That's what super-condamine can do. And you're going to get plenty of it. You're a lucky, lucky man, Mercer. You have me for a friend, and you have my needle for a treat. I do all the work and you get all the fun. Isn't that a nice surprise?"

Mercer thought, You're lying! Lying! Where do the screams come from that we have all heard broadcast as a warning on Punishment Day? Why did the doctor offer to cancel my brain or to take out my eyes?

The cow-man watched him sadly, a hurt expression on his face. "You don't believe me," he said, very sadly.

"It's not quite that," said Mercer, with an attempt at heartiness, "but I think you're leaving something out."

"Nothing much," said B'dikkat. "You jump when the dromozoa hit you. You'll be upset when you start growing new parts—heads, kidneys, hands. I had one fellow in here who grew thirty-eight hands in a single session outside. I took them all off, froze them and sent them upstairs. I take good care of everybody. You'll probably yell for a while. But remember, just call me Friend, and I have the nicest treat in the universe waiting for you. Now, would you like some fried eggs? I don't eat eggs myself, but most true men like them."

"Eggs?" said Mercer. "What have eggs got to do with it?"

"Nothing much. It's just a treat for you people. Get

something in your stomach before you go outside. You'll get through the first day better."

Mercer, unbelieving, watched as the big man took two precious eggs from a cold chest, expertly broke them into a little pan and put the pan in the heat-field at the center of the table Mercer had awakened on.

"Friend, eh?" B'dikkat grinned. "You'll see I'm a good friend. When you go outside, remember that."

An hour later, Mercer did go outside.

Strangely at peace with himself, he stood at the door. B'dikkat pushed him in a brotherly way, giving him a shove which was gentle enough to be an encouragement.

"Don't make me put on my lead suit, fellow." Mercer had seen a suit, fully the size of an ordinary space-ship cabin, hanging on the wall of an adjacent room. "When I close this door, the outer one will open. Just walk on out."

"But what will happen?" said Mercer, the fear turning around in his stomach and making little grabs at his throat from the inside.

"Don't start that again," said B'dikkat. For an hour he had fended off Mercer's questions about the outside. A map? B'dikkat had laughed at the thought. Food? He said not to worry. Other people? They'd be there. Weapons? What for, B'dikkat had replied. Over and over again, B'dikkat had insisted that he was Mercer's friend. What would happen to Mercer? The same that happened to everybody else.

Mercer stepped out.

Nothing happened. The day was cool. The wind moved gently against his toughened skin.

Mercer looked around apprehensively.

The mountainous body of Captain Alvarez occupied a good part of the landscape to the right. Mercer had no wish to get mixed up with that. He glanced back at the cabin. B'dikkat was not looking out the window.

Mercer walked slowly, straight ahead.

There was a flash on the ground, no brighter than the glitter of sunlight on a fragment of glass. Mercer felt a sting in the thigh, as though a sharp instrument had touched him lightly. He brushed the place with his hand.

It was as though the sky fell in.

A pain—it was more than a pain; it was a living throb —ran from his hip to his foot on the right side. The throb reached up to his chest, robbing him of breath. He fell, and the ground hurt him. Nothing in the hospital-satellite had been like this. He lay in the open air, trying not to breathe, but he did breathe anyhow. Each time he breathed, the throb moved with his thorax. He lay on his back, looking at the sun. At last he noticed that the sun was violet-white.

It was no use even thinking of calling. He had no voice. Tendrils of discomfort twisted within him. Since he could not stop breathing, he concentrated on taking air in the way that hurt him least. Gasps were too much work. Little tiny sips of air hurt him least.

The desert around him was empty. He could not turn his head to look at the cabin. Is this it? he thought. Is an eternity of this the punishment of Shayol?

There were voices near him.

Two faces, grotesquely pink, looked down at him. They might have been human. The man looked normal enough, except for having two noses side by side. The woman was a caricature beyond belief. She had grown a breast on each cheek and a cluster of naked baby-like fingers hung limp from her forehead.

"It's a beauty," said the woman, "a new one."

"Come along," said the man.

They lifted him to his feet. He did not have strength enough to resist. When he tried to speak to them a harsh cawing sound, like the cry of an ugly bird, came from his mouth.

They moved with him efficiently. He saw that he was being dragged to the herd of pink things.

As they approached, he saw that they were people. Better, he saw that they had once been people. A man with the beak of a flamingo was picking at his own body. A woman lay on the ground; she had a single head, but beside what seemed to be her original body, she had a boy's naked body growing sidewise from her neck. The boy-body, clean, new, paralytically helpless, made no movement other than shallow breathing. Mercer looked around. The only one of the group who was wearing clothing was a man with his overcoat on side-

wise. Mercer stared at him, finally realizing that the man
had two—or was it three?—stomachs growing on the
outside of his abdomen. The coat held them in place.
The transparent peritoneal wall looked fragile.

"New one," said his female captor. She and the two-
nosed man put him down.

The group lay scattered on the ground.

Mercer lay in a state of stupor among them.

An old man's voice said, "I'm afraid they're going to
feed us pretty soon."

"Oh, no!" "It's too early!" "Not again!" Protests
echoed from the group.

The old man's voice went on, "Look, near the big toe
of the mountain!"

The desolate murmur in the group attested their con-
firmation of what he had seen.

Mercer tried to ask what it was all about, but produced only a caw.

A woman—was it a woman?—crawled over to him
on her hands and knees. Beside her ordinary hands, she
was covered with hands all over her trunk and halfway
down her thighs. Some of the hands looked old and
withered. Others were as fresh and pink as the baby-fin-
gers on his captress' face. The woman shouted at him,
though it was not necessary to shout.

"The dromozoa are coming. This time it hurts. When
you get used to the place, you can dig in—"

She waved at a group of mounds which surrounded
the herd of people.

"They're dug in," she said.

Mercer cawed again.

"Don't you worry," said the hand-covered woman,
and gasped as a flash of light touched her.

The lights reached Mercer too. The pain was like the
first contact but more probing. Mercer felt his eyes widen
as odd sensations within his body led to an inescapable conclusion: these lights, these things, these whatever
they were, were feeding him and building him up.

Their intelligence, if they had it, was not human, but
their motives were clear. In between the stabs of pain he
felt them fill his stomach, put water in his blood, draw

water from his kidneys and bladder, massage his heart, move his lungs for him.

Every single thing they did was well meant and beneficent in intent.

And every single action hurt.

Abruptly, like the lifting of a cloud of insects, they were gone. Mercer was aware of a noise somewhere outside—a brainless, bawling cascade of ugly noise. He started to look around. And the noise stopped.

It had been himself, screaming. Screaming the ugly screams of a psychotic, a terrified drunk, an animal driven out of understanding or reason.

When he stopped, he found he had his speaking voice again.

A man came to him, naked like the others. There was a spike sticking through his head. The skin had healed around it on both sides. "Hello, fellow," said the man with the spike.

"Hello," said Mercer. It was a foolishly commonplace thing to say in a place like this.

"You can't kill yourself," said the man with the spike through his head.

"Yes, you can," said the woman covered with hands.

Mercer found that his first pain had disappeared. "What's happening to me?"

"You got a part," said the man with the spike. "They're always putting parts on us. After a while B'dikkat comes and cuts most of them off, except for the ones that ought to grow a little more. Like her," he added, nodding at the woman who lay with the boy-body growing from her neck.

"And that's all?" said Mercer. "The stabs for the new parts and the stinging for the feeding?"

"No," said the man. "Sometimes they think we're too cold and they fill our insides with fire. Or they think we're too hot and they freeze us, nerve by nerve."

The woman with the boy-body called over, "And sometimes they think we're unhappy, so they try to force us to be happy. *I* think that's the worst of all."

Mercer stammered, "Are you people—I mean—are you the only herd?"

The man with the spike coughed instead of laughing.

"Herd! That's funny. The land is full of people. Most of them dig in. We're the ones who can still talk. We stay together for company. We get more turns with B'dikkat that way."

Mercer started to ask another question, but he felt the strength run out of him. The day had been too much. The ground rocked like a ship on water. The sky turned black. He felt someone catch him as he fell. He felt himself being stretched out on the ground. And then, mercifully and magically, he slept.

3

Within a week, he came to know the group well. They were an absent-minded bunch of people. Not one of them ever knew when a dromozoon might flash by and add another part. Mercer was not stung again, but the incision he had obtained just outside the cabin was hardening. Spike-head looked at it when Mercer modestly undid his belt and lowered the edge of his trouser-top so they could see the wound.

"You've got a head," he said. "A whole baby head. They'll be glad to get that one upstairs when B'dikkat cuts it off you."

The group even tried to arrange his social life. They introduced him to the girl of the herd. She had grown one body after another, pelvis turning into shoulders and the pelvis below that turning into shoulders again until she was five people long. Her face was unmarred. She tried to be friendly to Mercer.

He was so shocked by her that he dug himself into the soft dry crumbly earth and stayed there for what seemed like a hundred years. He found later that it was less than a full day. When he came out, the long many-bodied girl was waiting for him.

"You didn't have to come out just for me," said she.

Mercer shook the dirt off himself.

He looked around. The violet sun was going down, and the sky was streaked with blues, deeper blues and trails of orange sunset.

He looked back at her. "I didn't get up for you. It's no use lying there, waiting for the next time."

"I want to show you something," she said. She pointed to a low hummock. "Dig that up."

Mercer looked at her. She seemed friendly. He shrugged and attacked the soil with his powerful claws. With tough skin and heavy digging-nails on the ends of his fingers, he found it was easy to dig like a dog. The earth cascaded beneath his busy hands. Something pink appeared down in the hole he had dug. He proceeded more carefully.

He knew what it would be.

It was. It was a man, sleeping. Extra arms grew down one side of his body in an orderly series. The other side looked normal.

Mercer turned back to the many-bodied girl, who had writhed closer.

"That's what I think it is, isn't it?"

"Yes," she said. "Doctor Vomact burned his brain out for him. And took his eyes out, too."

Mercer sat back on the ground and looked at the girl. "You told me to do it. Now tell me what for."

"To let you see. To let you know. To let you think."

"That's all?" said Mercer.

The girl twisted with startling suddenness. All the way down her series of bodies, her chests heaved. Mercer wondered how the air got into all of them. He did not feel sorry for her; he did not feel sorry for anyone except himself. When the spasm passed the girl smiled at him apologetically.

"They just gave me a new plant."

Mercer nodded grimly.

"What now, a hand? It seems you have enough."

"Oh, those," she said, looking back at her many torsos. "I promised B'dikkat that I'd let them grow. He's *good*. But that man, stranger. Look at that man you dug up. Who's better off, he or we?"

Mercer stared at her. "Is that what you had me dig him up for?"

"Yes," said the girl.

"Do you expect me to answer?"

"No," said the girl, "not now."

"Who are you?" said Mercer.

"We never ask that here. It doesn't matter. But since you're new, I'll tell you. I used to be the Lady Da—the Emperor's stepmother."

"You!" he exclaimed.

She smiled, ruefully. "You're still so fresh you think it matters! But I have something more important to tell you." She stopped and bit her lip.

"What?" he urged. "Better tell me before I get another bite. I won't be able to think or talk then, not for a long time. Tell me now."

She brought her face close to his. It was still a lovely face, even in the dying orange of this violet-sunned sunset. "People never live forever."

"Yes," said Mercer. "I knew that."

"Believe it," ordered the Lady Da.

Lights flashed across the dark plain, still in the distance. Said she, "Dig in, dig in for the night. They may miss you."

Mercer started digging. He glanced over at the man he had dug up. The brainless body, with motions as soft as those of a starfish under water, was pushing its way back into the earth.

Five or seven days later, there was a shouting through the herd.

Mercer had come to know a half-man, the lower part of whose body was gone and whose viscera were kept in place with what resembled a translucent plastic bandage. The half-man had shown him how to lie still when the dromozoa came with their inescapable errands of doing good.

Said the half-man, "You can't fight them. They made Alvarez as big as a mountain, so that he never stirs. Now they're trying to make us happy. They feed us and clean us and sweeten us up. Lie still. Don't worry about screaming. We all do."

"When do we get the drug?" said Mercer.

"When B'dikkat comes."

B'dikkat came that day, pushing a sort of wheeled sled ahead of him. The runners carried it over the hillocks; the wheels worked on the surface.

Even before he arrived, the herd sprang into furious action. Everywhere, people were digging up the sleepers. By the time B'dikkit reached their waiting place, the herd must have uncovered twice their own number of sleeping pink bodies—men and women, young and old. The sleepers looked no better and no worse than the waking ones.

"Hurry!" said the Lady Da. "He never gives any of us a shot until we're all ready."

B'dikkat wore his heavy lead suit.

He lifted an arm in friendly greeting, like a father returning home with treats for his children. The herd clustered around him but did not crowd him.

He reached into the sled. There was a harnessed bottle which he threw over his shoulders. He snapped the locks on the straps. From the bottle there hung a tube. Midway down the tube there was a small pressure-pump. At the end of the tube there was a glistening hypodermic needle.

When ready, B'dikkat gestured for them to come closer. They approached him with radiant happiness. He stepped through their ranks and past them, to the girl who had the boy growing from her neck. His mechanical voice boomed through the loudspeaker set in the top of his suit.

"Good girl. Good, good girl. You get a big, big present." He thrust the hypodermic into her so long that Mercer could see an air bubble travel from the pump up to the bottle.

Then he moved back to the others, booming a word now and then, moving with improbable grace and speed amid the people. His needle flashed as he gave them hypodermics under pressure. The people dropped to sitting positions or lay down on the ground as though half-asleep.

He knew Mercer. "Hello, fellow. Now you can have the fun. It would have killed you in the cabin. Do you have anything for me?"

Mercer stammered, not knowing what B'dikkat meant, and the two-nosed man answered for him. "I think he has a nice baby head, but it isn't big enough for you to take yet."

Mercer never noticed the needle touch his arm.

B'dikkat had turned to the next knot of people when the super-condamine hit Mercer.

He tried to run after B'dikkat, to hug the lead space suit, to tell B'dikkat that he loved him. He stumbled and fell, but it did not hurt.

The many-bodied girl lay near him. Mercer spoke to her.

"Isn't it wonderful? You're beautiful, beautiful, beautiful. I'm so happy to be here."

The woman covered with growing hands came and sat beside them. She radiated warmth and good fellowship. Mercer thought that she looked very distinguished and charming. He struggled out of his clothes. It was foolish and snobbish to wear clothing when none of these nice people did.

The two women babbled and crooned at him.

With one corner of his mind he knew that they were saying nothing, just expressing the euphoria of a drug so powerful that the known universe had forbidden it. With most of his mind he was happy. He wondered how anyone could have the good luck to visit a planet as nice as this. He tried to tell the Lady Da, but the words weren't quite straight.

A painful stab hit him in the abdomen. The drug went after the pain and swallowed it. It was like the cap in the hospital, only a thousand times better. The pain was gone, though it had been crippling the first time.

He forced himself to be deliberate. He rammed his mind into focus and said to the two ladies who lay pinkly nude beside him in the desert. "That was a good bite. Maybe I will grow another head. That would make B'dikkat happy!"

The Lady Da forced the foremost of her bodies in an upright position. Said she, "I'm strong, too. I can talk. Remember, man, remember. People never live forever. We can die, too, we can die like real people. I do so believe in death!"

Mercer smiled at her through his happiness.

"Of course you can. But isn't this nice . . ."

With this he felt his lips thicken and his mind go slack. He was wide awake, but he did not feel like doing anything. In that beautiful place, among all those companionable and attractive people, he sat and smiled.

B'dikkat was sterilizing his knives.

Mercer wondered how long the super-condamine had lasted him. He endured the ministrations of the dromozoa without screams or movement. The agonies of nerves and itching of skin were phenomena which happened somewhere near him, but meant nothing. He watched his own body with remote, casual interest. The Lady Da and the handcovered woman stayed near him. After a long time the half-man dragged himself over to the group with his powerful arms. Having arrived he blinked sleepily and friendlily at them, and lapsed back into the restful stupor from which he had emerged. Mercer saw the sun rise on occasion, closed his eyes briefly, and opened them to see stars shining. Time had no meaning. The dromozoa fed him in their mysterious way; the drug canceled out his needs for cycles of the body.

At last he noticed a return of the inwardness of pain.

The pains themselves had not changed; he had.

He knew all the events which could take place on Shayol. He remembered them well from his happy period. Formerly he had noticed them—now he felt them.

He tried to ask the Lady Da how long they had had the drug, and how much longer they would have to wait before they had it again. She smiled at him with benign, remote happiness; apparently her many torsos, stretched out along the ground, had a greater capacity for retaining the drug than did his body. She meant him well, but was in no condition for articulate speech.

The half-man lay on the ground, arteries pulsating prettily behind the half-transparent film which protected his abdominal cavity.

Mercer squeezed the man's shoulder.

The half-man woke, recognized Mercer and gave him a healthily sleepy grin.

" 'A good morrow to you, my boy.' That's out of a play. Did you ever see a play?"

"You mean a game with cards?"

"No," said the half-man, "a sort of eye-machine with real people doing the figures."

"I never saw that," said Mercer, "but I—"

"But you want to ask me when B'dikkat is going to come back with the needle."

"Yes," said Mercer, a little ashamed of his obviousness.

"Soon," said the half-man. "That's why I think of plays. We all know what is going to happen. We all know when it is going to happen. We all know what the dummies will do—" he gestured at the hummocks in which the decorticated men were cradled—"and we all know what the new people will ask. But we never know how long a scene is going to take."

"What's a 'scene'?" asked Mercer. "Is that the name for the needle?"

The half-man laughed with something close to real humor. "No, no, no. You've got the lovelies on the brain. A scene is just part of a play. I mean we know the order in which things happen, but we have no clocks and nobody cares enough to count days or to make calendars and there's not much climate here, so none of us know how long anything takes. The pain seems short and the pleasure seems long. I'm inclined to think that they are about two Earth-weeks each."

Mercer did not know what an "Earth-week" was, since he had not been a well-read man before his conviction, but he got nothing more from the half-man at that time. The half-man received a dromozootic implant, turned red in the face, shouted senselessly at Mercer, "Take it out, you fool! Take it out of me!"

While Mercer looked on helplessly, the half-man twisted over on his side, his pink dusty back turned to Mercer, and wept hoarsely and quietly to himself.

Mercer himself could not tell how long it was before B'dikkat came back. It might have been several days. It might have been several months.

Once again B'dikkat moved among them like a father; once again they clustered like children. This time B'dikkat smiled pleasantly at the little head which had grown out of Mercer's thigh—a sleeping child's head, covered with light hair on top and with dainty eyebrows over the resting eyes. Mercer got the blissful needle.

When B'dikkat cut the head from Mercer's thigh, he

felt the knife grinding against the cartilage which held
the head to his own body. He saw the child-face grimace
as the head was cut; he felt the far, cool flash of unimportant pain, as B'dikkat dabbed the wound with a corrosive antiseptic which stopped all bleeding immediately.

The next time it was two legs growing from his chest.
Then there had been another head beside his own.
Or was that after the torso and legs, waist to toe-tips,
of the little girl which had grown from his side?

He forgot the order.

He did not count time.

Lady Da smiled at him often, but there was no love in
this place. She had lost the extra torsos. In between tera-
tologies, she was a pretty and shapely woman; but the
nicest thing about their relationship was her whisper to
him, repeated some thousands of times, repeated with
smiles and hope, "People never live forever."

She found this immensely comforting, even though
Mercer did not make much sense out of it.

Thus events occurred, and victims changed in appearance, and new ones arrived. Sometimes B'dikkat took
the new ones, resting in the everlasting sleep of their
burned-out brains, in a ground-truck to be added to other herds. The bodies in the truck threshed and bawled
without human speech when the dromozoa struck them.

Finally, Mercer did manage to follow B'dikkat to the
door of the cabin. He had to fight the bliss of super-condamine to do it. Only the memory of previous hurt, bewilderment and perplexity made him sure that if he did
not ask B'dikkat when he, Mercer, was happy, the answer would no longer be available when he needed it.
Fighting pleasure itself, he begged B'dikkat to check the
records and to tell him how long he had been there.

B'dikkat grudgingly agreed, but he did not come out
of the doorway. He spoke through the public address
box built into the cabin, and his gigantic voice roared
out over the empty plain, so that the pink herd of talking people stirred gently in their happiness and wondered what their friend B'dikkat might be wanting to tell
them. When he said it, they thought it exceedingly pro-
found, though none of them understood it, since it was

simply the amount of time that Mercer had been on Shayol:

"Standard years—eighty four years, seven months, three days, two hours, eleven and one half minutes. Good luck, fellow."

Mercer turned away.

The secret little corner of his mind, which stayed sane through happiness and pain, made him wonder about B'dikkat. What persuaded the cow-man to remain on Shayol? What kept him happy without super-conda-mine? Was B'dikkat a crazy slave to his own duty or was he a man who had hopes of going back to his own planet some day, surrounded by a family of little cow-people resembling himself? Mercer, despite his happi-ness, wept a little at the strange fate of B'dikkat. His own fate he accepted.

He remembered the last time he had eaten—actual eggs from an actual pan. The dromozoa kept him alive, but he did not know how they did it.

He staggered back to the group. The Lady Da, naked in the dusty plain, waved a hospitable hand and showed that there was a place for him to sit beside her. There were unclaimed square miles of seating space around them, but he appreciated the kindliness of her gesture none the less.

4

The years, if they were years, went by. The land of Shayol did not change.

Sometimes the bubbling sound of geysers came faintly across the plain to the herd of men; those who could talk declared it to be the breathing of Captain Alvarez. There was night and day, but no setting of crops, no change of season, no generations of men. Time stood still for these people, and their load of pleasure was so commingled with the shocks and pains of the dromozoa that the words of the Lady Da took on very remote meaning.

"People never live forever."

Her statement was a hope, not a truth in which they

could believe. They did not have the wit to follow the stars in their courses, to exchange names with each other, to harvest the experience of each for the wisdom of all. There was no dream of escape for these people. Though they saw the old-style chemical rockets lift up from the field beyond B'dikkat's cabin, they did not make plans to hide among the frozen crop of transmuted flesh.

Far long ago, some other prisoner than one of these had tried to write a letter. His handwriting was on a rock. Mercer read it, and so had a few of the others, but they could not tell which man had done it. Nor did they care.

The letter, scraped on stone, had been a message home. They could still read the opening: "Once, I was like you, stepping out of my window at the end of day, and letting the winds blow me gently toward the place I lived in. Once, like you, I had one head, two hands, ten fingers on my hands. The front part of my head was called a face, and I could talk with it. Now I can only write, and that only when I get out of pain. Once, like you, I ate foods, drank liquid, had a name. I cannot remember the name I had. You can stand up, you who get this letter. I cannot even stand up. I just wait for the lights to put my food in me molecule by molecule, and to take it out again. Don't think that I am punished any more. This place is not a punishment. It is something else."

Among the pink herd, none of them ever decided what was "something else."

Curiosity had died among them long ago.

Then came the day of the little people.

It was a time—not an hour, not a year: a duration somewhere between them—when the Lady Da and Mercer sat wordless with happiness and filled with the joy of super-condamine. They had nothing to say to one another; the drug said all things for them.

A disagreeable roar from B'dikkat's cabin made them stir mildly.

Those two, and one or two others, looked toward the speaker of the public address system.

The Lady Da brought herself to speak, though the

matter was unimportant beyond words. "I do believe," said she, "that we used to call that the War Alarm."

They drowsed back into their happiness.

A man with two rudimentary heads growing beside his own crawled over to them. All three heads looked very happy, and Mercer thought it delightful of him to appear in such a whimsical shape. Under the pulsing glow of super-condamine, Mercer regretted that he had not used times when his mind was clear to ask him who he had once been. He answered it for them. Forcing his eyelids open by sheer will power, he gave the Lady Da and Mercer the lazy ghost of a military salute and said, "Suzdal, Ma'am and Sir, former cruiser commander. They are sounding the alert. Wish to report that I am . . . I am . . . I am not quite ready for battle."

He dropped off to sleep.

The gentle peremptorinesses of the Lady Da brought his eyes open again.

"Commander, why are they sounding it here? Why did you come to us?"

"You, Ma'am, and the gentleman with the ears seem to think best of our group. I thought you might have orders."

Mercer looked around for the gentleman with the ears. It was himself. In that time his face was almost wholly obscured with a crop of fresh little ears, but he paid no attention to them, other than expecting that B'dikkat would cut them all off in due course and that the dromozoa would give him something else.

The noise from the cabin rose to a higher, ear-splitting intensity.

Among the herd, many people stirred.

Some opened their eyes, looked around, murmured. "It's a noise," and went back to the happy drowsing with super-condamine.

The cabin door opened.

B'dikkat rushed out, *without his suit*. They had never seen him on the outside without his protective metal suit.

He rushed up to them, looked wildly around, recognized the Lady Da and Mercer, picked them up, one under each arm, and raced with them back to the cabin.

He flung them into the double door. They landed with bone-splitting crashes, and found it amusing to hit the ground so hard. The floor tilted them into the room. Moments later, B'dikkat followed.

He roared at them, "You're people, or you were. You understand people; I only obey them. But this I will not obey. Look at that!"

Four beautiful human children lay on the floor. The two smallest seemed to be twins, about two years of age. There was a girl of five and a boy of seven or so. All of them had slack eyelids. All of them had thin red lines around their temples and their hair, shaved away, showed how their brains had been removed.

B'dikkat, heedless of danger from dromozoa, stood beside the Lady Da and Mercer, shouting.

"You're real people. I'm just a cow. I do my duty. My duty does not include this. These are *children*."

The wise, surviving recess of Mercer's mind registered shock and disbelief. It was hard to sustain the emotion, because the super-condamine washed at his consciousness like a great tide, making everything seem lovely. The forefront of his mind, rich with the drug, told him, "Won't it be nice to have some children with us!" But the undestroyed interior of his mind, keeping the honor he knew before he came to Shayol, whispered, "This is a crime worse than any crime we have committed! *And the Empire has done it.*"

"What have you done?" said the Lady Da. "What can we do?"

"I tried to call the satellite. When they knew what I was talking about, they cut me off. After all, I'm not people. The head doctor told me to do my work."

"Was it Doctor Vomact?" Mercer asked.

"Vomact?" said B'dikkat. "He died a hundred years ago, of old age. No, a new doctor cut me off. I don't have people-feeling, but I am Earth-born, of Earth blood. I have emotions myself. Pure cattle emotions! *This* I cannot permit."

"What have you done?"

B'dikkat lifted his eyes to the window. His face was illuminated by a determination which, even beyond the edges of the drug which made them love him, made him seem like the father of this world—responsible, honorable, unselfish.

He smiled. "They will kill me for it, I think. But I have put in the Galactic Alert—*all ships here*."

The Lady Da, sitting back on the floor, declared, "But that's only for new invaders! It is a false alarm." She pulled herself together and rose to her feet. "Can you cut these things off me, right now, in case people come? And get me a dress. And do you have anything which will counteract the effect of the super-condamine?"

"That's what I wanted!" cried B'dikkat. "I will not take these children. You give me leadership."

There and then, on the floor of the cabin, he trimmed her down to the normal proportions of mankind.

The corrosive antiseptic rose like smoke in the air of the cabin. Mercer thought it all very dramatic and pleasant, and dropped off in catnaps part of the time. Then he felt B'dikkat trimming him too. B'dikkat opened a long, long drawer and put the specimens in; from the cold in the room it must have been a refrigerated locker.

He sat them both up against the wall.

"I've been thinking," he said. "There is no antidote for super-condamine. Who would want one? But I can give you the hypos from my rescue boat. They are supposed to bring a person back, no matter what has happened to that person out in space."

There was a whining over the cabin roof. B'dikkat knocked a window out with his fist, stuck his head out of the window and looked up.

"Come on in," he shouted.

There was the thud of a landing craft touching ground quickly. Doors whirred. Mercer wondered, mildly, why people dared to land on Shayol. When they came in he saw that they were not people; they were Customs Robots, who could travel at velocities which people could never match. One wore the insigne of an inspector.

"Where are the invaders?"

"There are no—" began B'dikkat.

The Lady Da, imperial in her posture though she was completely nude, said in a voice of complete clarity, "I am a former Empress, the Lady Da. Do you know me?"

"No, Ma'am," said the robot inspector. He looked as uncomfortable as a robot could look. The drug made Mercer think that it would be nice to have robots for company, out on the surface of Shayol.

"I declare this Top Emergency, in the ancient words. Do you understand? Connect me with the Instrumentality."

"We can't—" said the inspector.

"You can ask," said the Lady Da.

The inspector complied.

The Lady Da turned to B'dikkat. "Give Mercer and me those shots now. Then put us outside the door so the dromozoa can repair these scars. Bring us in as soon as a connection is made. Wrap us in cloth if you do not have clothes for us. Mercer can stand the pain."

"Yes," said B'dikkat, keeping his eyes away from the four soft children and their collapsed eyes.

The injection burned like no fire ever had. It must have been capable of fighting the super-condamine, because B'dikkat put them through the open window, so as to save time going through the door. The dromozoa, sensing that they needed repair, flashed upon them. This time the super-condamine had something else fighting it.

Mercer did not scream but he lay against the wall and wept for ten thousand years; in objective time, it must have been several hours.

The Customs robots were taking pictures. The dromozoa were flashing against them too, sometimes in whole swarms, but nothing happened.

Mercer heard the voice of the communicator inside the cabin calling loudly for B'dikkat. "Surgery Satellite calling Shayol. B'dikkat, get on the line!"

He obviously was not replying.

There were soft cries coming from the other communicator, the one which the customs officials had brought into the room. Mercer was sure that the eye-machine was on and that people in other worlds were looking at Shayol for the first time.

B'dikkat came through the door. He had torn navigation charts out of his lifeboat. With these he cloaked them.

Mercer noted that the Lady Da changed the arrangement of the cloak in a few minor ways and suddenly looked like a person of great importance.

They re-entered the cabin door.

B'dikkat whispered, as if filled with awe, "The Instrumentality has been reached, and a lord of the Instrumentality is about to talk to you."

There was nothing for Mercer to do, so he sat back in a corner of the room and watched. The Lady Da, her skin healed, stood pale and nervous in the middle of the floor.

The room filled with an odorless intangible smoke. The smoke clouded. The full communicator was on.

A human figure appeared.

A woman, dressed in a uniform of radically conservative cut, faced the Lady Da.

"This is Shayol. You are the Lady Da. You called me."

The Lady Da pointed to the children on the floor. "This must not happen," she said. "This is a place of punishments, agreed upon between the Instrumentality and the Empire. No one said anything about children."

The woman on the screen looked down at the children.

"This is the work of insane people!" she cried.

She looked accusingly at the Lady Da, "Are you imperial?"

"I was an Empress, madam," said the Lady Da.

"And you permit this!"

"Permit it?" cried the Lady Da. "I had nothing to do with it." Her eyes widened. "I am a prisoner here myself. Don't you understand?"

The image-woman snapped, "No, I don't."

"I," said the Lady Da, "am a specimen. Look at the herd out there. I came from them a few hours ago."

"Adjust me," said the image-woman to B'dikkat. "Let me see that herd."

Her body, standing upright, soared through the wall in a flashing arc and was placed in the very center of the herd.

The Lady Da and Mercer watched her. They saw even the image lose its stiffness and dignity. The image-woman waved an arm to show that she should be brought back into the cabin. B'dikkat tuned her back into the room.

"I owe you an apology," said the image. "I am the Lady Johanna Gnade, one of the lords of the Instrumentality."

Mercer bowed, lost his balance and had to scramble up from the floor. The Lady Da acknowledged the introduction with a royal nod.

The two women looked at each other.

"You will investigate," said the Lady Da, "and when you have investigated, please put us all to death. You know about the drug?"

"Don't mention it," said B'dikkat, "don't even say the name into a communicator. It is a secret of the Instrumentality!"

"I am the Instrumentality," said the Lady Johanna. "Are you in pain? I did not think that any of you were alive. I had heard of the surgery banks on your off-limits planet, but I thought that robots tended parts of people and sent up the new grafts by rocket. Are there any people with you? Who is in charge? Who did this to the children?"

B'dikkat stepped in front of the image. He did not bow. "I'm in charge."

"You're underpeople!" cried the Lady Johanna. "You're a cow!"

"A bull, Ma'am. My family is frozen back on Earth itself, and with a thousand years' service I am earning their freedom and my own. Your other questions, Ma'am. I do all the work. The dromozoa do not affect me much, though I have to cut a part off myself now and then. I throw those away. They don't go into the bank. Do you know the secret of this place?"

The Lady Johanna talked to someone behind her on another world. Then she looked at B'dikkat and commanded, "Just don't name the drug or talk too much about it. Tell me the rest."

"We have," said B'dikkat very formally, "thirteen hundred and twenty-one people who can still be counted on to supply parts when the dromozoa implant them. There are about seven hundred more, including Go-

Captain Alvarez, who have been so thoroughly absorbed by the planet that it is no use trimming them. The Empire set up this place as a point of uttermost punishment. But the Instrumentality gave secret orders for *medicine* —" he accented the word strangely, meaning super-condamine—"to be issued so that the punishment would be counteracted. The Empire supplies our convicts. The Instrumentality distributes the surgical material."

The Lady Johanna lifted her right hand in a gesture of silence and compassion. She looked around the room. Her eyes came back to the Lady Da. Perhaps she guessed what effort the Lady Da had made in order to remain standing erect while the two drugs, the super-condamine and the lifeboat drug, fought within her veins.

"You people can rest. I will tell you now that all things possible will be done for you. The Empire is finished. The Fundamental Agreement, by which the Instrumentality surrendered the Empire a thousand years ago, has been set aside. We did not know that you people existed. We would have found out in time, but I am sorry we did not find out sooner. Is there anything we can do for you right away?"

"Time is what we all have," said the Lady Da. "Perhaps we cannot ever leave Shayol, because of the dromozoa and the *medicine*. The one could be dangerous. The other must never be permitted to be known."

The Lady Johanna Gnade looked around the room. When her glance reached him, B'dikkat fell to his knees and lifted his enormous hands in complete supplication.

"What do you want?" said she.

"These," said B'dikkat, pointing to the mutilated children. "Order a stop on children. Stop it now!" He commanded her with the last cry, and she accepted his command. "And Lady—" he stopped as if shy.

"Yes? Go on."

"Lady, I am unable to kill. It is not in my nature. To work, to help, but not to kill. What do I do with these?" He gestured at the four motionless children on the floor.

"Keep them," she said. "Just keep them."

"I can't," he said. "There's no way to get off this planet alive. I do not have food for them in the cabin.

They will die in a few hours. And governments," he added wisely, "take a long, long time to do things."

"Can you give them the *medicine?*"

"No, it would kill them if I give them that stuff first before the dromozoa have fortified their bodily processes."

The Lady Johanna Gnade filled the room with tinkling laughter that was very close to weeping. "Fools, poor fools, and the more fool I! If super-condamine works only *after* the dromozoa, what is the purpose of the secret?"

B'dikkat rose to his feet, offended. He frowned, but he could not get the words with which to defend himself.

The Lady Da, ex-empress of a fallen empire, addressed the other lady with ceremony and force: "Put them outside, so they will be touched. They will hurt. Have B'dikkat give them the drug as soon as he thinks it safe. I beg your leave, my Lady . . ."

Mercer had to catch her before she fell.

"You've all had enough," said the Lady Johanna. "A storm ship with heavily armed troops is on its way to your ferry satellite. They will seize the medical personnel and find out who committed this crime against children."

Mercer dared to speak. "Will you punish the guilty doctor?"

"*You* speak of punishment," she cried. "You!"

"It's fair. I was punished for doing wrong. Why shouldn't he be?"

"Punish—punish!" she said to him. "We will cure that doctor. And we will cure you too, if we can."

Mercer began to weep. He thought of the oceans of happiness which super-condamine had brought him, forgetting the hideous pain and the deformities on Shayol. Would there be no next needle? He could not guess what life would be like off Shayol. Was there to be no more tender, fatherly B'dikkat coming with his knives?

He lifted his tear-stained face to the Lady Johanna Gnade and choked out the words. "Lady, we are all insane in this place. I do not think we want to leave."

She turned her face away, moved by enormous compassion. Her next words were to B'dikkat. "You are wise and good, even if you are not a human being. Give them all of the drug they can take. The Instrumentality will decide what to do with all of you. I will survey your planet with robot soldiers. Will the robots be safe, cow-man?"

B'dikkat did not like the thoughtless name she called him, but he held no offense. "The robots will be all right, Ma'am, but the dromozoa will be excited if they cannot feed them and heal them. Send as few as you can. We do not know how the dromozoa live or die."

"As few as I can," she murmured. She lifted her hand in command to some technician unimaginable distances away. The odorless smoke rose about her and the image was gone.

A shrill cheerful voice spoke up. "I fixed your window," said the customs robot. B'dikkat thanked him absentmindedly. He helped Mercer and the Lady Da into the doorway. When they had gotten outside, they were promptly stung by the dromozoa. It did not matter.

B'dikkat himself emerged, carrying the four children in his two gigantic, tender hands. He lay the slack bodies on the ground near the cabin. He watched as the bodies went into spasm with the onset of the dromozoa. Mercer and the Lady Da saw that his brown cow eyes were rimmed with red and that his huge cheeks were dampened by tears.

Hours or centuries.

Who could tell them apart?

The herd went back to its usual life, except that the intervals between needles were much shorter. The once-commander, Suzdal, refused the needle when he heard the news. Whenever he could walk, he followed the customs robots around as they photographed, took soil samples, and made a count of the bodies. They were particularly interested in the mountain of the Go-Captain Alvarez and professed themselves uncertain as to whether there was organic life there or not. The mountain did appear to react to super-condamine, but they could find no blood, no heart-beat. Moisture, moved by the dromozoa, seemed to have replaced the once-human bodily processes.

5

And then, early one morning, the sky opened.

Ship after ship landed. People emerged, wearing clothes.

The dromozoa ignored the newcomers. Mercer, who was in a state of bliss, confusedly tried to think this through until he realized that the ships were loaded to their skins with communications machines; the "people" were either robots or images of persons in other places.

The robots swiftly gathered together the herd. Using wheelbarrows, they brought the hundreds of mindless people to the landing area.

Mercer heard a voice he knew. It was the Lady Johanna Gnade. "Set me high," she commanded.

Her form rose until she seemed one-fourth the size of Alvarez. Her voice took on more volume.

"Wake them all," she commanded.

Robots moved among them, spraying them with a gas which was both sickening and sweet. Mercer felt his mind go clear. The super-condamine still operated in his nerves and veins, but his cortical area was free of it. He thought clearly.

"I bring you," cried the compassionate feminine voice of the gigantic Lady Johanna, "the judgment of the Instrumentality on the planet Shayol.

"Item: the surgical supplies will be maintained and the dromozoa will not be molested. Portions of human bodies will be left here to grow, and the grafts will be collected by robots. Neither man nor homunculus will live here again.

"Item: the underman B'dikkat, of cattle extraction, will be rewarded by an immediate return to Earth. He will be paid twice his expected thousand years of earnings."

The voice of B'dikkat, without amplification, was almost as loud as hers through the amplifier. He shouted his protest, "Lady, Lady!"

She looked down at him, his enormous body reaching to ankle height on her swirling gown, and said in a very informal tone, "What do you want?"

"Let me finish my work first," he cried, so that all

could hear. "Let me finish taking care of these people."

The specimens who had minds all listened attentively. The brainless ones were trying to dig themselves back into the soft earth of Shayol, using their powerful claws for the purpose. Whenever one began to disappear, a robot seized him by a limb and pulled him out again.

"Item: cephalectomies will be performed on all persons with irrecoverable minds. Their bodies will be left here. Their heads will be taken away and killed as pleasantly as we can manage, probably by an overdosage of super-condamine."

"The last big jolt," murmured Commander Suzdal, who stood near Mercer. "That's fair enough."

"Item: the children have been found to be the last heirs of the Empire. An over-zealous official sent them here to prevent their committing treason when they grew up. The doctor obeyed orders without questioning them. Both the official and the doctor have been cured and their memories of this have been erased, so that they need have no shame or grief for what they have done."

"It's unfair," cried the half-man. "They should be punished as we were!"

The Lady Johanna Gnade looked down at him. "Punishment is ended. We will give you anything you wish, but not the pain of another. I shall continue.

"Item: since none of you wish to resume the lives which you led previously, we are moving you to another planet nearby. It is similar to Shayol, but much more beautiful. There are no dromozoa."

At this an uproar seized the herd. They shouted, wept, cursed, appealed. They all wanted the needle, and if they had to stay on Shayol to get it, they would stay.

"Item," said the gigantic image of the lady, overriding their babble with her great but feminine voice, "you will not have super-condamine on the new planet, since without dromozoa it would kill you. But there will be caps. *Remember the caps.* We will try to cure you and to make people of you again. But if you give up, we will not force you. Caps are very powerful; with medical help you can live under them many years."

A hush fell on the group. In their various ways, they were trying to compare the electrical caps which had stimulated their pleasure-lobes with the drug which had drowned them a thousand times in pleasure. Their murmur sounded like assent.

"Do you have any questions?" said the Lady Johanna.

"When do we get the caps?" said several. They were human enough that they laughed at their own impatience.

"Soon," said she reassuringly, "very soon."

"Very soon," echoed B'dikkat, reassuring his charges even though he was no longer in control.

"Question," cried the Lady Da.

"My Lady . . . ?" said the Lady Johanna, giving the ex-empress her due courtesy.

"Will we be permitted marriage?"

The Lady Johanna looked astonished. "I don't know." She smiled. "I don't know any reason why not—"

"I claim this man Mercer," said the Lady Da. "When the drugs were deepest, and the pain was greatest, he was the one who always tried to think. May I have him?"

Mercer thought the procedure arbitrary but he was so happy that he said nothing. The Lady Johanna scrutinized him and then she nodded. She lifted her arms in a gesture of blessing and farewell.

The robots began to gather the pink herd into two groups. One group was to whisper in a ship over to a new world, new problems and new lives. The other group, no matter how much its members tried to scuttle into the dirt, was gathered for the last honor which humanity could pay their manhood.

B'dikkat, leaving everyone else, jogged with his bottle across the plain to give the mountain-man Alvarez an especially large gift of delight.

INCREDIBLE S-F
from
🅱🅱
BALLANTINE BOOKS

STARMAN JONES Robert A. Heinlein	**$1.50**
NORSTRILIA Cordwainer Smith	**$1.50**
FARTHEST STAR Frederick Pohl & Jack Williamson	**$1.50**
A FUNERAL FOR THE EYES OF FIRE Michael Bishop	**$1.50**
THE MAN WHO AWOKE Laurence Manning	**$1.50**
WARM WORLDS AND OTHERWISE James Tiptree, Jr., with an INTRODUCTION by Robert Silverberg	**$1.50**
MORE THAN HUMAN Theodore Sturgeon	**$1.50**
CYCLE OF FIRE Hal Clement	**$1.50**
THE TAR-AIYM KRANG Alan Dean Foster	**$1.50**